SECRETS
OF THE
SWAMP

Secrets
OF THE
Swamp

PENELOPE S. DELTA

Translated by Ruth Bobick

PETER E. RANDALL PUBLISHER
Portsmouth, New Hampshire
2012

First published in 1937 by Penelope S. Delta with the title
Sta Mystika tou Valtou (Secrets of the Swamp).

© 2012 English translation by Ruth Bobick

ISBN13: 978-1-931807-87-6

Library of Congress Control Number: 2012932665

Peter E. Randall Publisher
Box 4726, Portsmouth, NH 03802
www.perpublisher.com

Illustrator: D. A. Biskini

Jacket, book design, and map illustrations: Grace Peirce

Jacket image: Captain Agras / Tellos Agapinos; date: before 1906;
author: unknown; from: Pandektis Online Digital Thesaurus of
Primary Sources for Greek History and Culture, National Hellenic
Research Foundation

Jacket rondelle: detail from the illustration on page x

Chapter-heading icons:
Rifle and flag icons: Museum of the Macedonian Struggle, Salonika,
booklet.
Plant icon: Museum of Byzantine and Post-Byzantine Studies,
Venice, booklet.

CONTENTS

	Setting		ix
Chapter	1	The Roumoukli Plain	1
Chapter	2	To The Swamp	13
Chapter	3	The Lake At Giannitsa	27
Chapter	4	Two Children	39
Chapter	5	The Lower Huts	55
Chapter	6	Miss Electra	65
Chapter	7	Spying	84
Chapter	8	Work	96
Chapter	9	Kouga	115
Chapter	10	Battle At The Central Hut	133
Chapter	11	Thessalonika	145
Chapter	12	A Devil Of A Priest	160
Chapter	13	The School At Zorba	179
Chapter	14	The Large Hut At Kouga	197
Chapter	15	Nikiphoros	207
Chapter	16	New Arrivals	217
Chapter	17	Agras	229
Chapter	18	Captain Akritas	237
Chapter	19	Comitadjes	257
Chapter	20	Takis	283
Chapter	21	Bozets	297
Chapter	22	Matapas	311
Chapter	23	The Chapel At Kaliani	324
Chapter	24	Kourfalia	338
Chapter	25	Gregos	355
Chapter	26	Meeting At Kouga	373
Chapter	27	Fears	388
Chapter	28	Betrayal	396
Chapter	29	Jovan	404
Chapter	30	Martyrs	424
Chapter	31	Doctor Antonakis	435
Chapter	32	In The Water Of The Swamp	446
Chapter	33	"Again With The Years, With Time"	460
	Afterword and Notes		469

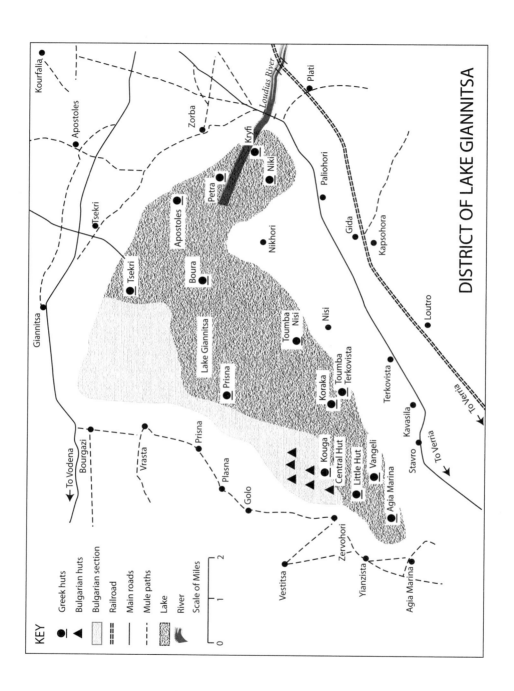

DISTRICT OF LAKE GIANNITSA

KEY

- Greek huts
- Bulgarian huts
- Bulgarian section
- Railroad
- Main roads
- Mule paths
- Lake
- River
- Scale of Miles

Scale of Miles: 0 1 2

Kourfalia
Apostoles
Zorba
Loudias River
Plati
Kryfi
Niki
Petra
Paliohori
Apostoles
Tsekri
Nikhori
Gida
Kapsohora
Tsekri
Boura
Giannitsa
Lake Giannitsa
Toumba Nisi
Nisi
Loutro
To Vodena
Bourgazi
Prisna
Vrasta
Prisna
Koraka
Toumba Terkovista
Terkovista
Plasna
Kouga
Central Hut
Little Hut
Vangeli
Kavasila
Stavro
To Verria
Golo
Agia Marina
Vestitsa
Zervohori
Yianzista
Agia Marina
To Verria

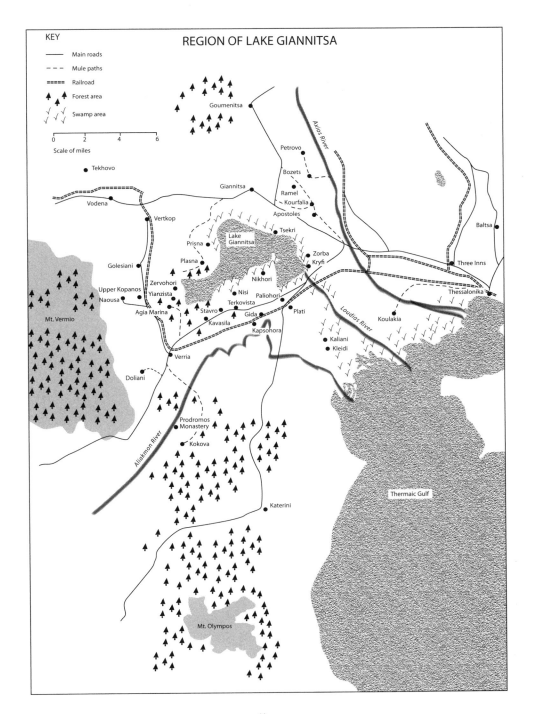

REGION OF LAKE GIANNITSA

KEY

— Main roads
- - - Mule paths
===== Railroad
🌲 Forest area
✓ Swamp area

Scale of miles
0 2 4 6

Goumenitsa

Axios River

Petrovo

Bozets

Tekhovo

Giannitsa

Ramel

Kourfalia

Apostoles

Baltsa

Vodena

Vertkop

Tsekri

Prisna

Lake Giannitsa

Zorba

Kryfi

Three Inns

Golesiani

Plasna

Nikhori

Zervohori

Upper Kopanos

Yianzista

Nisi

Paliohori

Thessalonika

Naousa

Terkovista

Agia Marina

Stavro

Gida

Plati

Kavasila

Koulakia

Kapsohora

Loudias River

Mt. Vermio

Verria

Kaliani

Kleidi

Doliani

Aliakmon River

Prodromos
Monastery

Kokova

Thermaic Gulf

Katerini

Mt. Olympos

vii

SETTING

Time: *October 1906–August 1907*

Place: *the Swamp at Lake Giannitsa in Turkish-occupied Macedonia*

Background: *a clandestine struggle between Greek and Bulgarian guerrilla forces for land under Turkish control*

Ultimate goal: *for the Greeks, the liberation of historic Macedonia and its union with mainland Greece; for the Bulgarians, liberation and Bulgarian sovereignty over greater Macedonia*

. . . the head of a child stood out . . .

1.

The Roumlouki Plain

THE SETTING SUN GAVE A ROSY HUE to the snowy peaks of Mt. Olympus, and cast a glow on the puddles in the muddy plain that extended, ashen and desolate, into the distance.

Leaping from one foot to the other, raising a glob of mud each time, a boy of about fifteen hurried along his way. The only living creature in that flat, deserted countryside, he seemed dauntless and indifferent to his arduous journey through the mud.

Occasionally he looked up from under his fur cap and searched around him; then lowering his forehead again, he resumed his soggy path.

Suddenly he stopped.

A little beyond, beside a bush swept bare by the wind, the head of a child stood out in the ash-grey plain. The child was thin, he had no cap, and his large almond-shaped eyes appeared very black in his pale face.

"Jovan . . . I knew I'd find you somewhere near here!" the older boy said in Bulgarian. "But what are you waiting for?"

The child didn't answer. Silently he stared at him with what seemed to be an expression of respect.

"Why don't you answer?" the older boy asked again. "What are you up to? A chore?"

Jovan slowly shook his head "no." Seven or eight years old, slight and under-nourished, he was barefoot and dressed in shabby clothes. His thick, unkempt hair fell onto his forehead, shading his eyes and making them seem still darker.

1

"You're not on an errand? Listen! I have some work for you. Will you do it for me?"

Once more, there was no reply.

Opening his jacket, the elder boy drew out a long, narrow sack.

"Look! . . . How about a little bread? And some cheese? Come! You'll eat well!" he said with a smile.

Jovan's hungry eyes darted from the bread and cheese to the other boy's face, then back to the bread and cheese. Yet he said nothing.

"Come on, I'll let you have all my cheese. And three pieces of candy. Do you want them?"

Jovan thrust his underlip forward proudly.

"I'll do it, Apostolis," he answered, "but for you, not for your candy or your cheese!"

"Bravo, Jovan! I knew you were first rate," Apostolis responded, laughing. "Take the bread and cheese, though. I've eaten; I'm not hungry. And the sweets, too. Listen, do you have the strength to go as far as Kleidi?"

"Of course!" Jovan exclaimed. "It's a half hour from here if I run."

"You must go tonight."

"I'll start right away!"

Apostolis regarded him with sympathy.

"You seem starved," he said. "Why doesn't your uncle give you enough to eat?"

Jovan shrugged one shoulder without replying.

"What do you want from Kleidi?" he asked.

"You'll have to hurry there."

Glancing towards the west, Apostolis added:

"You can't make it in a half hour. You'll need a full hour. However there's time before it's dark. But won't your uncle beat you if you're back late?"

Jovan shrugged his shoulder again.

"What do you want from Kleidi?" he repeated.

"You'll go to Thanasis . . . You know . . . the old man with the big plow. You'll say to him: 'Apostolis sends you word to prepare the bedding. Do you understand?'"

"I understand," Jovan answered, beginning to leave.

"Another thing!" Apostolis called out. "Tell him to give you some hot soup! . . ."

But Jovan had already taken off. Apostolis watched him—such a tot, jumping over the puddles while he hastily bit off mouthfuls of the bread and cheese he held in each hand.

"The poor child . . ." Apostolis murmured in Greek. "The poor, hungry child . . ."

He set off again at a fast pace himself, over puddles and through thick mud, heading for the sea.

* * * *

Twilight slowly descended onto the plain. A light breeze had risen; and Apostolis pressed on faster and faster towards the mouth of the Axios River.

If only a strong north wind would start up, he reflected, to dry the Swamp a little . . . The journey would be easier for the men. . . .

He threw a glance back at the muddy stretch behind him. In the dusk, the puddles and pools of water glistened.

"That deceptive south wind's of no use even if it does blow . . ." he murmured.

Deep in the night he reached a Greek fisherman's cottage. At one of the windows, an oil lamp was burning.

Inside, around a fire in the middle of the floor, five or six fishermen were squatting, warming their hands over the flames. Two women—a mother and daughter—bustled about, tossing onions into a pot hanging from the ceiling over the fire. In it, a savory fish soup was simmering.

"Welcome," the elder woman greeted him in the local dialect, smiling at the boy as he entered.

Raising their heads, the fishermen greeted him, too, in their easy-going manner.

"We've been expecting you. It's nearly midnight," the oldest of them said. His long white moustache extended down to his beard.

"Am I late, Lambros?" Apostolis asked. "I couldn't set out earlier. I was waiting for Demos, but he didn't appear."

"Demos left with the other boats," the old man answered, pronouncing his s's heavily and swallowing syllables like the other natives. "He arrived early and went off with our lads."

"They started as soon as it grew dark—as if they were going fishing," Lambros's daughter explained, tossing a handful of salt into the pot. "They said you should go on . . . that you'd meet up with them."

The fishermen had gotten up and put on their wool jackets and caps.

"Let's be on our way!" Lambros declared. And addressing his wife:

"Be sure the soup's spicy!"

All together, with slow movements and stooped shoulders, they headed towards the coast.

Two boats with broad keels were waiting at the shore.

Climbing inside, the fishermen drew towards the open sea.

* * * *

"Do you see anything, Apostolis?" Lambros asked.

Bent over in the prow, trying to pierce the black night with his gaze, Apostolis replied:

"Nothing . . . Perhaps tonight will be lost as well."

"Can't you see the other fishing boats?" a rower inquired.

"Not one of them . . . I only hear Mitros somewhere beyond— but he's not visible either . . ."

"Shame on you! Your eyes have the reputation of seeing in the dark!" Lambros mocked him.

"When nothing's there, how can they see anything?" Apostolis responded. And he added: "The Master might have been mistaken about the ship."

"The Master mistaken? Not on your life!" Lambros exclaimed. "Forward lads!"

The boat advanced silently.

Time passed.

"Our three fishing boats . . ." Apostolis whispered.

"Where?" the closest man questioned him, lifting his oar from the water.

"Towards the prow . . . the three of them . . ." And cupping his hands to his mouth, Apostolis called out in a low voice: "Demos . . . did you catch any fish?"

From the darkness another voice arose, also low.

"Nothing yet . . ."

Once again, slowly, quietly, the fishermen dipped their oars into the water.

A little more time elapsed.

All at once, Apostolis flung himself back and lifted up the first oar.

"Not a word!" he murmured.

His command flew like lightning from one to the other. Complete silence spread over the water.

Staring out and listening intently, Apostolis strove to penetrate the dark expanse before him.

A few seconds went by, full of agony.

Suddenly a virile voice cut the eerie silence.

"Who's there?" it asked fearlessly. "Are you Koulakia fishermen?"

Several voices replied at the same time:

"We are! Welcome! . . ."

A joyful whispering swept over the water's surface.

The fishermen were now rowing furiously to approach a boat that appeared like a phantom. Hands reached out from it to catch and clasp their own. Gun barrels gleamed in the faint starlight, while rows of criss-crossed cartridges could be made out on the men's chests. Another four fishing craft drew near the foreign boat.

"Welcome!"

"It's good to be here!"

"For days now, we've been waiting for you."

The virile voice, bold and commanding, sounded again.

"How many boats are there?"

"Five in all," Lambros answered.

"Five altogether? Then one can lead us to shore and the other four go back to the ship."

"Where's the ship, Captain?" Lambros inquired.

"About a mile from here, straight ahead. The men, weapons, and ammunition have to be unloaded. Ask for the captain—Captain Tasos . . ."

There was a hushed exchange of instructions, orders, and explanations.

Meanwhile, following Lambros closely, the foreign boat touched land.

Three men armed to the teeth disembarked.

"Welcome!" a delighted Lambros exclaimed once more, shaking their hands a second time . . . "Who's Captain Nikiphoros?"

"I am," the tallest one said in the fearless voice that had been heard in the dark. "And this is Captain Kalas, along with his second-in-command Captain Zykis.[1] Will we wait for the boats here?"

"They'll be arriving soon. Come to my cabin to warm yourselves and have something to eat. "

"I say it's better to await our men here," Captain Nikiphoros recommended to his companions.

Both of them agreed.

* * * *

A sailor and two other armed men from the foreign boat removed a few rifles and two or three heavy cases, then climbed aboard again to go help unload the ship.

"Leave your own rifles here," a fisherman suggested.

"A Cretan never parts with his rifle," one of the armed men responded in a characteristic Cretan accent.

"Well spoken," Lambros said approvingly. "Go quietly now, so no Turkish soldier gets wind of you . . ."

The sailor began rowing and the boat disappeared once more in the night.

A couple of fishermen set up watch further off, while the three commanders sought information from Lambros.

"Do you have guides for the lake at Giannitsa?" Captain Kalas wanted to know.

"You bet your life we have," Lambros replied, nodding. "Apostolis is here, and we also have Demos!"

"Who is that boy?" Captain Nikiphoros asked, motioning toward Apostolis who was gazing at him, spellbound.

But all at once the boy retreated bashfully.

"It's Apostolis, who I just mentioned."

"That child?" Captain Kalas exclaimed.

"That child? Test him and see," the fisherman answered, smiling. "He's the best guide this side of the Axios River. And he knows the Roumlouki plain as no one else does!"

In a hushed voice he called out:

"Apostolis!"

Apostolis approached shyly, proud and happy that he'd answer the captains' questions.

"Don't be hesitant," Captain Nikiphoros said encouragingly. "Tell us, can you lead us to the lake at Giannitsa?"

"I can," Apostolis replied.

"Are there Greek villages in the lake area?"

"Yes. However they're scared. The Bulgarians have killed many of the villagers. Now Captain Agras[2] has arrived at the Swamp."

"He's here? . . . Where? . . . When did he come?"

"About two weeks ago. He entered the Swamp . . . "

"The lake at Giannitsa?"

"Yes. We call it the Swamp. With Captain Agras here, we'll put up a fight, ourselves! . . . "

"In which part of the Swamp is he? Do you know?"

"No. But I've heard about him."

He looked up in the direction of the Axios River.

"We need to set off soon, though," he added. "It's a long journey and we have to reach the village before daybreak."

"Which village?"

"Kleidi. I've sent a message. They're expecting you."

* * * *

The first boats pulled up. Men disembarked and weapons were carried onto shore. In less than half an hour, all the supplies had been secured to the men's backs.

Lambros had brought the three officers to his cottage. While the two women cheerfully served them bowls of fish soup, the commanders warmed their hands and feet over the central fire in the increasingly smoky room.

At the start of their careers, lacking experience, they were constantly seeking information.

"Don't worry, Captains," the fisherman's daughter said with a smile as she refilled their earthen bowls. "Captain Manolis the Curlyhead will tell you everything. The Master took care of it all."

"Which Master? We didn't meet any Master," Captain Kalas responded.

The girl laughed.

"That's what our lads call the Leader," she replied.

Lambros nodded toward the river and winked.

"The fighters call the General Consul 'Master,'" he said.

"Who? Koromilas?" Captain Nikiphoros inquired.

"Ssh . . . Don't say the name!" the fisherman's daughter whispered. "Yes, he's the Master."

Demos and Apostolis, the two guides who'd been present during the conversation, were urging them to leave.

"There's a long way ahead. And we must reach Kleidi before dawn."

The captains took up their weapons; and after bidding the hospitable fishermen good-bye, they set off.

* * * *

The entire armed division made its way in the dark—a long line, one behind the other. Apostolis proceeded in front with a short-barrelled rifle they'd given him. Stepping lightly, he instinctively chose the driest footpaths in the soggy plain, guiding them without hesitation or uncertainty.

The commanders and their men followed closely—with the second guide placed toward the middle in case anyone wandered off and got lost in the mud or pools of water.

No one spoke or smoked. In that flat, desolate countryside, every noise carried and every spark betrayed a human presence.

With gestures Apostolis informed the next-in-line if he was to stop, drop down, or turn back. He in turn communicated the command the same way to the third-in-line, and the third to the fourth, and so on to the tail end.

The forces of the two captains, about fifty altogether, traveled in absolute silence and pitch darkness.

After walking for two hours, they paused to rest a few minutes, sitting down on the ground.

Everyone had a knapsack on his back to keep the food, clothing, and equipment he needed.

From behind their cloaks to prevent their being detected, a few of them lit portable burners to prepare coffee or tea to warm themselves, and others smoked a cigarette . . . Afterwards they all stood up again and resumed their course in the same order in the dark, with the guide in front.

Far off, something seemed to be growing lighter. Apostolis raised his hand and the column of men came to a halt.

He licked his finger and held it up to determine which way the wind was blowing.

Directly in back of him, Captain Nikiphoros leaned over to inquire:

"What's the matter?"

"That's Kalyvia ahead of us; however, we won't stop. It's a village with Turks," the boy whispered.

"Why are you seeking the direction of the wind?"

"So our scent doesn't reach the village. The dogs would betray us with their barking. We'll pass to the right since it's a west wind blowing."

Nikiphoros smiled.

"Don't tell me you know the winds, too, you rascal!" he whispered. "If we come out of this alive, I'll take you on my ship."

"You're in the navy, Captain?" Apostolis inquired, enchanted.

Nikiphoros nodded "yes," and they continued on their way.

* * * *

Suddenly a shadow was projected before them. Automatically Captain Nikiphoros raised his rifle.

With a laugh, Apostolis brushed it aside.

"It's our guards from Kleidi," he said. "They've been watching for us. There! The other one."

A second shadow drew up to the first. Both had Gras rifles.

"Welcome," they said in hushed voices, glad to see them. "Why did you delay so long in arriving? . . ."

"We've been out there at sea," Nikiphoros replied. "A dead calm kept us almost at a standstill."

The guards were looking uneasily towards the village as the men gathered around them, curious.

"You still have a distance before you reach the village," the first one said. "Don't waste time, Captain."

With friendly good-byes, they separated. And falling back into place, the human column set off again on its silent march.

Day was starting to dawn in the east when they arrived at the first houses at Kleidi.

There, too, guards were keeping watch. The signal of the approaching Greek force was relayed without a word, and villagers came out to meet them and take over.

One, evidently in charge, was an old man whose eyes were shining and lips trembling from emotion.

"Mister Thanasis," Apostolis murmured, introducing him. "He's arranged for you to stay the night . . ."

In silence, communicating by means of signs, Thanasis split the men up to be hidden and cared for in Greek homes. He led the officers and a couple of others to his own house, where the low round table, a feature of the Macedonian villages, had been set for them.

Thanasis was overjoyed.

"We've been awaiting you for some time now. Why are you so late?" he asked.

"The calm suspended us at sea," Captain Nikiphoros explained again. "If the wind hadn't risen tonight, we'd still be idling. And our food and water were exhausted."

With a smile Thanasis nodded towards Captain Kalas, a large man leaning against the wall, half-asleep.

"Yes," Nikiphoros said, "we're all dead tired. We only want to sleep . . ."

Thanasis clapped his hands and a middle aged woman entered, shy and eager to please.

"We've prepared food for you, Captains. Bless you! Pass into the guest room!"

* * * *

When Thanasis remained alone, he opened up a door facing onto the courtyard and had Apostolis come in.

"Give me an account now," he said.

"Let me ask you, Mister Thanasis," Apostolis replied. "Did Jovan get here?"

"Certainly he did. He was ready to collapse, all worn out from running so hard. Where did you find that child? He's a gem!"

"What message did he give you?"

"He informed me that Apostolis sent word to prepare the bedding. I understood. But how did you know they'd arrive today?"

"I saw that the wind was rising and figured 'today or never!' And I sent him to you. Did you give him something to eat?"

"No! . . . Why? He didn't ask for food."

"I told him to ask for some soup. However he's proud. The poor child was so hungry! What time did he get here?"

"Toward sundown."

"What? He must have run the whole way!"

"Where did you find him? Who is he?"

"He's Bulgarian. He stays with his uncle somewhere near Kalyvia and tends his sheep."

"You can trust him?"

"I once saved him from a Turk who wanted to beat him for grazing his uncle's sheep in someone else's pasture. I rescued him from his uncle as well—Angel Pio, the beast who dispatched him to the pasture and then denied it. From that time on, he's been devoted to me. And I make use of him. He'll do what I tell him!"

"Well enough. Get some sleep now, yourself. You can lie down on the fleece rug near the fireplace. Tomorrow's another long journey to the Swamp . . ."

"Thanks, Mister Thanasis, but I prefer the stable where your wife won't wake me when she cleans up," Apostolis replied.

"Suit yourself!" Thanasis said good-naturedly.

He opened the door to the courtyard and the guide passed back outside.

2.

To The Swamp

"Apostolis! Apostolis!"

Apostolis sat up on the straw where he'd been lying and rubbed his eyes. Could he still be dreaming? Or did he really hear his name?

"Apostolis! . . . Wake up! . . . Listen!"

This time he clearly heard the words whispered in Bulgarian. And he recognized the childish voice.

"Jovan!" he exclaimed. "Where are you?"

High up at the stable window, which had no glass or shutters, he saw the outline of a child's head against the sky.

"Why did you climb up there, Jovan? Come inside! . . ." he called to him.

Jovan scrambled down from the outer side of the window, and ran around the stable to enter by the door.

Flushed and panting, he appeared very excited.

"What time is it? How do you happen to be here in broad daylight?" Apostolis asked in Bulgarian.

"It's past noon! The men have gone out to the coffee-house! . . ." Jovan answered hurriedly.

Situating himself in a cross-legged position next to the pile of straw where Apostolis sat stretching himself, he added:

"Listen! Tell Mister Thanasis that . . . that the person who arrived yesterday is wandering around the village! The bey[3]—or another Turk—will see him . . . And then . . ."

Apostolis flew to his feet and started towards the door. But a sudden thought turned him back.

13

"Who arrived yesterday?" he questioned him suspiciously. "What do you know? What have they told you?"

Jovan shrugged his shoulder.

"They didn't tell me anything. No one knows . . . But I do!" he replied.

"What do you know?"

Jovan glanced behind him, then drew closer and whispered:

"The tall one with the blue eyes . . . who stands very straight . . ."

"Where did you see him? What is it that you know?" Apostolis demanded.

"I saw him last night . . . with many others . . . And just now on the road," the child murmured hesitantly.

"Last night? . . . Where were you?" Apostolis grew angry.

"Here . . . I was waiting for you . . . Don't get mad . . . I wanted to tell you . . . to tell you . . ."

All at once, Apostolis' anger subsided.

"What would you like to tell me?"

"To tell you that . . . I want to work with you!"

Jovan's eyes had filled with tears.

"What work could you do?" Apostolis asked him kindly.

"I can also show the way to those who kill the Bulgarian comitadjes,"[4] Jovan answered.

Apostolis gazed at him thoughtfully and scratched his head.

"What do you know about Bulgarian comitadjes?"

The child raised his shoulder again, but didn't reply.

"What will your uncle do to you for staying out all night?" Apostolis continued.

Once more, the child shrugged his shoulder.

"Don't they hurt . . . the beatings? . . ." Apostolis teased him.

Jovan caught hold of Apostolis' belt.

"Tell Mister Thanasis . . . If the bey sees the stranger, he'll call out the army! . . ." he exclaimed.

Apostolis feigned indifference. Inside him, though, uneasiness was mounting.

"If he sees who?" he inquired as though he wasn't paying attention.

Jovan began to be distressed.

"Why are you acting like you don't know? If the bey sees him, he'll understand what's happening. Because he's not like one of us—he doesn't bow his head like we do. He walks . . . like this!"

Throwing back his head and shoulders, he swaggered for a few steps. Then, returning to Apostolis, he persisted:

"Send Mister Thanasis. Other Turks are in the village too, besides the bey."

A moment longer Apostolis vacillated. But Jovan's thin, anxious face revealed such anguished impatience that all of a sudden he was persuaded.

"All right!" he said. "Stay here and wait for me. I'll be back."

* * * *

He left the stable seemingly unconcerned. However from there he ran up to the house and entered the large room used for entertaining—which served as kitchen as well.

"Mister Thanasis?" he inquired of the middle aged woman who was washing vegetables.

Missus Thanasis raised her head:

"Welcome child," she responded agreeably.

"I'm looking for Mister Thanasis. Can you tell me where he is?" Apostolis asked again, more insistently.

"As if I know! He went out. Perhaps to the coffee-house . . ."

Apostolis didn't stay to listen further. Racing outside, he sped to the coffee-house at the turn of the road. There, in fact, he found Thanasis playing backgammon with another villager. Apostolis bent down to his ear and whispered something to him.

Thanasis sprang to his feet in alarm.

"My wife needs me for something!" he told his companion.

And he set off as rapidly as his old legs would carry him.

"Where?" he questioned Apostolis when the two of them were in the road.

"I don't know. He's wandering about the village! . . . You go in one direction; I'll take the other. We'll see who discovers him first!"

* * * *

Apprehensive and unsteady on his feet, Thanasis hastened off. He examined windows and doors—whatever opening caught his eye—and searched up and down the sideroads, seeking the newcomer from the villagers he encountered. It was a bitter cold October afternoon, yet beneath the fez[5] that covered his head—a sign of the Turkish occupation—his forehead was perspiring from exertion and emotion.

A villager stopped him, worried and scared.

"Mister Thanasis!" he exclaimed. "Your guest is strolling about in the square! He says he's not afraid. But what will become of us? Hurry and restrain him."

"Where is he?" Thanasis asked anxiously.

"Heading towards the orchards! Catch up with him before a thunderbolt descends on us!"

Thanasis rushed away in the direction the villager had indicated and came out into a wider road. Sunshine was drying up what remained of the previous days' puddles. In front of a chapel, he saw a man staring up at the stone carving above the door, seemingly carefree.

At once he approached him.

"For God's sake, Captain Nikiphoros! Conceal yourself! Return home with me. Don't roam any farther. Some Turk might see you!"

"And what if he does?" the other responded with a smile.

"You're not experienced about these things! You'll be responsible for our undoing!" the old man said, gasping for breath.

Nikiphoros smiled again.

"All right," he replied, "let's go back. It was such a beautiful day, and I was tired of being enclosed in the room . . ."

A swarm of children chasing after each other, darted down the slope.

"Lower your shoulders, Captain," Thanasis whispered. "It won't do to stride along so fearlessly. Some Turk will take note of you and report it to the bey. Alas for us, then—all of us!"

"You have a bey here?"

"Certainly! Rakmi-bey. This is his village. But he doesn't bother us. We're all Orthodox Christians and he only asks that we pay our taxes regularly. However, woe to us if he learns"—and he threw a frightened look around—"that you're here and that we're hiding you! . . . "

The two men quickened their pace. Every so often Captain Nikiphoros forgot himself and straightened up, whereupon Thanasis gave him a signal to put his head and shoulders down.

"What a state of things!" the young man murmured. "To belong to a bey . . . Men treated like a herd of animals!"

"There's one good thing about it, though," Thanasis declared. "At least he saves us from the Bulgarian comitadjes, Captain!"

From a side road, Apostolis appeared before them.

"This way, make haste! . . ." he exclaimed. "Two Turks are approaching."

All together, they slipped into an alley and headed for Thanasis' house.

* * * *

Next to the fireplace in the large guest room, a heavyset Captain Kalas was sitting with his second-in-command and two of their men, conversing with the mistress of the household. Over a glowing log, a pot was hanging. From inside it, the smell of fresh vegetable soup spread throughout the room.

"You're treating us again today, Missus Thanasis?" Captain Nikiphoros inquired as he shook off his heavy cape. "We've become a burden to you . . ."

"Our honor . . . our honor, Captains . . ." the housewife responded shyly.

Her husband cut in to address the men:

"Rest up, Captains. You have another journey before you tonight."

And he turned in order to ask Apostolis how long it would take for them to reach the Swamp.

But the boy had left.

"He'll return," Thanasis said with a nod of his grey head. "He'll be guiding you there . . ."

Upon leaving, Apostolis had proceeded straight to the stable.

He discovered Jovan as he'd left him, seated cross-legged on the straw. Making a place for himself next to the child, Apostolis had him confess what he knew.

It wasn't difficult. Jovan answered all his questions.

"Where did you see us last night?" Apostolis began.

"Here," the child said, and he pointed to the stable door. "I was waiting for you, hidden here so Thanasis' wife wouldn't notice me."

"You were waiting for us? Who do you mean by us?"

"I understood that you'd gone to bring the captains. It's not the first time."

"How do you know?"

Jovan shrugged his shoulder.

"I know," he said simply.

Apostolis shoved his cap back and scratched his head.

He was bothered.

"Listen," he said to the child. "Do you tell these things to others?"

"Who would I tell them to?" Jovan inquired.

"Let's say . . . to your uncle!"

Jovan flung back his two shoulders.

"He's a comitadje!" he exclaimed, hate resounding in his voice.

"And you, what are you?" Apostolis continued.

Jovan raised his large black eyes and gazed at the boy opposite him. But he didn't speak.

Hesitantly, Apostolis said:

"All this . . . that you saw last night . . . You won't reveal it?"

"No!"

"Not to anyone?"

"I don't know anyone."

"Swear that you won't tell."

Apostolis had intersected his index fingers to form a cross; and the child kissed it, after first crossing himself.

Both of them were moved.

"Listen, Jovan," Apostolis said. "I'll put you to work with me."

"I'll do what you say."

"First explain where you were today and what you saw."

"I was here ... in the street ... in the neighborhood. The captains were asleep. The old lady was cooking quietly, so as not to wake them. In a while they woke up. She set the table for them and they ate . . ."

"How do you know?"

"I saw them through the window, from up on the roof across the way."

"How did you get up there?"

"It wasn't hard! . . . I don't have shoes . . . I climbed up."

Apostolis looked at the child's bare feet, swollen from the cold. Old blood had dried up on unwashed sores.

"Did anyone come?" he asked.

"A bunch of them came—everyone of importance. They were seeking news. They wanted to learn about the war."

"What war?"

"The one the captains fight to kill the comitadjes. It's called . . . it's called . . . " He paused to remember and then said two Greek words with a foreign accent: "Our Struggle." And he added in Bulgarian: "They said it again and again!"

Apostolis was taken back.

"How do you know all this?" he questioned him.

"I heard it. They'd closed the window, but I went in by the open door and listened from the next room."

Apostolis stared at him suspiciously.

"You're dangerous!" he burst out.

Jovan showed no agitation. His large black eyes—full of contemplation and uncertainty—were fixed on the elder boy's face. He didn't answer, though.

Apostilis went on:

"Why did you stay to see and hear all this?"

"To tell you about it,"   the child replied. "You were tired and had gone to sleep. I thought you'd want to know. So I watched and listened."

Instinctively Apostolis put his arm around the child's thin shoulders and hugged him. Tears rose in Jovan's eyes. He squeezed the older boy's hand that was on his shoulder.

"Listen, Jovan," Apostolis said. "I'll give you some work . . . You'll do what I tell you—do you hear?"

The child nodded "yes."

"Then go back to your uncle's. You'll get a beating . . . Are you worried?"

Jovan made a negative gesture.

"Say to him . . . say that you lost your way . . . that you slept at a neighbor's . . ."

Jovan raised his shoulder again.

"What do you want me to tell him?" he asked.

"Nothing. You're to find out from him."

"Find out what?"

"Learn where the comitadje Apostol Petkoff is—if he's in the Swamp . . . Are you familiar with the Swamp? If I tell you, will you know where to come and find me?"

"I'll know!"

"You've been there?"

"Many times!"

Startled, Apostolis inquired:

"Why did you go there?"

"Angel Pio sent me two times . . . And I discovered the hut of Captain Matapas."[6]

"What!" Apostolis exclaimed. "You informed your uncle?"

Hate returned to Jovan's eyes. His lips shot out disdainfully.

"No!" he said. "However I'll show it to you, if you want."

"Show it to me. And another thing: do you know a landing cove by the name of Tsekri?"

"I know it."

"Can you give the call of a wolf?"

"I can."

"Go to your uncle's, then. Do his work, graze his sheep. But find out where Apostol Petkoff is hiding and come to Tsekri. Howl like a wolf, and I'll meet up with you."

"I'll come!"

"Go now. We'll be leaving in a while, ourselves."

"Good-by, Apostolis."

"So long, Jovan."

The two boys parted. The child went out secretly, edging against the wall. Pensive, the older boy entered the house and huddled unobserved in a corner of the room.

* * * *

Thanasis was relating stories from his life to the captains. A little apart, arranging dishes and glasses on shelves in a cupboard, Mistress Thanasis followed every word.

Thanasis was in the midst of his tale:

"Imagine us, Orthodox Greeks, wearing our legs out to build roads for the Turkish artillery to pass over and strike . . . Who? . . . The Greek army!"

"But you were no longer young in '97[7] at the time of the war, Mister Thanasis. How did it happen that the Turks forced you into labor?" one of the men asked.

"As if they cared who was young or old! Don't you—a Cretan—know the Turks?" the old man replied. "They wanted laborers. And if the work didn't go fast enough, they thrashed us! Later, when disaster struck—when the Greek army beat a retreat and we heard about it here . . . What despair! . . . What mourning!"

"Tell the commanders what they did to you for giving the signal to water down the mud! . . ." Mistress Thanasis ventured to say from back at the cupboard.

But the old man interrupted her.

"No matter! What I went through isn't of concern to the captains," he said, putting an end to the subject. "Now we're interested in who defeats who in this war!"

Turning to Captain Nikiphoros, he inquired:

"Are you acquainted with any of the captains from the Swamp?"

"No . . . My work was of a different nature . . . I'm in the navy," Nikiphoros replied cautiously.

"You were working for our Struggle?"

". . . No. I was on a naval warship. However I learned how desperately Macedonia needed help, and I volunteered. It's the first time I've undertaken this kind of fighting . . . But do you know the captains?"[8]

"Yes. They've all passed by and slept here on their way to and from the Swamp. Only poor Captain Kapsalis didn't return—he was killed in a clash with the Bulgarians. Courageous fighters, all of them!"

"So they all came here to you?" Captain Kalas asked.

Thanasis slapped his hand against his thigh. "To me? Old Thasasis? Wasn't I one of the first to take an oath to the Struggle! . . . Even before they killed our first martyr Captain Zezas,[9] the Greek Committee had initiated me. I've often gone to Thessalonika to see the Master."

He winked and gestured toward the east. "Do you know him?"

"I do. Before arriving here, I passed by Thessalonika," Captain Nikiphoros answered, standing up.

"And what did he tell you?" Thanasis asked.

"We all take our orders from him," the captain said in his even-tempered way, "though it's not for us to discuss them."

Then casting a glance around the room, he inquired:

"Isn't it time we set off? Where is Apostolis?"

"Here I am, Captain!" the guide replied, coming out from his corner. "It's best for everyone to get ready. The sun set an hour and a half ago. However we can't start before another half hour."

"Why not? It's already night."

"Yes, but a Turk could still be in the back alleys. When we leave, we'll leave in safety."

The commanders smiled at the boy's decisive tone. Observing it, Thanasis felt some uncertainty behind their smile and made a reassuring motion to them not to be in a hurry.

"You can trust what Apostolis tells you," he said. "No one's at home in the Swamp like he is. Have faith in him—and don't worry, Captains."

* * * *

It was a dark night with a strong north wind blowing. A proud Apostolis proceeded first, armed with his short-barrelled rifle. Cartridge belts criss-crossed his chest. Behind him, one after another, the commanders and men formed a long, shadowy line.

Light-footed, the guide led them safely, avoiding inhabited areas and pastures where shepherds grazed their sheep—above all, Albanians hostile to Greeks.

For hours they continued their course in silence.

All at once Apostolis raised his arm. Nikiphoros halted, as did the second, third, and fourth in line, up to the very end.

"The railroad passes here," Apostolis murmured in Nikiphoros' ear. "Let me have one of your men. We'll go on alone to investigate, in case a Turkish sentry's on duty. Meanwhile, conceal yourself! Lie down on the ground—I'll be back."

Stealthily, sometimes on all fours and at times crawling, Apostolis forged ahead. A short distance behind, Captain Nikiphoros' man did the same.

Presently Apostolis stopped him.

"Wait and keep watch," he said. "I'll go myself now."

Quick and nimble, Apostolis was truly adept. He seemed to blend right into the surroundings, advancing in the dark until he arrived at the train track. His eyes pierced the night, catlike, as he searched up and down the track—wherever a human form could be.

Nothing. No one . . . Solitude everywhere . . .

Springing to his feet, he rushed back.

"It's free! Quickly! We'll cross over! . . ."

They crossed . . . Bent down, the entire human chain moved along quietly and passed over the iron track, overcoming the first hurdle.

"We'll travel at a distance from Plati," Apostolis whispered to Nikiphoros. "Then there's the Loudias River bridge. When we're almost to it, I'll continue on ahead again and see if the Turkish army's on patrol."

"Isn't there another road?" Captain Nikiphoros questioned him.

"No, Captain. Except for the narrow pathway we're taking, it's all Swamp—all mud and water. We'll go over the bridge. And don't worry, we'll succeed!"

They succeeded.

The Loudias River, which flowed from Lake Giannitsa to the sea at the Thermaiic Gulf, had but two bridges—one at the railroad crossing, the other at the Thessalonika-Verria carriage road.

Apostolis considered the second bridge less likely to be guarded; moreover it put them out closer to the Swamp.

With the same precautions as at the train track, he went on alone to survey the scene. Convinced that no one was around, he led the two forces safe and sound over this last hurdle and delivered them, near now, to the lake.

Thick fog covered the Swamp. The air was heavy from fumes and the stench of rotted grass. The soggy ground stuck to their feet. Humidity and cold dug into their bones.

Downcast, the men plodded along. Low plants and reeds obstructed their path. The commanders paused and then pushed on, clenching their teeth. So this damp, murky Swamp was Lake Giannitsa, where they'd live an amphibious life for days, weeks, and months on end—and perhaps even die!

Agile and sure-footed, Apostolis wove his way inside the plants and reeds, gaining a foothold wherever there was a speck of dry land. And silent and gloomy, the men followed him.

* * * *

Dark forms rose before them, discernable in the faint light of dawn. Notified in advance, Greek rebels from the lake divisions had come out to meet the newcomers and guide them to the Swamp's nearby landing cove.

Happy to finally see them, they reached out to clasp the tired men's hands, to welcome them and assist with the unloading.

The commanders stared without speaking. Were these the fighters of the Swamp—these emaciated, sallow figures? Would it be with them that they'd struggle against the Bulgarians? And would they become the same way themselves in a matter of time?

Apostolis had struck up a conversation with one of the rebels.

"Captain Manolis the Curlyhead isn't with you? . . . Why?"

"He's not here. He went to Ramel."

"What for? He should be at the Swamp!"

"He went on an investigation. But we'll take you ourselves. The lads are waiting with the boats at the Kryfi landing cove."

On their way, the commanders questioned the rebels, seeking information about any recent outrage.

"You're asking about crimes, Captains?" the fighter who appeared to direct the others responded with a smile. "We have them every day! That's why we're here." A tall, pale man in his thirties, he'd been ravaged by the Swamp fever.

"Where are you from?" Captain Nikiphoros asked. "And what is your name?"

"Vlandis—from Roumeli."

"How did you get this way? You seem to be of a strong constitution. Did you become ill here?"

Vlandis smiled.

"All of us who spent the summer here suffered. The fever attacks us every so often. And the flies run rampant, Captain. Still, you've arrived at a good time. In winter the fever lets up." He smiled again encouragingly. "You'll see! You'll manage—half of you here, half there . . . We'll rid the place of Bulgarians."

* * * *

They'd reached the landing-cove at Kryfi.

The landings were secret inlets opened up in the thick reeds at the edge of the lake. The lake bed sloped upwards toward the shore; and boats headed up the incline with their prow forward, half out on the ground. Thus it was possible to enter and depart from dry land. Without these secret openings, the oarsmen could flounder in the reeds for hours and fail to locate the shore. The cove at Kryfi was situated at the point where the Loudias River emerged from the lake.

It was there that the newcomers encountered the canoe-like boats, flat underneath, that circulated in the lake's shallow water among the reeds and aquatic plants. Each had one or two oars, but no oar-locks.

Used as a rudder, the oar in back served to propel the boat as well—being driven like a pole down to the bottom of the lake.

More rebels were waiting at the landing, thin and pale with sunken eyes and yet a smile on their lips.

"Welcome! We're few now. We need reinforcements!" they greeted them. "With the summer's heat, fever consumed us! . . ."

All were eager to lend a hand—to carry supplies and transport weapons and ammunition.

The new men followed them, their spirits fallen. Then together, old and new fighters crammed into twenty-five or so boats. In a long file they ascended the current of the river and drew towards Kryfi, the hut hidden among tall, thick reeds, with its blue and white Greek flag flying overhead.

.

3.

The Lake At Giannitsa

THE LAKE AT GIANNITSA was a perfect hiding place for fugitives, rebels, and bandits, for anyone who was persecuted, pursued, or condemned. A large lake overflowing in the winter with water descending from the surrounding mountains, it became a swamp in the summer with rivers running dry. Covered in the heat with thick green vegetation and in the cold with dry reeds—overgrown and inaccessible—the lake was nearly impregnable.

The Turkish army had never entered Lake Giannitsa, known as a refuge for brigands.

When the Bulgarian comitadjes made the decision to get the upper hand in the region—revolting against Turkish authority and turning Greek Macedonia Bulgarian[10]—they hid inside the lake. Taking possession of the reed huts the fishermen had built inside the water, the comitadjes set forth on raids by night and disappeared into the lake by day, terrorizing the Greek villages and population that remained loyal to Greece and the Patriarch.

Macedonia at the time was a mixture of all the Balkan nationalities—Greek, Bulgarian, Romanian, Serbian, and Albanian—as well as the Christian and Muslim faiths. All lived jumbled together under Turkish occupation.

The Macedonian language itself was a mixture of Slavic and Greek, interspersed with Turkish words.

As in the Byzantine past, the population had become so entangled it was difficult to distinguish a Greek from a Bulgarian, the two prevailing identities. The ethnic consciousness was simply Macedonian.

However when the Bulgarians proclaimed their religious independence—recognizing the Bulgarian Exarch instead of the Greek Patriarch in Constantinople as leader of their church; and when a synod declared them schismatic in 1872, Macedonia separated into patriarchal Greeks and exarchal Bulgarians. Fellow townsmen and villagers, even families, became divided.

The fierce Bulgarians organized and sent out bands with military commanders dispatched from Bulgaria, under the pretext of freeing Macedonia from the Turks. Subjecting everyone who wasn't exarchal to a reign of terror, they caused the suffering villages to change from patriarchal to exarchal from one day to the next, in order to survive.

For their part, the Turks remained indifferent to the Christian in-fighting, though not to the revolutionary declaration of the Bulgarian comitadjes. And in their flight before the Turkish army, the Bulgarian forces escaped to the unassailable reeds of the Swamp. The lake became a nest of comitadjes.

A few Greek forces had succeeded in entering the lake and establishing themselves in scattered huts—although their presence proved insignificant, lacking real strength. Greek captains, too, had often sought to protect the Greek villages in the area from comitadje attack, but to no avail. Except for the wooded western shore held by the Bulgarians, the rest of the countryside was an open plain, providing no cover for a rebel band.

Greeks and Bulgarians fought furiously to drive each other out of the Turkish controlled lake territory. And besides fighting one another, they had to guard against their common enemy, the Turkish army, which pursued the rebel forces relentlessly—whether Greek or Bulgarian.

Whoever controlled the invulnerable Lake Giannitsa became master of the scene, while whoever strove to put up a defense outside the lake was condemned to failure.

Thus the Greek band of Captain Georgakis had been completely destroyed at Petrovo, a heavily populated Greek village north of the lake in the Axios Valley. A brave Macedonian rebel, Captain Georgakis knew the region well, but Bulgarian villagers betrayed him. Encircled at Petrovo by the Turkish army, he was killed along with all his men. As punishment to the village that sheltered him, the Turks threw its leaders into Turkish prisons.

Prior to the scourge of Bulgarian activity on the lake, which unleashed the Greek-Bulgarian hatred, the lake had not been permanently inhabited. Villagers from the surroundings penetrated the water to fish, hunt, or cut the Swamp reeds—especially a native grass used for covering roofs, filling saddles, and weaving floormats and baskets. The lake also swarmed with leeches that the villagers sold abroad for bloodletting purposes, mainly to Austria which received large quantities of them.

The lake vegetation was extremely rich. A variety of shrubs grew in thick clusters, while flat-leafed waterlilies proliferated wherever the water was stagnant. Swamp weeds with thick outstretched leaves stood next to grasses two or more meters high, which rustled with every breeze. And reeds were everywhere! Shooting up to four meters above the water—a green wall in the summer months and dry and yellow in the winter—they concealed every suspicious whisper, swishing and whistling in the wind.

Here and there atrophied trees sprouted from time to time, or a willow drooped a mournful branch over the water. Beeches too, dense along the western shore, assured the comitadjes of protection.

The lake also teemed with wildlife—with countless fish, eels, frogs, and water-snakes; with wild ducks, geese, water-hens and other fowl; and with foxes, martens, wild boar, even wolves that descended during the winter. Sounds known and unknown filled the air. There were whispers, chirps, and cackles; screeches, howls, humming and droning—sounds that multiplied in the silent water, creating a mysterious, surreal atmosphere.

At intervals in the deeper water of the real Lake Giannitsa, wide open spaces existed without reeds, grass, or plants. It was there that the water-fowl roosted at night, before flying away each morning in search of food from the fields around the lake. Except for this deeper water where no growth managed to reach the surface, vegetation and wildlife were ever-present.

The Loudias River flowed through the dense reeds, opening up two natural waterways each five or six meters wide.

Natural paths from smaller branches of the river were formed as well[11]—narrower passages where boats could be concealed. However the current in them wasn't powerful enough to prevent the reeds from reappearing every so often.

Everywhere else, in order to communicate with each other and the shore, the fishermen were compelled to open up "foot-paths" about a meter wide. They cut the reeds as far down as possible in the water, so that the flat-bottomed canoes could make their way. Nevertheless the plant life was so tenacious that these footpaths too, if not constantly cut low inside the water, soon disappeared again under the growth without leaving a trace.

The lake with its plant and animal life had long been utilized to the advantage of the villagers who lived in the area. Yet from the time that small Greek bands succeeded in entering the Swamp, the shooting, the frequent clashes with the Bulgarians, and the attacks against those suspected of sympathizing with the Greeks, put such fear into the villagers that one by one they abandoned their huts and the lake. As a consequence, the wooded western section remained to the Bulgarians and the bare, exposed eastern side to the Greeks.

All the while, the comitadjes terrorized the countryside freely from their concentration of strength. In the Giannitsa district, there were both fervent Greek and fervent Bulgarian villages, together with those of mixed population. But no one was able to prevent the Bulgarian killings, which increased all the time.

At that point, the secret headquarters of the Macedonian Struggle in Athens decided to act by dispatching strong Greek forces to occupy the lake.

Captain Agras, a lieutenant fresh out of Officers Training School, had already arrived—stationed at Naousa. However upon sizing up the situation, he understood that no work would be effective if it didn't first dislodge the Bulgarians from their "nest." Without hesitating, he took leave of his easier mission at Naousa and immersed himself and his corps of select evzones[12] at Lake Giannitsa.

Fifteen days later Captains Kalas and Nikiphoros arrived, the former an infantry lieutenant, the latter a young naval officer who'd been put in charge of a land force for the first time.

Captain Kalas, who was general commander of the Greek mission, installed himself and his men at the Kryfi hut in the southeastern section of the lake. Two days later Captain Nikiphoros departed from Kryfi and headed north to another lake hut, Tsekri.

Constructed of reeds and wood of poor quality from the lake trees, the huts resembled those found in the wilds of Polynesia. Their foundation consisted of a skeleton of supports thrust down into the bottom of the lake—in a long, narrow, rectangular shape. Between them, reeds and wood were piled up, rising above the lake water to form the "floor." Another set of supports, erected upon the floor, had reeds and grass woven around them to create the huts' walls. And the walls supported a conical roof, also covered with reeds and grass, which allowed the rain to roll off and not flood the interior.

The fishermen had used the huts to store equipment and food, and as a place to sleep out on the lake. Around their primitive shelter, they extended the floor on all sides—or rather they extended the layer of stacked wood and reeds without a roof. On this open deck, they could sit outside to get some air, or fish or work.

In these crude dwellings, the two newly-arrived forces settled in with their captains.

Just as Captain Nikiphoros reached Tsekri, he ran up against a brutal Bulgarian crime.

At Ramel, a Bulgarian-speaking and dominated village in the Axios Valley north of the lake, a patriarchal Greek named Giovanni had succeeded in awakening the intimidated villagers' consciousness of their Greek heritage. As a result, a large part of the village renounced the exarchal schism and became patriarchal again.

From then on, Giovanni found no peace. The Bulgarians regularly sent word to him that his days were numbered; and he received letters signed by Apostol Petkof threatening his life.

The most terrifying of the comitadji commanders, Apostol Petkof seemed to be present everywhere and to be involved in all the killings. Yet no one could capture him, or even meet up with him. Like an evil spirit, he was continually felt but never seen. Spreading fear all around, he'd grown into almost a mythical figure.

Giovanni's frightened neighbors advised him to go into hiding. One youth, above all, told him to flee. And he pressured him to such an extent that he finally convinced him. Early one morning Giovanni loaded his family—his wife, his five children, and his aged parents—on two oxcarts and left.

A half hour outside the village, the comitadjes ambushed him and slaughtered them all. Apostol Petkof's classic letter was found pinned to Giovanni's body, with the warning that all those who failed to obey him would end up the same way.

It was an obvious betrayal—and the betrayer had to be caught. Someone inside the village had informed the comitadjes of Giovanni's plan to leave, and told them where to await him to kill him.

But who the informer was, no one knew.

Among the Greek rebels at the lake was a Cretan—Captain Manolis, nicknamed "the Curlyhead."

When he heard what had happened and learned that the betrayer hadn't been captured, he announced:

"I'll find him!"

And he set out from the Swamp for Ramel to interrogate the villagers.

* * * *

When Captain Nikiphoros approached Tsekri, the morning after his men had arrived at the hut with Apostolis, he discovered it in turmoil.

Armed youth were coming and going, passing from the hut to the deck, gesturing and speaking all the while. A few climbed into canoes to go out and meet their commander. Each wanted to be the first to report the news to him.

However the somewhat cold manner with which Nikiphoros followed all this anxiety, cut short even the boldest among them, so that only murmuring was heard.

As the commander's boat drew alongside the reed floor that served as a deck, Nikiphoros stepped up onto it with his customary calm.

"What's the matter?" he asked the men who'd gathered. "Why all the uproar?"

A little apart, all eyes and ears, an alert and curious Apostolis was watching and listening.

One young man with curls overflowing from his cap, came up to Nikiphoros.

"Welcome Captain. I'm Manolis the Cretan. And I've brought you a guest."

From the other side, someone held out a letter to the commander.

"A boy delivered it. It's news from the General Consulate about the crime. And it's urgent."

"What crime?"

"It concerns Giovanni, who they killed."

"It's about Ramel!"

Captain Nikiphoros, who'd traveled directly from Kryfi, hadn't heard anything. Not understanding, he opened the letter.

It was from the Center in Thessalonika.

As his reading progressed, Nikiphoros' face expressed horror.

"How savage . . ." he murmured.

And noticing his men looking at him, excited and impatient:

"A frightful crime occurred nearby . . ." he said.

All at once, ten voices erupted. The men's tongues had loosened:

"At Ramel!"

"They killed Giovanni!"

"They killed them all!"

"Even his parents!"

"He betrayed him, the contemptible . . ."

"Who?" Captain Nikiphoros inquired, startled. "The letter didn't say."

"Haven't I told you I brought you a guest?" the Curlyhead replied. "I went to Ramel and made an investigation. I found him for you!"

"Where is he? . . ." Nikiphoros asked, more and more shaken.

A number of men dashed into the hut and reappeared, dragging a youth whose hands were tied.

"Captain Manolis brought him to you for a trial, Commander!" they exclaimed.

Captain Manolis related how he'd gone to Ramel, questioned the villagers one by one, and had them each swear to tell the truth. He explained how he'd satisfied himself that this neighbor of Giovanni's—the one who'd urged him to flee—was the informer. Without disclosing his discovery to the guilty youth, the Curlyhead had summoned him along with some other villagers to the Tsekri landing cove, supposedly to show the way to the murderers. But once there he'd let him know the truth, tied him up, and transported him to the hut.

All the while Manolis spoke, the commander stared at the prisoner—at his evasive eyes and rigid mouth . . . Fear that the Greeks would torture him had drained all his color. His eyes darted to and fro, seeking a means of escape.

Apostolis didn't miss a word that Captain Manolis said, or remove his gaze from the Bulgarian. And he kept edging toward the prisoner.

Captain Nikiphoros interrogated the youth:

"You! Did you betray Giovanni?"

The Bulgarian didn't answer.

"Did something take place between the two of you in the past?" Nikiphoros questioned him again.

Seeing there was no reply, he asked:

"Does anyone here speak Bulgarian?"

"I do," Apostolis said, raising his hand as if in school.

"Ask him, then, whether he had anything against Giovanni . . . Some quarrel? . . . Or complaint? . . ."

Apostolis translated. But the prisoner turned a glance full of hate upon him, and again he didn't speak.

"Ask him if he revealed that Giovanni would leave in the morning," Captain Nikiphoros ordered.

Once more Apostolis translated. And once more the Bulgarian remained silent.

Apostolis warned him:

"Say what you have to say! They're trying you."

The Bulgarian's lips opened, uncovering his teeth which were clenched to such a degree that they ground together. His expression hardened still more.

"Ask him why he doesn't speak. His position is growing worse!" Captain Nikiphoros declared.

Again Apostolis translated, but without any result.

"Put him inside the hut," the leader commanded. "I'll look into it further."

"What more do you need to know, Captain?" the Curlyhead responded as two of the men dragged the Bulgarian back into the hut. "Ten villagers swore that he left secretly in the night and betrayed Giovanni. It was only after the slaughter that he returned . . ."

"Can't you see from his deceitful look, Commander?" Captain Pandelis added. Among Nikiphoros' newly-arrived men, he was his deputy-commander and one of his choice youth. "His face testifies to what he doesn't say!"

A racket with loud voices arose from the hut. Suddenly the Bulgarian burst forth, tied as he was. Running to the edge of the deck, he threw himself into the water.

At the same time, a shot rang out. Blood appeared; and then in the lake below, water closed over the body.

All this happened in a couple of seconds.

"Who fired?" the commander demanded.

"I did!" Pandelis answered. "We couldn't let him escape. He was a dangerous criminal."

The men had climbed down into the boats and were searching for the body.

They discovered it a short distance away, face down in the reeds, with the youth's head in the water.

He was dead. His teeth remained clenched and his lips distorted with hatred and fury.

Nikiphoros rebuked Pandelis.

"You killed him before we were sure!"

Captain Manolis, who was close by, laughed.

"You're new to this, Captain. You still feel compassion. When you've cut off some heads, you won't be upset about such things."

Captain Nikiphoros shuddered.

"Those aren't civilized words."

The Curlyhead smiled.

"Who said we came here for a civilized life?"

"We're here to discipline them and instruct them," the commander responded.

A little put to shame by his scolding, Pandelis declared:

"We won't succeed with the gospel and the cross, Captain!"

"I don't want to spill blood," Nikiphoros said grimly. "Captain Zezas didn't kill. He's our example."

"He himself didn't kill, Commander," Pandelis replied. "But why don't you ask the captains here whether his men did?"

Nikiphoros made no answer. All those around him were quiet.

Until Captain Manolis spoke up:

"This is a hard fight . . ."

Again the commander said nothing. With slow, heavy footsteps, he walked inside the reed hut.

"It's a darn hard fight . . ." Pandelis added in a low voice.

"The commander will find out for himself," the Curlyhead said. "He thinks he's dealing with men. However these are beasts—or worse! They torture whomever they capture!"

The others drew near to listen. Sitting in a circle, they recounted what they'd heard about the comitadjes' crimes.

"Whether you fall into Bulgarian or Turkish hands, you won't have an easy time of it," the Curlyhead maintained.

"The Bulgarians are worse. The Turks are more humane," Captain Pandelis interjected.

"Is that your opinion?" the Curlyhead responded. "Why not ask me?"

"You're a Cretan. Cretans and Turks never could suffer each other. We know that!" Evangelos, a dark-eyed youth exclaimed.[13]

"That's how you see it," the Curlyhead replied. "What about the martyrdom of Boubaras? You can't say it happened in Crete!"

"Who is Boubaras?"

"There you go, greenhorn! . . . Boubaras was a fearless young patriot from Macedonia. When two of our captains entered the Struggle,[14] he guided them up a steep, wild mountain. There were about a hundred Greek fighters, pursued by three hundred Turkish soldiers. Boubaras was a crack guide, though, and the captains gained a strong position.

"The Turkish soldiers got the worst of it. Those that weren't killed were put to flight. However a huge army came out and seized the roads and water sources. Our own men fled; but on the mountain, an unarmed Boubaras was captured."

"And did they kill him?" Nicolas, a Macedonian, asked.[15] "Out with it! Did they kill him?"

"If only they had! They wanted him to reveal where the captains had gone. He knew, yet he wouldn't say. They tied him to a tree and tortured him! . . . No response! More torturing—along with mutilation. 'Will you speak?' the officer said to him. 'I won't!' he answered. So they untied him and hurled him down. Little by little, they broke all the bones in his body."

"Did he inform on them?"

"He? . . . Not a word! But he cursed them and declared: 'I expected this, you scum! However I was born a Greek and a Greek I'll die! You'll learn nothing from me!' He died as they carved him up. Until the end he insisted: 'You won't get anything out of me!' When he was dead, the Turkish officer marveled and exclaimed: 'A devil of a patriot! Any country can be proud of such men!'"

"He slaughtered him, though!" Nikolas said angerly.

"Certainly! Do you think they'd let him go?" the Curlyhead replied. "And to think Pandelis considers the Turks more humane!"

"Then each of us must save a bullet in battle," Captain Pandelis cautioned. "And if he's wounded and knows there's no hope—if our men flee and leave him in enemy hands, whether Turk or Bulgarian—he can use it on himself!"

Seated apart, Apostolis listened silently, his sharp eyes fastened upon one after the other of the men. Attentive to their every word, he remained calm and unperturbed—as though he'd spent his whole life among such atrocities.

4.

Two Children

Tsekri was built beside one of two tributaries of the Loudias River, which formed a navigable road before it. One of the largest huts, it had sheltered other forces—some that remained at the lake and others that just passed by. Captain Agras had stopped there with his men upon arriving in Macedonia, then gone on to Naousa before returning to clear the lake of comitadjes.

In addition to the large Tsekri hut with its deck surrounded by an embankment for defense, there was another, smaller hut next to it that had a storehouse for provisions and ammunition, along with an oven for baking bread.

But as all this stood in a primitive and neglected condition, it was in need of repairs.

All day the commander and his men drove themselves to patch up the large hut—to close the holes with grass and reeds, level the uneven floor with dirt and straw, and fix the roof that had gaps in places. That way they'd be able to sleep lying down at night, one next to the other, enveloped in their cloaks and covers.

It was a chilly night in October.

The men lit a fire in the middle of the hut floor—which had been coated with clay to prevent the wood and reeds from igniting. After they'd prepared some legumes and eaten, they lay down to sleep.

To guard against a surprise Bulgarian attack, the commander stationed sentries a few meters beyond the large hut, in the shallow water full of vegetation. Once he'd assigned replacements to succeed them every two hours, he settled down to sleep, himself.

Beside the entrance with only an oilcloth for a door, Apostolis watched the tanned, tired, unshaven captain spread his blanket down, wrap himself in his cloak, adjust his cap, and try to become comfortable. A naval officer trained—like Miss Electra said about her father—"in the cleanliness and orderliness of his ship," he'd be sleeping on the reed floor in the dampness of the lake. Beds and mattresses didn't exist for the huts. In the crude facilities of the Swamp, it was a luxury for the rebels to have straw bedding.

It's good enough for us, accustomed as we are to the hard life of the Struggle, the boy thought to himself. But for him?

The commander extinguished the oil lamp, plunging them all into darkness.

* * * *

Absorbed in his thoughts, Apostolis couldn't fall asleep.

His work was finished and tomorrow he'd leave. He'd accomplished his mission of guiding Captain Nikiphoros and his force to the Swamp. Now that the commander had arrived at his destination, in the morning a boat would take the boy to the landing-cove and put him out on shore. His life of wandering would resume.

I'll go to Zorba . . . And then?

He visualized the village school—the teacher, the children at their desks, the blackboard . . . He could hear the teacher's ardent voice and see her brown eyes flashing with enthusiasm as she told her pupils in a hushed tone: "You're Greeks! Be proud! Greece is an old and glorious civilization! . . ."

Miss Electra . . . Was she beautiful? he wondered.

He couldn't say. What it meant to be beautiful, he really didn't know. All the women he knew were dark, thin, and drained from work and the sun. Miss Electra had pale skin and long, slender fingers . . .

Whether she was beautiful or not, he wasn't sure. He only knew that when he entered her warm classroom and heard her tell the children in her low, passionate voice: "You're Greeks! Be proud! . . ." something inside him softened and tears came to his eyes. He felt deep down the desire to give his life, like so many others had—for Greece, for its people and for Hellenism.

He would set off now for Zorba and see Miss Electra. Perhaps she'd have some instructions for him . . . another mission. At peace, he dropped off to sleep.

* * * *

At daybreak everyone was up and about. Apostolis volunteered to make coffee. While the men bustled in and out of the hut—taking care of the boats, the ammunition, and any weapons that needed cleaning—he squatted down and lit some freshly-cut wood in the clay-coated center of the floor. Clouds of smoke billowed up all around.

The huts had neither flue nor window. When a fire was burning, the smoke proved suffocating. In order to breathe, the men had to sit or lie down lower than the smoke rising up toward the roof.

"Isn't there any dry wood here?" Captain Pandelis asked, coughing.

"See to it that wood is cut today and put out in the sun to dry," the commander replied from the hut entrance, where he was enjoying the October sunshine.

A wolf howled in the distance, then a second time closer . . . And the howling stopped . . .

No one took any note of it; they were all caught up in their work. Only Apostolis had pricked up his ears like a hunting dog at the first howl, before turning his attention back to the pot of brewing coffee.

* * * *

The sun was high when he climbed into a flat-bottomed canoe with two newly-taught oarsmen, who wanted to practice their rowing on the way to the Tsekri landing-cove.

"So long! Come back again!" the commander had said to him. He'd tried to give him a gift for all of his hard work as a guide, but offended and red-faced, Apostolis refused.

To accept money? For showing the way to a Greek force?

Captain Nikiphoros therefore presented him with a small, silver cross.

"To remember me by . . ."

This Apostolis accepted. As a remembrance it pleased him as nothing else would have. Not money, though! . . .

* * * *

In the still water, the two men and the boy proceeded towards the shore without a sound, while scrutinizing every bush and bed of reeds in case an enemy might be lurking there.

The yellowish fall foliage hadn't yet fallen from the trees, shrubs, and reeds. In places, the thick vegetation remained green.

Sometimes the men exchanged an observation in low voices.

"We're new to this. It takes time to get the feel of the Swamp," one of them was saying.

"This part of it is free of Bulgarians," Apostolis responded.

"I wonder if you can ever be sure . . ." the first oarsman murmured.

"Of course not. But their nest is behind us in the western section of the lake, concealed by the forest," Apostolis said. "They don't venture out much in the open. Instead of taking us on, they work in the dark to be safe."

Upon reaching the landing-cove, they separated. Apostolis leaped to the ground, and the men started back to the hut. The boy headed to the right, in the direction of the plain.

* * * *

Solitude all around. No one in sight.

Apostolis walked slowly until the boat grew distant and disappeared behind the reeds.

Then he halted, let forth a long, drawn-out jackal's wail, and settled himself in front of a bush to wait.

Suddenly a child appeared almost at his feet. Bounding over to Apostolis, he dropped down beside him.

"I didn't know if you heard me, you took so long to come!
. . ." he said in Bulgarian.

Apostolis reacted calmly:

"The boat had to bring me to shore. It wasn't up to me, Jovan."

Jovan looked at him with his large, black eyes wide-open, not
daring to utter a word. Apostolis saw the admiration in his gaze,
combined with something like fear or respect. Laughing, he asked:

"Did you learn anything?"

It was without expecting much of an answer that he inquired.
So he was taken back when the child replied:

"Yes! I found out!"

"About Apostol Petkoff?" Apostolis exclaimed.

"Yes! He's hiding at Zervohori. He wasn't at Ramel!"

Once more Apostolis was taken back.

"What do you know about Ramel?" he questioned him.

"Didn't they kill a patriarchal Greek there with all his children? And wasn't Apostol Petkoff's letter pinned to him?" Jovan
replied in turn. "Well, the letter was chief Apostol's—but he's at
Zervohori."

"How did the letter get pinned to the dead body, then? . . ."

Jovan shrugged his shoulder with his customary motion.

"He gives all those letters out to the comitadjes," he answered;
"and they leave them on the dead bodies. That way it seems like
Apostol is everywhere and it scares the patriarchal Greeks."

Now it was Apostolis who looked at Jovan with what resembled awe and admiration.

"Where did a tot like you learn all this?" he asked.

Jovan blushed from the emotion and joy he felt at the older
boy's words. He stole a sidelong glance at him and said softly:

"You told me to find out where Apostol Petkoff was. I did,
and I came to tell you."

"But how did you find out?"

Jovan put his arms around his knees and gazed thoughtfully
out at the plain before him.

"How did you learn all this?" Apostolis repeated.

"I discovered it at Zervohori. Angel Pio sent me," the child replied.

"Your uncle? What did he send you to do there?"

"I lied to him when he began to beat me for not returning for two days. I said I'd been searching for a Captain Yianni in the Swamp, a patriarchal Greek who was there with a band of rebels."

"What Captain Yianni, Judas?"

Wide-eyed and uncertain, Jovan stared at him.

"I told him the fishermen from Kourfalia were talking about it—they're all comitadjes. Angel Pio believed it and wanted me to find him . . . 'Without a boat, how can I find him?' I asked. And he sent me to Zervohori."

"To Apostol Petkoff?"

"No! To a Toman Pazarenze. I had a letter . . ."

"What did the letter say?"

"It was sealed."

Apostolis gave him a shove.

"You're a fool! At such times you open letters!"

"And then?" the child responded seriously.

"You'd show it to me!"

"What would you do?"

"What would I do? . . . In other words, you feared a beating!"

Jovan gazed at him, growing more and more perplexed.

"Didn't you tell me to discover where Apostol is?" he asked.

"He might have written it in the letter. Use your head!"

Jovan hugged his knees tighter.

"I thought I should listen and learn, and then take a canoe to find Apostol in the Swamp. Angel Pio said to me: 'If I get you a little boat, will you find the patriarchal Greek?' I answered 'yes,' and he wrote Toman Pazarenze for them to give me one."

"Did they?"

"A crowd had gathered at Toman's—fierce, bearded comitadjes. One of them was shaven and wore a gold ring on his middle finger. After Toman read the letter, he handed it to him and they spoke together in low voices. I watched them secretly and saw that the shaven man was looking at me. He came over and put his hand on my shoulder. 'You didn't hear the name of the patriarchal Greek right,' he said. 'It's not Captain Yianni, but Captain Agras.'"

Apostolis gave a start.

"What?" he exclaimed.

" . . . And he asked me whether I could find him in the Swamp. 'I'll find him,' I replied. Then he said he'd give me a canoe and had them bring me clothes and shoes."

Apostolis became angry.

"Hey, Judas! Who are you working for?" he demanded. "For your uncle or for me?"

Distressed, the child replied:

"For you. But why do you call me Judas?"

"Because you're Bulgarian!"

He looked at Jovan and softened before his crestfallen face.

"But you're not a traitor. I won't insult you—don't be upset. However, who was the shaven man with the ring?"

"It was Apostol Petkof."

"What are you saying? You saw him, then? How do you know that's who it was?"

"Everyone called him 'chief.' When they took me in another room, a woman got me clothes and helped me dress. It was Pazarenze's wife. I pretended I knew the shaven man was chief Apostol. From her, I learned that it was."

"Your clothes came from him?" Apostolis questioned the child.

"He told them to give me some."

Hesitantly Apostolis said:

"You shouldn't have accepted them if you're not working for him."

Instantly Jovan flew up and started to undress. Apostolis stopped him.

"Never mind," he told him. "I don't have any others for you yet. But I'll manage to find some and then you'll return these. Sit down," he added, drawing the child up close to him again; "and tell me the rest. Did they give you a canoe?"

"Yes."

"What did you do with it?"

"I brought it."

"It's here?"

"Yes! Inside the reeds . . . at the landing-cove nearby."

Apostolis paused to consider . . .

"Listen," he said shortly. "Will you promise not to speak about all this?"

He had him swear upon Captain Nikiphoros' silver cross this time—which he kept hanging from his neck by a string.

"Pay attention, now," Apostolis said. "You'll come with me and we'll find Captain Agras! . . ."

"I'll show you the way," Jovan interrupted.

"What! You know where he is?"

"I know!"

"Can you take me there?"

"I can!"

Apostolis trembled all over from excitement.

"Don't tell me you saw him?"

"I saw him! I've just come from there—from his hut!"

Apostolis breathed heavily.

"How did you find him?" he asked, restraining the emotion that took his breath away.

In turn, Jovan sought to recall.

"How did you find him?" Apostolis repeated in a louder voice.

Frightened, the child stared at him.

". . . I shouldn't have? . . ."

Lowering his threatening fist, Apostolis stuffed his hands under his knees.

"Tell me," he went on, more in command of himself. "You swore! You mustn't lie."

"I don't want to lie to you, Apostolis. Why are you mad?"

Softly, reassuringly, controlling his nerves and suspicions, Apostolis replied:

"I'm not mad. But I don't know you well. Besides you're Bulgarian . . . Did you inform Apostol that you saw Agras?"

Tears welled up in the child's eyes, and two flowed down onto his pinched cheeks.

"How could I inform him when I came right here!" he murmured.

Touched, Apostolis threw his arm around the child's neck and said in a soothing tone:

"Don't cry. Come on, I believe you! Yet why did you go to find Captain Agras? And how did you discover where he was?"

"The chief told me where to go."

"He knows? How is it that he knows?"

"There were battles. Not big ones, but the comitadjes' boats can't get through to Agia Marina anymore—the village where they have storehouses."

"Who told you that?"

"I was talking with Toman Pazarenze's wife, the one who brought me the clothes. She told me everything."

"How stupid! To have such conversations with an infant like you!"

"I acted like a Bulgarian. I lied. I said that I'm trusted by Angel Pio—that I'm his nephew . . . And they know he's a fierce comitadje."

"Eh . . . and you are! Aren't you?" Apostolis cut him short.

Jovan didn't answer. Sorrow spread over his pale face. His lips trembled, about to break into sobs.

Smiling, Apostolis jostled him and hugged the child.

"Come on, don't make a fuss. I won't tease you anymore . . ." he said. "You know your uncle's a criminal and that you mustn't listen to him. Come, I consider you my own loyal helper. Tell me, did Apostol inform you how to find Captain Agras?"

"He wasn't sure. He said gunshots came from the direction of Agia Marina. But I went into the reeds and searched and found him."

"You saw him?"

"I did!"

"You told him Apostol is aware of his hiding place."

"No! I wanted to let you know first!"

"What is Captain Agras like? . . . big? dark? fierce?"

"No! He laughs all the time! I didn't understand what he said very well because he spoke fast . . ."

"Bulgarian?"

"No, Greek!"

"You understand Greek?"

Hesitantly Jovan replied:

"I don't remember it well . . ."

Apostolis bent over and looked him in the face.

"You mean you spoke it once?"

"I don't know . . . But I understand if they speak slowly to me."

"Did you understand what Captain Agras said to you?"

"I understood that he said . . ."

And the boy repeated in Greek: "This child is sick."

His accent was foreign, yet he pronounced the "d" softly, not in the hard Slavic way.

"What did you answer?"

"I answered: 'No, not sick.' And he laughed again and pulled my hair. He said something to a villager who was cutting reeds with a sickle to open up a road in the water; and the villager asked me in Bulgarian where I came from. I didn't want to say. Then Captain Agras spoke again so quickly I couldn't understand. And he had the villager explain it to me."

"Yes? . . . What was it? . . ." Apostolis responded impatiently.

"He wanted me to go and tell the comitadjes hiding in their forest that he—Captain Agras—was at the Lower Huts. And he dared them to come and take him on."

"He said that? A brave man, no doubt about it!" Apostolis exclaimed.

And fascinated, he asked:

"What did you reply?"

"I didn't say anything. Then Captain Agras raised his voice and repeated: 'Do you hear? Inform them!' I answered back in Greek: 'I won't inform them!' Laughing again, he took a bowl, put some meat in it, and handed it to me. 'Eat,' he said. 'You're hungry.'"

"You ate?"

"Yes! I didn't want to leave. It was wonderful being near him. All the time he laughs and jokes with his men. And when a villager cutting reeds got tired, the captain jumped in the water himself, grabbed the sickle, and cut whole armfuls of reeds. I decided you should know about it. So I came."

Pensive, Apostolis gazed out at the lake that stretched peacefully before them. All at once he sprang to his feet.

"Let's go!" he said decisively.

Jovan got up immediately.

"To Captain . . ."

"Hush! . . ." the other boy whispered.

Together they set off in a hurry, following the shore of the lake.

Two fishermen crossed their path and, in passing, bid them good day.

"Where are you off to, boys?" they asked in the Macedonian dialect.

"To Zorba," Apostolis answered, "to school."

"At this hour?"

"Yes—we're late," Apostolis said.

But when they reached the curve of the lake, rather than drawing left to find the road to the village, they turned right towards the landing-cove.

No one was there when they arrived. To the side in the reeds, Jovan's little boat was waiting. The two boys climbed inside; and using the oars as poles, they made their way out of the reeds. Finding a tributary of the river, they proceeded to the southwest.

Jovan acted as guide. Apostolis observed that he was steering towards the southern shore.

"Why don't you head more towards the middle?" he asked. "The water's deeper. Besides, it's a short-cut to the Lower Huts."

"Inside the reeds, there are other huts. I don't know who they belong to," Jovan answered.

Apostolis stopped rowing and got up to see.

"Where?" he questioned him.

"They're low; they don't appear," the child replied. "But I know of a new path that leads near Toumba. Neither Greeks or Bulgarians will notice us, if they're theirs."

Apostolis rowed steadily, while Jovan steered them through the tall reeds, making a rudder out of the back oar.

However they were but children, the sun was still high, and they had a distance to go.

Sweating, Apostolis lifted his oar out of the water.

"I say let's stop and have a bite to eat," he said.

He wasn't about to admit that he needed a break. But casting a glance toward the front of the boat, then behind, and afterwards up at the sky, he asked:

"Are we still far?"

"Yes," Jovan answered. "We haven't even gone half way."

"Where is the first Toumba hut?"

"In that direction . . ." and he gestured to the left to show him.

"Did we pass it?"

"Not yet!"

Apostolis took out a handwoven handkerchief with a prominent red A embroidered in one corner, and wiped the sweat from his face.

"I say let's eat," he repeated.

Jovan didn't reply. Seated in the stern, with the wet oar on his lap, he stared at Apostolis.

"Why don't you speak? Aren't you hungry?" the older boy asked again.

"No," the child murmured.

Apostolis leaned over and looked him in the face again.

"I suspect that you're always hungry," he said. "You're skin and bones."

Jovan remained quiet.

Apostolis understood.

"You don't have anything to eat?" he said. "Is that it?"

The child gazed at him with the sad eyes of a hungry dog.

"Don't worry," Apostolis said protectively. "We'll share what I have."

He didn't have much. A half loaf of bread, a little sheep's cheese, and a small bunch of grapes in a long, narrow sack—what they'd given him at the Tsekri hut before he departed. He divided the bread and cheese, taking care that the portions were equal, and gave half to Jovan.

The hungry child began to devour the food.

Apostolis watched him with compassion.

"Why don't your own people feed you enough?" he asked.

Jovan didn't answer.

"Why do you stay with your uncle and not your parents?" Apostolis went on questioning him.

"I don't have any parents," Jovan replied.

"What? You have no mother?"

"No!"

"And your uncle took you into his house? Then why, since he took you in, does he give you so little food?"

"He says I don't work enough!"

"But you tend his sheep for him, don't you?"

"I do. However he says that isn't work and I'm not capable of anything else."

Apostolis flared up:

"How can you be capable of heavy work if he leaves you without food?"

Jovan made no reply.

The two boys continued eating in silence.

Jovan finished first. With his hands spread out over the oar still on his lap, he sat admiring Apostolis—who ate slowly and seemed to enjoy every mouthful.

Timidly he said his name:

"Apostolis . . ."

"Yes?"

"Apostolis . . . do you have a mother?"

Becoming serious, the older boy replied:

"No. I don't have either a mother or a father. I'm alone."

"You don't even have an uncle?"

"No! I'm a foundling."

"What does that mean?"

"That they found me!"

"Who found you? . . . Where?"

"How am I supposed to remember?" Apostolis responded with a laugh . . . "I was a baby. Babies don't remember."

Again, the boys were silent.

And once more Jovan asked hesitantly:

"If you don't have a mother, who made that beautiful letter for you?"

He pointed to the thickly woven handkerchief lying on the other boy's knees, with its red A embroidered in one corner.

"This? . . ." Apostolis picked it up and looked at it, perhaps for the first time attentively . . .

". . . Miss Electra embroidered it and gave it to me . . ." he replied.

"Who is she?"

"The teacher at the school at Zorba."

"Is she nice?"

"Very nice. She taught me to read."

He'd finished eating. Stuffing the grapes back in the sack he kept inside his shirt, he took another look at the sun shining overhead.

"Come on, Jovan. Chin up!" he said. "Where will this new path lead us?"

"To a branch beyond . . ."

"Beyond Nisi?"

"Of course—beyond the second Toumba, too."

"But who opened up this narrow path that cuts off so much distance?"

Jovan didn't know.

For some time the two boys rowed without a word.

And again Jovan spoke up.

"Apostolis . . ."

"Out with it!"

"Since you're a foundling, where did you get food?"

"As if I should know! Sometimes here, sometimes there
. . . The fishermen by the sea are all good men . . . For as long as I
remember, they've always shared their food with me. Later I was
working."

"What kind of work?"

"When they fished with lines, I set the bait on the hooks. I
helped them drag the trammel net; and I sorted the fish when they
took the nets out . . . You can always find work if you want to."

The child stared at him, reflecting.

"And your shoes? . . . and your coat? . . . Did the fishermen
give them to you?" he asked.

Apostolis was startled.

"These? The ones I'm wearing? Certainly not! I bought them."

"With money?" Jovan inquired.

"Of course with money! With what else? Pebbles? . . . I work!
For years now I've been working!"

Jovan didn't presume to ask anything else. Quietly the boat
glided along the still water of the path, among the tall walls of
reeds which closed off the lake to both sides of them.

However, Apostolis was also reflecting. This time, he broke
the silence first, himself:

"Perhaps you'd like to join with me, Jovan?"

Jovan's large eyes filled with happy tears. His lips quivered,
and his breath was taken away.

"Could I? . . ." he murmured, trembling all over.

"You bet you could! You're smart . . . not at all lazy . . . In fact,
you're pretty sharp! But you'll have to leave your uncle."

Jovan was so overcome he couldn't say a word.

"And you'll have to learn Greek . . . You can't be Bulgarian
anymore," Apostolis added.

Jovan let out a sigh that swelled his narrow chest.

Apostolis misunderstood.

"I don't work with Bulgarians," he declared abruptly.

Softly in a low voice, the child said:

"Neither do I . . ."

"Well, you accept then?"

The tears Jovan had been holding back, burst, overflowed, erupted in a flood.

"Oh! Take me with you, Apostolis! . . ." he murmured between sobs.

Apostolis was stirred, too. Protectively he reached out and stroked the child's head.

"Don't worry," he said to him. "If you come with me, you won't be without food or a coat or shoes. And you'll return the ones you're wearing to Apostol Petkof. They're Bulgarian."

"I'll do what you tell me," Jovan replied obediently.

"This work . . . that we're doing today . . . and that you did yesterday . . . It doesn't pay—you have to understand that! We do this work for the sake of a Greek Macedonia. But I have other work as well—of all kinds! . . . And I'm a carpenter. I'll make you my apprentice."

Charmed, the child asked:

"You have a hammer?"

"A hammer and a saw, a plane, a screw-driver—and nails! . . ."

"Where do you keep them?" Jovan wondered.

"Miss Electra keeps them for me when I'm not using them."

"The teacher?"

"Yes. I fix all the desks at her school."

The two boys rowed on. From time to time, they paused a few minutes to rest, and then took up their oars again . . .

Emerging from the narrow path onto a waterway that was deeper, the boys continued to row—Apostolis firmly and Jovan more wearily.

The sun lowered before them and sank behind the mountains. Dusk descended. Little by little it grew dark, until night engulfed them.

5.

The Lower Huts

"Who is it? . . ."

Day was dawning . . . The man's strong voice resounded over the water.

The click of a trigger was heard. Below, the dipping of an oar suddenly fell silent.

However no one appeared. Reeds everywhere . . . shadows . . . brambles . . . Then somewhere close by, the frightened flight of a water-hen.

A boyish, immature voice rose up from inside the reeds.

"Don't draw, Mister Evzone! It's a Greek! . . I'm Apostolis the guide!"

"Come out from the reeds! . . . Where are you? . . ."

A boat emerged from inside the foliage and entered the waterway flowing slowly to the east. Inside it, a man was standing, well-armed. A second man in a cloak sat rowing.

At the same time, from the opposite side of the water another canoe turned, trampled some reeds, and also passed out into the open. Only two children were in it. The smallest, pale and thin, was weak from lack of sleep. His two hands clung to the side of the boat.

"Which of you is Apostolis the guide?" the man asked.

"I am," the bigger boy replied. "We've come from the northern shore. Night overtook us on the water."

"Who are you seeking?"

"Captain Agras."

"Do you have something to show to identify yourself?"

"No. But I guided Captain Nikiphoros to Tsekri. I was with him for three days and nights . . ."

"How do I know that?"

"He gave me this cross," Apostolis answered, drawing it out of his shirt. "Here, take a look!"

"How can I be sure this cross is his? . . . Say the password!"

Apostolis didn't know it. However, he kept his composure.

"I don't know the password," he said, "because there was no need to say it at Tsekri. Take me to your commander. I have important news for him."

"Who's to assure me you're trustworthy? . . ." the armed man began.

The other one with the cloak interrupted him.

"For shame, Nasos!" he exclaimed. "Don't you see they're babies? If the commander heard you, he'd give you a hell of a dressing down!"

The first man still hesitated a moment before deciding.

"All right," he said. "Follow us with your boat!"

He let out a call, and another responded from beyond the reeds.

"A visitor!" Nasos shouted.

Rowing slowly, the oarsman ascended what little of a current there was, while Apostolis followed, working his oar steadily.

Another canoe appeared before them, with an armed oarsman. Nasos and his companion moved their boat out of the way so the two boys could pass.

"They're searching for the commander," Nasos explained. "They say they've come from Tsekri. You take charge of them, Mihalis. We're on duty . . ."

With curiosity, Mihalis looked at the two children.

"Aren't you Apostolis the guide?" he asked.

"I am," a pleased Apostolis answered. "How do you know me?"

"Didn't you lead us from the sea to the Swamp? You remember Captain Kapsalis, don't you? I was in his force until he died."

"You fought with him in the battle where he lost his life?" Apostolis asked eagerly . . .

"It happened that he'd dispatched me as a messenger when they killed him. Otherwise I'd be dead too. Now I'm with Captain Agras. Come, I'll show you to the hut."

In a triumphant good-by to Nasos, Apostolis took off his cap and bowed.

Nasos laughed.

"My job is to question you. I'm on guard," he said. "It's Mihalis that knows you as a guide. So long now . . ."

Jovan had observed all this scene quietly, gripping both sides of the boat to support himself. He was trembling, fearful that someone might speak to him and he wouldn't know what to say.

Smiling, Apostolis nodded to him not to worry and caught up the oar.

In the lead Mihalis steered his canoe along narrow, curving, twisting paths where the reeds blocked the view at every turn. The boys trailed him, tired and hungry.

At one turn, a large hut was suddenly revealed. Well-built, it had a high embankment surrounding its deck, making it a veritable stronghold.

Canoes were moored all around, while anxious men rushed in and out of the hut, readying knapsacks, weapons, cartridges, and bread . . .

One person stood out, calm and cheerful amidst the activity. Somewhat short, he wore knee breeches and boots and had a cartridge belt with a row of leather pockets strapped over his rebel's tunic. A pair of binoculars was hanging from his neck onto his chest. His thick, curly hair remained loose, without a cap.

Standing at the edge of the deck, he had his hand on a short-barrelled rifle.

To counter the water's glare, he squinted as the canoes with Mihalis and the boys drew near. Recognizing Jovan, he straightened up.

"The little Bulgarian!" he exclaimed. "What! You're here again?"

Uneasy, Jovan bent down to Apostolis' ear:

"That's Captain Agras!" he whispered in Bulgarian.

Impressed, Apostolis remained silent.

The boats pulled alongside the deck, and Mihalis and the boys climbed up onto it.

Agras approached them.

"Why do you bring me such chicks when we're about to set off on a campaign, Mihalis?" he asked with good humor.

Mihalis sought to justify himself.

"I don't know the child," he answered, "but the older boy is no chick. He's Apostolis the guide, who knows the Swamp inside out."

"You're a guide?" Agras responded, taking stock of the boy.

"I am!" Apostolis replied proudly. "I come from Tsekri, where I guided Captain Nikiphoros and his force."

"What are you saying?" Agras exclaimed. "So reinforcements have arrived? And this little Bulgarian? What's he to you?" he added, nodding towards Jovan who could barely stand on his feet.

"He's my apprentice. He's Bulgarian-speaking, but devoted to me," Apostolis replied again. "He's the one who discovered you were at the Lower Huts, and then came to tell me and show me the way here. I have some news that will interest you, Captain Agras. Apostol Petkoff, who's supposed to be at Kourfalia and Botzets, is hiding at Zervohori."

"At Zervohori? Here? Right under our nose?"

Agras stopped short and asked:

"Who told you?"

Apostolis pointed to the pale child next to him.

"This one! He went and found him. And he saw him! Petkoff put him on your trail, Captain Agras, in order to spy on you. The chief's aware you're at the Swamp and he wanted information."

Apostolis threw out his chest:

"However Jovan's loyal to me," he continued. "He came to tell me yesterday and led me to your hut. Night caught us on the water!"

"So that's the reason the child's in such a state?"

Agras made a sign to Jovan.

"Sit down," he said, shoving a bunch of straw to him. "Hey! The boy seems more dead than alive!"

"We're hungry," Apostolis confessed, a little shamefaced. "We've had nothing to eat since lunch yesterday . . ."

Agras motioned to one of the men who'd gathered to listen:

"Hot coffee, and bread and cheese . . . and whatever else you have!" he ordered.

A couple of men hurried to bring food. And while the two famished boys gobbled up their bread and cheese, Agras resumed his questioning.

"Where and how did this infant learn that Apostol Petkoff is hiding at Zervohori?" he asked.

Briefly Apostolis gave him an account of as much as he knew about Jovan. He related how his uncle had sent him to find a non-existant Captain Yianni, and how Apostol Petkoff told him he'd confused the name Yianni with Agras—who was at the Swamp and held the road to Agia Marina, the village with Bulgarian storehouses.

Agras laughed, in good spirits.

"So they've gotten wind of us! . . ." he said to his men.

And turning once more to Apostolis:

"Does the youngster know if Petkoff is informed about our strength, or that we took the Agia Marina and Vangeli huts?"

Apostolis translated the question.

"No," Jovan replied. "He didn't know much—he only said that Captain Agras was somewhere near the Agia Marina village."

"Well enough!" Agras exclaimed upon hearing Apostolis' answer. "But tell me, do you know where a hut called Kouga is located?"

"Yes," Apostolis answered. "Near Zervohori. However, it was such a wreck that the fishermen abandoned it . . ."

Delighted, Agras raised his hand and made a sign to an old man sitting on the embankment beside the hut.

"Pascal," he shouted out to him, "our troubles are over! This boy knows where Kouga is."

Old Pascal got up slowly and took his time walking over to the commander. He was wearing a felt cap that covered his head and ears and extended down to the back of his neck.

"What did you say?" he inquired in Bulgarian.

A robust youth, heavily-armed, had approached to hear.

"Captain Gonos," Agras called out. "Tell him that this boy can find Kouga."

Captain Gonos looked at Apostolis without much faith.

"You can find it?" he asked with a Bulgarian accent, groping for words.

Somewhat confused at encountering so much Bulgarian, Apostolis remained quiet. Mihalis, standing next to him, slapped him on the back.

"Hey, kiddo," he said, laughing; "don't you know Captain Gonos,[16] who's fought in battle after battle and holds the Prisna hut? The fact that he's Bulgarian-speaking doesn't make him a Bulgarian! No Bulgarian comes near here."

Silently Apostolis fixed his eyes on old Pascal.

"He's become one of us now!" Captain Agras said cheerfully, patting the old man on the shoulder. "We don't mistreat anyone, do we Pascal? And you have firsthand experience of Bulgarian clubs and knives."

But the old man didn't understand. His gaze rotated from the commander to Apostolis.

In a couple of words Captain Gonos explained to him in Bulgarian that this boy, and he gestured toward Apostolis, knew where Kouga was.

With disbelief the old man stared at him.

"Where is it?" he asked.

"Near Zervohori," Apostolis replied in Bulgarian.

"I know it, too," the old man said with a guffaw. "However you can't find it anymore."

"What did he say?" Agras inquired.

"That he knows where it is . . . but that it's impossible to find now," Gonos translated haltingly.

"He can't find it because the reeds and waterlilies have covered up the paths," Apostolis stated.

Agras took stock of him again, looking him up and down, and smiled.

"If I told you to find it, would you be able to?" he asked.

"Kouga? Certainly, Captain. You'll need to reopen paths, though, to arrive at Grounandero."

"What's that?"

"A waterway that winds around to the Bulgarian huts like a snake—or as we say, like the intestines of a pig. It's near Kouga. If you clear the old fishermen's paths from here, you'll get there faster."

"Can you locate these paths again? . . ."

"I can. The reeds will be lower and greener."

Agras gave him an affectionate slap.

"I'll take you as a guide!" he declared in good spirits. "But you're not to boast to Pascal. Because he'll let you have it and that's not to our interests. Besides, he's a good man who knows all the Bulgarian huts and every inch of the Swamp."

Looking over at the hut, he shouted:

"Captain Teligadis!"

A hardy lad of about twenty to twenty-five appeared, who was armed like everyone else.

"Teligadis, go inform the Agia Marina hut to send us all the villagers we've recruited," he ordered. "We'll go out and clear the paths."

* * * *

That day was engraved in Apostolis' life with indelible colors. It seemed to him that he grew two feet. All day long he remained close to Captain Agras, to his second-in-command Captain Teligadis, and to Agras' select evzones whose names he'd learned—Andonis, Nikos, Pavlos, Yiorgos, Demos, Kostas, and others.

He'd spoken with Pascal, who really did know the Swamp as if it were his home. And Mihalis had related the old man's history to him. A Bulgarian, he'd been captured and beaten by one of two quarreling factions. Therefore he hated all the Bulgarians and had come to Captain Agras, proposing to serve as his guide in the labyrinth of the lake.

During the whole day Apostolis had seen the villagers—who'd never been mobilized before—laboring in the dense, entangled forest of reeds. For the first time, Captain Agras had persuaded them to work for a day's wage to open up paths for the Greek forces. He'd even jumped into the shallow water himself, beside the twenty or so villagers. Although unaccustomed to a sickle, he'd cut down armfuls of reeds with a determination, will, and spirit that renewed the strength of the tired men.

In the midst of Captain Agras' youths, Apostolis saw and breathed an atmosphere that was fearless and free. It caused him, too, to raise his head, throw back his shoulders, and stand erect and self-confident.

When in the evening they all returned to the Lower Huts, the men separated—half to Vangeli, the others to Agia Marina. While the tired workers sat down to eat the lentil stew prepared by those left guarding the huts, a beaming Apostolis was welcomed back by Jovan.

"I thought you'd never return—that Apostol Petkoff would kill you . . ." he whispered.

"Let him try. The commander gave me a pistol," Apostolis announced with pride.

He showed it off to him, stuffed into his belt like Captain Agras' force had theirs.

After the men had fallen asleep, the two boys were left side-by-side in their corner. Whispering, Jovan related as much as he'd understood of the rebels' and villagers' conversation.

He'd learned that Pascal was a real Bulgarian—who'd first been with the comitadjes. But during a quarrel, they'd tied him up, slashed his arms and legs, and cut off his ears. That was why he wore a cap covering his head. Old Pascal had gone over to the Greeks then, who were known not to torture their prisoners. He'd offered to guide Captain Agras' force into the most secret parts of the Swamp.

And Captain Gonos was a Macedonian from Giannitsa. At the beginning of the Struggle, when he thought the Bulgarians wanted to free Macedonia from the Turks, he'd fought at their side. But once he discovered they planned to turn Macedonia Bulgarian, he split with them and formed his own force. And when Captain Agras went to Naousa with his few evzones, he'd joined with him.

As soon as Captain Agras re-entered the Swamp, Captain Gonos did, too. He settled at Prisna, a hut close to the comitadjes. His one wish was to drive the Bulgarians out of Zervohori and the huts they'd built near it, in the wooded section of the lake and at the shore.

But the captains didn't know how to find the Bulgarian huts. And the fishermen were afraid to guide them. Only Pascal, who they paid well, consented to show them the way.

"And do you know . . ." Jovan whispered to the older boy. "Do you know that Captain Agras is a Greek officer? From the Greek army? . . ."

"Who told you?"

"One of the men said that he wasn't used to bowing down— that he was a free citizen of Greece. It was only because of his love for his officer . . ."

He paused to remember a difficult word, and then pro- nounced it in Greek: ". . . for his *lieutenant* that he'd come here. I asked a village rebel who knew Bulgarian what lieutenant meant. 'Nothing,' he said. 'Forget it.' And he told another fighter to be careful when he spoke before the little Bulgarian—that I wasn't to know who the commander is, or about the Greek army. But I heard them talking, and I know that the commander's an officer."

Apostolis reprimanded him:

"You shouldn't eavesdrop!"

"No?" Jovan responded apprehensively.

"No, never! Miss Electra told me that. She says it's not right."

Jovan leaned over to Apostolis' ear again.

"If I didn't listen, how would I have learned that Apostol was hiding at Zervohori?"

His words bothered Apostolis.

"Miss Electra said never to eavesdrop. But I think it doesn't matter with the comitadjes. With our own men, though, you shouldn't."

And he added, "Besides, maybe you didn't get it right. You mustn't repeat it to anyone."

Jovan stopped short, deflated.

"What else did the men say?" Apostolis continued.

"That Captain Agras realized it wouldn't be enough just to attack the Bulgarians, as long as the comitadjes held the Swamp. He felt it was useless to strike them from outside. So he came here himself and captured the two huts. Now he's after Kouga, to be closer to Zervohori. Did you find it, Apostolis?"

"Not yet. We have to open up roads, since they've disappeared in that area. However I know where it is."

And he asked: "Has Captain Agras fought any battles?"

"They spoke so fast I couldn't make it out," Jovan answered. "But the men all seem to love their captain, and one who was enthusiastic called him 'the best officer in the Greek army.' The villager looked at me again then and whispered something to the others."

Apostolis turned toward the child, worried.

"Listen, Jovan," he said in a low but sharp tone. "It doesn't matter that you told all this to me. However, if you repeat it! . . ."

Tears quivered in Jovan's voice as he asked:

"Do you want me to swear not to talk?"

"No," Apostolis said sternly. "You did yesterday. See to it that you keep your word."

The two children were quiet. Apostolis heard Jovan sniffling for a while, swallowing his tears. But he didn't say anything to him. Troubled by what he'd heard, he was angry at Captain Agras' men for speaking out so carelessly. After all, there could have been a Bulgarian listening somewhere . . .

Finally he fell asleep, next to the already slumbering Jovan.

6.

Miss Electra

Everyday the black, tar-coated canoes set out from the Lower Huts with the village workers and armed rebels to open up roads in the lake—curved, twisted, secret passages inside the thick, woody area towards the Bulgarian huts.

Everyday in water up to their knees, Captain Agras' evzones guarded the recruited villagers as they cut down reeds and uprooted shrubs. They covered the entrances to paths with false clusters of branches and leaves to prevent the Bulgarians from discovering them on one of their patrols and setting up an ambush.

Yet the work was slow, the workers few, and the cutting of reeds and uprooting of bushes strenuous. All the while they continued to spy on the Bulgarian huts. However they didn't find Kouga.

"They must have destroyed it," the men said.

But Pascal shook his head "no," and they kept heading north, opening up more paths.

"It's to the left, beyond Grounandero, Captain Agras," Apostolis insisted. "I know where it is. We still haven't reached there."

Meanwhile they'd distanced themselves from the Lower Huts. With only seven canoes and twelve evzones, Captain Agras ran the risk of falling into a Bulgarian trap, which would thwart his plan and expose his villagers to the comitadjes' revenge.

One evening at the Vangeli hut, he summoned his officers, evzones, and Pascal to a council. Each one presented his view, while the commander listened. Finally he spoke himself.

His force was limited, he said, and their boats too few to undertake a successful assault on the Bulgarian huts. Moreover their work was now far from the Lower Huts, so that each day they lost time coming and going. It would be wise to build a small hut at the halfway point and fortify it to serve as a refuge.

But even this wouldn't be enough. On a couple of daring patrols he'd made to the Bulgarian hideouts, he'd learned how strong and well entrenched the comitadjes were. Their complex of huts was impressive; and they had a complete fleet of boats to transport them.

"We lack men, our canoes are insignificant, and help is far away," he stated. "We need reinforcements." And casting a glance around that stopped at Apostolis:

"Will you go to Captain Nikiphoros and tell him to come to our aid?" he asked the boy.

Apostolis, who'd been following the discussion from the beginning, became agitated.

"I will if you send me, Commander. However we're approaching Kouga. Don't remove me from here. Just a little work remains and we'll find it."

Agras stared at him thoughtfully.

"If you don't go, who will tell him? We have too few fighters to be deprived even of one," he murmured.

Apostolis pointed to Jovan, sitting crosslegged to the side, taking it all in.

"Send him, Commander," he said in a choked voice. "He's capable of doing it."

"That tot?" Agras responded, caught by surprise.

"That tot went and discovered Apostol Petkoff at Zervohori. He's the one who learned all the information I gave you about him," Apostolis said, stirred up. "And both before and since, he's done any number of tasks for me—besides leading me here. Send Jovan, Commander. You won't regret it. What's more, he knows Bulgarian; and as little as he is and as much of a tot, he'll pass where someone else would run into an obstacle."

Agras didn't reply. Pensive, he looked at Jovan, who returned his gaze with his large black eyes.

All around, the men were arguing, murmuring, expressing their doubt.

"What does this infant know?"

"He'll need a nanny with him."

"He'll bring us all down . . ."

Nasos—who'd been on guard and met the canoe with the two boys when they arrived that dawn at the Lower Huts—shook his head slowly in disbelief and declared:

"Nor will Captain Nikiphoros ever think that this toddler comes from you."

Apostolis flew to his feet.

"I'll give him a sign," he exclaimed.

Hastily unbuttoning his jacket, he took out a cross on a string and extended it to Agras.

"Look, Commander! This cross is a gift from Captain Nikiphoros. If Jovan shows it to him, he'll recognize it and believe him right away. Have faith, Commander, and send Jovan. I know he'll do the job well! . . ."

Rubbing his chin and pondering, Agras stared at the child—whose black eyes didn't leave his own. All at once, the commander made his decision. He stood up, took the cross from Apostolis' hands, and walking over to Jovan, passed the string around his neck.

"Do you understand Greek?" he asked him.

The child blushed.

"I understand," he replied.

"Do you know where Tsekri is, a landing-cove . . ."

"I know it," Jovan interrupted.

"It's a long distance . . . and I can't give you a canoe . . ."

Jovan shrugged his shoulder.

"However, perhaps someone can accompany you . . ." He turned to a middle aged villager, brown from the sun, the only person outside his force that he had at the meeting . . . "Theodore could go with you—he's from Plati . . ."

Jovan broke in. Speaking slowly, he searched for the Greek words.

"There's no need . . . I know the way . . . I'll go more quickly by myself. Just put me out on land . . ."

The deputy-commanders approached Agras.

"It doesn't make sense," they cautioned. "It's not acting soundly . . ."

But the captain had decided. He smiled with good-humor at Jovan.

"Tomorrow at daybreak," he said, "a boat will bring you to shore. I'll give you instructions in the morning."

It was a short and fitful sleep that Jovan had that night. The thought of his work and responsibility, the pride that swelled up in him, held him in a state of constant excitement.

Before day had dawned he was up and about. He washed himself, combed his hair, and adjusted his belt in order to be presentable and clean.

When the boat had deposited him on a deserted part of the southern shore of the lake, he felt grown-up and free.

He was used to being alone, but not to freedom. Enough times he'd gone where he wanted, always though with the knowledge that he'd pay for it with a beating or lack of food, or worse.

Now he was alone again, yet without the worry of having to face Angel Pio's anger. What's more, he was working for Apostolis—and it was confidential work that made him feel proud.

For weeks now, he'd lived with Greeks and heard Greek spoken. He'd learned the language and understood it all. Still, to be safer, Apostolis had translated every sentence of Captain Agras' into Bulgarian for him; he'd explained every instruction. And when the captain wanted to give him money for the road, Apostolis had offered good advice:

"It won't do, Commander. He's too young to have earned money. If anyone catches him, it will raise suspicions that he stole it or that he was paid by the rebels to run errands."

Thus they provided him only with food in a sack, which was hanging at his side.

Apostolis, who knew the Swamp thoroughly, had completed the directions for him—where he was to stop to rest, where to sleep, and what to reply if they questioned him. Now he'd begun his journey, alone and on his own—a man already.

* * * *

The children had been let out of school. Gathered around the teacher like sparrows, they were shrieking and chattering all at once. One child was justifying himself, another seeking information or advice, another complaining of an injustice, and still another receiving a last hug.

The teacher listened to them all. She answered, consoled, and hugged each one of them; she had time for and said good-night to every child.

"And now, you must start off," she said.

Glancing up at the clouds that were tumbling down, fluffy and pink in the sunset, she added:

"It won't rain anymore tonight. The stars will be out and the road will dry up. Tomorrow . . ."

A boy who'd gone outside with a long stick he was beating against his hip, rushed back into the courtyard and interrupted her.

"Miss Electra! Miss Electra! Someone's asking for you outside."

"Asking for me? What does he want? Let him enter inside."

"He looks like a beggar. He's little. He seems very poor . . ."

"Bring him inside. Wait! I'll come myself . . ."

Leaning against the frame of the courtyard door to support himself, a child was standing. He wore a woolen jacket, heavy cape, and shoes like those of the villagers. But he was so muddy it appeared he'd sunk into the Swamp. His knees were shaking, ready to give way.

Casting his gaze upon her, he murmured with difficulty:

"Miss Electra?"

"Yes. That's who I am . . . Come inside and sit down . . ."

The child started to straighten up, but his legs swayed and he fell down upon the damp ground.

. . . his legs swayed and he fell down . . .

A swarm of children surrounded him. One tried to pull him, another to lift him up, a third to unbutton his clothes.

The teacher made a path among them; and with the help of just an older girl, she picked up the unknown child and brought him into the school.

No one wanted to leave now. Curious, they all crowded into the classroom—the bigger children eager to help, the smaller ones all eyes and ears, driven back to the doorway where the older pupils had relegated them.

The stranger tried to say something. But only his lips moved. No sound came out. His eyes were closed, and beneath the dried mud on his face and head, his color was yellow.

"A little tea, Evangelia! . . . And hot! . . . Quickly! . . . Put in a spoonful of brandy so that he comes to!" the teacher murmured, feeling the child's pulse.

Evangelia hurried out of the room, while other eager hands removed the stranger's shoes and cape and rubbed his frozen feet.

She returned with a small cup. The teacher knelt down next to the child, and spoonful by spoonful poured the hot tea between his pale lips.

Jovan opened his eyes and saw the woman's head leaning over him.

"Miss Electra?" he asked again.

"Yes, child . . . What do you want? What are you seeking?"

But Jovan had closed his eyes again, as if he'd gone to sleep.

The teacher got up and dispatched all her pupils, except for Evangelia.

"Be on your way, children. You can see that he's sleeping. After he's rested, he'll be able to tell us what he wants. Tomorrow at eight, we'll have our lesson again. Good-night."

When the last pupil had left and she'd shut the courtyard door, the teacher went back to the classroom where they'd placed the unknown child down. Evangelia awaited her.

"You can bring the brazier with the hot coals into my room and undo the bed covers. Then heat some water on the hearth. We'll wash him, first of all," she said.

While the girl readily set off to make the preparations, the teacher knelt down again and softly, gently, stroked the unknown child's forehead.

He turned, observed her, and repeated:

"Miss Electra?"

"Yes! That's who I am. What is it that you want, child?"

Jovan made an effort to raise himself on his elbow and threw a glance around him.

"Are you alone, Miss Electra?" he inquired.

"Yes, all alone . . ." She glanced toward the door to assure herself that Evangelia had gone. Bending down closer, she asked in a low voice:

"Did someone send you? Who?"

"Apostolis . . ." the child whispered.

Miss Electra bent over still closer.

"From where did he send you?" she asked.

"From the Lower Huts . . . from Captain . . ."

The teacher put her hand over his mouth. Evangelia was coming back.

With a natural, composed voice, the teacher said to her pupil:

"Help me, Evangelia, take him to the wash-tub. When we've cleaned him up, we'll put him in my room. And then you can go home so your mother won't worry . . ."

"Bah, Miss Electra, I'll stay with you. I won't leave you alone with so much work," Evangelia protested.

Her eagerness was such that Miss Electra found it difficult to send her away. Only when her worried mother arrived to learn why her daughter was late, and when the girl had made certain that the unknown child—now lying clean and wrapped up in a warm robe among pillows—no longer needed her, did Evangelia decide to follow her home.

Night had descended. Miss Electra closed the windows and doors and went back to her bedroom. The stranger was finishing up a bowl of soup—the teacher's meal.

Taking the bowl, she sat down next to him.

"What is your name?" she inquired in Bulgarian.

"Jovan," the child replied in Greek.

"But you're not Greek, are you?" the teacher responded in Greek herself. "You have a foreign accent."

The child didn't answer. His large almond-shaped eyes examined her face with curiosity and admiration.

She was about twenty years old, tall and slim with thick black hair in a braid around her head, like a crown on her forehead. Her eyes were brown, almost gold, and they flashed beneath her black eyelashes, lively and imposing.

Miss Electra was accustomed to being obeyed. Her eyes commanded even when her lips were silent, even when they smiled maternally as now.

She extended her hand—a white hand with long, slender fingers—and stroked the child's forehead.

"We're alone here, Jovan," she said softly. "Speak to me . . . Tell me . . ."

Jovan sat up, ready to jump down.

"Miss Electra, you must take me immediately to Tsekri," he said, trembling from emotion.

Restraining him with both hands, she had him lie down again in bed.

"Tell me first. Why did Apostolis send you to Captain Nikiphoros?"

Jovan gave a start.

"Do you know . . . Do you know Captain Nikiphoros?"

"I'm asking the questions now," the teacher replied with a calm authority that didn't allow for opposition. "Tell me, why did Apostolis send you to Captain Nikiphoros?"

"For help," Jovan answered, subdued.

"Who seeks it? Captain Kalas?"

"No. Captain Agras."

"He's settled at the Lower Huts?"

"Yes, but he only has a few men."

"How many?"

"Twelve."

"That's all?"

"Twelve rebels. He also took some villagers—but he says they're still not trained for war. He wants more men."

"Has he been fighting?"

"Not yet. But he'd like to."

The teacher had asked all this in a composed manner, as if she were quizzing a pupil on addition tables, or the future tense of a verb.

Pensive, she gazed at Jovan, who faced her with a look full of doubt, anxiety, and questions of his own.

"Since he's not fighting, I'll take you tomorrow," she said to him fondly.

Jovan was thrown into turmoil.

"Not tomorrow! Miss Electra," he cried out.

In his agitation he abandoned Greek, which was difficult for him, and continued in Bulgarian. His sentences tumbled out, one after another.

"We have to go right away. I should be there now. I'm not worthy. I traveled back and forth because I didn't have a canoe . . ."

Tears filled his black eyes and rolled onto his pale cheeks.

"Where did you turn back from?" the teacher inquired.

"From Tsekri. I went straight there. The landing-cove was deserted. I waited and no one appeared. I saw that I was losing time. Apostolis had told me: 'If you don't succeed, go to Miss Electra. She'll take you.' And I came."

Startled, the teacher asked:

"When did you start?"

"The day before yesterday."

"Where did you set out from?"

"From the shore . . . near the Lower Huts."

The teacher was shaken.

"You traveled all that way alone?" she exclaimed.

"Was it far?" the child asked.

"What are you saying? At least you found a cart?"

"I didn't go by the road . . . Apostolis said it was better not to speak with anyone. I came over the plain."

"You went to Tsekri? And then back here?"

Jovan didn't reply. Her surprise seemed strange to him.

She bent down and observed him close up. Her eyes were warm. They both soothed and disturbed him.

"How old are you?" she asked.

"I don't know."

"Don't you have a mother?"

"No."

"Or a father either?"

"No. Neither."

"Do you have someone? An aunt? An uncle? Brothers and sisters?"

"I left the house of . . . of my uncle," Jovan replied, on guard.
"Why?"
"Because I wanted to work with Apostolis."
"What is your uncle's name?"
"Angel Pio."
"The comitadje Pio! He's your uncle!" Miss Electra exclaimed.
Jovan was ashamed. Once more tears sprang to his eyes. As was his custom when he didn't want to reply, he shrugged his shoulder.
"How is it that you're with Apostolis?" the teacher inquired.
"I wanted to work with him," Jovan repeated.
"You? A Bulgarian child?"
The teacher leaned over again and looked into his eyes, which didn't avoid meeting her own.
She reached up and pushed back her hair.
"Are you very tired, Jovan?" she asked gently.
Like a whiplash her words brought him to, reminding him of his work.
"Let's go, Miss Electra; let's go to Tsekri right away," he begged, flinging back the covers.
"Apostolis had you come to me," she said, covering him up again. "You'll do as I tell you. At such an hour we won't find a canoe. Tomorrow . . . Tomorrow perhaps we will. Sleep tonight. You're exhausted."
She stroked his hair. And bending over suddenly, she kissed him on the forehead.
"Sleep," she repeated. "I'll come and lie down close by."
Going out, she entered the classroom and sat at her desk, a wood plank table with a drawer.
By the light of a candle, she wrote a note in a large, firm, easy-to-read handwriting:

"Evangelia, I had to set off early to accompany the child who lost his way and couldn't find his village. You give the lesson to the small children, dismiss the older ones, and come again tomorrow at eight. With affection, Electra."

Leaving the paper unfolded on the table, she took up the candle and passed into the kitchen. From the loft she removed a mattress, rolled it out, and placed it over her shoulder. Picking up the candle again, she returned to her room.

Quietly, she spread the mattress on the floor and leaned over Jovan.

He was awake, following her every move with his gaze.

"You're not asleep?" she said. "Is there anything you want?"

Sitting down next to him, without waiting for an answer she pursued her own train of thought and asked:

"The villagers that Captain Agras recruited. Has he armed them already?"

"A few," Jovan replied.

"How many?"

"Only six."

"Why didn't he arm the others? Do you know?"

"They say he doesn't have the rifles."

"And you were on your way to ask Captain Nikiphoros for some?"

"Both rifles and men."

Once more the teacher remained absorbed in thought. All at once, she got up again.

"Sleep now," she told him. "Tomorrow I'll wake you myself."

She extinguished the candle and lay down upon the mattress, dressed as she was.

* * * *

Day was just breaking when Jovan awoke to the stroke of an unknown hand on his head.

It jolted him, for he wasn't used to caresses or to warm beds. But in the candlelight he saw the woman's face bent above him, and he remembered.

He burst up.

"It's time!" he cried.

"Yes! Dress quickly. I've brought you coffee. Drink it. You can eat your bread while we're walking."

She was wearing a dark blue overcoat of a heavy wool fabric that filled her out and made her seem twice her size. A blue handkerchief was tied around her head. It too was puffed up—from her thick braid, it seemed.

Hastily Jovan dressed in his now clean clothes, put on his shoes, and went out to the road with the teacher. In each hand, she was carrying a long, thick wax-candle, wrapped in rose-colored paper.

"Close the door softly, without making any noise," she said in a low voice, "so we don't wake up the neighborhood."

* * * *

They set off on the well-traveled road, deserted at that hour; and when they'd left the houses of the village behind, she put the two candles over her right shoulder and addressed Jovan:

"Tell me, how did you go from the Lower Huts? And how were you able to find me?"

With uncertainty, he looked up at the two candles.

"Give me one at least to carry," he entreated her.

But she refused.

"It won't do," she answered. "You'll damage it, and then how will our young men celebrate the Feast the day after tomorrow?"

* * * *

Her sharp eye perceived the shadow before she saw the Turkish policeman step out from behind a cluster of shrubs. All at once, without calling attention to it, she lowered the candles so that one hung from each hand by the wick.

"Good-morning, Sergeant," she called out to the policeman in Turkish.

"Good-morning to you, Teacher," he replied with a bow, placing his hand on his heart and then on his forehead. "Where are you off to so early with your church candles?"

"Up to the Apostoles Village, where our little church is poor. We have a Feast the day after tomorrow . . ."

"You're determined to go so far? . . ."

"Eh, what's such a journey to us, Sergeant? We're used to it, you and I . . ."

Flattered, the policeman smiled. After exchanging a few more pleasantries, he drew on to the village, while she headed toward the plain with her companion.

"Is that Turk your friend, Miss Electra?" Jovan inquired when they were at a distance again.

The teacher's eyes flashed.

"No Turk is a friend of mine," she answered. "However we live under Turkish occupation . . . And we have the Bulgarians as a common enemy."

She lifted the candles back onto her shoulder and added:

"Tell me now how you came."

As they walked, Jovan related to her how Captain Agras' canoe had left him on shore, and how he'd traveled straight in the direction of the sun. At the start it had been easy and fun, since the plain was dry and deserted. He'd eaten and slept among the bushes, then resumed his way. Running for the most part, he'd followed his shadow with the sun behind him.

But the sun had set early in back of some black clouds and it began to rain. He went on running, and when he got out of breath and his legs were worn out, he sat down for a little while before going on again. However, the rain didn't let up and his cape was heavy so that he could barely make his way in the dark.

Finding a hayloft, he'd entered it secretly and slept on the hay. At dawn, he set out again, running as much as he could and stopping to catch his breath when his legs wouldn't carry him any longer. He'd gone on and on.

While he knew those parts, he didn't know them all that well. Moreover, it had rained all day and his cape weighed down on him. At night he'd lost his way and wasn't sure where to go. He didn't realize that the Loudias River bridge, where the main road passed, was nearby.

But he'd heard Turkish conversation and tramping—a Turkish patrol heading for the bridge.

He'd trailed them at a distance; and upon reaching the bridge, he climbed underneath it to escape the rain, lying down on some stones. At daybreak he'd found his path without difficulty. Following the shore of the lake, he arrived at the Tsekri landing-cove.

No one was there. He gave the wolf signal, as he'd done to inform Apostolis on another occasion. But this time no one came. Then he lost heart and turned back to Zorba . . .

"And your legs still held up?" the teacher responded.

"Not very well," Jovan admitted. "My bread was gone, too . . . I'd been hungry the day before . . . I didn't judge well . . ."

"And there was a lot of mud, wasn't there? Your feet would have gotten stuck in it."

"Yes, they did . . . I fell twice . . ."

"Did you hurt yourself?" Miss Electra asked.

"I don't remember . . ."

"What? You don't remember if you hurt yourself?"

"I don't know how I fell . . . Only when I came to I was soaked . . . I'd sunk in the mud both times."

The teacher regarded him with emotion.

"The poor child . . ." she murmured.

"Won't Apostolis scold me for taking so long, Miss Electra?" he asked her apprehensively.

"No, no! How did you ever cover so much ground so quickly with such little legs?"

Her voice was so pleasant, just like the touch of her hand. A delightful, up to then unknown sensation pervaded him.

Ah . . . how nice, how good Miss Electra was . . .

With no experience of affection, of sympathy or kind words, it seemed to him as if he'd been living in a dream since yesterday— a dream in which the Madonna had descended from an icon to speak to him and brush back his hair from his forehead . . .

The teacher's voice awakened him from his reverie.

"To the left at once, inside the bushes . . ."

They descended hurriedly into a ditch and sat crouched down in back of some thick shrubs.

In a short time conversation sounded on the road behind them.

The teacher watched from inside the branches.

"They're villagers . . ." she whispered. "But it's better if they don't see us. When they've gone, we'll head directly for the Swamp."

Leaving the frequented road, they cut toward the lake. It was deserted—peaceful and quiet. They sank in mud up to their ankles; and passing north of the Apostles landing-cove, they approached the Tsekri inlet.

* * * *

Endless mud, water, reeds . . . Desolation . . . No one . . .

The teacher examined the countryside. Discovering a gully, she climbed down to the bottom with Jovan.

Suddenly two gunshots, one after the other, burst forth.

Frightened, the child turned toward the teacher, who smiled at him calmly. In her hand she was still holding a smoking pistol. Taking her time, she put it away in her overcoat pocket.

"They'll come now . . ." she said softly.

They waited in silence.

Quiet . . . Solitude . . .

All at once a voice erupted from the reeds and called out in Greek:

"Anyone there?"

The teacher emerged from the gully.

"White hawk!" she declared and proceeded to the landing-cove.

Jovan followed her. From the reeds, a canoe with two armed oarsmen appeared and plunged onto the muddy shore.

"Hello!" they greeted her. "Enter quickly. The commander's waiting for you before he starts off."

"For where?" the teacher inquired.

"Enter inside, Miss Electra, and hand me your candles," the first armed man answered.

He took them, and with a smile weighed them in his hand.

The teacher climbed into the canoe and sat down, gathering her overcoat around her carefully.

Curious, Jovan was attentive to her movements; and he listened to the words she exchanged with the men as if they were close relations.

She motioned to him to sit next to her, then asked again:

"Where is the commander going?"

"On a tour in the direction of Nihori, Nisi, and I don't know where else. He makes a round of all the villages," the oarsman replied, thrusting his oar into the ground and pushing the boat out into the water.

The teacher shook her head.

"It's no time for him to leave . . . Not today," she murmured.

The canoe had entered the reeds again, along a snake-like path. The oarsman who was seated did the rowing, while standing behind in the stern, his companion steered the boat with his oar.

As the hut was near, it wasn't long before they arrived. A narrow path let them out into the wide waterway in front of the deck.

A tall, shaven young man awaited them, with his rifle lowered to the floor. Here and there, five or six other men were sitting crosslegged, all of them armed.

The youth extended his hand to help the teacher up onto the deck.

"It's good you came early," he told her. "In an hour you wouldn't have found me. I'm expecting lads from the nearby huts in order to set off on another tour."

"We'll talk about it, Captain Nikiphoros," she replied with a smile. "I must speak to you."

They stepped into the hut together, while Jovan stood outside. He saw her remove her overcoat and unfasten five strips of cartridges hanging from her belt. Then she poured out a profusion of cartridges from interior pockets sewn into the coat's lining. After she'd untied the kerchief on her head, she took out another strip of ammunition from inside her braid. In the meantime one of the oarsmen had brought in the two candles, ripped off the paper, thrown it in the corner with the wicks, and leaned two rifles against the wall of the hut.

Jovan watched it all in amazement. Once more Miss Electra became slim and graceful as she'd been the evening before.

In the midst of explaining something to Captain Nikiphoros, she nodded toward where Jovan was standing, making occasional brief gestures.

Nikiphoros said something to her; and leaning toward the door, she called out:

"Jovan, come inside."

Timidly he approached and stopped before the commander, looking at him while nervously twisting his fingers one inside the other.

The commander stared at the child, rubbing his smooth-shaven chin.

"You've been at the Lower Huts? With Captain Agras? How long were you there?" he asked.

"It's been two weeks . . . maybe longer," Jovan answered.

"Tell Captain Nikiphoros the instructions Captain Agras gave you," the teacher ordered him.

And she smiled encouragingly.

"He wants to attack the comitadjes," Jovan said slowly, groping for words, "and he doesn't have the fighters, or the rifles, or canoes."

He met the teacher's gaze and with more courage, added:

"He asks you to come and help, Captain Nikiphoros . . . And to come quickly."

Pondering, hesitant, Nikiphoros continued to stare at him.

"All right," he said. "But who are you? Miss Electra doesn't know you, and you don't even speak Greek. How can I believe you? . . ."

Rapidly Jovan stuffed his hand into his shirt at the neck and drew out a string with a silver cross.

"Apostolis told me . . . told me to show you this."

"This?"

Nikiphoros took hold of it, Puzzled, he exclaimed:

"I gave this cross to my guide Apostolis!"

"Yes," Jovan replied, trembling all over. "And Apostolis told me: 'If Captain Nikiphoros doesn't believe I sent you, this will change his mind.' Apostolis wanted me to show it to you, Commander."

Nikiphoros turned to the teacher:

"The cross has persuaded me," he said decisively. "I'll set off immediately for the Lower Huts."

He summoned his men outside:

"Is there a guide for the Lower Huts?"

Jovan raised his hand.

"I know where they are," he said shyly. "I took Apostolis . . ."

"You know how to find the larger waterways? And the paths?"

"I also know a new shortcut."

Captain Nikiphoros didn't delay in carrying out the decision he'd made. In no time at all he'd given his orders and the men were ready.

"A canoe will take you to the Apostles landing-cove," he informed Miss Electra. "It's closer to Zorba."

Jovan was watching and listening.

Miss Electra tied the kerchief on her head, put on her over-coat, and bid him good-by.

"If you return this way, come to my school," she said. "I'll teach you to read."

From the deck of the hut, amidst the commotion of the prep-aration, Jovan saw her go off in the canoe. Something was torn inside him. Along with Miss Electra, his dream was fading away—of the Madonna who stepped out of her icon to stroke his hair with her long, slender fingers . . .

7.

Spying

"Captain, do as you're doing and you'll fall into their hands. Then you won't escape."

"This is the work we came for. We knew we weren't going on a holiday," the captain replied.

"I've suffered at their hands. I know what awaits you."

"It's victory or death!" the captain exclaimed with spirit. And striding over the side of the boat, he climbed up onto the deck.

Behind him Pascal followed, more slowly and heavily, shaking his head.

"I'll guide you . . ." he muttered, "but it's not meant for me to fall into their hands again . . ."

Captain Agras gave him a lively smile that exposed his well-set white teeth.

"Don't worry, Pascal. If we're brought down spying or fall into some trap, I promise I'll fire a gunshot into your head before planting a bullet in my own. Provided that you want it!"

Pascal made no answer. Hunched over and moving slowly, he continued to follow the young captain.

Agras threw back his shoulders.

"We can't be preoccupied with death if we want to succeed."

[All this was translated back and forth for them.]

And standing in the canoe, the oar still in his hand, Apostolis drank in Agras' words.

How could you not go through fire and water for such a leader?

One of the men on the deck smiled warmly upon hearing the commander.

"Any information, Andonis?" Agras asked him.

"Two pieces of news, Commander! Someone's been seeking you here, and someone else is waiting for you at the Lower Huts."

"Here? Who has discovered our secret Little Hut?" Agras responded.

Seeing a young villager approach, he called out:

"How did you ever find me here?"

The villager greeted him with deep respect, bowing down.

"I'm a Macedonian," he said. "I learned about your daring feats and I came to enlist in your force."

"Well spoken! Come right away. I have need of brave youths. What is your name?"

"Stelios."

"Are you armed?"

"No! I thought you'd take care of that."

"There are a number of things I don't have. However, something will be found for you. Courage is what's essential. But are you aware of what it means to enlist in my force?"

"I know that you're attacking the Bulgarians. And I have grievances with them."

"Good! To be with me, though, means whole days without eating and nights without sleeping. It means being exposed to the cold, to hard labor and to suffering. You go where you're in danger of losing your hide. When there's work to be done, sleep and food don't count for me."

"I know all that and I accept it," the villager answered. "Six months isn't that long."

Agras' manner changed.

"Six months? Why do you say six months?" he asked.

"I have in mind to enlist for six months, Captain. Then I'll be free to leave, if I want."

"Aha!" Agras exclaimed. "So you think you'll live? Bah, you're not for my band. We expect to die every day, not to live! Be on your way. You're not for us."

He turned to his men who had drawn near:

"Right, lads?" he asked. "Is there one of you who plans on waking up tomorrow?"

They were all evzones, the pick of the crop, youths seasoned by the bold reconnaissances of their commander, who didn't hesitate to steal up to the Bulgarian huts even at night. Trained with a rifle and prepared for fierce body to body combat—at times inside the water—they were frequently wounded but always victorious.

The men laughed.

Captain Teligadis, the second-in-command, declared:

"For our part, we surrendered our life to you, Commander. Send us where you will. It's enough that you're leading us."

He said it with both affection and pride.

Agras gave him a fond slap on the shoulder.

"Bravo! That's the way I feel you all are."

And addressing Andonis who stood next to him, full of life and vigor:

"Who did you say was waiting for me at the Lower Huts?"

"Captain Nikiphoros."

"The devil!" Agras exclaimed. "Why didn't you inform me earlier?"

He caught sight of Apostolis, straining to make his fifteen year-old frame reach that of the men.

"Apostolis," he called out to him, "the little Bulgarian didn't deceive us. He was able to find Tsekri. Quick, let's be on our way. I won't leave anyone behind at the Little Hut. Hurry with the boats! It's already dusk, and we have an hour and a half journey ahead of us!"

The villager was standing there dejected.

"Take me with you, Captain," he begged.

"I'll assign you the task of opening up paths. How would that be?" Agras asked.

"Take me into your force," he said hesitantly.

"You'll show yourself if you're worthy of joining us, Stelios," Agras replied. "Come, enter your canoe and follow us. Start rowing, all of you!"

* * * *

In a few minutes, the Little Hut lay deserted.

The first canoe led the way, slipping silently through the still water. Inside, armed rowers listened intently to the sounds of the lake—to the cry of a water-hen or the scraping of an oar—their attention fixed upon the shadows of the reeds. Behind, in a dark line, other tarred canoes followed.

Furtive and somber, the men dipped their oars into the water, without a word. Every shrub might conceal a comitadje ambush. Every cry of a bird or wild animal could be a signal, and every turn a trap. No one smoked. Each fighter was on the lookout, with his finger on the trigger.

As the fleet entered a larger waterway, the oars sped up in the deeper water. The danger of an ambush decreased as they approached the Lower Huts. The Bulgarians, fearful of the now familiar Captain Agras, didn't dare come near his hide-out.

A shadow appeared, and the barrel of a gun glistened.

From inside the first canoe, joyfully the signal was given.

And then: "We're here, Demos."

"Welcome back. Visitors are waiting for you," Demos answered.

In a couple of minutes the boats had docked, and the men disembarked. Hands were extended, handshakes and greetings exchanged.

The two leaders looked each other over, sizing one another up.

Nikiphoros was tall and lean, a man of few words and those words spoken slowly and with deliberation. Agras was short and quick, all energy and action.

Both were courageous and fearless, united in their aims and dedication.

"You wanted me. I came," Captain Nikiphoros stated simply. "The child guided me . . ."

"Really? Where is he?" Agras wanted to know.

A bashful Jovan was standing a little apart, glued to Apostolis' side.

"Bring him here, Apostolis," Agras called out.

Pale and frightened, Jovan drew near.

"What took you so long? We'd given you up for lost," Agras exclaimed.

Briefly, Apostolis repeated as much as Jovan had been able to confide to him in the few moments they'd been together.

The child didn't venture even to look up.

Nikiphoros placed his hand on Jovan's hair.

"He's a good boy . . ." he said. "He led us this far without going astray in the maze of paths . . . Eh, Jovan? . . . And he knows a secret shortcut to save time . . ."

Commanders, sub-commanders, and men had all gathered around to listen in astonishment. Captain Nikiphoros' words focused everyone's attention upon the previously insignificant child they knew as the "little Bulgarian." Until then he'd evoked only indifference, even disdain, among the evzones and Greek-Macedonians from the Lower Huts.

Suddenly this child became a hero. He'd brought them the help of Captain Nikiphoros and part of his force—as well as rifles, revolvers, cartridges, and hand grenades.

"Who's to stop us now, Commander?" Captain Teligadis responded, stroking the boy's head, himself.

"Starting tomorrow . . . the Bulgarian huts!" Nasos said menacingly, his fist clenched.

"Zervohori, get prepared," Captain Teligades added. "Let's inform Captain Gonos!"

"Bravo, Jovan. We owe it to you. Long live Jovan!" some of the men shouted, half-serious, half-laughing.

Unused to kind words, the shy little Bulgarian was overwhelmed by their outburst of praise. Burrowing next to Apostolis, he tried to hide from the rebels' approving, flattering glances.

"Over there," he entreated in a whisper, indicating a spot apart. "I have to tell you about Miss Electra . . ."

In the meantime, the two commanders had entered the hut. Seated cross-legged on the floor, they set about developing a strategy to destroy the Bulgarian activity on the lake.

"The capture of their central hut will require a carefully worked-out plan, along with a hard fight," Agras said. "Night and day I've spied on them, and I know. If we don't establish and fortify ourselves near them, we won't succeed. And I have neither the men nor the boats to do so."

Nikiphoros stretched his long legs out before the fire in the clay-coated center of the hut.

Taking his time, he replied:

"All right . . . But I need to return to Tsekri first . . . to organize my work there . . . Moreover before I leave, I'd like to see their huts up close . . ."

"Let's go early tomorrow. What do you say?" Agras interrupted.

Immediately a course of action was determined upon, and men were chosen to accompany the captains on the reconnaissance. The others would remain at the Lower Huts under a deputy commander.

Very early they started out with Pascal as guide. Apostolis was left behind, beside himself at not being included in the commanders' undertaking.

* * * *

The spying took place under the strictest of precautions. Two oarsmen rowed in silence, in the prow and the stern, taking care not to slap the oar in the water or strike a root or plant where the noise would be heard. Below in the broad, flat-bottomed boat, both the rebel captains kept watch, huddled together and half-reclining. Rifle in hand, each of them was prepared for an unexpected attack. Every movement had to be precise and controlled, since the canoes overturned easily.

The lake resonated with live as well as mysterious sounds— the whistling of the wind in the reeds, the rustling of branches and leaves, the cackling and chirping of birds, the fluttering of ducks, the paddling of frogs, and the slithering of eels among the water shrubs. The sounds of plants and animals covered up the presence of men. A complete series of canoes with armed comitadjes could be hiding inside the reeds. Those on patrol had to be ready at all times for a clash.

The commanders went by the Little Hut without stopping and ascended north towards the Bulgarian complex.

All at once Captain Nikiphoros extended his arm.

"Look . . ." he whispered.

They were passing by the narrow, twisting waterway known to the fishermen at the lake as Grounandero. It had deeper water; however on both sides where it was shallow, shrubs with thick, broad, scaly leaves formed a firm surface that could endure a heavy load.

Broken reeds and branches, crushed leaves, and recently trampled plants testified to the passage of men who'd stayed there. Traces of boats drawn up, of footprints and reclining bodies—along with scraps of food—showed not only that men had hidden there and dragged their boats onto the shrubs, but that there had been many of them and that they'd lingered for hours, perhaps days.

Agras leaned over to see for himself, and then laughed.

"They realize that I come by here often, and they set a trap," he said. "Alas! they've lost their time in vain. I didn't pass by either yesterday or the day before."

"They must have remained quite a while waiting," Nikiphoros declared. "It's heavily trampled all around."

"Bah," Agras responded. "Two days at the most. I came by in the evening three days ago and no one was here. With the cold, though, they would have had a hard enough time of it last night! What a pity!"

And he laughed again, unconcerned.

The oarsmen were proceeding even more cautiously now. Lying down in the canoe, his head the height of the upper edge of the boat, Pascal searched before him, to the sides, inside the reeds, and behind the bushes. Motionless and silent, he was totally absorbed in scrutinizing all around. His restless eyes dug into every secret corner, shadow, and hollow.

He held up his hand slowly and the oarsmen stopped rowing. A second motion of his hand, and the oarsmen sank down in the boat. It glided on a meter or two without a sound. Pascal stretched out his hand, grabbed hold of some reeds, and drew the canoe sideways so that it disappeared among the green vegetation. Then the old man raised a few branches and covered the boat.

Quietly a large enemy canoe issued forth from the reeds to the left, slipped slowly in front of the prow of the hidden boat, and was lost again in the reeds to the right. Four armed Bulgarians were inside.

No one had fired. Ready to shoot, Agras' oarsmen awaited a sign from their commander. But it wasn't given.

A few minutes elapsed. The canoe didn't return.

As the rebels' boat emerged from the reeds, Pascal whispered:

"To the left into the path they came from."

"Why didn't we fire?" Captain Nikiphoros inquired, curious.

"Because they'd hear us at the huts," Agras replied. "Do you want to see them? We're almost there."

Nikiphoros did; and the boat continued to slip noiselessly through the narrow path between the reeds that rose like a hedge on both sides of them.

When they'd reached a certain point, Pascal separated the reeds again and the boat disappeared behind their wall.

Distant conversation could be distinguished, yet nothing was visible in back of the reeds.

Agras bent over to Nikiphoros' ear.

"Would you like to get a good view?"

"Of the Bulgarians? Of course. That's what we're here for."

Agras lifted his feet slowly over the side of the boat. Keeping steady so he wouldn't splash and make a noise, he climbed down into the water.

In that area, the water was shallow. It hardly reached his knees. He nodded to Nikiphoros to come, too; and the two leaders tred lightly, imperceptibly. Parting the reeds carefully to prevent any from breaking and betraying them, they inched their way toward the voices.

The men had remained in the canoe with Pascal, ready to jump into the water at the first signal. They were familiar with their commander's reconnaissances and knew that he always proceeded up to the enemy huts alone, or with just one other person.

Agras took the lead, with Nikiphoros right in his footsteps, holding back the reeds his companion handed to him.

Agras stopped and Nikiphoros did the same.

Agras sank down into the water, and Nikiphoros followed suit.

Only their heads passed among the thick reeds now.

Before them a few steps to the right, the barrel of a gun was shining in the sun.

It was the Bulgarian lookout post.

Distancing themselves from it, the two men drew silently to the left and advanced toward the Bulgarian conversation—up to their necks in the water.

From inside the reeds, they finally saw the well-concealed hut. On the deck with its embankment, a handful of men were smoking and talking. Warmly dressed, they wore fur caps and were heavily armed.

Side by side in the water, the two Greek commanders watched. Without uttering a word, Agras pointed out to Nikiphoros what he wanted him to notice.

The Bulgarians were carefree in what they said. But neither of the Greeks knew Bulgarian, although they did heed one name—Apostol—that was repeated.

For a short time, the two men remained there watching.

Afterwards, with equal care they withdrew. Keeping their eyes on the hut and the lookout guard—revealed by the glare of his gunbarrel—the two commanders backtracked to their hidden canoe.

When they'd returned to the Little Hut, soaked through, they lit a fire in the middle of the floor and sat down to dry themselves. Surrounded by their men, the two commanders exchanged observations.

"Surely Apostol directs them," Captain Nikiphoros commented. "His name kept occurring."

"Did you see their hut with its floor?" Captain Agras asked. "It's constructed better than ours. It floats, instead of resting on the bottom of the lake. When the rivers pour down and the lake floods, their floor will just float along as the water rises. While ours . . ."

"We'll drown inside our huts like mice, Commander," one of the evzones who'd accompanied him said. "But don't worry. Let us drown. It's enough that we're with you."

"Their embankment is better than ours, too," Nikiphoros remarked.

"And the roof of their hut," Agras added. "Our roofs are inadequate, I know. If only I had the men and time! . . ."

"You've recruited villagers. Why don't you take on more? . . ."

"They'd have to be taught from scratch," Agras replied. "And I lack the time . . . If we don't locate Kouga, how will we get a foothold and make a base? . . ."

"Decide that there's no Kouga, Commander," Captain Teligadis said, raising his voice.

Pascal heard the word and guessed what he was saying. Nodding affirmatively, he declared in Bulgarian:

"There is a Kouga and we'll find it."

"What did he say?" Nikiphoros inquired.

Mihalis translated.

"We must locate it," Agras said. "Without Kouga, we can't embark upon any serious undertaking. They won't tolerate our building new huts close to them. And without a refuge we can't attack them. As long as they have their huts here, no Greek force can survive, either at Naousa or in any of our villages. That means Bulgarian propaganda and terrorism will wipe out patriarchism and Hellenism from Central Macedonia."

"Where exactly is this Kouga? Does anyone know?" Nikiphoros asked.

"Pascal knows. Eh, Pascal? . . ." And Agras had Mihalis translate for him.

While Mihalis did so, the commander whispered to Nikiphoros:

"Tomorrow I'll take the boy. He insists it's more to the east than where we've been searching . . ."

* * * *

The next day Captain Nikiphoros and his force departed from the Lower Huts. He'd left Tsekri without notifying the Center in Thessalonika, and he needed to rush back.

"Before you attempt a military operation, inform me and I'll come immediately with my men," he told Agras.

Those remaining looked on sadly as their new friends got ready to leave and made their departure.

* * * *

The isolate, monotonous life at the lake was full of danger and deprivation. Without enjoyment or even rest for the poorly-nourished fighters—who scarcely knew sleep—any new conversation or the visit of a friend brought intense as well as rare pleasure.

Agras perceived how downcast his men were and immediately gave them some busy-work to distract them. He dispatched a canoe to spy at the southern shore, and another with villagers and an armed guard to open up a new path towards Toumba. With the canoes that remained, he headed north with his evzones and whatever villagers could fit in the boats—bound for the Little Hut, his secret hideout.

This time they took Apostolis with them. Proud, the boy was carried away by a desire to make great sacrifices and undertake the most dangerous feats.

He'd parted with Jovan early in the morning, to Apostolis' displeasure and Jovan's burning tears. Captain Nikiphoros was bringing the child to Tsekri with him.

"What am I to do with such an infant in this desolation?" Captain Agras had said to Nikiphoros. "The fever that grips us every so often will destroy him. Take him and place him with some good Orthodox soul to raise . . ."

"You'll go to Tsekri," Apostolis instructed Jovan. "From there, make your own way to Zorba. You know the road now. Eh? You'll find Miss Electra there and tell her that I've sent you. Don't worry—in her hands, you'll experience only good. She'll teach you to read and show you what work you can do to earn money . . .

"Another thing, find a means to return the clothes you're wearing to Pazarenze as soon as possible. Ask Miss Electra. She'll know what to do. She's clever. And she understands such matters."

He winked at the child to divert him from his tears, then slapped him affectionately on the back of the neck.

"Cheer up, Jovan. Either you'll visit me or I'll come to see you. And we'll be together again. So long, my little friend."

8.

Work

CAPTAIN AGRAS HAD DIVIDED HIS WORKERS into two groups, half guided by Pascal, the other half by Apostolis. The boy hastily cut down reeds and stuffed them into the water, ignoring the dampness and cold, even the sound of branches breaking, which could betray him to some Bulgarian sentry post.

Mihalis' heavy hand fell upon his shoulder from time to time.

"Hey kid, softly," he whispered to him. "You'll bring about our ruin . . ."

With clenched teeth, Apostolis answered:

"I can smell it, I tell you. It's here close by! If we stretch out our hand, we'll touch Kouga."

And he continued by himself inside the reeds, leaving the workers to widen the path for the boats.

"What is it you smell? What do you see?" Mihalis asked. "The water-birds have returned to the Swamp. It's almost time for the sun to set. Yet no hut has come to light."

"Don't you notice, though, that the reeds are slimmer, as if new? And that the bushes have become spaced out, like we're approaching deeper water? A branch of the river is close by . . ."

He cut down a few more reeds, proceeded some ten meters, and buried his head among the stalks. Speechless from joy, he turned triumphantly to Mihalis, who'd followed, and pointed to show him.

Mihalis bent forward and viewed the open waterway making its way slowly between the walls of reeds.

"Call the commander . . ." Apostolis stammered, unable to continue from his excitement.

While Mihalis rushed back, he drew on ahead, reappeared among the last reeds, and searched up and down the waterway.

A little to the left, darkened with time, the rains, and abandonment, a deserted "floor" was rotting away, without hut or embankment.

Behind him, armful after armful of reeds were now falling rapidly, until suddenly the prow of a canoe emerged.

Inside, Captain Agras was sitting with two of his men, each with a rifle in his hand.

"Get inside, quickly," the commander murmured.

And he caught hold of Apostolis' arm.

"Bravo!" he exclaimed with his boyish, good-natured smile.

Apostolis saw that he had tears in his eyes.

That same moment from another side-path, a canoe with Pascal and his oarsmen arrived.

The old man gestured toward the half-rotted "floor" and broke into a grin that, with the gap in his teeth, split his face in two.

"Didn't I tell you?" he muttered in Bulgarian as he approached Agras and entered his boat. "I knew very well where Kouga was . . ."

Captain Agras gave a sidelong glance at Apostolis. However, he didn't speak.

All together, they climbed up onto the floor.

It was old, abandoned, and in wretched condition. Water, overflowing from the wreckage, had soaked it throughout—a dark, moldy ruin.

* * * *

Like a conqueror Agras strode from one end of the floor to the other, crosswise and lengthwise. He'd seized the only base that put him near the Bulgarian installations. Smiling, he rejoiced as he contemplated how to drive the enemy out.

"Now you can build a hut here near them," Pascal said to him. "I told you I'd lead you to Kouga. You see?"

Mihalis translated; and Agras raised his head. From within the dry, thinned out leaves of the reeds, he could distinguish the central Bulgarian hut. It was low, well-constructed, and concealed inside the thicker vegetation of the lake.

"Will you give me a gift, Captain?" the old man asked, his wily eyes narrowing into slits from wrinkles that deepened as he smiled.

Agras' glance crossed with Apostolis'.

"Tell him 'yes,' I'll give him something," he said to Mihalis.

And passing beside Apostolis:

"Let him take the credit now that he's asking for payment," he murmured. "It's enough that you know we'd have saved six or seven days' work, had we listened to you."

* * * *

Apostolis almost burst at the commander's words! What if another took the credit? He'd found Kouga himself right where he knew it to be—near the Bulgarian huts.

Along with the men, he quickly stuffed up the holes in the floor with reeds, leaves, and roots, according to the commander's directions.

"Because we'll settle in tonight," Captain Agras declared. "Seeing that we've set foot here, we can't leave now."

And he explained why:

"The hut's on a tributary of the river that's a Bulgarian passageway. Every moment one of their patrols could pass by. But they won't escape us now. We'll catch them like mice if they appear!"

Shivering, he drew his cloak around him.

"It's grown cold," he said, "and we don't have a roof over us. Is there anyone that wants to leave?"

No, not one of them, they answered. Only Pascal sought to return to the Little Hut.

"It's chilly and the deck is soaked. What's more, my rheumatism is acting up," he told Mihalis.

A strong shudder permeated Agras' whole body. Gathering his cloak tighter, he exclaimed:

"All right, be off! But you'll need a canoe and we don't have any extra ones! Who will bring it back to us?"

Apostolis flew to his feet.

"I will, Commander!" he responded. "I know Bulgarian, and I can pass for a Bulgarian. If they capture us . . ."

"You should go also, Commander," Captain Teligadis interrupted. He'd been eyeing him carefully while he spoke. "The fever has gripped you again. It's not right for you to stay here."

Agras' teeth were chattering and he was trembling all over. However he didn't cease smiling.

"Are you joking? Leave Kouga to the enemy now that we've discovered it?"

"Don't worry. I'll guard it with the others," Teligadis replied. "Remember what you suffered a few days ago when the fever grabbed hold of you . . ."

"And you think I'd retreat to the back line for a little fever and let you face the danger?"

Laughing, he slapped Teligadis' shoulder.

"No more of this! The fever's an enemy, too. But either we— or the Bulgarians—will attack. Moreover we'll defeat them or they'll defeat us. For me to leave, though, is out of the question. Fix me a cup of tea and no more worrying."

He turned to Apostolis:

"Take the old man," he ordered, "and then come back. We have need of both you and the boat. Go now! Make haste!"

* * * *

In a state of upheaval, Apostolis rowed with one oar while Pascal worked the other, drawing towards the Little Hut as fast as possible. The boy was in turmoil because of his affection and admiration for the commander, his haste to return to Kouga to help, his anger towards Pascal, and his longing to sacrifice his life for the ideals that inspired such youths . . .

For they were all brave youths surrounding Captain Agras. There was his next in command Teligadis, Nikos who guarded the Lower Huts in his absence, Mihalis, Nasos, Andonis . . . all of the twelve evzones that had accompanied him to the Swamp. And there were the natives too, the villagers he'd energized—arming them, encouraging them, and training them to use a rifle. Instead of fearfully awaiting a Bulgarian attack, they were to strike the enemy themselves. On a couple of occasions, he'd been told, Agras had encountered Bulgarian patrols on his bold reconnaissances and there had been firing between them. Each time the Bulgarians retreated, which amounted to a victory for the commander.

Pascal's whisper interrupted his train of thought.

"Will you really go back?" he inquired.

"Certainly, I'll go back! Do you think I'd leave the commander in the condition he's in?" Apostolis replied with some disdain.

The old man shook his head back and forth.

"The captain's fearless," he murmured, "but he lacks good sense. He doesn't keep his head. He'll fall into their hands and end up badly. What he does isn't sensible! He goes down under their nose—he's asking for trouble!"

"But if he were sensible, Mr. Pascal," Apostolis answered, "he wouldn't be Captain Agras. He'd be Pascal!"

The old man didn't lose his temper. He just shook his head again, with his cap descended to the nape of his neck.

"He doesn't understand . . . I do," he whispered. "And I paid for it. I know what devils they are . . ."

Apostolis made no answer.

Silently the canoe glided along the darkening path.

* * * *

It was late at night when Apostolis arrived back at Kouga alone and presented the signal to the sentries.

Wrapped in their cloaks, the men had lain down on the damp floor with its sprinkling of dry reeds and gone to sleep. A little apart, Captain Teligades was boiling water on the burner he'd concealed behind his coat to prevent the flame from appearing.

Reclining next to him, covered up to his neck, Agras was moaning softly.

Apostolis tied the canoe up and stepped onto the deck.

"He's better," Teligades replied to his uneasy question. "The shivering's passed. I'll give him another warm drink and he'll be able to rest. But it's the second time in a few days the fever has seized him like that. The Swamp will devour him too," he added sadly.

It was time for the guard to change. Teligadis woke up replacements and sent them to relieve the earlier shift—who returned and settled down on the floor. Complete silence reigned.

Only Teligades and Apostolis continued to watch over the sick commander until sleep overcame him, whereupon the two of them lay down and slept themselves.

* * * *

The night passed without incident.

* * * *

In the morning a lively Agras was among the first up, full of spirit and determination, ready for the most daring action as if he'd never suffered during the night.

"The fever's come and gone," he replied to those, worried, who inquired about him. "Now let's see what we need to do next."

He called a council with Teligadis and the rest of his force to discuss whether to make an assault on the Bulgarians, or wait in case one of their patrols passed by. The latter way, they'd be able to weaken the enemy's resistance before attacking them with their limited number of fighters.

They decided to wait.

Agras summoned Apostolis and Mihalis.

"We don't have the strength—either the men or canoes—should we need to attack or pursue the Bulgarians. The two of you, set off together and go to Captain Kalas and to Captain Nikiphoros. Tell them to be prepared to come. At any minute I could call upon them for assistance."

Agras' instructions for the captains were short and precise—but urgent.

"Start right away," he stressed to Mihalis. "Get there quickly and return. "We can't be deprived of a single rifle or canoe."

Agras' word was law. In an instant his will was imparted to his men, who stood ready to brave any danger to execute one of his commands.

* * * *

"I know a secret path . . . We won't lose time . . ." a panting Apostolis said to his companion as the two of them rowed with all their might. "It passes behind Toumba . . . into this waterway . . ."

His sharp eyes dug into the reed walls to the right, searching for the sign he'd left when he came by the first time with Jovan.

"There it is!" he exclaimed happily.

He guided the canoe into the reeds where two stalks were leaning towards each other, their dry leaves entangled as if blown together by the wind.

A couple of rows of now yellowish reeds concealed the beginning of the path. Pushing them carefully aside, the two men steered the canoe in-between and arrived at the secret shortcut.

"Now let's be off. Take heart and do your utmost! We'll get there quickly," Apostolis said.

But as much as they labored, it had grown dark when they reached Tsekri.

* * * *

Captain Nikiphoros was consulting with two dignitaries from Bozets. They'd come to report that their village had become a hotbed of Bulgarians—that the worst comitadjes had taken asylum in it, hidden, supported, and fed by the Bulgarian villagers. The few Greeks who lived there were exposed to constant danger. The heroic young teacher Miss Evthalia risked her life everyday, as did Father Chrysostomos, the patriarchal priest. They wouldn't give way, but it was necessary for Captain Nikiphoros to realize what a snake pit Bozets was—and Kourfalia and Ramel . . .

A youth entered and interrupted the speaker who, worry-beads in hand, was enumerating the exarchal Bulgarian villages where every so often another crime occurred.

Troubled, Captain Nikiphoros raised his head.

"What is it?" he asked.

"Someone's asking for you, Commander . . ." the young man murmured. "And he says it's pressing . . ."

"Who is it? What does he want?"

The youth bent down and whispered something in his ear.

Captain Nikiphoros turned to the dignitaries.

"Let me reflect on all you've told me. We'll see what can be done. Meanwhile . . . I have some work that demands immediate attention. Send Dr. Antonakis[17] to me. He knows the situation, and he's at Bozets. He'll report my decision and the steps we'll take. The signal's a pistol shot. When the boat approaches, the password is 'cross/star.' Go now."

* * * *

A little aside on the deck, two men stood enveloped in their cloaks, one big and tall, the other short.

Nikiphoros let the visitors from Bozets embark; and when the canoe was at a distance, he approached the two newcomers and led them into the hut.

By the light of the oil lamp, he recognized Apostolis.

"What! You again!" he exclaimed.

And addressing Mihalis:

"Did you bring a letter from Captain Agras?"

No, Mihalis didn't have a letter. However he presented the captain's message orally—his command for the other leaders to be prepared to rush with help as soon as called upon. They'd finally found Kouga, he reported, but it was a miserable floor without any defense or even a roof. It would go badly for Captain Agras, if the Bulgarians made an assault. He was in need of aid—of men, weapons, and boats—in order to strike the nearby Bulgarian huts first, and not let them anticipate him. Moreover he was ill. Last night the fever had gripped him again . . .

Captain Nikiphoros rose from his seat.

"I'll set off, myself," he said. "I won't wait for him to call me . . ."

He stopped to ponder. And making up his mind, he declared:

"I have work to do here in the frightened villages. Yet Agras' undertaking is critical . . ."

He stopped again for a moment, and then ordered:

"Depart at daybreak, Mihalis. Head for Kouga and tell Captain Agras I'll come without his sending me another message. I'll also inform Captain Kalas. As for you, Apostolis, I have a job for you. Grab a bite to eat and get some sleep. I must write something now. In the morning at dawn you'll both start out, each in a different direction."

* * * *

Very early, Apostolis was the first to rise. Rested, washed, and tidied up, he waited on the deck for the commander to summon him.

All around, men were in constant motion: cleaning their weapons, carrying cartridges to the canoes, transporting bread from the nearby oven, and washing clothes—but at a distance so as not to dirty the hut's water.

Tsekri was a bee-hive from the break of day, providing there hadn't been a tour of the villages the night before.

Apostolis watched the activity as he stroked the pistol Captain Agras had given him, kept tucked in his belt. If only he were grown himself and worthy of enlisting in a rebel force, of embarking on marches, skirmishes, and battles! . . .

"Apostolis!" the commander called out.

The boy bounded inside the hut—erect, alert, energized.

Captain Nikiphoros held a letter in his hand.

"You'll go at once to the landing-cove," he said. "There you'll leave the canoe and proceed on foot to Zorba. Take Miss Electra aside and give her this. I didn't write an address . . ."

Casting a glance toward the door, he added in a low voice:

"You'll tell her yourself . . . that it's for the Master . . . Do you understand?"

With his eyes, Apostolis made a sign—yes. In a whisper, he added:

"For the Center."

Nikiphoros smiled.

"You're sharp, all right!" he said to him. "But see that the letter arrives in her hands."

"If she asks me anything, do you have any instructions?"

"If she asks . . . She won't, though . . . Just inform her that two dignitaries from Bozets were here yesterday evening. She'll understand . . . She's experienced."

* * * *

That Miss Electra was experienced, Apostolis knew better than anyone else. Not even Captain Nikiphoros realized how many times she'd used him in the past to bring rifles, pistols, cartridges and handbombs into the school's secret hiding place during the night. From there, by countless means she'd managed to smuggle them to the huts.

Now it would be the letter . . .

Striding along the edge of the lake, avoiding the regular road, Apostolis drew towards Zorba. Half-hidden inside the reeds scattered over the dry land, he was mapping out a complete strategy in his head.

Because he was aware that Miss Electra would make use of him. Knowing him well, she understood that whatever she entrusted to him he would carry it through. Being young—and speaking both Bulgarian and Turkish as he did—he could pass anywhere, even where an adult would find it difficult . . .

* * * *

The school was calm and quiet when Apostolis reached it. The children had dispersed to their homes for the mid-day meal.

In the kitchen, Miss Electra was seated with Jovan before the spotless wood table.

The child let out a cry when he saw Apostolis and jumped down. But he stopped, bashful, and looked anxiously first at the teacher, then at his friend.

"Welcome, Apostolis," a delighted Miss Electra greeted him, extending her hand.

And with a glance towards the whitewashed walls and sparse furnishings, she added:

"There's no chair! Hurry! Bring a stool from my room, and we'll treat you to our pilaf. We just sat down to eat, ourselves."

The three of them settled around the table and exchanged news. Jovan forgot his food. He couldn't take his eyes off Apostolis. Every so often Miss Electra nudged him to wake him from his enchanted state.

"For heaven's sake, eat! Your pilaf will get cold."

But how could Jovan tear his attention away from Apostolis, who was relating how they'd discovered Kouga, a rotted floor entirely unprotected on a waterway which served as a Bulgarian passage. As sick as he was, Agras hadn't hesitated to seize it with a handful of men and boats, almost without ammunition. Kouga was so close to the Bulgarians that their central, largest hut appeared from inside the foliage—thinned-out at that time of year.

"Will he stay there unprotected?" Miss Electra asked, disturbed.

"They brought him cartridges from the Lower Huts. Moreover Captain Nikiphoros will go right away, maybe tomorrow, with his whole force to join him," Apostolis replied.

Glancing at Jovan, he said in a low voice meant for the teacher's ear:

"I need to speak to you privately, Miss Electra . . ."

"Run to my room, Jovan," Miss Electra ordered the child. "On the window-sill you'll find the basket with the apples Evangelia gave us. Choose the six ripest ones and return with them. There, take a plate."

Obedient, Jovan climbed down from his stool, took a plate from the table, and left the kitchen with his head down.

"Speak rapidly," the teacher said.

Apostolis thrust his hand into his shirt and removed Nikiphoros' letter.

"For the Master," he said succinctly.

She took the letter and examined it on each side.

"The envelope doesn't have an address," she remarked. "Therefore it's important. Didn't Captain Nikiphoros give you any instructions for me?"

"No, he said that you'd know—that you were experienced. Only he wanted me to inform you that yesterday evening two dignitaries from Bozets visited him."

"I know! I understand," Miss Electra cried out. "It's about the October and November murders—and now the killing of the notable at Ramel and his whole family.[18] The comitadjes have gone too far."

"What! Ramel again?"

"Yes! The poor village has had its share of crimes! And they wrote to the teacher in Bozets . . ."

"To Miss Evthalia?"

"Yes, to Miss Evthalia—to say if she didn't stop fanaticizing the children and parents, that's how she'd end up. They threatened to burn her alive inside her school. However, they don't realize who they're dealing with!"

"She's heroic like you, Miss Electra!" Apostolis responded.

"She's heroic, yes; but I'm not. She lives in the midst of comitadjes in a Bulgarian stronghold. I . . . I have many of my own; and the lake is near with the captains a step away. But she . . . I can imagine why the dignitaries went yesterday. They would have asked Captain Nikiphoros to come out into the villages so the orthodox could take courage again. Is that what they sought?"

"I don't know. He didn't tell me. He said you would understand."

Miss Electra didn't answer. Pensive, she kept turning the letter around in her fingers.

"Will you send it, Miss Electra?" Apostolis inquired.

The teacher looked up.

"Certainly," she murmured. "But how?"

"The same way—with the train . . . You know . . ."

"No . . . It won't do for you to go again . . . They'll take note of you . . . Let me think . . ." She raised her head and looked around in the direction of the door.

"What happened to the child? Is he lost? Jovan!" she called.

No one answered.

The teacher smiled.

"He must be crying . . ." she said with affection. "The poor boy . . ."

"Crying? Why?"

"That's what he does every time he thinks I dismiss him . . ."

With the letter in her hand, she went out of the kitchen. In a short time she returned pushing Jovan before her, his eyes red.

"Imagine—crying!" the teacher said, stroking the child's thick, brown hair. "And just when I'm preparing secret, confidential work for him . . ."

Apostolis' eyebrows shot up to the middle of his forehead. Silently, he gave her a questioning look.

"Yes," Miss Electra replied. "Jovan will take the letter you brought me, Apostolis. But you'll help, too."

She removed her silver watch from her leather belt.

"We have an hour until the children arrive for their lesson," she announced. "Come, Apostolis, let's draw up a plan. And you, Jovan, listen and pay attention. Today you'll show us if you're worthy of the new clothes I made for you—and of our returning the Bulgarian ones you're wearing."

* * * *

The two boys started out early, with the pale November sun still high above their heads.

Jovan was nervous and withdrawn. Apostolis encouraged him.

"Why do you have doubts? What you did before was much more difficult—your going from the Lower Huts to Tsekri. This is easy, if you keep your eyes open."

Jovan kept silent.

The older boy gave him a shove.

"Don't be foolish," he said. "You're not a greenhorn! So what do you fear?"

Again the child didn't reply.

With conviction, Apostolis declared:

"I'm certain you'll succeed. Besides, you're small and no one suspects little children . . . Still, even if they do catch you, there's no name written on the envelope. 'For the Master!' What does that mean? Which Master? Only don't forget if they ask you, that you're the nephew of the Master of Kastoria. Remember? What's his name?"

"Karavangelis, Germanos Karavangelis."[19]

"Good. And where are you heading?"

"To Monasteri to find my mother."

"That's right! All this is in case they question you. Otherwise . . ."

"I know . . ."

"Don't be afraid then. Captain Nikiphoros isn't so stupid as to call a spade a spade, as Miss Electra told you. Everything is written secretly so that no one will understand, if the letter falls into foreign hands . . ."

* * * *

The two boys hurried along, occasionally exchanging a few words. They passed the carriage bridge of the Loudias River and drew to the south, leaving the main road that went to Verria.

When they'd traveled a short way, Apostolis stopped.

"You go alone from here on," he instructed Jovan. "Plati is visible now. They know me there. It's better they don't catch sight of me. I'll be waiting for you under the bridge. You saw how to climb down. Eh? Or whistle if it's deserted and I'll come up. So long, now. But mind you, act as though you're stupid. Pretend to go right, and try to take the train that's heading left. And don't forget! The right cheek first, then the left, and the forehead last of all. Okay?"

"Don't worry . . ." Jovan murmured.

He left with his head lowered.

* * * *

The child hastened off, almost running, stretching his thin little legs as much as he could.

Now that he no longer had Apostolis beside him, he became bolder. From the time he was small, brought up on beatings and punishment as he'd been, he'd grown adept at sly tricks and wheedling. He was accustomed to using all sorts of maneuvers to escape Angel Pio's hands. But feeling safe close to Miss Electra and Apostolis, he'd lost those qualities and become a child eager to learn new things.

"I'll never lie to you," he'd told Miss Electra the day before, when he broke a pane of glass with the broom while sweeping up the classroom. "Even if you beat me, I won't tell you lies."

It was the same with Apostolis. He'd be ashamed to deceive him.

Now, alone in the plain, he felt all his old resources returning as he conjured up no end of schemes to succeed in his mission.

* * * *

The sun was sinking in the west toward the mountains when he entered the station.

The train hadn't arrived. From the other side of the track, three children were playing a game where they kicked a flat stone. Jovan paused and watched them, but his attention was directed towards the west.

From a distance, he heard the chugging of the engine. Taking a flat stone himself, he began to jump and kick it with one foot toward the track.

The Turkish employee, who had a red and a green flag in his hand, saw him and shouted:

"Get away from there! And you others, all of you—scram! The train's coming . . ."

Jovan picked up his stone, rushed away, and stopped at the station, his eyes and mouth open like a country child viewing the iron beast for the first time.

The train was pulling up, screeching and smoking. Passing Jovan, the locomotive came to a halt a little beyond.

A couple of villagers approached with their baggage, and a couple of others got off at the station. With the activity, Jovan hid among them and found himself before the luggage car.

Like a dim-witted child, he tried to climb up the steps. A porter caught his arm and pulled him down.

"Where are you going?" he inquired in Turkish.

With large, frightened eyes, Jovan stared at him, scratching his right cheek, his left one, and then his forehead with his wrist.

"Where are you going, climbing up that way, you rogue?" the Turk repeated, growing angry.

Speechless as though bewildered, Jovan went on staring at him, scratching his right cheek, his left one, and his forehead, one after the other.

"Don't you know any Turkish?" the porter asked, exasperated.

Jovan didn't reply.

The conductor was walking a little beyond, unconcerned. The Turk called out to him:

"Look here. A youngster who doesn't understand the language. You know Bulgarian . . . Perhaps he'll respond to you . . ."

Jovan looked at the conductor with the same fearful eyes.

Kindly the man inquired in Bulgarian:

"Are you Bulgarian?"

"Yes . . ." Jovan murmured in the same language.

And slowly he scratched his right cheek, his left one, and then his forehead again.

The conductor's eyes flashed. Turning to the porter, he said to him in Turkish:

"He seems slow-witted and you've scared him. Let me speak to him in his language."

"Better you than me," the Turk said innocently, shaking his head.

And he was off to his work.

The conductor continued questioning the child in Bulgarian, supposedly indifferent:

"Where do you want to go? . . . What are you searching for here?"

Jovan looked at him. Fearfully he rubbed his right and left cheeks again and then his forehead, like a stupid, startled child.

Hastily, furtively, the conductor made the same movements with his index finger and said in a low voice in Greek:

"Run further down, behind the baggage-car . . ."

"Which one?" Jovan asked, also in Greek.

"The one with the trunks . . . and wait for me . . ."

Jovan hurried off. In a few seconds the conductor leaped down from another car, a short distance away. He found Jovan huddled next to the baggage-car. When he'd assured himself they were alone, he approached the child hurriedly.

"Where are you from?" he questioned him softly.

"From Zorba," Joven replied.

"Miss Electra?" the conductor responded.

"Yes!"

"A letter?"

"Yes!"

"Give it to me quickly . . . Hide at the wheels . . . Take it out secretly . . ."

In a twinkling, Jovan had removed the envelope from inside his shirt and thrown it down. The conductor bent over as if to examine something on the wheel. Gathering it up, he stuffed it inside his sleeve and stood up again.

"To the General Consulate?" he murmured.

"The Master . . ." Jovan answered.

"All right, stay here. The train is leaving. When it's gone, be off yourself. Greetings to Miss Electra—from Christos . . . She knows . . ."

With rapid footsteps he climbed onto a car again. Almost immediately, the train departed.

From the ground where he'd seated himself, Jovan observed the bustle of the station. Before long everyone had scattered, both travelers and employees.

He got up himself, passed beyond the station, and stepped out onto the main road.

Running, he reached the carriage bridge. The sun was setting. Apostolis awaited him, alone, on the road.

"Did you succeed?" he asked.

"Yes!"

"To whom did you give it?"

"He said to tell Miss Electra: 'Greetings from Christos.'"

"Good! You fell into the hands of the smarter one. He always manages to accomplish all he undertakes, even the most difficult tasks."

Cheerfully, he slapped him on the back of the neck.

"You see how foolish you were to be scared. I knew you'd succeed," he said. "Now let's get started."

* * * *

The two children sped off in the deserted plain towards Zorba.

It was night when they arrived. The door of the school was unlocked and Miss Electra was waiting for them. On the kitchen table, two cups, plates, and bread and cheese had been put out. On the charcoal stove, a coffeepot was steaming.

"Sit down to catch your breath and relax. Have a glass of milk. I went myself to get it from the village," she said to the boys. "Then you can tell me what happened, Jovan."

She was heartened and in good spirits. She could rest easy once she'd heard them arriving and Apostolis announced: "Greetings from Christos."

Because she knew it was risky to entrust such important work to so small a child. But the work she undertook could never be done without risks.

She listened to Jovan's narration as he scratched his right cheek again, his left one, and finally his forehead, reenacting the scene with the Turk where he'd pretended to be frightened and dazed.

"I wasn't sure if he really was a Turk," he explained to her. "However, he didn't answer to my sign. When the other one came and made the same motions with his finger as I had, I was so glad, Miss Electra . . . For I feared the train might leave before anyone understood me. Now I know. Another time I'll do better."

"You succeeded this time," the teacher said, bending over to plant a kiss on his uncombed hair.

"Moreover you've earned your clothes," she added smiling.

She rolled out a mattress she'd taken down, down from the loft, and covered it with sheets and blankets.

"Undress and sleep here, both of you," she told them. "I'll lock up and then go to bed myself. Tomorrow we'll talk some more."

9.

Kouga

BUT THE NEXT DAY while they were talking, muffled gunshots sounded in the distance. Apostolis and the teacher raced outside.

"The noise is coming from there," Miss Electra said, pointing west.

"Good God! It's Captain Agras! I wonder if Captain Nikiphoros has set off?" Apostolis responded. "Or if Captain Gonos will get there in time from Prisna? Or whether Captain Kalas was notified?"

Jovan had followed them. Pressing his two hands over his mouth, he stared first at Miss Electra and then at Apostolis, pale and frightened.

"Did they kill him?" he murmured.

No one answered.

The firing had stopped. Miss Electra became even more uneasy.

"He has only a few men . . . and you say that Kouga is at a crossing . . . A surprise attack . . . with the enemy nearby . . . Listen, Apostolis," she said decisively: "Run to Nikhori. They'll have heard the gunfire and the village will be aroused. Nikhori has brave lads. Gather as many as have rifles. Tell them I sent you . . . and rush to the Lower Huts to learn what happened. Then . . . wait and see! But don't lose a moment. Captain Agras might need help right away . . ."

Apostolis didn't stay for a second order. He'd run off, straight to the Kryfi landing-cove.

There he fired a shot and waited.

No reply was forthcoming. He fired another shot.

In a short time, a voice arose from inside the reeds.

"Hello-o-o! . . . Who is it?"

"Apostolis the guide. Come quickly!"

A canoe appeared. An oarsman armed with a rifle and pistols was alone inside.

"Gunfire erupted at Zervohori," he told Apostolis, approaching with his boat, "and Captain Kalas grew anxious. His deputy commander[20] was insistent upon their leaving; however Kalas wouldn't allow it. Moreover he was right. It wasn't anything—the gunfire's stopped. What is it that you want?"

"Take me across to Nikhori. I have work there . . . an order of Miss Electra's," Apostolis answered.

Jumping into the canoe, he grabbed the second oar.

"I'll guide as many young men as show up . . ."

"You're going to Zervohori?"

"First to the Lower Huts. And then we'll decide."

"But the firing's quieted down!"

"You never know what's happening . . ."

As if to confirm Apostolis' words, shots issued forth in quick succession. Repeated volleys—muted from the distance, yet persistant—testified to a battle raging in the direction of Zervohori.

"Hurry! Hurry!" Apostolis exclaimed. "Captain Agras is fighting at Kouga."

The oarsman rowed with a fury. A fighter himself, he knew what a swift dispatch of reinforcements meant.

"Give me your rifle," Apostolis entreated. "At Nikhori I won't find one . . ."

* * * *

There was considerable activity at Nikhori, with canoes drawn up on the landing-cove, armed men leaping onto the ground, and more armed youth arriving from the village.

Among them, tall and erect, Captain Nikiphoros stood hastily arranging the men in line for a march.

The volleys continued to fall like distant thunder.

Apostolis leaped onto the shore of the lake, himself—carrying the oarsman's rifle and wearing his cartridge belt.

"Commander . . ." he began.

Nikiphoros turned and saw him. He saw the oarsman as well, upright in the canoe; and he recognized him.

"You're from Kryfi?" he called out.

"Yes!"

"Go back. Tell Captain Kalas that you met me, and that I'm on my way to the landing-cove at Terkovista with my men and a force from Nikhori—by land to be safe. Tell him to come himself with his deputy commander. It's urgent!"

He turned to those in line again and ordered:

"Forward—at a fast pace!"

Apostolis slipped in among them and followed.

He no longer had work now at Nikhori, since Captain Nikiphoros had anticipated him and assembled the village force. In the distance, the battle continued to rage. One round of firing succeeded another. The tumult reached the edge of the lake over the reeds and vegetation, drowning out the other lake sounds.

Apostolis' heart pounded. What could be happening on the half-rotted floor of Kouga, with no roof or embankment to protect Agras and his men?

Oh, to arrive in time! Not to be too late! With his weapon and cartridges, he'd be an extra rifle for them. And he'd do his job, he swore to it. Only let him arrive in time for the battle . . .

Ahead in the lead, Captain Nikiphoros was proceeding along the shore of the lake, down into muddy ditches and often inside the water. Neither fatigue nor any obstacle could stop him . . . Just let them get there, let them get there . . .

"If we took the regular road, we'd travel more quickly with less labor," someone said to Apostolis. "Look at all the mud and reeds . . . and then our stumbling ..."

"The commander is wise," Apostolis whispered back. "In broad daylight, the Turks would notice so many armed men passing by the villages . . . Did you consider that? To undertake a journey on land this way requires courage, you know . . ."

"Well spoken . . . If the Turks become aware of us, they'll wipe us out . . ."

The fierce firing hadn't let up. Agony was written on everyone's face. Nikiphoros pushed ahead, quickening his pace and drawing the human chain along.

Until the volleys ceased . . . The gunshots grew sporadic and stopped altogether. Some of the men secretly crossed themselves. The fighting had endured for more than an hour. What could the present silence portend?

* * * *

The march lasted three whole hours. When they reached the Terkovista landing-cove, the November sun had disappeared behind the peaks of Mt. Vermio.

A pistol shot brought a canoe to the shore. However, there were many men. Nikiphoros entered the boat with all those that would fit inside and headed for the Lower Huts. Once there, he sent out other canoes to transport the entire force.

Only a few had remained at the Lower Huts to protect them from an assault. Their worry had been acute when the first shots rang out in the morning. Most of Agras' men had set off for Kouga the evening before, with Pascal guiding them. The ones left behind had heard the big battle, but knew nothing about it. How had it ended? Was Agras the victor? Or could the Bulgarians have destroyed him?

* * * *

It was night by the time the last rebels arrived at the Vangeli hut.

Without losing a moment, Nikiphoros supplied large canoes with weapons, packed them with men, and drew for Kouga in the dark, with just Apostolis as guide.

"Are you certain you know the way?" the captain had asked anxiously.

But all the men replied for him, declaring that he knew the paths even better than Pascal.

Apostolis alone remained silent. For the first time, he hesitated. He knew the paths, it was true, even better than Pascal. Yet in the dark among the thick, mysterious vegetation would he find them again? As the sole guide, he'd be responsible for so many youth . . . If he lost his way? If he threw them into some trap?

Standing in the prow of the first canoe, his eyes dug into the dark as he led them silently by means of signs inside the labyrinth of narrow, twisting paths opened up among the reeds. And faithfully and obediently, the oarsmen responded, turning a corner when he extended his arm, stopping when he raised it, and rowing once more when he signalled.

* * * *

Without a word, the commander and his men continued in the canoes that way for two hours.

At a turn, dim light was cast onto the water.

Overjoyed, Apostolis pointed and whispered:

"The Little Hut!"

It was the hut Agras had built to facilitate his patrols and ensure communication with the Lower Huts.

"Stop, so we can ask," Captain Nikiphoros ordered.

Two men were on guard in the dark, one on each side of the hut.

Nikiphoros saw the flash of a gunbarrel as it lowered.

"Friends here. Don't draw!" he said.

"Give the password!" they called out.

"Cross/star! . . ." Nikiphoros replied.

The gunbarrels were raised.

"Welcome!" they greeted him.

The canoes pulled up alongside the deck, and the two shadows approached.

But no one got out of the boats.

"What happened at Kouga?" Nikiphoros asked.

"We don't know. We thought you'd bring us news . . ."

"It's from Tsekri that we've come. We're on our way to help,"
Nikiphoros said. "If it's bad news, we'll return. Otherwise, if you
don't see us, it means all is well."

He gave the signal for them to start off.

Now Apostolis was sure of where he was going. Since he'd
found the Little Hut, he knew every curve of the path and every
new road opened up.

The closer they came to Kouga, however, the more quietly
and cautiously the oarsmen proceeded, and the stiller the men sat.

Apostolis took the last secret path and the boat silently entered
the waterway. The men, hunched down and bent over their rifles,
were ready to fire at the first command.

Under the pale light of the stars, the barrel of a gun glistened
among the reeds.

"Who is it?" a voice sounded.

From their tense chests a sigh escaped—deep and heartfelt—
and passed over the water.

"Our own men! They're safe!"

The sentry heard it and waded out in the water to meet them.

"Who are you, comrades?" he asked.

"From Tsekri! . . . Captain Nikiphoros . . . What's the news
here?"

The guard had reached them. Delighted, he clasped their outstretched hands.

"Good news," he answered. "We beat the scoundrels. But we
have two wounded."

Impatiently, Apostolis had caught up an oar and was rowing
towards the darkened Kouga a little beyond. On his feet now, Captain Nikiphoros was trying to penetrate the darkness himself with
his gaze.

The canoes drew alongside the "floor." Scattered shadows
rose and approached. A cheerful, happy Agras stood in front, surrounded by his men.

Nikiphoros leaped out first. Grasping the hand Agras held
out to him, he squeezed it, very moved.

"We heard the volleys . . . and hurried here . . ." he said, his voice cracking. "We didn't know what was happening—if we'd find you alive! . . ."

Agras embraced him.

"It looked bleak for a moment," he responded with a smile. "There were so many of them. But we managed—eh lads?"

They'd all been sitting cross-legged on the floor, conversing in the dark. It was a cold, damp night, yet they couldn't light a fire. Without a roof, it would be visible from a distance and betray them.

From behind a cloak, the men had boiled water and prepared tea.

Wrapped up to their necks in their coats and sipping the warm drink, the new arrivals listened to Agras' account of the battle.

"Yes," the commander was saying, "we escaped cheaply. Moreover we were tired, for we'd been up all night. Isn't that so, Gonos? Thank God you were here! Tell them about it!"

But a pleased Gonos slowly shook his head.

"You tell them, Commander. You'll do a better job of it . . ." he replied with his foreign accent that bothered him.

Aware of it, Agras made a point of encouraging him to talk— insisting that his accent was useful as it enabled the commander to know, even in the dark, that he had a fearless youth beside him.

Agras continued his account:

"So we set off last night for Zervohori—eighteen of us in all with Captain Gonos—over paths that Pascal knows well. Since a northwind was blowing, when we reached the village we traveled through the southern part to keep the dogs from picking up our scent. We circled Toman Pazarenze's house, where Apostol Petkoff was supposed to be hiding. Right, Apostolis?"

Apostolis was listening with bated breath, seated among the men.

"Yes!" he replied. "Jovan saw him there. Did you catch him?"

"As if we could catch him! It seems the fox never sleeps two nights in the same place. He lives in fear! We burned Pazarenze's house, as well as two or three others to serve as an example and punish the murderers of seven mule-drivers from Naousa. We didn't get Apostol, though. The bird had flown . . ."

"Pazarenze? What did you do to him?" Nikiphoros asked.

"We sent him hostage with some others to Agia Marina to be guarded there. Let them dare kill any of our men now!"

"You should have done away with them, Captain," Gonos murmured.

Agras threw back his head, crowned by his curly hair that stood out against the sky.

"Bah! Why? They, too, consider they're doing their duty when they kill us. If they're more brutal than we are, it's a curse in their blood. Maybe they're not to blame, if they were born that way . . ."

The men in the circle were muttering disapprovingly.

"The way you're going, Commander . . ."

"You're not asking Pascal . . ."

Hearing his name, the Bulgarian leaned over to inquire what they'd said.

Captain Gonos translated for him.

With displeasure, the old man shook his head.

"Everyday I tell him, 'You'll bring about our undoing, Captain! . . .'" he declared in Bulgarian.

"What did he say?" an evzone asked.

However Nikiphoros interrupted:

"In the morning we heard gunshots."

"That's another matter," Agras responded with spirit. "Our day today has been full of adventure, from last night's expedition on! Those first gunshots you heard were a clash of one of our patrols with theirs—which resulted in their taking flight. It appears that they'd seen the flames from the houses burned at Zervohori and put out a patrol this morning."

"And the battle?"

"Now that was something! The Bulgarians had heard the shooting from their huts; and it infuriated them because they didn't know what it was or where we were. They don't imagine we've seized Kouga. Thus they dispatched a strong force in canoes—exactly what we'd been waiting for so many days. When they entered this waterway, we let them approach. One after the other, they ran smack into our gunshots! Our guards had seen them and slipped back to inform us.

"At first they tried to withdraw in fear. However there were many of them and we were few. They perceived it and began firing away themselves . . ."

"And you, uncovered like this?" Captain Nikiphoros broke in.

"We'd gathered some reeds to fortify ourselves, although it didn't help much. Still, the Bulgarians had no cover either in the narrow passageway. What happened? We fought it out! They greatly outnumbered us, as I said. What's more, we lacked the canoes that had transported the prisoners to the Lower Huts.

"Assessing our plight, I sent boats inside the reeds with Gonos in order to strike them from the rear. Then how they fled! They all took off rowing at top speed! If only we'd had five more canoes, not one of them would have escaped! But we don't—we're poor!"

"You're an indestructible rock of will and daring, Agras!" Nikiphoros exclaimed with emotion.

Agras started to laugh again, but grew serious.

"Two of our lads were wounded. I had them brought to the Lower Huts so a doctor could attend to them. I didn't suffer anything myself. Those two unlucky ones paid . . ."

Seated to the side, a silent Apostolis listened and watched, attentive and thoughtful.

From the time he was small, he'd followed and been exposed to the Struggle. He'd counted the corpses of villagers killed and tortured; he'd attended funerals and listened to laments and curses. Yet never before had he encountered ideas like Agras's when he justified his enemies, or feelings like Nikiphoros's when he praised his fellow commander while brushing aside his own disdain of death.

He'd known brave leaders who were bold and good. However it was the first time that he'd experienced first-hand—that he'd come into contact with—civilized men in this ferocious Struggle.

Nor was he prepared for such behavior. He'd grown used to jealousy and rivalry between the fighters. What's more, he'd learned to believe and declare that every Greek was good and every Bulgarian bad.

Agras's words that the Bulgarians considered it their duty to kill Greeks, took him by surprise. But they also opened up new worlds to him—of justice and a willingness to forgive . . .

Wrapped up in his cloak, lying next to Captain Gonos among the sleeping men and commanders, he tossed and turned without falling asleep. And then there was Captain Nikiphoros . . .

Each time he recalled Nikiphoros's description of Captain Agras, he was overcome. Yes, he was a rock of will and daring! But wasn't Nikiphoros one also? In order to bring help to Agras as speedily and safely as possible, he'd raced along the swampy shore in daylight with all his force, almost under the Turks' noses. Not only did he fail to praise himself—he seemed not even to realize what a bold and dangerous feat it was.

Until this point, Apostolis had idolized Miss Electra alone as a higher being! That made it all the more confusing now. Because Miss Electra wouldn't accept that either Bulgarians or Turks might consider it their duty to kill Greeks. She was all of one-piece. She hated them both as worthy only of being destroyed.

When she remembered her father, killed by the Turks in '97, she grew furious, with fire in her eyes . . . And he, Apostolis—he too hated the Turks equally with the Bulgarians.

* * * *

At daybreak, with life and activity resumed on deck, Apostolis prepared coffee and cut up bread for the men. As he looked first at one leader and then at the other, he asked himself which of the two he loved the most—the tall, blue-eyed, well-groomed Captain Nikiphoros, or the small, curly-headed, unkempt but perpetually cheerful Captain Agras.

The latter's thin face and weak, sunken brown eyes, testified to his sleepless nights, to his sickness, his labor, and his worry. His spirits, though, remained unaltered. He never became impatient or out-of-humor, nor did he complain about the life full of hardship and deprivation at Kouga.

Nikiphoros had observed his unhealthy appearance.

"You won't hold up long in such a state," he told him. "If you want to continue this strenuous work, it would be well to go to the Lower Huts for a while to rest up and recover . . ."

But Agras interrupted him.

"Leave after our success yesterday? Let them come and take Kouga away from us?"

With his boyish, spontaneous manner, he threw his arm around Nikiphoros' shoulders.

"Don't mention it to me again, my friend!" he exclaimed.

"At least, build a hut," Nikiphoros said.

"That I'll consent to, Yianni," Agras replied. "Today in fact—since you and your men are here with us—we can do it quickly and quietly, so that those cursed Bulgarians don't see or hear us. Look! Their central hut is visible farther on inside the reeds . . ."

* * * *

By evening the hut with its roof was in place, and a wide defense embankment of reeds, roots, and mud had been constructed around the deck.

Kouga had been converted from an open, dangerously exposed raft, into a fortified refuge for the rebels.

"Thanks to you, we've fixed up our shelter!" Agras said to Nikiphoros. "Now I won't ask you to stay any longer."

Captain Nikiphoros had rushed off to them from Tsekri. It was necessary for him to return to protect it in case the Bulgarians attacked. He had to provide support for the patriarchal Greek villages as well.

"I'm waiting for the Master's answer," he told Agras. "I wrote to inform him that we were leaving Tsekri in order to come to your aid—but we set off without receiving his instructions."

The two commanders agreed on how to communicate as rapidly as possible in the future.

And with Pascal as guide, Nikiphoros departed with all his force. He left Agras supplied with ammunition—with cartridges and hand bombs—and with as many men as the Lower Huts and the southern villages along the lake had sent. Gonos started off at the same time.

Apostolis remained at Kouga with two other guides, former fishermen who knew the old roads of the lake but not the new ones.

Therefore he went out two or three times a day with them on searches and patrols to show them the new paths opened up, paths that confused the already complicated maze of lake roads even more.

Some days later, returning from a reconnaissance near the Bulgarian huts with Captain Teligadis, Apostolis heard Turkish conversation inside Kouga.

Amazed, he turned to Teligadis.

The captain laughed in a carefree manner.

"It's Halil-bey, the commander's friend," he said. "Now and then he visits him at the Lower Huts. He'll have found out about Agras' success at Zervohori and is here to congratulate him."

"But where did the commander learn Turkish?" Apostolis inquired.

"Why, he doesn't understand a word of it!" Teligadis replied. "Don't you hear Mihalis interpreting? Halil-bey doesn't know any Greek, or the commander Turkish. However the Turk admires the commander's daring and fearlessness; and they have a common enemy in the comitadjes. The bey's estate is south of Terkovista; he's seen their criminal acts. And from time to time he sends us tobacco . . ."

At that moment the two men emerged from inside the hut— the good-sized Turkish bey, who was richly-dressed in his long coat, smart trousers, and shiny boots; and the thin, poorly-nourished Greek rebel with his torn clothes, unruly hair, and lively but sunken eyes.

As worn out by hardship and fever as he'd become, he was nonetheless erect, upbeat as always, and undaunted. Behind them Mihalis followed close-by, ready to serve as interpreter.

The Turk addressed him:

"Tell your commander that whenever he wants help, he has only to make a sign and I'm prepared to send both men and arms to him."

Mihalis translated.

"Say to the bey that I appreciate his offer," Agras answered in turn. "But we're accustomed to handling our work ourselves— above all, when it's a matter of shedding blood . . ."

Mihalis translated again.

The Turk smiled and bowed courteously.

"Your leader is proud," he responded. "He might, though, have need of something else . . . a doctor, for example. He doesn't appear so well . . ."

"We have a doctor too, thank-you," Agras replied. "However if the need presents itself, I'll turn to the bey's good will for help."

They separated with handshakes and mutual compliments.

When the Turk's canoe had departed and was lost inside the reeds, Agras threw back his shoulders, stretched himself, and laughed.

"We'll do our job better alone," he said, "even if the bey is a good and faithful friend. And now lads, be about your work! You, Mihalis, seeing that you've been there before, hasten to Kryfi and to Tsekri. The other time Captain Kalas didn't succeed in getting here. This time, however, he must. The day after tomorrow we'll attack the Bulgarians' central hut, and we require more men, boats, and cartridges."

Next he instructed Captain Teligadis:

"You'll make an assault on the back part of the hut, while I charge it from the front. Go with Apostolis and a few others before it's dark and draw as near to it as you can. See what the situation is up close and report back to me. In the meantime, I'll ready things here."

But Apostolis couldn't get near the central hut.

From a distance, Teligadis had noted unaccustomed activity—the arrival and setting off of canoes, men, and cases.

"They're up to something," he said. "Let's go to Zervohori and find out."

But they couldn't approach Zervohori either. Sentries stood on guard, while many canoes were pulling up and taking off.

From inside the reeds and trees, the Greeks watched without being able to make sense of what they saw.

Apostolis suggested that they leave and descend more to the south, so he could set off alone in the deserted part of the lake and scout around.

The others accepted his suggestion.

Silently they turned south and went down to the shore above Yianzista, where Apostolis disembarked by himself.

With his hands in his pockets and whistling a Bulgarian war song, he headed north in the direction of Zervohori.

On his way he met fishermen and villagers, without evoking any suspicion or curiosity.

At Zervohori there was a big commotion. A band of comitadjes had arrived, and safe places to stay were being arranged for them. As there were many men, they were split up and directed to different homes.

Avoiding them, Apostolis approached some women in the midst of the blackened walls of a burnt-down house. With their hands on their hips, they were staring sadly at the commotion in the square beyond.

"What!" Apostolis exclaimed, as if taken back. "Who burned down this lovely house? I remember it from last year when I passed by . . ."

He spoke Bulgarian like a native, with the local accent.

A woman looked him over from top to bottom.

"Where are you from?" she asked.

"From Vertkop," Apostolis said at random. "I'm traveling to Kourfalia and . . ."

The woman shook her head.

"Don't go by the Swamp," she broke in with a frown.

"Not by the Swamp? How should I go, then?"

"Better to make a round of the lake than venture inside it. They'll kill you, too."

"Why? Who will kill me? Chief Apostol? He only kills Greeks."

"The chief isn't here. That's the reason they've created havoc."

"Who's created havoc?"

"The Greeks—curse them."

Apostolis opened his eyes and mouth, and he raised his eyebrows up to his thick hair.

"The Greeks? Here? In our refuge?" he responded.

The woman pointed to her middle-aged companion, seated farther down on some blackened stones that had fallen. On her lap, she held a little bundle of clothing.

"Ask Mistress Pazarenze. It was her house. They set fire to it and captured her husband Toman," the woman said.

Mistress Pazarenze overheard her and began a soft lament, rocking her head back and forth.

Apostolis went up to her.

"When did they burn it down?" he asked sympathetically.

"A number of days ago . . . I don't know anymore . . ." she murmured.

Breaking off her lament, she started to cry.

"If they hadn't taken Toman away, I could endure their burning the house down," she said sobbing.

Apostolis sincerely pitied her. With compassion, he said:

"They might not harm him . . . It's rumored some of them don't kill . . ."

Sonia Pazarenze motioned toward the lake.

"A devil's joined up with them." And interrupting her words with moans, she added:

"Alas, they haven't caught him! They don't know where he's hiding. Our men can't escape him! He blocks all the roads and terrorizes them! Agras is his name. Our boys tremble when they hear it. See! He burned down our house, along with three others. And that's not all! Look! Today, right inside the ruins, I discovered these little clothes."

One by one, she unfolded and displayed them to Apostolis. He recognized Jovan's clothing.

"I gave these to Angel Pio's nephew," Mistress Pazarenze continued. "I dressed him with my own hands. They killed the child and threw his clothes in the ruins of my house. Ah! What bad luck has befallen us! . . ."

"Don't worry, Sonia," a woman spoke up, wrinkling her black eyebrows. "Our brave boys have come now! Not much time remains to them anymore."

"They'll attack them, eh?" Apostolis asked, feigning eagerness. "They'll give it to them?"

"Of course they will!" the woman replied angrily. "Only let them rest up tomorrow, and the next day they'll strike and fix them. Moreover, they'll bring that devil back, and we women will skin him alive . . ."

"So they know where he's hiding?" Apostolis inquired, growing more and more eager.

"They'll find him," the woman responded. "A few days ago he was at some rotted floor called Kouga. Curse him! Let him sink and be swallowed up by the river! He's hiding somewhere around there. They'll find him, I tell you. Many comitadjes have arrived now; they've brought rifles, and we've got canoes . . . We'll make mincemeat of the Greeks. And we'll tear that criminal Agras apart!"

Apostolis had all the information he wanted; however he asked still a few more questions. But the women could only tell him that other comitadjes were on their way to reinforce the huts toward Zervohori—before they tracked down and attacked the demon who was plaguing them so.

Pretending he had time on his hands, Apostolis strolled below, then turned back again and exchanged several more words with the women. When they'd dispersed to attend to their work, he headed off too and drew south. As soon as it was deserted, he ran down to the edge of the lake. Teligadis and his companions were waiting for him, with the canoe concealed inside the reeds. Making a loop to avoid encountering Bulgarians, they returned to Kouga.

It was dark when they arrived.

* * * *

An oil lamp was burning behind the oilcloth door. Bundled up in his cloak and covers, Agras lay on the floor engaged in a discussion with some of his men.

His eyes were shining, lit up by the fever. But his mind worked incessantly as he set up plans with them—determining the part each would play in the attack two days later.

Captain Teligadis raised the oilcloth and stepped inside.

"You're sick, Commander," he said, "and unfortunately I have some bad news for you."

Agras sat up. Wrapping his cover tighter, he leaned his back against the wall of the hut.

"Speak," he ordered. "In two hours I'll be well. What did you learn?"

Teligadis gave him a brief account of what he'd heard from Apostolis.

Agras listened attentively until the end, then turned to Andonis who was standing beside him:

"Call the guide," he commanded.

Apostolis entered and stood before the sick leader, concerned and respectful.

"Repeat to me what you heard and saw," Agras said.

Apostolis related his conversation with the distressed women he'd met in the ruins of Zervohori, without neglecting to report the interpretation they'd given to Jovan's clothes thrown there.

The commander didn't interrupt even once.

When Apostolis had finished his narration, again Agras didn't reply or ask anything. Pensive, he continued to lean against the reed wall, his feverish eyes fixed upon the glowing embers in the center of the floor.

Making his decision, he said suddenly:

"Teligadis, prepare the men and canoes. We'll strike early in the morning. We won't wait for them to attack us whenever they choose. It's win or lose—them or us."

And trembling from fever, he lay down once more as close to the embers as he could to warm himself.

10.

Battle At The Central Hut

DAY BROKE ON NOVEMBER 14, 1906.

Agras was the first one up, energetic and in good humor. His fever had gone; and paying no attention to his illness, he arranged for the attack.

In a large canoe Apostolis waited for him, oar in hand, silent from his intense pleasure.

Pascal hadn't returned. And the village guides didn't sufficiently know the new paths. He remained the only guide with experience. The commander—who intended to surprise the central Bulgarian hut at Zervohori—had honored him by taking him in his own boat up front.

The rebels numbered just eighteen, all crack fighters though. Brave youths completely dedicated to their commander, they'd come to Macedonia resolved to beat back the Bulgarians. There were but seven canoes.

"A daring undertaking, without any hope of help reaching us," Captain Teligadis exclaimed, fastening on his cartridge belt and placing hand grenades in a row in the bottom of his canoe. "Yet when has the commander ever taken danger into account?"

Andonis leaped into the first canoe, next to Apostolis.

He was carrying a Mannlicher rifle and had two pistols tucked under his belt.

"So? We didn't come here to live!" he replied, exhilarated. "Didn't the commander tell Stelios: 'Every day we expect to die' when he took him into his force? And today his words might well come true . . ."

"Don't worry!" Christos declared in his Cretan accent from the next boat. "If it's our fate, we'll die. If not, no bullet will touch us . . ."

Armed men were approaching and dividing up into the canoes, two in the smaller ones, three or more in the others.

Agras gave his final instructions to the recruited villagers. Trained with a rifle now, they were to guard Kouga and defend it from any Bulgarian assault. The commander was the last to leap down into his canoe.

"If Captains Gonos and Kalas appear, send them to us . . ." he ordered.

* * * *

The boats started off, each three meters apart.

Agras led with Andonis, with Apostolis serving as guide.

No one spoke. They rowed in silence, careful not to splash, hit anything hard, or set a waterbird to flight, which would reveal their presence.

Drawing near to the huts, they entered the reeds that Apostolis separated, attentive not to break any.

The canoe glided along without a sound.

Seated in the middle Agras directed the procession that followed, by means of gestures.

Captain Teligadis and two other men were right behind them.

With a sweep of his arm, Agras motioned him to turn aside in order to strike the hut from the rear.

At once, Teligadis and three other boats split off and disappeared in the reeds, circling around the central hut. Agras proceeded towards the entrance with the last three canoes.

They were now so close that Bulgarian conversation could be heard; and the Greeks observed cigarette smoke rising up into the calm atmosphere.

Agras bent over to Apostolis' ear.

"What are they saying?" he whispered.

"They're planning tomorrow's attack on Kouga," the guide answered, keeping his voice low.

Agras nodded and looked towards the back of the hut. Teligadis wasn't visible. The canoes had become lost inside the reeds.

Apostolis stopped at a sign from the commander.

Holding their breath, they waited.

Suddenly a volley from behind the hut shook the air. At the same time, another volley responded from Agras' canoes. The central hut burst into an uproar—with cries, confusion, fear . . .

"Alas, alas!" the Bulgarians wailed.

"Forward! Fire quickly! Teligadis, the hand grenades!" Agras shouted.

With all his strength Apostolis pushed the canoe forward, driving his oar into the bottom of the lake.

But the water was shallow, and the broad-leafed plants dense. The dugout bogged down every time it moved.

"Forward! Forward!" Agras yelled. "Teligadis! Throw the hand grenades . . ."

Frightened and confused, the Bulgarians had also begun firing. From the two sides, the gunshots were deafening. But the Greeks took aim, while the startled Bulgarians sought cover in back of their defenses, firing haphazardly almost without looking.

With great labor, inch by inch Agras' canoes advanced inside the thick growth. All of a sudden, the commander's voice thundered:

"The bombs! Throw them! What are you waiting for?"

Teligadis' unruffled voice sounded from within the deafening shots:

"We threw them. They didn't go off . . ."

Agras plunged into the shallow water. Followed by his youth and Apostolis, he charged the entrance to the hut. It was slippery with mud; and plants got tangled up around the men's legs. Yet nothing could stop Agras. He proceeded in the lead, struggling against the hurdles of the Swamp, constantly emptying his rifle and encouraging the others.

"Forward, lads! Forward!" he shouted. "We need a better hut in order to sleep tonight. Take it from them . . ."

Teligadis had appeared at the back of the hut, bloody but unsubdued. Together, he and his men were firing from inside their canoes.

Christos the Cretan goaded the Bulgarians by crying out:

"Cowards! Hiding behind your defenses, are you? Come out and fight us, if you dare!"

One, who knew Greek, replied:

"We'll send you to Zervohori for the women to skin alive!"

"I'll send your heads to my village for our girls to see how ugly you are!" Christos yelled back, tossing a final hand grenade.

But this one didn't explode either.

Seeing the bombs roll like balls without bursting into flame, the many and well armed Bulgarians reorganized and caught up their places, shooting all the while.

At the same time, gunfire rose from the nearby Bulgarian huts, where reinforcements had arrived from a quarter of an hour away.

Bullets were now raining down on the rebels, fired off by the enemy under cover.

Agras' men, exposed and unprotected in the water, dropped one by one. The battle was as uneven as it was fierce.

A bullet hit Agras' hand. Another penetrated his right shoulder. With a glance, the commander counted his youth. Half remained. The undertaking had failed.

Ordering a withdrawal, he shouted:

"The dead! We'll leave nothing to them!"

And ignoring his wounds, under a hail of bullets he began gathering up those who'd fallen. Along with his men, he raised a sunken canoe to the water's surface, lay the dead inside, and dragged it away. He was the last to withdraw, still turned toward the Bulgarian hut with his weapon in his good hand, determined to resist until death.

However the intimidated Bulgarians had gone into hiding. Many had been struck down; and the rest were so frightened and thrown off balance by the enemy's boldness that they didn't pursue them.

When they reached Kouga, the Greeks took stock.

Of Agras' eighteen men, only nine were left.

That day left a deep impression on the rebels at Kouga. Nine of them—a half—were dead, the others severely wounded.

Agras himself had his right shoulder pierced through and a finger severed from his left hand. But he was undaunted, refusing to leave to have his wounds treated at the Lower Huts. All day he stayed with his men, speaking to them, consoling them, bolstering them up.

Their failure had shaken them. The hand-grenades hadn't exploded. They'd been sent defective equipment. Elsewhere, too, cartridges supplied to the captains had proven deficient. The governing authority was neglecting them, abandoning them to their fate, forsaking them. What, then, could they expect? From where would help come? Nine of them remained . . .

"Won't nine men be sufficient for us to hold a fortified hut like Kouga?" Agras broke in impetuously. "Who doubts it? Let whoever is hesitant go straight to the Lower Huts where there's safety. Captain Teligadis and I will be enough to defend Kouga."

"And I!" Apostolis called out. With his head bandaged and a Mannlicher rifle in his hand, he sprang up and stood next to Teligadis.

"And I!" Mihalis exclaimed.

"And I!"

"And I!"

"And I!"

Evzones from mainland Greece, freedom fighters from Crete, native Macedonians—all flew up as one, electrified, and surrounded their leader.

"We're with you, Captain! We'll all stay."

Agras smiled at them, and his smile was filled with affection.

"I knew not one of you would leave," he responded. "All your talk was anger that we didn't succeed in capturing their central hut. Still, what could we do? The bombs didn't go off! The next time the Master will send us better ones. Meanwhile, let's prepare the defense for tomorrow. Those in the best shape will go out on patrol to take over the paths . . ."

* * * *

But as the day passed, the men's weariness became more perceptible. Their inadequately bound wounds pained them, darkness weakened their morale, and melancholy pressed down upon them with the descent of night.

Burning from fever, his cheeks red and his eyes glazed, Agras drew himself up and leaned back against the reed wall. Lively and cheerful, he related stories to his men to entertain and inspire them. One was of the heroic Captain Bouas[21]—who'd been wounded in the leg yet had fought furiously until he had to be carried away.

A youth who'd suffered a bullet in the leg himself, commented sadly:

"But he was crippled and returned to Greece. He couldn't become a rebel again."

Calmly, Agras answered:

"This is the *Struggle.* They'll strike us down, and we'll do the same to them."

"But they're beasts!" Christos exclaimed in his Cretan accent. "Didn't they burn all our eastern huts before our own men rebuilt them? . . ."

Agras laughed.

"As if their sins were the only ones! What do we do, I wonder? The day before yesterday, didn't we set Zervohori in flames? Doesn't Mistress Pazarenze have a soul too—the poor woman Apostolis saw sobbing and moaning in the ruins of her house after we'd seized her husband? And the other women who cursed us so . . ."

"What will you do to Pazarenze, Commander?" Andonis inquired.

Agras pushed back his curly hair with his injured hand. His wounds ached and his temples throbbed from fever. But he didn't want to show it.

"We'll send him back to his wife. I didn't have time to think about him yesterday or today."

"He's a dangerous one, Commander," Mihalis protested.

"I know it," Agras answered, unconcerned. "That's the reason we're still holding him. However let's resolve this once to do it—then afterwards . . ."

"Give Christos his head to ship to Crete so the women of his village can see a Bulgarian mug for themselves," Andonis said with Christos' Cretan accent. As always, he was in high spirits.

Everyone burst out laughing.

"Yes, give it to me!" Christos said.

"You watch out instead that the Bulgarians don't first dispatch your own head to the girls of Zervohori, seeing that you're a handsome one," Agras joked.

And growing serious, he added:

"We're not out to be savage. We're to fight honorably, don't forget it."

"You'll never crush them that way, Commander," another evzone said.

"Why not?" Agras inquired.

"Because you show pity instead of destroying them. Besides, there's so many of them."

"Didn't I say there were?" the commander responded indifferently.

"And when they overrun us?"

Agras shrugged his shoulders.

"Brave fighters don't meet such a fate. One fearless fighter puts down all those that are scared."[22]

A clamor, with laughter and footsteps, sounded on the deck. Each man grabbed his gun.

By the light of the flickering lamp, a tall, manly figure appeared at the door, filling its frame.

"Hello, Yianni!" Agras called out, welcoming him. "The gunshots spoke and summoned you!"

Stirred, Captain Nikiphoros approached without a word and clasped Agras' hand, while his men entered the hut one by one, spreading throughout it.

"How many have you brought us?" Agras asked. He, too, was stirred.

"Twenty-two. With me, twenty-three."

"Once more, you arrived first, Yianni! But how did you get here so quickly?"

Nikiphoros spoke with emotion.

" . . . I'd received your message . . . However you were to stage your attack tomorrow, so I figured we'd be in time . . . When we heard the firing, we raced to reach Kouga. Pascal guided us by snakelike roads and paths impossible to describe . . . We were fearful we'd be late . . ."

Agras smiled.

"It's not too late. Tomorrow the Bulgarians will besiege us; and as you see, we're a little worn out . . ."

"Captain Teligadis, the battle was a hard one, eh?" Nikiphoros asked.

"The bombs didn't go off," Teligadis replied, adjusting the bandage on his forehead. "Otherwise no one would have escaped. The commander made an assault from the front of the hut, while I did the same from the rear. We were capturing it right on target. But the wretched grenades failed us . . ."

"Moreover reinforcements had made it to the nearby huts," Agras added.

And he continued:

"I'd been notified by Captain Panayiotis[23] that Bulgarian reinforcements would descend on us from behind, if we didn't drive the comitadjes from their hut. But I thought we'd be able to seize it before they arrived. There wasn't time to wait, though, as the Bulgarians will take the offensive tomorrow. We needed to anticipate them . . . Captain Gonos didn't appear—which means they blocked his way . . ."

Each of the men had his own interpretation of the failure.

"If Captain Kalas had come . . ." one began.

"What happened to Kalas?" Agras asked Nikiphoros.

However Nikiphoros didn't know. He'd rushed to Kouga without contacting him.

"At any rate, you got here in time, Yianni. Again, you and I will manage when they make their big attack tomorrow," he said fondly.

* * * *

The next day, it dawned, the sun rose high in the sky, and midday arrived without the enemy showing up.

When night fell and the Swamp grew dark, the guards took up their posts. Yet no Bulgarian approached.

Despite its failure, Agras' bold undertaking had terrified them. A patrol guided by Pascal, which drew up almost under their huts, reported back that they'd suffered both heavy casualties and a loss of morale. For a few days at least they'd stay quiet.

Thus Nikiphoros persuaded Agras to go down to the Lower Huts with the other wounded to be looked after by a doctor.

Nikiphoros left nearly all his men with Captain Pandelis to protect Kouga and the nearby huts, along with one of Agras' deputies—Nikos—and as many of Agras's men as remained able.

He himself accompanied Agras down to the Vangeli hut, where the seriously wounded fighters were being cared for.

Agras became tired and stiff from sitting still in the canoe.

Upon seeing him, his men at the hut all gave him a warm greeting.

Inside, four villagers were huddled around the fire. They neither rose when Agras entered nor greeted him.

To his surprise, Agras observed that their hands were tied. He recognized them as the villagers they'd captured at Zervohori.

"Why have you tied their hands?" he asked indignantly.

"Because they try to get away," a rebel replied. "That one," and he pointed to a heavy-set man, "jumped into the water. We had a difficult time finding him again inside the reeds. Since we tied them, we've had some peace."

Agras went up and spoke to the prisoners.

"Aren't they treating you well?"

No one answered.

"Someone translate . . ." Agras called out.

"Bah! They all understand Greek, Captain," Mihalis said. He'd received a chest wound and come to the Lower Huts with the first of the wounded.

"Why don't you answer?" Agras asked the heavy-set Bulgarian who, with his head down, was staring at him from under half-closed eyelids.

Once more, he didn't speak.

One of them, still a child, was sitting to the side. He'd been crying and his eyes were red.

Agras questioned him:

"Why are you crying? Did they harm you?"

In a low voice, he replied:

"You'll torture us and kill us!"

"Who told you that?" Agras wanted to know.

"Toman Pazarenze," the youth answered, indicating the hefty man with his head down.

"You're Pazarenze?" Agras said to him. "Do you have a wife Sonia?"

Pazarenze didn't respond. From under his eyelids, he glared at Agras.

"We don't torture and we don't kill prisoners," the commander declared affably. "We'll even set you free. It's enough that you promise not to raise a gun against us anymore."

The prisoners were shocked. A couple of them couldn't believe their ears, three gave their promise, and the younger one began to cry again.

Pazarenze alone kept silent.

Agras summoned the villager Stelios.

"Take all four of them in a large canoe," he ordered. "Put them down on dry land—then untie their hands . . ."

Drawing Teligadis aside, he added:

"Go along in case anything occurs on the way. I entrust them to you . . ." And speaking more softly: "See to it that they're blindfolded, and follow the secret path of Captain Panayiotis. They can be released at Yianzista. You're responsible for them . . ."

Standing beside Nikiphoros, he waited for the men to enter the boat. When all the prisoners were seated inside, he addressed Pazarenze:

"Tell Sonia that we Greeks returned her husband to her. She shouldn't forget it if our men fall into her hands."

Silently he watched the boats leave. Two of the rebels approached him, taken back by what he'd done.

One, Mihalils, spoke up: "Better to do good and have it wasted than not to do it at all," he declared.

"But you forget you're dealing with wild bears that will tear you apart, Captain," the other inserted.

Thoughtfully, Agras replied:

"The young one who was crying won't attack us again. If we gain one person, do you count that so little?"

"Pazarenze?"

"I'll admit myself that he's a devil."

"Why did you let him go?"

Agras shrugged his shoulders.

"That's the way it is," he said.

With a laugh, he went on:

"Let one pardon be wasted."

He stepped into the hut.

"Where is the doctor?" he asked. "My confounded hand hurts."

The doctor—who operated by trial and error—was already there. He'd been brought from the south of the Swamp, where he served the Greek villages. Full of good-will, he had primitive medical notions.

Entering the hut, he made Agras remove his shirt, then examined his shoulder and left hand. One bullet had taken away a finger, and another had passed through his right shoulder and come out in back. This wound was the most serious. The doctor began to sterilize it, without setting down the cigarette he was smoking.

"Tell him to throw it away and wash his hands first," an exasperated Nikiphoros whispered to Agras.

But Agras smiled.

"Don't worry," he responded. "We're rebels. What's a little smoke!"

He allowed the doctor to treat him in his own, make-shift way.

11.

Thessalonika

IT WAS LATE WHEN THEY ALL LAY DOWN TO SLEEP on the reed floor.

Agras, however, couldn't rest. His mind was on Kouga.

By the light of the oil lamp, he tore a sheet of paper from his notebook and wrote:

> "Dear comrade from Mani,[24] As soon as you receive this, come to the Vangeli hut as quickly as possible. Agras."

Very early in the morning he summoned Vangelis, a trustworthy Macedonian from Naousa—a giant in height and fearless in spirit.

"You're courageous and strong," he said to the youth. "You've proven it in battle. Show me now if you can also travel swiftly."

Calmly Vangelis took the paper and concealed it inside his shirt.

"Where do you want it to go, Captain?" he asked.

"To Naousa, into the hands of Captain Panayiotis."

The Macedonian didn't wait further. He climbed into a canoe with an oarsman and left.

All day Agras remained lying down. They'd cut weeds and straw from the Swamp and spread them over the reeds on the floor, so it wouldn't feel so hard to him. Yet the whole day fever consumed him; and his inflamed wounds gave him pain.

It was past midnight when, still awake, he heard conversation. Sitting up, he saw Captain Nikiphoros and Teligadis talking with someone at the door of the hut.

"Who is it, Yianni?" he called out.

Nikiphoros turned, then stepped aside and a man dressed as a villager entered. Small, lean, and dark from the sun, he went up to the wounded Agras and bent over him.

"Panayiotis! I knew you'd come right away!" Agras exclaimed. And he added:

"Your entire work in the western Swamp is in danger!"

"Don't worry," Captain Panayiotis replied, unperturbed. "We'll put them in their place. Didn't I send you a message, though, not to strike the Bulgarian huts without first seeking reinforcements?"

"The cold weather compelled me to act," Agras responded. "We were suffering at Kouga. Besides, I didn't want to let them attack us whenever they chose . . ."

"What about the other captains?" Panayiotis inquired.

"Nikiphoros came. We were able to transport the wounded . . ." Agras replied with his boyish, upbeat smile.

And reflecting, he added:

"Do what you think best now about Zervohori, Captain Panayiotis."

The following day Captain Panayiotis departed with his force and a Naousa fisherman as guide, one who knew all the huts. Agras waited in agony, confined as he was to the Lower Huts, while Captain Nikiphoros scouted around inside the labyrinth of lake paths.

But nothing was heard all day and night.

Suddenly at six in the morning, a rifle shot sounded, followed by successive volleys testifying to a battle. Then there was silence again—and once more volleys from the land and the upper part of the lake.

Agras ground his teeth together.

"To think I'm stuck here!" he groaned in a fury.

However the gunshots had stopped. Hours went by.

Late in the evening, a clamor arose. Captain Panayiotis had arrived, exhausted and drenched, with all his cartridges and those of his men spent.

"They're well fortified, all right," he said, frowning, "with weapons better than ours and huts able to support one another."

"But why are you soaked that way?" Agras asked.

"Why? I fell in the water!"

"How on earth did that happen?"

"The shooting was underway, when I noticed a Bulgarian canoe starting to rush off. Standing, I drew my rifle and fired. Our dugout overturned and the three of us landed in the water. The boat sank; however we managed to retrieve it and the shoot-out continued. From the western shore, the Turks were alerted and joined in with volley after volley. Our bullets gave out and my men retreated. All this took place near the Zervohori landing-cove—it didn't extend to their huts."

"Kouga! Hold on to Kouga!" Agras burst out.

Wild from the fever and from Panayiotis' account, he repeated again and again:

"We can't lose Kouga! If we do, they'll defeat us!"

Understanding the significance of the hut, the next day Captain Panayiotis set off for Kouga as soon as Nikiphoros returned from his patrols. Among his force he included recruits from the Greek villages—those who'd been trained with a rifle.

All day Agras raved under the effect of his strong fever, his mind constantly on Kouga.

"If he doesn't get away from here, he'll die," Captain Teligadis said. "The fever will consume him."

Alarmed himself, Captain Nikiphoros contacted the Central Command in Thessalonika.

And he told Agras, "If you don't leave the Swamp and see a doctor, I wash my hands of you."

But Agras treated his words lightly.

Then the command came from the Center in Thessalonika. Captain Agras was to report right away to the General Consulate—so that willing or not, he was compelled to obey.

He called Apostolis who was also at the Vangeli hut, recovering from a slight head wound.

"Do you know where Halil-bey's estate is?" he asked.

"Kavasila? Yes, I know," Apostolis answered. "It's a little further than Terkovista."

"That's right. Can you go and find him?"

"I'll go, Commander."

"I want to give you a letter. Are you able to set off today?"

"Immediately!"

He removed the bandage from his head, and the doctor replaced it with an adhesive. In order to hide his half-healed wound, he put on his cap, then headed for the Terkovista landing-cove to be let out on shore.

It was still day when he reached Kavasila.

Following Captain Agras' instructions, he informed the servants who opened up for him, that Razmi-bey had sent him with a message for Halil-bey.

Without any difficulty, he was led to the bey's office.

The bey was alone.

Silently, Apostolis took out Captain Agras' letter and presented it to him.

Halil-bey couldn't read Greek, and Agras didn't know how to write in Turkish. Halil started to clap his hands, but Apostolis made a motion that stopped him.

"Better not to call anyone else, Bey," he said. "The letter is from Captain Agras who seeks your help."

"Is that what he's written? How do you know?" Halil questioned him.

"I'm from the Swamp. The commander is ill . . ."

"Read the letter to me!" the bey ordered.

Apostolis read and translated it:

"My friend," Agras wrote, "the other day you offered me your help. I'm wounded and ill and need to go to Thessalonika to see a doctor. I ask you to find a way to get me there without the Turkish police arresting me . . ."

"By the Prophet!" Halil-bey exclaimed. "Was it he who raised such havoc a few days ago in the Swamp? The gunshots never let up. We thought the whole lake was ablaze! Tell me, is he badly wounded?"

"He is," Apostolis replied, "both in his hand and shoulder . . . He also has a high fever . . ."

"I should have guessed it was Captain Agras when I heard the volleys . . ." the bey murmured.

He walked up and down the room a couple of times, before sitting down again at his desk.

"Listen," he said to Apostolis. "I'll provide you with the clothes of a Turkish villager. Tell your leader to wear them and come out to the Terkovista landing-cove. One of my men will be waiting for him. And he shouldn't worry about anything. Tomorrow at ten, have him be there."

* * * *

The next day at ten Agras disembarked in the mud at Terkovista, dressed in the villager's clothing sent by Halil-bey. His wounded arm was in a sling, he had a cloak draped over his shoulder, and his face appeared flushed from the fever.

Only an oarsman and Apostolis accompanied him. He'd refused to take any other escort, confident he was being dealt with honorably—the way he dealt with others.

Uneasy, the oarsman kept his gaze on him, dallying his oar in the water, uncertain whether or not to leave the commander with just Apostolis, a child.

He saw a Turk approach, greet Agras, and set off with him. After making his cross secretly, he departed himself.

Not knowing Turkish, somehow or other Agras reached an understanding with the Turk without Apostolis' assistance. He followed him on foot to the carriage road, calm and free of worry, relying on Halil-bey's word.

And he was right.

In the road before him, two horses and a groom were waiting. Agras mounted one, the Turk took the other, and Apostolis trailed them on foot with the groom.

The sick commander and his Turkish escort proceeded slowly.

. . . Agras disembarked . . . dressed in the villager's clothing sent by Halil-bey.

When they arrived at Halil-bey's estate, the doors opened wide and Halil-bey himself came out to greet his rebel friend. He welcomed him with a profusion of Turkish compliments, none of which Agras understood.

"What is he saying?" he asked Apostolis a little hesitantly.

"He wants you to sit down and rest, and he thanks you for entrusting your fate to him, Commander. He says you'll leave together today, and that you shouldn't be worried about anything now—that he'll bring you himself to the Greek Consulate in Thessalonika."

"Give him my own thanks," Agras answered, "and tell him I know that once a Turk gives his word, he doesn't break it."

* * * *

Seated in a third class carriage of the train bound for Thessalonika, Apostolis was contemplating—trying to unravel his thoughts that were all tangled up.

Captain Agras had entered the first-class carriage with Halil-bey, unsuspecting and fearless as ever, putting his trust and faith in the good.

But if Halil-bey betrayed him? If sitting beside him, he killed him?

"Once a Turk gives his word, he doesn't break it," the commander had said; and the commander would know. However Miss Electra knew too. And Miss Electra always insisted: "Don't ever put faith in the word of a Turk!"

Miss Electra hated the Turks as much as the Bulgarians. True, the Turks had killed her father in the war of '97. But no promise had been made. It was a war. An officer in the navy, he'd enlisted with enthusiasm and landed with a force of volunteers at Ai-katerini in Macedonia. They were to attack the Turks from the rear and put them between two lines of fire.

Miss Electra had related the undertaking to him many times; and she'd repeated how the foolish Athenian newspapers had announced it in advance, so that everyone was aware of it. Thus informed, the Turks were waiting at Ai-katerini for the force to land. As soon as it advanced a little, they attacked and destroyed it with much superior strength, killing every last man along with the mission's commander.[25]

Her lips always trembled and her eyes flashed whenever she described this tragic history. With passion in her voice, she exclaimed:

"Turks! Let there be as many Turks as I know, myself!"

She said this because she didn't really know any—that is, she didn't have relations with any. She avoided even speaking to one.

The Turks must be bad, he reasoned, since Miss Electra hated them so. What Miss Electra said was the gospel for him.

But now Captain Agras had entrusted his life to Halil-bey, a Turk! Moreover, he'd declared that once a Turk gave his word, he didn't go back on it . . . Perhaps it was necessary to always bind a Turk by his word? The Turks who'd killed Miss Electra's father certaintly hadn't made any promises, since they were enemies at war . . .

* * * *

With confused thoughts and impressions, Apostolis descended at the Thessalonika train station and followed his commander. With Halil-bey, they got into a carriage and headed for the city.

Seated beside the driver, every so often he placed his hand on his belt and felt his hidden pistol, a gift from Captain Agras. In order to defend his leader in any danger or attack, he was prepared to fire and to give his blood.

Nothing happened, though.

It was night when the carriage pulled up before a large white building on a corner—the Greek Consulate.

A shared wall separated the Consulate's long, narrow courtyard from the Metropolitan Mansion of the bishop, which stood at the far end of the garden with an imposing marble stairway.

A small door in the shared garden-wall made secret comings and goings easier between the two buildings—generally clandestine visits from Greeks and specifically from Macedonian fighters.

The carriage stopped before the Consulate courtyard, and Halil-bey stepped out with Agras and Apostolis. An Albanian guard with a gold-handled Turkish sword at his side, received them.

He bowed low to Halil-bey like he knew him, but looked disdainfully at Agras with his Turkish villager's clothes, hesitating to allow him to pass. Halil-bey had to assure him: "He's with me!" for the guard to take the three of them to the Consulate, reached by means of an outer staircase.

Inside, a man in civilian clothes emerged from the entrance of a room that was all lit up, looked at Agras with startled eyes, and greeted Halil-bey.

They exchanged a few words with much bowing and ceremony. However, Apostolis couldn't hear what was said because the guard kept him at the door.

The bey protested he didn't want to go upstairs to visit the General Consul, where the man in civilian clothes invited him. He had no time, he said; he'd return the next day. And with a new round of handshakes and compliments, he went outside with the official and climbed back into his carriage.

Hastily the official reentered and closed the Consulate door. Running to Agras, he embraced him and said in a stunned voice:

"You traveled in Turkish clothes! What folly! You who don't know any Turkish! If someone spoke to you, what would you do?"

Agras laughed, indifferent as always about such things.

"If we had to reflect on all this, my dear Theodore,"[26] he replied, "it wouldn't be worth living . . ."

"Come upstairs and rest. The Consul will be anxious to see you," Theodore said.

Arm-in-arm they ascended the inner stairway.

* * * *

The guard had stayed below with Apostolis near the door of the Consulate. He observed the boy from head to toe with curiosity, keeping his hand on the handle of his sword.

"Is your master a Greek?" he inquired. "Why is he dressed as a Turk?"

"And you, what are you?" Apostolis countered suspiciously.

The guard chuckled.

"For the General Consul to have me here, I must be of some good," he answered.

Then he added:

"Is your master a rebel leader?"

But taken back by the unknown surroundings he was experiencing for the first time, and excited by the thought that the General Consul—the Master as he was known by all the fighters—was nearby, Apostolis remained silent. As always, he was cautious with strangers.

The guard gave him a friendly slap on the back of the neck.

"You, a puppy, hold back with me?" he responded good-naturedly. "Don't you know that the Consul sends me on the most secret work?"

"What work?" Apostolis asked, longing to hear and learn what went on at the Consulate.

"Ah, you've found your tongue?" the guard said mockingly.

Footsteps and conversation on the floor above were heard.

The guard stood at attention, facing toward the stairs.

No one appeared, and the conversation grew distant.

"The Consul!" the guard informed him in a low voice, mechanically grabbing hold of the handle of his sword again.

"He stays so late?" Apostolis inquired eagerly.

"So late? When there's work to be done, has the Consul ever paid attention to time?" the Albanian replied with pride. "But now he's at home. The Consulate's here below and his quarters are above."

"And you? What is your job?" Apostolis asked.

"I'm a guard. One of three. We keep watch at the Consulate and accompany the Consul when he goes out . . . I also do other work," he inserted with a sly wink.

Apostolis didn't dare ask. But he was so anxious to find out that he remained with his mouth open, staring at the Albanian.

The guard wanted nothing more than to converse.

"Today," he volunteered, "I went, we would say, to assist two girls onto shore . . ."

He winked again.

"They had trunks for customs . . . that by no means were to pass through . . . They were heavy . . . I told the customs officer: 'Two silver coins for you, and I'll take care of them!' The officer looked the other way while I took the trunks. But I was carrying a large handkerchief as well, with goods inside. A corner of it got away from me . . . and the goods scattered! . . . Lead, you see . . . they fell and made a racket."

"Were they bullets?" Apostolis asked, startled.

"Cartridges," the guard answered, chuckling to himself.

And he continued:

"The customs officer turned around . . . I brought out my pistol. 'It's nothing,' I said. 'They're olives . . .' Pistol in hand, I gathered the scattered goods and went out. On the ground where the olives had fallen, I left two more silver coins . . ."

Chuckling to himself again, the Albanian gave another wink.

"That's the way we do our work," he went on, puffing up his chest and beating it with self-satisfaction. When the consul says: 'Look to see that the trunks get out, Ali, without going through customs!' they get out without going through customs."

"What was inside the trunks?" Apostolis inquired, breathing heavily.

The Albanian narrowed his eyes in a cunning smile.

"They contained heavy goods . . . which go 'boom boom!'" he replied proudly.

"Rifles? Where do you put them?" Apostolis asked, more and more excited.

Footsteps sounded again on the upper floor. This time they headed in the direction of the stairs and descended.

Once more the guard stood at attention. Apostolis removed his cap, stretched himself as tall as he could, and stepped beside the Albanian. The boy was all eyes and ears as he faced the stairway.

Three men came down. First, next to Captain Agras who'd changed into civilian clothes, was a tall, white-haired, white-bearded gentleman with a youthful face. Erect in his bearing, he had a dignified smile and a resolute manner.

Apostolis understood that it was the General Consul—the Master Koromilas[27]—leader and soul of the Macedonian Struggle. Ardent feelings arose in him . . .

A few steps behind, Theodore followed with his hat in his hand, all respect and deference before his leader.

The guard removed a soft, gray, stylish hat from the hat-rack at the entrance and held it out to the consul. Taking it, Koromilas continued his conversation with Agras:

"I'll let you off at the doctor's house. He'll be your host and provide for you . . ."

However Agras had caught sight of Apostolis, and he put his hand on his shoulder.

"This one is also with me," he said. "I'd like the doctor to examine him as well."

The consul approached. Brushing the boy's hair back from his head-wound, he inquired:

"He's wounded, too?"

And addressing Apostolis:

"How did it happen you were in the battle?"

From his turmoil, Apostolis couldn't speak.

Agras answered for him.

"He's my guide. In our Struggle, Consul, there aren't children or women. They're all brave fighters; and as you know better than I do, the women and children succeed in making their way where our path is obstructed . . ."

"I know, I know," the consul replied, smiling. "Just today two girls brought in loads . . . eh, Ali? We managed and they got out without passing through customs."

The guard had bowed halfway to the floor, with a smile that revealed all his white teeth.

But the consul wasn't in the habit of wasting words on praise and compliments.

"The carriage, Ali—quickly."

"It's waiting for you, Master," the guard replied with another bow.

Indeed, the carriage was waiting outside. The consul helped Agras up into it, then summoned a bashful and overwhelmed Apostolis.

"Enter inside," he ordered him. "You'll go with your commander to the doctor's."

Bidding Theodore good-by, he leaped into the carriage himself, like a young man, and sat down beside Agras.

* * * *

"If I live a hundred years more, I won't forget that drive!" Apostolis said that same evening to the doctor's children. They'd taken charge of him and led him to one of the rooms to sleep, in a household always ready to put up rebels and persecuted Greeks. He proceeded to describe the ride to them:

"Imagine! . . . I, Apostolis the guide, sitting opposite the Master and Captain Agras! Every time we passed a streetlight, I saw the Master's white hair and beard and his noble face . . . Ah, how impressive he is! And next to him, the most courageous fighter of the Swamp, Captain Agras! Do you understand what that means?"

Yes, the doctor's children understood. A string of secondary school children used to all the savagery and heroism of the Struggle, they were accustomed to hearing and keeping secrets, to seeing off and providing refuge to officers and rebels, and to transmitting letters and conveying weapons and cartridges to hiding-places in schools. They'd met both Miss Electra from Zorba and Miss Evthalia from Bozets—as well as Father Chrysostomos . . ."

"The priest from Bozets?" Apostolis asked, surprised.

The boys exchanged glances and burst out laughing.

"Yes, the one who poses as a priest," Kostas, an older child, answered. "All those that have beards aren't priests," he added, winking at his brothers.

The oldest of the children, Harilaos, straightened up.

"You're not to speak about these things," he reprimanded his brother.

But Kostas wasn't listening. He wanted to tell what he knew.

For the doctor's children knew everything and everyone. They'd met Captain Nikiphoros and Captain Matapas. They knew Captain Kapsalis as well, killed in a fierce battle with the comitadjes that past April—and many more . . .[28]

"Do you know the captain the Turks captured in a clash near Kilkis and put in prison?"[29] Kostas asked Apostolis.

No, he didn't.

"He pretends to be a doctor in the prison. We go and visit him sometimes . . ." Alekos, one of the middle boys, informed him.

"And we'll help him break out," Kostas confided to Apostolis in a low voice, "the way we set his bravest fighter Aristeidis free. Do you know how he got away?"

Apostolis had no idea.

So Alekos related it to him:

"When their prison terms are almost finished, those who've served long sentences are given the task of carrying the garbage outside in large baskets. In front of the door, a guard digs down into them with an iron bar to make sure there's nothing else inside. Well, two Greeks approaching the end of their sentences hid the iron bar one day, put the prisoner inside the basket, and covered it with a blanket. Then they piled garbage up over it and took him to the door.

"The guard searched for the iron bar without success. Growing tired of looking, he ordered: 'Go—pass!' So they went to the outer wall and emptied the garbage along with the prisoner down below. He took off, but wasn't familiar with Thessalonika. Entering a house—which chanced to be Greek—he was asked who he was! 'Take me to the Consulate. I'll reveal who I am there,' he replied. They brought him to the Consulate, where he was kept hidden in the basement and then helped to escape . . ."

"That's how we'll set his captain 'the doctor' free, too. Only don't let on about it," Kostas added.

Apostolis had no desire to do so. He'd been involved in secret matters, himself. Yet all of these doctor's children knew so much that it astonished him, and made him dizzy. Only when they asked him about the battle at the Swamp, where he'd been wounded in the forehead and Captain Agras had been struck, was he able to take the upper hand again. For he'd seen and lived the battle. And first on his knees and then upright, attacking make-believe canoes and leaping into imaginary water, he enacted it for them. He showed such spirit, such thunder and bluster—repeating the commands: "Forward, lads!" and "Gather the dead; we'll leave nothing to them!"—that the boys' mother arrived on the scene.

With a hug for each child and a smile for all, she had both her own children and their guest get some sleep—and dream of new battles, victories, and glory.

12.

A Devil Of A Priest

THE NEWS WAS BAD. Apostol Petkoff had been making a round of the lake villages, leaving a bloody trail behind him. Where he didn't have time to finish, the blood-thirsty comitadje Hadzi-Traio took over. Two men from the Apostles village and five fishermen from the Swamp had paid with their lives for the sin of being patriarchal Greeks. In all the open countryside, comitadjes were threatening the Greek population—burning their property, killing, torturing, and terrorizing them.

"Agras mustn't find out about it. He'll try to leave," the doctor said to his wife. "Tell the children not to breathe a word. Because the captain's wounds haven't completely healed, and I fear the malaria, above all, will render him incapable of continuing his work if he doesn't take care . . ."

The children said nothing, although they were itching to speak with Captain Agras to learn his view about what was happening, and then discuss it among themselves.

Late in the afternoon on the fourth day, there was a rap on the door. The devoted old houseservant opened up and was greeted in a friendly manner by a girl who asked for the doctor.

No one was at home. The doctor was on a sick-call, his wife had gone out, and the children hadn't returned from school.

At that point, the girl requested to see the "sick visitor." Faithful Missus Morfo brought her up to the guest's room.

Captain Agras was reading, seated beside the window in a rocking chair, enjoying the last rays of the setting sun behind the faint peaks of Mt. Vermio.

He heard the door open and beheld a young woman about twenty years old, dressed in a navy blue outfit with fox fur at the neck.

"Captain Agras?" the girl asked with some emotion.

Agras stood up. His arm still hung limp; however his shoulder had almost mended. He wore his jacket without his injured arm passing through the sleeve.

"That's who I am," he answered, a little uncertain. "Miss . . .?"

"Electra Drakou."

"The heroic teacher from Zorba?" Agras interrupted in surprise.

"Teacher, yes. Heroic, though, no. I've never done anything heroic," Miss Electra replied smiling.

"We're the ones to judge that," he said, more and more moved by her.

And extending his sound arm:

"I want to shake your hand," he added.

He made her sit in the rocking chair by the window, and pushed another chair up next to her.

"Tell me quickly. For you to leave your school and come to find me, you have something important to relate," he said anxiously.

Yes, Miss Electra had important news for him. She'd stopped at the Consulate and been taken to the General Consul. After listening attentively to her, the consul had instructed her to go herself to the doctor's. She was to see Agras and present her message directly to him, as he knew the Swamp and could tell her what should be done.

Because there had been disagreement among the captains.

In the meantime, some strange acts of revenge had occurred. At Naousa, Verria, and above all to the north, dangerous comitadjes were discovered dead—four or five of them, all killed the same way with a stab in the heart. No rebel force had passed by there. Certainly, Captain Nikiphoros hadn't proceeded that far. For the northern villages were too distant for him to reach, punish the comitadjes, and return to the Swamp by daybreak. Besides, a rebel force wouldn't conduct isolated murders like that; it would burn down the comitadjes' village as punishment.

Everyone in the countryside had begun to murmur the name of Captain Garefis again—the famed Garefis who'd personally killed two of the worst comitadje leaders inside their hut, and wounded a third. But Garefis had died a couple of days later from a bullet in the stomach, fired by comitadjes or hit by cross-fire. No matter, they said—Garefis had come back to life.

They were whispering it in the Greek villages and rejoicing, although they still sought help and action from the rebel forces.

Miss Electra had relayed all of this to the two officials in charge of administering the western districts.[30] Both of them had listened to her, serious and silent—one with a mysterious smile half-concealed by his moustache, the other all seriousness and more inscrutable.

When they'd heard her out, the serious one declared that, of course, Garefis hadn't come back to life. However the comitadje chiefs needed to be eliminated; they were holding the Greek communities in a state of terror.

Regarding the villages at the lake, they called in two others with authority[31] and had her provide details of the captains' disagreement. That is, Captain Kalas, who was critical of Agras' daring assaults, had quarreled with his deputy commander—who was now leaving with the sick Captain Panayiotis to return to Greece.

Meanwhile three thousand Turks had encircled the lake and proposed an agreement to strike the Bulgarians.

Captains Nikiphoros and Kalas both went to the Lower Huts in the western district for negotiations, but Captain Kalas didn't want to co-operate with the Turks.

"Why! Why!" Agras burst out. "Let's first drive the Bulgarians from the lake, and then see about the Turks."

"That's how the other captains felt, too," Miss Electra reported, "but Captain Kalas was suspicious and didn't want to."

Captain Nikiphoros had requested to be transferred himself to Kouga with his men, in order to restrain the Bulgarians and assault them in their refuge. So far Kouga had been holding out, but reinforcements were badly needed.

However Kalas disapproved of violent action. The General Commander of the lake couldn't decide to take the lives of so many men upon himself, as Agras had done with his attack at Zervohori.

Captain Matapas had come down from Olympus to persuade Kalas to change his mind. To no avail! He refused to go along with such madness. He'd undertake a defensive position, he said— nothing more.

Agras flew to his feet.

"When do you depart?" he asked.

"Tomorrow morning."

"We'll set off together. My friend Halil-bey will get us to the Swamp safely."

In vain, the doctor tried to dissuade him from leaving before his wounds were healed, before he'd regained his strength and recovered from the malaria. Very early Agras went off with Miss Electra, and by nightfall he was at the Tsekri hut.

The assembled captains held a council there, with the majority voting for Agras' aggressive action. Any improper acts on the part of rebels were investigated, and the decisions sent off to the Center.

The next morning Agras departed again, this time headed for Kouga with Apostolis.

* * * *

A real building had been raised upon the old Kouga—a new hut higher than the tallest reeds, proud and provocative!

More than thirty villagers had labored all the while Agras was away, transporting wood beams, reeds, grass and earth from the southern shore. The large hut was to be up and ready when the commander arrived.

"What is this monster?" Agras exclaimed in surprise.

Delighted, the deputy-commanders exchanged glances.

"Don't you deserve such a hut, Commander?" Teligadis responded. "After your attack of mid-November, you should have a palace."

The men surrounding him showed their pride. The hut was stationary; beams had been driven into the bottom of the lake. Between them, a thick bed of reeds and Swamp grass had been piled up above the shallow water to form the floor. The well-constructed walls were protected from the rain, like the roof, by a thick layer of grass.

They had indeed built a hut to evoke envy in the neighborhood.

Agras admired it too, so as not to disappoint the men who had worked on it with such good will. But unconsciously with his eye, he measured the height of the roof protruding defiantly above the dry reeds of the Swamp—and also the low embankment. Because of the difficulty of carrying so much earth from the Terkovista landing-cove to Kouga, it had been restricted to three or four handspans, which only bodies lying flat could defend.

Vangelis, the giant from Naousa who'd done the work of ten—"the Macedonian" as Agras called him—declared:

"You have a right to such a hut, Commander. With eighteen men you put fear into the Bulgarians in the Zervohori huts. The day before yesterday, two hundred Turks tried to capture them and were driven back."

"Two hundred Turks? What!"

"It's true! The Turks encircled the lake from the northwest section. Didn't you know, Commander?" Teligadis asked. "Two hundred of them wanted to make an assault on the Bulgarian huts, but they didn't do anything. The Bulgarians attacked them and they fled . . ."

"The Bulgarians forced them to flee?" Agras reflected. "Don't rejoice; it means they've received reinforcements and that our turn will come."

"What if it does?" Vangelis boasted. "We're here."

And he displayed his formidable arm muscles.

Agras however remained absorbed in thought. Given his small force, he was considering whether defensive action inside his large new hut would be possible behind the low embankment.

"Apostolis!" he called out.

When the boy presented himself, he said to him:

"Again it falls to you, Apostolis, to be a messenger for me."

"Go to Toumba where Captain Panayiotis has just left, to Tsekri to see Captain Nikiphoros, and from there to Kryfi to Captain Kalas. Tell them all to send us support. Terkovista will take care of providing food and ammunition by means of the usual villagers and carriers. But we need men."

Kouga's position, like a wedge thrust into the complex of Bulgarian huts, was a provocation the Bulgarians couldn't bear.

Nor could Agras bear to leave Kouga. His fate had been tied up with that of the hut. If Kouga were lost, he'd be lost himself . . .

* * * *

Uneasy, Apostolis hastened toward Kryfi with a village oarsman. At the Toumba hut, Captain Panayiotis had gone off, ill. And those on guard said:

"We're not strong here. We're hardly able to defend ourselves. How can we help you, given our own plight?"

At Tsekri, Captain Nikiphoros had received him and listened with his pensive, quiet air—rubbing his shaven chin and contemplating for some time.

He sat down and wrote a long letter then, which he entrusted to Apostolis to take to Thessalonika himself, to the General Consulate.

"But I have a message to deliver to Kryfi, too," Apostolis said.

"Go to Kryfi," Nikiphoros replied. "See what you're able to do there. And when you reach the shore, head for Thessalonika—with Miss Electra's help or alone, however you can. But I won't wait for an answer. I know they'll approve of my setting off immediately for Kouga. I can't let Captain Agras be killed. If they give you a reply at the Center, bring it directly to me there."

Apostolis drew south with his oarsman and arrived at Kryfi at midday.

For two days now he'd been away from Kouga. That morning, leaving Tsekri after sleeping at the hut, he'd heard gunshots erupt toward the western part of the lake and then stop suddenly.

Had the men clashed with enemy patrols? Or had the Bulgarians, strengthened as they were, attacked Kouga?

As clean, tidy, and disciplined as the Tsekri hut had been, Apostolis found Kryfi to be the opposite.

All the captains were at odds. And Captain Panayiotis, who he encountered there, could scarcely stand from his weakness and rheumatism. Sick and exhausted, he'd suffered hemorrages; and the lake leeches had sucked up more of his blood. In addition, he was so infested with lice that he couldn't sleep. Pale, weak, and worn out, he was about to leave the lower lake.

Apostolis didn't have the heart to ask him for assistance, he seemed so tired and ill.

Only when Captain Panayiotis had departed did he present Agras' message to Captain Kalas—there to take over Kryfi which, like Toumba, remained without a commander.

Captain Kalas listened to Apostolis in silence, tapping a cigarette on his nail before lighting it. He had no help to send, he said. There were very few men with him. However he'd see about it . . . he'd take care of it . . .

Will he go? a worried Apostolis wondered.

With a heavy heart the guide set off from the hut and got out at the Kryfi landing-cove, where he bid the oarsman good-by and drew towards Plati. There he boarded the train for Thessalonika with his pass from Halil-bey. Around seven in the evening, as before, he arrived at the station.

It was the start of December and bitter cold.

* * * *

He proceeded straight to the Metropolitan Mansion as if to see the bishop, and then to the Consulate by means of the secret door in their shared garden wall.

The General Consul had gone out. However Ali took Captain Nikiphoros' letter; and together with Apostolis, he delivered it directly to the Master who was dining at a friend's house.

Afterwards he let Apostolis off at the doctor's—to give him news of Captain Agras.

When Apostolis got there, he found the swarm of boys all excited.

No, their father wasn't home, they replied when he sought him.

"Do you know why?" Alekos asked.

But Kostas cut him off.

His father had left. His father had work. His father . . .

The older boys took him off to the side so the younger ones wouldn't hear, and Kostas confided to him:

"Didn't I tell you we would set the captain free? Well, we did! We got him out of prison."

"Inside the garbage?" Apostolis inquired, caught up by the boys' excitement.

"No, certainly not! Do you think these things always happen the same way? He went freely," Kostas added with a broad gesture, "yesterday, on St. Nicholas' day."

Dying to learn more, Apostolis listened to the boys' narration as they interrupted one another to include some forgotten point.

"Everything was planned for weeks. They'd closed him up in the Seven Towers prison, a fearful, terrible dungeon! An Albanian guard distributed loukoumi . . ."

"And the candy had a drug in it . . ."

"There were two boxes of it, one with a drug and the other without . . ."

"Why?" Apostolis asked.

"So he could also offer it to those who weren't to be put to sleep . . ."

"You brought the loukoumi to him?"

"No, no! The druggist prepared it all. He's our own man! Well, the Albanian treated the other guards, and it took hold of them. One after the other, they dropped off to sleep. Opening up all the doors, the Albanian got the captain out, and then ate the loukoumi with the drug, himself . . ."

"Why?" Apostolis inquired again.

"To pretend that the captain had drugged him as well. And so he fell asleep. Today he received an awful beating when they discovered the prisoner had fled. He didn't talk, though—poor fellow."

"From patriotism?" Apostolis asked.

"Patriotism? But he's not a Greek!" Kostas exclaimed.

"From bought patriotism," Harilaos said, rubbing his thumb and forefinger together.

"Where did the captain go?" Apostolis wanted to know.

"He came straight here," Kostas answered, "and arrived at almost two in the morning. It was dark outside. No one saw him."

"We were all waiting . . ." Alekos began.

But Kostas broke in again.

"Immediately we took him . . . to another house. What's more, it's good we did! The police suspected us. They appeared today and made a search."

"What does that mean?"

"That they ransacked the whole house to make sure we weren't hiding the prisoner. Not anymore! He'd escaped!"

Apostolis thought he knew many secrets of the Struggle. Yet compared to the doctor's children! . . .

That evening, upon returning to the Consulate and being given a place to sleep in the basement, he stayed awake for some time. He wanted so much to do something important for the Struggle himself . . .

* * * *

Apostolis had hoped the General Consul would give him a reply for Captain Nikiphoros right away.

But in the morning when Ali led him up to the Consulate, he was received by a high official with a military air about him—Mr. Zoés.

"We've designed another mission for you," he said. "You're Apostolis the guide—yes? You know the countryside backwards and forwards—yes?"

"Yes, I do!"

"You guided Captain Kalas and Captain Nikiphoros?"

"Yes, I did!"

"Then go down to Koulakia . . . You can find some oxcart going there?"

"There's no need. I'll travel by foot."

"As you wish. Go directly to the school and ask for the teacher, Miss . . ."

He took out a directory, but Apostolis anticipated him:

" . . . Miss Aspasia," he said.

Mr. Zoés raised his head.

"You know her?" he questioned him.

"Yes!"

"Good. Tell her I've sent you. You'll remain at the school until word reaches you. After that, head for Kleidi and from there to the mouth of the Loudias River, or wherever they instruct you . . ."

"I know."

"And you'll guide the men the Center sends . . ."

"I know. To Kleidi to Mister Thanasis. From there to Kryfi in the Swamp."

"Fine. Set off at once. And learn if Captain Panayiotis has managed to depart for Greece. Have Thanasis inform us. Do you understand?"

* * * *

For Apostolis, accustomed to trudging back and forth through the mud of the plain, it was a sport to take the miserable but well-trod road between Thessalonika and Koulakia.

Not at all tired, he arrived at Koulakia in good shape and made his way to the school.

There was but one school in Koulakia, a Greek one. As in the villages at the mouth of the Axios River, scattered over the Roumlouki plain, and in the districts down to the Greek border,[32] the Bulgarians couldn't gain a foothold.

Here and there, though, they did have sheep-folds. Moreover woodcutters and villagers stood ready to rise up at a command from Bulgaria to form comitadje bands that extorted, destroyed, and killed—and then returned to their work so that the Turkish army discovered them laboring away peacefully. However from the lake and below, they weren't able to create communities or open schools.

When Apostolis reached the Koulakia schoolhouse, he found the children gathered together in the classroom, with Miss Aspasia in her chair. She gave him a nod and an abrupt greeting:

"Sit down. Wait."

It was a cold December day and the classroom wasn't warm. With red noses, the children were blowing on their hands that were swollen from the cold. Curious, they stared at the stranger who stood discretely in a corner, waiting for the lesson to finish.

The teacher looked at him out of the corner of her eye while he stood there. As soon as the lesson ended and the children were dismissed, she approached him:

"Who are you seeking, Apostolis?"

"You, Miss Aspasia. The Consulate sent me. You're to instruct me."

But Miss Aspasia didn't know anything. Confused and uncertain, she stared at him.

In a few words, Apostolis explained to her why he'd gone to Thessalonika, and how the Consulate had told him to come to Koulakia.

"I don't know a thing," the teacher said to him. "However, you can't stay here. You'd better go to my house. My mother will provide for you; and I'll be there as soon as the children leave for the day."

Yet the winter sun set and night descended without the teacher showing up.

Patiently Apostolis waited for her, seated next to the hearth. Miss Aspasia's mother, an old woman with a kerchief around her head, was cooking tomatoes with oil inside a pot blackened by years of usage. At the same time, speaking in the local dialect, she recited her daughter's virtues to him.

"If' it wasn't for my Spasia, who'd dare be called patriarchal? From when the Bulgarians burned Nisi, I tell you, no one calls himself Greek. My Spasia bolsters them all up, I tell you . . ."

"Did you see the fire, Missus Vassilou?" Apostolis inquired.

"As if I didn't see it! Certainly I saw it! They burned all the houses! They turned them to ashes—and they were all patriarchal! We left then and came here. My Spasia studied in Athens. They sent her here, an infant, a sixteen year old girl. She took over in the village and told the men not to be afraid. And she went out at night . . . Don't ask . . . her pockets were full . . ."

With her hand, she made a sign of shooting and winked.

"And cartridges hanging from her skirts . . ."

She stopped in alarm. Someone was beating on the door.

"Right away! Right away!" she called out, feigning cheerfulness.

However she hurridly crossed herself, frightened.

"Right away!" she repeated.

With trembling footsteps, she walked to the door and opened it.

"It's you, Takis? You scared me!" she responded with relief.

It was a boy eight to ten years old. Stuffing his head between the half-opened door and the old woman, he saw Apostolis seated next to the fireplace and motioned to him.

"Come!" he said in a half-whisper. "Miss Aspasia wants you."

Apostolis sprang up. Passing Mistress Vassilou who was still trembling, he went out onto the road.

"Where is she?" he asked in a low voice.

"At the school. I was cleaning up the class and she came in and told me to run and get you. And I ran!" the child answered.

Together, they entered the school courtyard.

Miss Aspasia appeared at the door, holding its shutter half-closed.

"Thank you, Takis. I don't need you any longer. Hurry home now," she said to the boy.

Letting just Apostolis inside, she shut the door.

The room was lit by a candle burning on the sole table within it, before a wicker chair—the teacher's seat.

In the window recess, a priest with a thick black beard was sitting. His headdress descended to his black, bushy eyebrows, shading his large, intimidating eyes that were full of fire. He sat motionless in the window alcove, but his glance rotated from the door to the window and back again.

"This is Apostolis the guide," Miss Aspasia announced, approaching.

The priest pointed toward the window.

"And the little one, who is he?" he asked.

"Takis? Don't ask! He's an orphan, without anyone in the world. I took him into my house and he shares what my mother and I have to eat," Miss Aspasia replied.

"Is he from Koulakia?"

"He is now. I'm not sure where he's from. He was with Bulgarian bear trainers, woodcutters, coal-merchants, and who knows what else. Last April when two of our captains crossed the Aliakmon River at the passage near the monastery, the child was with the Bulgarians they captured. An accident occurred, and the boat—that is to say, a raft—sank at the passage . . ."

"I know," the priest cut in, frowning.

"All of them drowned—all Bulgarians," Aspasia continued. "Only the child escaped because he wasn't on the boat. They brought him to the monastery to the south, near . . ."

"So he's Bulgarian?"

"No, he's ours. The Bulgarians carried him off, it appears, from some slaughter."

"Which slaughter?" the priest exclaimed.

He stood up all of a sudden, shaken.

Very tall and lanky, he had a beard that seemed heavy for his thin face, in which his large eyes were glowing.

"Don't question me about details," the teacher answered. "They brought him to me one day, and I pitied the child and took him home. But do you know him? Why do you ask?"

"Because I'm seeking the lost child of . . . of a friend of mine," the priest answered. For a moment, he stopped short.

Then, sweeping the air with a quick movement of his arm, he went on:

"We'll speak of it again. Our work first. Apostolis, can you guide me to Kaliani in the dark?"

"To the village?"

"To the church."

"I know it. It's above the road, a little out of the way," Apostolis replied.

"How will we cross the Loudias River?"

"By dugout."

"We'll find one there?"

"We will," Apostolis declared.

He stared at the priest and hesitated. Who was he and what did he seek? Moreover who was ordering him—Apostolis—to be his guide?

Miss Aspasia noticed his distrust and understood it. Lowering her voice, she said:

"Command of the Center. You'll go."

Apostolis looked up again and met the priest's large, black eyes.

Then the man smiled, and his beard moved strangely, all in one piece. Softly he said:

"Message of Mr. Zoés—of the Consulate. Kleidi . . . Kryfi . . . Understand?"

"I understand," Apostolis replied.

Briefly, hurriedly, they bid Miss Aspasia good-by and set off.

* * * *

It was a dark night. The rugged road, muddy and full of holes, was for foot-travelers and mules only. It was slippery, which often meant sinking to the ankles in the mire.

The priest and Apostolis walked along without speaking, the first holding his robe high, the second light and supple, with his unbuttoned cloak thrown over his shoulders.

It was very dark, but Apostolis could see in the night. He observed the priest's thick, strong, city-bought boots with curiosity. They didn't fit in with the homespun gaiters and knee length Macedonian breeches that appeared below his raised robe.

Tall but lean, he'd have to be very powerful. He strode through the mud with great, decisive footsteps that it wouldn't be easy to interrupt—that is, if he didn't call for it himself.

Who was he, and where did he come from? Apostolis didn't even know his name. If he chose to address him, what would he call him? "Father?" "Teacher?"

His restless mind wasn't satisfied with vague estimates and guesses. He liked to know. His senses were alert, sharp—ready to grasp every point that would put him on the tracks of this mysterious priest. From the time he was small, he'd made it his job to try to fathom what was most secret, understand what was most inscrutable, and solve complex problems. Moreover this priest presented a problem to him. When they'd reach the Loudias River and he'd ask him where he wanted to cross it, perhaps something would come to light.

However they arrived at the river past midnight, with not a soul in sight.

It began to snow lightly.

Apostolis stopped for a moment, as if perplexed. Some discussion was called for—questions and answers.

The priest stopped, too, and waited.

Apostolis went through the motions of searching up and down the river. In a few minutes, he returned to the priest and scratched his head.

"There's no boat," he murmured.

Not even for a moment did the priest hesitate.

"Can you swim?" he asked.

Apostolis could. But he wasn't about to admit it to accommodate him.

"The water is deep in the winter . . . And it's cold. It's snowing . . ." he said as though startled.

"Can you swim?" the priest repeated, this time in a threatening manner that didn't allow for any objection.

Apostolis drew back.

"If you're not tired, Teacher," he suggested, "let's continue a little further . . . to where the Loudias River meets the tributary. We'll find a boat there, and the water's shallower."

"Let's go to the tributary," the priest replied more pleasantly.

They started up again, following the shore toward the mouth of the Loudias River.

It was all seriousness with this devil of a priest! The guide would go to the sea—to inferno if he wanted it. But the older man wouldn't tolerate discussion . . .

Apostolis stole a look at him, striding through the mud with long, resolute footsteps that recognized no obstacle.

They came to the part where the two waterways joined. A little to the side was a wood shack, covered with straw. Apostolis knocked on the door a couple of times. From inside, a sleepy voice replied in Turkish:

"Who is it?"

"Open up, Traiko! It's me, Apostolis . . ." the guide answered.

The door opened and a fisherman with a fez appeared, still half-asleep.

"Come inside," he said hospitably; "it's cold . . ."

"You come outside," Apostolis responded. "Father . . . Father . . . wants to cross to the other side . . ."

He turned to his companion, waiting for him to give his name. But there was no reaction.

"Do you have a boat?" the priest asked the fisherman in his imperious way that was more military than clerical—and that silenced all opposition.

Seeing the long black robe, the fisherman was taken back.

"I have," he said, bowing and crossing his hands on his chest.

"Then ferry us across," the priest ordered. "And don't put us out here, but up above where the road passes."

The fisherman bowed again. Grabbing an old, worn cloak from his straw mattress, he descended to the river with the priest and Apostolis.

The snow had ceased, but the weather was raw.

A sizable boat with a broad keel was drawn up onto the ground. The fisherman tried to push it, but it was glued to the mud.

"You pull and I'll push," he said to Apostolis.

However the priest brushed him aside. Catching hold of the boat by the seat, he lifted it up and shoved it into the water.

The fisherman watched, stunned. For a moment Apostolis remained spellbound. But the priest raised his robe and climbed into the boat, nodding for them to do the same.

"Forward," he said, "we don't have time to lose."

Submissive, the fisherman rowed down to the shallower water and crossed to the opposite side. Following the shore, he ascended the river again, passing into deeper water toward the road.

The motion of the boat made Apostolis drowsy. Feeling the day's strain, he fell asleep in his seat. But the priest's heavy hand shook him by the shoulder.

"Quickly, the boatman can't find the road," he said. "Where is it?"

"I can't see; it's overcast," the fisherman excused himself.

Apostolis could, though. They'd gone beyond the dark line of the road—which he distinguished faintly in the wet plain—and had to reverse directions. The cold smarted. The fisherman all at once wrapped himself tighter in his cloak that had holes in it.

They approached the shore and the priest set foot in the water.

Turning, he put something that jingled into the fisherman's hand.

"Buy a new cloak," he said.

Apostolis made out two gold coins in the darkness.

"Light a match, Traiko, and see," he whispered.

The fisherman lit one and looked. He extended his two arms, raising his face in prayer.

"God! ... God!" he murmured.

The priest was already at a distance.

Apostolis ran up to him.

"Teacher, Traiko thanks you . . ." Apostolis began.

But the priest continued along his way as if he hadn't heard; and Apostolis didn't dare say anything further.

He was reflecting, however, wondering how this priest found two gold liras in his pocket. The priests in Macedonia had no liras to give, not even loose change. It was doubtful if they had money from time to time.

Apostolis trudged along the muddy road next to the priest, weighing and pondering the matter.

* * * *

In the early morning hours, they observed a couple of cottages grow lighter.

The priest halted.

"Where is the church?" he asked.

Apostolis stretched out his arm.

"There," he said, pointing in the general direction. "But we have to enter the village to go to Father Elias and get the keys . . ."

The priest interrupted him.

"Take me to the church," he ordered.

No deliberation was possible. Apostolis turned to the right, outside the village. In a short while they reached an elevation, with the chapel half lit up in the dawn.

The priest stopped before the door, took out a key and opened it.

"Enter inside," he commanded.

It was dark. Neither oil-lamp nor candle was burning. The cold dug into one's bones.

Stepping inside, the priest shut the door.

"Is Kleidi far?" he asked.

"No. But the road is bad," the guide answered.

"Well, go to sleep," the priest said. "I don't have any mattress to give you. However, a rebel has to learn to sleep even on paving stones."

And he laughed. His deep, hearty laughter resounded warmly through the deserted church.

In the dark, Apostolis wrapped himself in his cloak and huddled next to the wall. He heard the priest go up to the door and lie down himself.

Apostolis didn't want to fall asleep. The thought of the unknown priest occupied him.

Yet he'd been walking all day and he was exhausted. His heavy eyelids closed by themselves as sleep caught hold of him.

He awoke with a start. A ray of sun had come in through the window and fallen on his face. Sitting up, he glanced around him at the strange church. Then he recalled.

He searched for the priest. But he'd gone. The door was closed and he was alone. He sprang up. What time could it be? And where was the priest?

He rushed to the door. It wasn't locked. However the key was missing. Attached to his cloak, he discovered a piece of paper ripped from a notebook. A few words were written on it in pencil:

"Go to Kleidi. They're expecting you. You'll receive orders there."

No signature. Curious, Apostolis took a look around the church. Under a corner pew, he came upon a well-folded black bundle and opened it up. It was a robe, with a priest's headdress and a long black beard enclosed inside.

Refolding them, he put the bundle back where he'd found it and stepped outside.

13.

The School At Zorba

IT HAD SNOWED WHILE APOSTOLIS WAS SLEEPING. Everything was white, with the sun sparkling directly overhead.

So he'd slept soundly. The priest had managed to leave without his realizing it.

Apostolis was a little ashamed he'd let him disappear without learning who was hiding under the cassock. His first thought was to follow the man's footprints in the snow and find him, then go on to Kleidi as he'd been ordered in the note and Mr. Zoés had specified.

However, he didn't discover any footprints. He made a round of the church outside. No tracks appeared in the freshly-laden snow. The priest must have gotten very little sleep, or none at all. And the snow that had fallen covered up all traces of his flight.

A hungry Apostolis had no money to buy bread in the village. Only at Kleidi at Thanasis' would he find food.

But such a little thing didn't put him at a loss. Quickly he took the snow covered footpath and drew for Kleidi.

"A devil of a priest! . . ."

Then he wasn't a priest at all, since he'd left beard, robe, and headdress behind. Was Miss Aspasia aware of it? he wondered.

Recalling the man's smile, with his beard moving all in one piece, he hit his head with his fist:

Stupid! How utterly stupid he'd been! Clearly, it wasn't a priest!

* * * *

179

At Thanasis' they were waiting for him. The message had arrived for him to eat, rest up, and be at Lambros' cottage the next night.

"Who delivered the message?" Apostolis asked.

Thanasis didn't know his name. He was an unknown villager dressed as a Turk, although he spoke Greek like a native. He'd left this note . . .

Removing a paper folded up in his handkerchief and tied with a knot, Thanasis showed it to Apostolis. It was a sheet torn from a notebook, similar to the one the priest had attached to Apostolis' cloak. The guide took out his own note and compared the two. They were alike and so was their large, legible handwriting—in pencil on both papers.

The second message read:

> "Command of the Center, The guide Apostolis is to be at Lambros' cabin tomorrow evening."

Again, no signature.

"Therefore we were expecting you," Thanasis added.

But seeing a thoughtful Apostolis folding up the two notes to put in his pocket, he seized them.

"It won't do," he said. "The letter carrier . . . the one who brought the note, said to burn it!"

Ripping up both papers, he threw them onto the burning coals in the fireplace.

When Apostolis arrived at Lambros' cabin at dusk the next day, he discovered the fishermen gone.

"The northwind is blowing," Lambros' daughter explained. "The boats set forth, supposedly to fish but really to meet a ship that's bringing us rebels and picking up the captains that are departing."

"Which captains?" Apostolis inquired. "From the Swamp?"

"I don't know," the girl replied. "However our men got them from the lower lake. Your instructions are to wait here. We've prepared food for you."

Late at night the boats showed up with some youth—most of them from Crete—replacements for those who'd returned ill to Greece.

Out at sea, the fishermen had met up with the ship, where the captains were taken aboard. Now they were on their way down the coast.

Thus the sick Panayiotis would have succeeded in leaving. Thanasis could inform the Center in Thessalonika.

"Now to Kleidi," Apostolis declared.

The human chain formed a line and drew for Kleidi in the snow. From there they headed for Kryfi the next night; and Captain Kalas received them at daybreak.

Apostolis' mission had finished. On foot, he traveled to Zorba to see Miss Electra to learn if they'd sent any further order for him.

Miss Electra's school served as his "headquarters." All his instructions went there that weren't given to him directly.

He calculated he'd arrive at midday and that Miss Electra would take care of him. As always, she'd say: "Sit down and share our stew or soup."

Upon entering the kitchen, however, he discovered only Jovan setting the table with three plates as if he knew Apostolis was coming.

As soon as he saw Apostolis, he let out a cry. Flushed and happy, he wrung his hands together and stood gaping at him.

Apostolis was also happy, yet he didn't like to show it. He gave the child a playful shove.

"You knew I'd be here and put out three plates?" he asked in Bulgarian.

"No," Jovan replied in Greek. "We weren't expecting you. For days now there's been no news of you. And Miss Electra wants . . ."

That same moment, Miss Electra appeared in the kitchen with a priest. He was short, thin, and seemed very small in his robe. His scrawny beard had white hairs intermixed with the black ones. His eyes, though, were lively and youthful, as if in protest against the white of his beard.

"Well, Apostolis! Where have you been?" Miss Electra exclaimed. "Exactly when I needed you. Three benches are ready to fall apart, and one has lost its fourth leg. Father, this is Apostolis—our carpenter," she added, addressing the priest. "He's been missing for a while . . ."

Miss Electra spoke on and on; however to Apostolis who knew her well, she seemed preoccupied. The guide had kissed the priest's hand and they'd all settled down to eat, once a blessing had been given.

Miss Electra continued speaking to the priest about this and that in the village—about the children, their parents, and the lessons—although her mind was obviously elsewhere. The priest answered in monosyllables.

Just as the meal ended, Miss Electra turned to Jovan:

"Run to the grocer's and get some loukoumi to treat our guest. Never mind the coffee! I'll make it!"

After putting some money in his hand, she removed the coffee-pot from the shelf. But as soon as the door closed, she forgot both coffee-pot and coffee.

"When did you leave Kouga?" she asked Apostolis.

"It's been a number of days," he replied. "Why?"

"I wonder if they know there about the slaughter at Tekovo?"

"I don't know about it, myself. When did it happen?"

"On St. Nicholas' day," Miss Electra said.

"No, the day after!" the priest corrected her. "It was the seventh of December. Apostol Petkoff killed them."

"Who did he kill?" Apostolis inquired.

"Eight villagers. They tied them to trees and tortured them . . ."

Running footsteps sounded.

"Hush!" Miss Electra responded. "Don't talk about it before Jovan. When he hears about slaughters, he becomes frightened . . ."

The door flew open and Jovan rushed in and closed it again.

"Comitadjes! . . ." he whispered.

He was very pale and his lips trembled. In his outstretched hand, which also shook, he still held the money Miss Electra had given him.

"Comitadjes? Where?" Miss Electra asked, without losing her self-possession.

"In front of Petroff the coal dealer's. They're searching for a priest . . ."

"Apostolis . . ." Miss Electra said, arching her eyebrows slightly.

Taking Jovan by the hand, she led him into her room.

"Tell me, what did you hear?" she asked.

The child's words tumbled out:

"There were many of them—six or eight—I didn't have time to count. They were looking for the priest from Bozets. They went to catch him, but they didn't find him . . ."

Hastily Miss Electra began to undress the child.

"Did they see you?" she questioned him.

"No! I saw they had knives in their belts and were carrying axes, and I hid."

"Good. I'll put you to bed and you'll pretend to be sick. If they come, you'll speak Bulgarian to them. You're a fisherman's son and you have a fever. You'll tell them you haven't seen a priest here. Don't be afraid of anything. What else did you learn?"

"They went to the school of a Miss Evthalia at Bozets to search for the priest there. She said he wasn't at Bozets. They threatened her. She told them she didn't know where he was. They said they'd kill her. That's all I heard. I came back . . ."

In the adjoining classroom, hammering started up. Miss Electra opened the door and found Apostolis settled on the floor, with his tools beside him and nails in his mouth, fixing a bench.

"Climb into bed quickly, Jovan," the teacher said. "I'm going to prepare you a hot drink."

She shut the door. And leaning over Apostolis, she asked in a low voice:

"Ready?"

He nodded "yes" and the teacher stepped into the kitchen.

The coals were still burning in the fireplace. Removing a sack of sand from the shelf, she hurriedly scattered it before the hearth up to the door, spreading it with a little broom. Then she cleared the plates from the table, took a pinch of camomile from the drawer, and put it in a little cup. Filling the coffee-pot with water, she placed it on the coals.

All of this was done rapidly, without any noise. Her attention remained fixed on the door, her ear strained toward the road.

Footsteps were approaching. Someone pounded on the door.

"Come in!" the teacher said calmly in Turkish.

The door opened before those outside had time to hear her. Two strangers entered, along with a villager from Zorba.

Miss Electra greeted him in her accented Bulgarian.

"Good-day, Petroff. What is the matter? What do the men want?"

Through the open door, her sharp glance had detected two men at one corner of the school and another two shadows at the other.

Comitadjes had encircled the school.

The hammering inside the classroom had stopped.

Miss Electra threw a couple of fresh coals onto the fireplace and brushed the soot from her hands, gazing steadily at the three men.

"Miss Electra," Petroff began, somewhat ill-at-ease, "these men want to know . . . Perhaps you saw a priest . . ."

"A priest!" the teacher repeated. "Aren't you aware that Father Elias never comes to us?"

"Not Father Elias . . . Another priest . . ."

"From Bozets. We're asking about a patriarchal priest," one of the strangers snapped.

"From Bozets? And you're searching for him here?" Miss Electra inquired, unruffled.

"Did you see him?" the Bulgarian asked abruptly.

"No, I didn't. But why are you seeking him here?"

The hammering started up once more.

The two strangers ran toward the classroom. Miss Electra laughed.

"The benches are being repaired," she said to Petroff. "Why did you bring these men here? Who are they?"

"One, the short one . . . he's to be feared. Don't get him angry," Petroff warned in a low voice.

"What do they want from me?" Miss Electra asked disdainfully.

Petroff cast a fearful glance towards the door, without answering.

Leaving the coffee-pot on the coals, Miss Electra entered the classroom with him.

The two Bulgarians were examining Apostolis—who'd taken the nails out of his mouth and was answering them with composure. Where was he from? Oh! from far away, from Vertkop. His father? No, he didn't have one. Nor a mother. He was a foundling. Well if he had a father or mother, would he be working like a dog this way? Rushing from village to village to make a little money? Undertaking such journeys? . . . Last name? No, he didn't have any. They called him Apostol, Apostol the carpenter.

Why was he working at a Greek school?

Apostolis chuckled. Well, poor fellow that he was, he took a job wherever he found work . . . "Eh, Petroff?"

The coal dealer nodded affirmatively. Yes, true enough. The boy also worked for him and throughout the village, repairing whatever was broken. Moreover, he was a good craftsman.

"Our own lad," he whispered behind his hand to the short Bulgarian next to him.

"Did you see a priest by any chance?" the other Bulgarian inquired.

"No, I still haven't had time to go to Father Elias," Apostolis answered as if apologetic. "But I'll go this evening . . ."

"I don't mean Father Elias. It's a stranger—a patriarchal priest—that I'm asking about."

"No, I didn't see one."

"Search the house," the short Bulgarian said, "together—you Rango, and Petroff."

As they were leaving the room he asked Miss Electra, who was standing, still calm, beside him:

"Is there anyone else at the school?"

"There is," she replied. "I have a sick child . . . Ah! I forgot his hot drink!"

She ran into the kitchen where she'd set the water to boil—now overflowing from the coffee pot and spilling onto the coals.

The Bulgarian was right behind her.

"You're a Greek?" he demanded.

"Yes," Miss Electra said, smiling.

Steadily she poured water over the camomile, while the Bulgarian watched her with a frown.

"That is, you make propaganda here?"

With a questioning look, the teacher responded:

"What propaganda?"

"Don't you gather the children here and teach them Greek? . . ."

"But it's my job!" the teacher said with a laugh. "I'm paid to do it. Tell me, what is your work?"

"We'll burn you alive inside here! We have no use for Greeks."

Miss Electra remained unflustered:

"Since we're here, what do you expect us to do? They pay me. The Turks accept our school; they gave us a permit. We're in order . . ."

"You teach the children to hate Bulgarians!"

"I? Go into my room and you'll find a Bulgarian child I took in out of compassion—and am caring for as well! We have an order to help all those that are suffering. The child is sick with a fever. He's in my bed. Come and see. I'm preparing the hot drink for him . . ."

Together they entered her room, where a pale Jovan was lying with his large eyes fastened upon Petroff and the other Bulgarian. The two were searching everywhere—under the bed, beneath the mattress, inside the cabinet, even in the drawers.

The teacher rolled her eyes.

"Will a man fit in the drawer?" she asked.

Without replying, the second Bulgarian said to the short one in charge:

"We didn't find a weapon."

"No," Petroff murmured, "I told you she's a peaceful woman. Only she's Greek . . ."

From the open door Apostolis had been following the search, occasionally pounding a nail into the bench.

Miss Electra bent over the bed and gave the camomile to Jovan to drink. With her eyes, she communicated to him not to be afraid.

And leaving the strangers with the child—with Apostolis in the next room—she returned to the kitchen with the empty cup.

From the window, she noted shadows coming and going. They'd surrounded the school. For how long, she wondered?

Footsteps were heard running. The shutter of the door sprang towards the inside, and a third unknown man entered.

"The Turkish police!" he shouted.

The two Bulgarians raced into the kitchen with Petroff and took off without a word to the teacher, murmuring directions between them. Only Petroff stayed behind, trembling all over. He sat down in a chair.

"Excuse me, Miss Electra," he said to her. "I didn't want to bring them here . . . but they pressured me . . . They were carrying knives and axes . . . They claimed to be woodcutters . . . Who knows what they are, though! Excuse me, Miss Electra . . ."

Restraining her anger, she replied:

"All right, all right, Petroff. We're neighbors. However, I thought you knew our school doesn't hide weapons."

"Of course, I know. But would they listen? I wish you well, Miss Electra. If the policeman comes, don't say I was with them . . ."

"Send me a sack of good coal tomorrow," the teacher broke in.

"And you won't inform on me?" he asked, opening the door.

"We're not informers," the teacher remarked sharply.

She shut the door behind him.

All at once her appearance changed. Sparks shot from her eyes, and she raised her clenched hands in two white, threatening fists.

"Betray who, and to whom! . . ." she moaned, gritting her teeth. "Bulgarian scoundrels! Turkish scoundrels!"

The hammering had recommenced. Pushing her hair back with her two hands, she took a deep breath and walked into the classroom.

"They've gone," she announced quietly.

Apostolis made an inquiring sign. She shook her head "no" and entered her bedroom.

"Don't get up," she told Jovan, who was staring uneasily at her. "The children will be arriving. Let them say you're sick when they return home."

His color hadn't come back. In a low voice, he asked:

"Did they hurt you, Miss Electra?"

"No, no, child."

"And the priest?"

"Now! . . . Where! . . . He's been gone for some time!" she exclaimed.

Jovan didn't ask anything else. He found it difficult to do so when he felt they were concealing something from him. Mentally, though, he tried to figure out when and how the priest had left without the Bulgarians on the road seeing him. He'd scrambled up the hayloft himself to enter the school. But could the priest go out that way? And his own little body that he squeezed in everywhere—could it be compared to the priest's with his long black robe and headdress?

The children appeared and had their lesson. After it was over, the chatter began. Woodcutters, it was said, had come to the village. But Thanasis knew that they were comitadjes . . . And Evangelia did too . . . and Pascalis and Morpho . . .

Miss Electra interrupted them:

"Even if you do know, it's better to forget it, children. The Bulgarians in our village greatly outnumber us. Your lesson, our work, and not so much talk."

"They were searching for a priest . . ." Morpho whispered to her.

"Well, let them go to Father Elias. We don't have a church or a priest of our own," the teacher said.

Smiling, she sent them on their way and closed the outer door.

* * * *

A peacefulness enveloped the school again. Only Apostolis' sporatic hammering sounded in the kitchen, where he'd transferred the broken benches in order not to disturb the lesson.

It had now grown dark. Miss Electra put three bowls of soup on the kitchen table and sat down to eat with the two boys. She was lively and carefree and told them stories of the Greek Revolution of 1821. Yet both of them wanted to hear of more recent events—like the feats of Captain Akritas and some of the other captains that everyone was excited about.[33]

"They didn't work in this territory," Miss Electra responded.

"What was it Evangelia said today—that Captain Garefis came back to life?" Jovan asked hesitantly.

"She was talking nonsense," Miss Electra replied. "Unfortunately the dead don't return to life. And Garefis died."

"But she said that Captain Garefis killed a comitadje . . ." Jovan murmured.

"That was far away. We don't really know what's happening. They tell us many things."

And she added:

"What about us here? There's been firing back and forth in the Swamp all these days and we haven't learned what's going on—if our captains are fighting, or if their huts have been captured. The Bulgarians are supposed to have brought a large force into the western section . . ."

"Shall I go and ask, Miss Electra?" Jovan inquired again hesitantly. "I know how to get there alone . . ."

"No, that won't do," the teacher answered him. "All the village thinks that you're sick, don't forget. But you, Apostolis . . . perhaps you could go?"

They exchanged a secret sign.

"I'll leave tomorrow," Apostolis declared.

"Yes," Miss Electra agreed, "tonight get to sleep early. You, Jovan, climb into my bed. If the comitadjes return, they need to find you there, as if you're sick. Do you hear? Go and lie down now."

Without objection, the child bid them good-night and disappeared. Miss Electra took out a mattress and left to place it down beside her bed.

"Try to fall asleep, Jovan," she said. "I have to correct the children's papers. Afterwards I'll lie down to sleep, too."

Carrying the candle with her, she walked out and shut the door.

The classroom was empty.

Miss Electra seated herself at a bench, her hands clasped before her, and listened. Every so often she consulted her watch. A quarter of an hour passed, a half hour. She extinguished her candle and approached the closed window.

Nothing could be heard. Groping along the wall, she located the door and went out of the classroom into the dark kitchen.

"Apostolis . . ." she whispered.

"Here I am," he replied, also in a whisper. "All's well . . . It's deserted outside. Moreover he's ready . . ."

"Did you give him food?"

"Yes! Bread and cheese for the road as well, like you told me. He doesn't want anything else. He says he has money."

"Now's the time. Do you need light? I can't see a thing."

"No! I can see, Miss Electra. Only help me. The sand's been gathered."

Feeling the ground before the hearth, Apostolis removed a rough piece of wood from among the floor boards, exposing a metal loop.

"Over here . . . quietly . . . in case it creaks."

Together they gripped the loop and lifted up a trapdoor.

"Good . . ." a hushed voice said from the hole. "I'll come up."

"Be careful the stairs don't squeak," Apostolis cautioned.

Catching hold of the ladder that rose up through the hole, he leaned it against the edge of the opening.

Once the priest had climbed up, they drew it out in the dark and reclosed the trapdoor.

Again no light was lit. Searching, the priest found the teacher's hands and kissed them.

Touched, she said to him:

"Are you wearing the fez?"

"I'm wearing it—and the vest, coat, and shoes. Just give me a sack to put my robe and headdress in."

"I'll prepare it for you," Apostolis volunteered. "And I have some dry grass to put over the top. Hand them to me."

While Apostolis arranged the clothes inside the sack in the dark classroom, Miss Electra received the priest's final instructions.

"Have the Center send the rifles from Giannitsa. Our mule drivers know how to conceal them well with plenty of dry grass. Besides, we need lots of it to cover roofs in the parish, and wrap and hide weapons."[34]

Apostolis walked quietly inside.

"The sack is ready," he whispered. "Let's be off, Father."

The priest got up.

"Merry Christmas," he said to Miss Electra.

"Take care, Father Chrysostomos," she murmured.

Without a sound, she opened the door and the three of them passed out into the courtyard.

Apostolis went alone to the road, surveyed it, and reappeared.

"It's clear," he said. "Are we off to Petra?"

"No—to the Apostles landing-cove. I left a canoe on the shore . . ." the priest answered.

For a second Miss Electra stood at the half-closed outer door, watching as the two shadows disappeared into the black night. Then she locked the door and entered the school.

* * * *

Apostolis proceeded at his customary quick, steady pace, stepping wherever there was firm ground or rock. His companion followed in his footsteps, dressed as a villager with the sack thrown over his back.

They headed straight for the lake, leaving the village houses and occasional scattered fishermen's cottages behind them.

When they reached the water, they drew north in the direction of the Apostoles cove. Everywhere it was dark and deserted. Now they could travel and converse more freely. Not a soul was around to hear them.

"All night I walked on my way here," the priest began, "and I arrived at Tsekri before daybreak. I found just Manolis the Curlyhead returning from night patrol. He brought me to the Tsekri hut to sleep . . ."

"Was Captain Nikiphoros there?" Apostolis broke in.

"No, he hadn't returned from Kouga. The last news I received, Agras was sick and couldn't carry on any longer. What's more, every day they're attacked. Their hut is high, visible from far away—a target for the Bulgarians. In fact as I slept, a volley woke me."

"Did it last long?"

"No. Two rounds, a few shots here and there, and it stopped. The Curleyhead said gunfire erupts every day."

"Yes! Miss Electra said the same thing. It means we hold Kouga, doesn't it?"

"Certainly we hold it. But how much can our lads endure? Captain Agras is in a wretched state. Others with him are sick and wounded."

"New men have come . . . I guided them," Apostolis informed him.

"Kalas should go to Kouga himself," the priest declared.

* * * *

Their conversation stopped.

They'd reached the Apostoles landing-cove. Dragged half onto the ground, an empty canoe awaited them. They pushed it into the water, waded over, and climbed in. Standing at the prow, Apostolis took up the oar.

But as soon as they arrived at the larger waterway inside the reeds, the priest spoke:

"Stop rowing and sit down. I have something to say to you."

Apostolis did as he was told.

"Do you have a mission?" the priest asked.

"No! I'm at your service."

"Then spend some time at Zorba. Mingle with the Bulgarians, fix their broken furniture, and put them off track."

"Did they see you come to Zorba?"

"No! I arrived at night and went directly to the school. However it seems they were suspicious and had been on my trail. Do you know who it was that was seeking me at the school?"

"There were two of them."

"Was one short? . . . Dark? . . . Fierce? . . ."

"Yes."

"I heard him and recognized his voice. It was Botsos—one of the most blood-thirsty comitadjes. He lives in Bozets, but he's involved in all their crimes. And he always escapes. When the Turkish army shows up, he's back laboring in his field. I know him, though, and he knows me. If we don't get rid of him, we'll suffer a crushing blow. He's trying to eliminate me, too. We'll see who succeeds. That's why I came. We need both weapons and help. Go to Kouga and tell Nikiphoros."

"What do you want me to say?"

"That all the villages on the eastern side of the Swamp are being left to their fate. They're all Bulgarian strongholds, except for Petrovo which is ours. Father Manolis—while he lives—and a courageous villager are in control there. No Bulgarian force dares to approach this heroic village! As long as Captain Nikiphoros was at Tsekri, he went out in the night to bolster up the patriarchal population. We had support. Now we've been abandoned."

"I'll tell him, Father Chrysostomos."

"Have Nikiphoros come himself, or else send us a brave leader who will impose his authority . . . Like the Eviscerator."

"Who is he? I haven't met up with him at the Swamp."

"That's not his name. It's what the Bulgarians call him, terrified as they are. No one seems to have seen him. However he's very much alive and active. Our people say Captain Garefis has come back to life; the Bulgarians call him the Eviscerator. He goes about his work systematically—with a knife driven into the heart of every murderer. No witnesses. No one knows him. Right up to the northern villages, he's disposed of those comitadje leaders whose hands are steeped in blood, one by one. Yet there's no rebel force of ours in that territory . . ."

"Could it be Captain Matapas?"

"No! Matapas is at Olympus. Someone who knows . . . revealed to me that this new Garefis kills these comitadjes from revenge. If we had such a fighter in our eastern villages, we'd be saved."

"I'm to tell Captain Nikiphoros to return to Tsekri, or send the unknown avenger to you?"

"I wonder if he knows him? If only he does! Let him judge whether it would be more effective to come himself or send another. Tell him the needs of our villages—that we're suffering from the Bulgarians' atrocities and the Turkish authorities' indifference. In fact last September the Bulgarians killed the Turk Riza-bey, and they still haven't caught the murderers. He was a friend of Halil-bey's . . ."

"From Kavasila?" Apostolis interrupted.

"Yes!"

"I know him! He's a friend of Captain Agras'. When the captain was wounded, he brought him to Thessalonika . . ."

"Well, this Halil-bey asked Captain Panayiotis to go out and hunt down Bulgarians with him. He wanted to take back Riza-bey's blood, since the Turkish officials weren't doing anything."

"And did he?"

"No! Panayiotis had turned over the operation of the western Swamp to Agras. But he introduced Halil-bey to him."

"Then the beys are helping?"

"When it's in their interests, they help."

The priest paused for a while before continuing:

"We have both guides and messengers that are Turkish. Aren't you aware of it?"

"I am. But they're paid," Apostolis said with contempt.

"Eh, certainly they're paid. Why else do you think they do it? They're not Greeks."

"They hate us as much as the Bulgarians."

"Sometimes they're faithful, provided that you pay them regularly."

"And if the other side pays more?"

Pensive, the priest replied:

"I don't believe they're out to deceive us. Without doubt, some of them do. We have to be careful. They're useful to us, though—that is, if they aren't in on our plans or realize who's been initiated . . ."

"Father Chrysostomos . . . You're not a priest . . ." Apostolis said all of a sudden.

"Who told you that?"

"I can't say the name. However I heard it at the home of a great patriot. Is it true?"

"My beard has grown sufficiently," the priest said smiling. "And I've learned the religious part. What does it matter who I am?"

"I encountered someone else disguised as a priest . . . He left his false beard and robe behind. Perhaps you're acquainted with him? He's tall, lean, and incredibly strong. By himself, he lifted up a boat that was stuck fast in the mud and threw it back into the water. Who is he? Do you know?"

"No. Many pretend to be priests these last years in Macedonia. And to do the work we do, we must have both good health and plenty of muscle. As short and thin as I am, I can stay awake for three nights in a row and walk twelve straight hours. But tell me, where did you meet this man disguised as a priest?"

"It's not for me to tell, Father Chrysostomos. I've given an oath not to disclose what I'm doing."

"You're right! Each of us performs his mission, but without commenting about it or repeating what he sees. Now take me to Tsekri."

14.

The Large Hut At Kouga

THAT DECEMBER THE COLD WAS FIERCE.

The rebels' stay at Lake Giannitsa, always difficult, became painful. The huts with their walls, roof, and floor of reeds couldn't protect them from the cold. When the men lit a fire inside, the smoke had no outlet and it choked them. If they opened the door, the hut froze. In order to breathe they were compelled to sit very low or lie on the floor near the fire, beneath the smoke.

However the fight between the two enemies continued, fierce and relentless, as each sought to drive the other from the Swamp.

The tall Kouga hut, which could be seen from far away, put the Greeks at a disadvantage. The Bulgarians shot off volleys from a distance, without approaching in their canoes and being perceived. The bullets tore through the reeds and struck whoever chanced to be standing in the hut.

For their part, the Greeks maintained their aggressive action by conducting raids on the Bulgarian huts. But these were built low and didn't appear among the reeds, so that the boats had to get up close to find them. As a result, the raids proved more dangerous for the attackers than for those under assault.

On guard, the Bulgarians had lookouts and patrols everywhere. Often surprise attacks developed into unexpected hand-to-hand battles.

Agras and Nikiphoros had built other, smaller huts here and there around Kouga, and assigned sentries to defend them. Exposed to the cold inside the water, the sentries awaited the enemy from one moment to the next.

This inactivity and uncertainty among the reeds proved so nerve-racking that the commanders were forced to change the guard every hour. Inside the huts, the men remained on edge, constantly expecting Bulgarian gunfire. Those supervising them were perpetually in motion; and the two commanders had to rotate staying awake at night to keep watch.

All the men had grown wild-looking and unkempt, with long hair, beards, and torn, worn-out clothes. Only Nikiphoros and Captain Pandelis still managed to seem somewhat tidy despite their rebel beards.

Life was hard for everyone. But Agras with his constant fevers and unhealed wounds, had reached a state of complete exhaustion.

"You must leave!" Nikiphoros repeated over and over to him. "You'll never get well in the Swamp, while if you leave and regain your health, your work, too, will go better."

Agras would laugh, take up his rifle, and set off on a patrol. Returning with a high fever, he'd lie down on the floor for a few hours, then be up again in the morning to resume his work.

Yet even he began to lose his calm. A volley had killed one of his evzones, and the following day another round of gunfire from inside the reeds mortally wounded a second—the courageous and irreplaceable Andonis.

They put him in a canoe and were preparing to send him to the Vangeli hut to see the doctor, when another boat arrived with a villager and a priest.

They'd come from Nisi, the priest said, to meet the commanders.

Observing the wounded youth, the priest bent over him. Andonis opened his eyes and saw the robe.

"Say a blessing, Father, so that my sins are forgiven," he murmured.

By the time the priest had finished, the youth was no longer alive.

They lifted him up onto the deck again and brought him into the hut.

Commanders and men were all despondent. Andonis was one of their finest youths, and a particular favorite of Agras's.

That morning Agras had awakened feverish. Bundled up to his ears in his cloak, he'd seated himself near the fire.

Once they'd placed the dead youth down, Agras called the priest over.

"Sit and eat with us, Father," he said, his spirits low. "What is your name?"

"Father Yianni. I'm from Nisi."

"Well be seated, Father Yianni. Later you can read the last rites. The lads will bury my poor Andonis tonight at Nisi, where they'll accompany you. It's no time to go now, in daylight."

"What information do you bring us?" Captain Nikiphoros inquired, seeking to change the conversation in order to raise the men's morale.

"Both good and bad news," the priest answered. "Toman Pazarenze from Zervohori has been killed . . ."

"What!" Agras exclaimed. "I'd given him his life and freedom!"

"That was wrong, Captain Agras," Father Yianni replied. "He was one of the worst of Apostol Petkoff's comitadjes who took part in the Tekovo slaughter, where eight brave village youths were tortured and killed! You shouldn't have given him his life. It's good he's gone."

"Who killed him?" Agras wanted to know.

"A friend of Captain Manolis'."

"Manolis the Curlyhead?" a startled Nikiphoros asked.

"No, another Manolis—from Thrace."[35]

"Who is he?" Captain Teligadis spoke up.

"You haven't heard of him?" the priest responded. "Here in the Swamp, didn't you learn about the killing of Stavrakis, who kept an inn at the crossroads to Verria and Thessalonika?"

"It seems I heard something when I was in Thessalonika," Agras said. "Tell us more,"

"Certainly you would have! There was a big commotion! This Stavrakis was a Bulgarian who posed as our friend. Many of our lads pass through the village there . . . secretly, of course. And Stravakis knew it . . ."

"But wasn't he killed back in October," Nikiphoros interrupted, "at a funeral, I believe?"

"Yes, in the center of Thessalonika, right out in the open. This Manolis put an end to him, once he'd determined Stavrakis betrayed us."

"How did Manolis escape?"

"Just listen! He was quick and clever and took refuge inside a house. During the night he slipped out and made his way to Captain Gonos' force in the Swamp. Somewhere or other he met up with a friend of his, an officer I think, who was intent on doing away with Pazarenze. The two of them traveled together to Zervohori."

"What were their plans?"

"To settle old accounts."

"They both had accounts with Pazarenze?"

"No. Manolis went to support his friend, the officer."

"What is his friend the officer's name?" Nikiphoros inquired.

"It's a mystery! Manolis won't reveal it."

"How do you know, Father, that he's an officer?" Agras asked.

"It's obvious. He's tall, lean, strong . . . made of iron. He stands straight, with his head held high! And his eyes are full of fire! When he gives an order, his voice . . . his every word is like a command!"

Both leaders laughed.

"So that's how an officer is recognized!" Agras joked. "Wouldn't it have been better simply to ask him who he is?"

"Ask him? As if anyone would have the nerve! He stares at you and his eyes bore right through you. Yet he's secretive himself! . . . How could you ask him anything!"

"Where did you see him, Father Yianni?"

"At Nisi. He and Manolis spent a night with me. It was right after the Tekovo slaughter—and our retaliation. This friend of Manolis' took Pazarenze's life, maybe more lives."

"But what score did he have to settle with Pazarenze? Didn't you inquire?" Agras persisted.

"No one asks him anything, Captain—I told you! I did question Manolis, though; and he said his friend had avenged a Vasilis from a little village that no longer exists between Naousa and the Swamp. The comitadjes destroyed it to get back at this Vasilis for going off to fight with Captain Zezas. They killed Vasilis' mother and wife and took his child.

"Eventually the friend of Manolis'—who's also a friend of Vasilis'—learned about it and tried to find him. But Vasilis had disappeared, gone mad, or died—I don't know which. Manolis' friend set off after Pazarenze then, for destroying Vasilis' family. He went to Zervohori to a coffee-house filled with Bulgarians, and summoned Pazarenze outside to challenge him . . .

"Pazarenze attempted to take out a knife. Impossible! Manolis' friend is as powerful as a wild beast. He seized him by the neck; and in an instant he'd strangled him like a chicken."

"Another Garefis!" Captain Teligadis marveled.

"Yes, another Garefis! . . . What's more, it's not as if Pazarenze was a lightweight! He's a beast himself, a huge man. Yet who could get the better of this unknown friend of Manolis'—this Hercules! Pazarenze's neighbors ran after him; however he beat them off and rushed to the swamp, hiding in the reeds. He managed to reach the canoe where Manolis was waiting for him, and they were on their way! It was night when they appeared at my place in Nisi."

"Why didn't they come here to us?" Agras inquired.

"They might not have known how to get here. And you can't say it was planned! After discovering a path to Yianzista, they went on to some Greek huts, and from there our men directed them to me . . ."

"Where are they now?" Nikiphoros asked.

"Who knows! The two of them left as suddenly as they'd come. I put out mattresses for them, and in the morning when I woke, they'd gone. No one had seen them . . . They seemed to have evaporated."

The food was ready. The captains sat around the fire with Father Yianni.

"You said you had both good and bad news for us, Father Yianni," Captain Nikiphoros reminded him. "To which category does Pazarenze's death belong?"

"To the good, of course. It removed one of Apostol Petkoff's worst accomplices."

"But not Apostol Petkoff!" Captain Teligadis inserted.

"What is the bad news, Father Yianni?" Nikiphoros inquired again. "Anything from here?"

"No, from elsewhere. More deaths! Another frightful slaughter! . . . The Bulgarian Center in Sofia sent comitadjes out to murder the bishop of Drama. The plot was well-organized, and they would have succeeded had he not been making a round of his district. Frustrated, the murderers turned all their vengence upon the bishop's unarmed village . . ."

Conversation and footsteps sounded on the deck outside. Mihalis appeared at the door of the hut.

"Apostolis the guide is here," he announced.

"The boy? Send him in! Have him come to our table!" Agras said—referring to their lack of one. His teeth were chattering from the fever. He huddled as close as he could to the fire burning in the middle of their circle.

Mihalis stepped aside, and Apostolis entered.

"Welcome!" the two commanders called out together.

"Sit there, next to our guest Father Yianni," Agras added.

And he drew even closer to the fire.

"What brings you to us?"

Apostolis' sharp glance had halted before Andonis' body lying to the side, covered with a cloak. Then he eyed the unknown priest. Who could he be?

"I'm here to get news," Apostolis said, on guard; and he sat down cross-legged beside the priest.

"Did you hear? They killed Pazarenze," Captain Teligadis informed him.

"Where? Who?" Apostolis exclaimed.

"Some friend of a new Captain Manolis."

The name aroused Apostolis' curiosity.

"Of the one who killed . . ."

"Stavrakis, yes."

When Father Yianni explained how, in killing Pazarenze, this friend of Manolis' avenged a Vasilis who'd lost his child to the comitadjes, Apostolis pricked up his ears.

"Was the lost child called Takis?" he asked eagerly.

The priest didn't have time to answer.

A volley split the air, followed by a second one. Immediately Father Yianni fell back.

All at once the hut was in an uproar. Officers and men raced out onto the deck. Flat on their stomach behind the low embankment, they shot off batteries blindly inside the reeds, aiming in the direction of the sudden bullets.

But there was no answer. Nor was anything further heard. And it was in vain that two boats set off on a search with Teligadis. They returned without encountering a single Bulgarian.

Meanwhile the priest had breathed his last.

The bullets had pierced the reed walls of the hut and crossed to the opposite side, above the shoulders of the captains who sat surrounding the fire. One hit Father Yianni in the head.

All the men were dispirited. This state of things couldn't go on. Their nerves were frayed. The large hut had become a target. In order to walk, or even sit, it was necessary to stoop over to avoid a bullet striking them out of the blue, as had been the case with poor Father Yianni.

Silently Agras watched his men wash the priest's bloody face, wrap him in his robe, and place him down next to the dead Andonis.

Captain Nikiphoros took Teligadis aside.

"We can't move in daylight," he said. "But as soon as it gets dark, Apostolis will guide the canoes with the dead men down to the Lower Huts—and take the commander away as well. As sick as he is and with such cold weather, he can't remain here any longer."

"He won't want to leave!" Captain Teligadis replied.

"This situation can't continue," Nikiphoros stated decisively. "Our hut is a decoy. They'll go on killing us without our realizing where the bullets are coming from. We have to pull the hut down tonight and build it up again lower. For us to do so, though, the sick commander must be gone."

"He won't consent to leave," Teligadis repeated.

"I'll speak to him myself," Nikiphoros said.

Lying on his back, propped up next to the fire, Agras had closed his eyes and was trembling from the fever. With his suffering, he moaned softly.

Nikiphoros felt his burning forehead and called out his name.

Agras opened his eyes.

"What is it?" he asked.

"Apostolis is setting off in a short while . . . He'll guide the boats transporting the dead men . . . I say you should go with them."

"I? . . . With the dead? . . . Why? . . ." Agras responded, dazed from his strong fever.

"You won't go with the dead . . . They'll take you to the Toumba hut," Nikiphoros said.

Agras had leaned his head to the side and closed his eyes again.

"I'm not leaving here . . ." he murmured.

Those were his final words. He no longer answered to what Nikiphoros said to him.

"In the miserable state he's in, he won't even understand . . ." Nikiphoros told Teligadis. "We'll carry him to a canoe, and two men will accompany him to the large Toumba hut."

That was what happened. Agras had neither the strength nor the will to resist when they picked him up and put him in a canoe.

Gloomy and silent, standing on the outer deck next to the faithful Teligadis, Nikiphoros observed the boats grow distant in the icy dark.

When they'd disappeared, he turned, shook his shoulders like he wanted to throw off a weight, and strode into the hut.

Agras had neither the strength nor the will to resist.

"Now, to work!" he declared to Teligadis, who had followed him.

The work was strenuous, time-consuming, demanding . . . It wasn't easy in just one night during such bitter cold to tear down such a hut in the dark and construct another.

However once Captain Nikiphoros made up his mind about something, nothing could prevent him from seeing it through.

Without noise, with scarcely any tools or light, thirty of them pulled down reeds, walls, beams and roof in one night; and with the same materials constructed a new, low hut that didn't rise above the reeds of the Swamp.

Nikiphoros worked right along with them, ignoring his weariness, the labor and the pain. And seeing their commander outdo them all, the men competed among themselves as to who would strive the hardest and be the most help to him.

Yet when they wanted to remove the embankment to bring it closer to their low hut, it couldn't be done. The cold had turned the mud to stone. They would need picks to break it up, and silence was crucial to their success.

In the morning at daybreak, the exhausted, muddy, soaked men—at peace now—lay side-by-side in their humble hut, able to sleep the kind of sleep they'd not enjoyed for some time.

15.

Nikiphoros

APOSTOLIS HAD A HARD JOB FINDING KOUGA again when he returned the following evening. Searching for the tall hut, wherever he turned he saw only dry reeds.

A pleased Nikiphoros greeted him when he finally located it.

"If you had a problem, the enemy will be even more at a loss," he said.

And he requested news from the outside.

Upon hearing the message for help from Father Chrysostomos of Bozets, he frowned.

"I'm aware that they need support and encouragement. Yet how can we leave Kouga and all the western lake to the Bulgarians? Captain Agras is away now. I'm alone here."

"He wonders if you can send someone the Bulgarians call the Eviscerator . . . No one knows his name, but he's killed comitadjes one after another."

"The Eviscerator? Who is he?"

Apostolis repeated what the priest from Bozets had told him, adding:

"Our men call him Captain Garefis, as if the Captain has come back to life and is avenging all the murders they've committed."

"I don't know him," Nikiphoros said. "However if the Center does, Father Chrysostomos can ask for him there. No such person has worked in our region. In any case, I can't leave Kouga, since the greatest danger is here. The villages will have to be patient. I'll remain at the hut."

The defense of the western lake stands out as a heroic page of the Macedonian Struggle. In seeking to take over Kouga, the Bulgarians sent out patrols to destroy it; while the Greeks, who based their action upon the hut, dispatched patrols of their own to combat them. Every day there were clashes, sometimes at a distance and sometimes up close.

The Bulgarians constructed another hut between their cluster and Kouga; the Greeks responded by building one between Kouga and the new Bulgarian hut. Each half-appeared to the other among the reeds, now thinned out from the cold.

For more security, Nikiphoros put up two more huts on the opposite side of Kouga, one of which he made into a storehouse.

Canoes with villagers traveled back and forth daily with earth for the embankments, along with reeds, dry grass, wood, and food supplies. And every so often Agras sent them cartridges and grenades to replace the ammunition burned up in everyday skirmishes.

The cold intensified. Thick snow covered the Swamp, crushing the reeds and revealing friendly and hostile huts. Another Bulgarian one popped up, constructed without their taking notice of it.

Nikiphoros stationed sentries further and further from Kouga, so near to the Bulgarians that their conversation was audible. Greeks and Bulgarians frequently exchanged insults and curses from inside the reeds.

The patrols multiplied, with Captain Nikiphoros leading them.

One night on a reconnaissance with three canoes, he got lost and couldn't find the path. They'd approached the Bulgarian complex and were in danger of coming out at an enemy hut—or being spotted from a lookout post or falling into a trap. It was with the utmost labor that they maneuvered their way back again through the reeds.

Another time, the captain set off with two canoes in such cold that the water began to freeze and it was impossible to go on.

Captain Pandelis, who'd accompanied Nikiphoros, warned:

"We'll be stuck if we don't return to the hut."

In fact, the water was thickening all around them.

"How far away are we?" an oarsman asked.

"Two hours," Nikiphoros replied.

The oarsman wasn't so sure.

"It will take us longer," he said. "The boat won't budge."

They had to break the ice in order to get loose. However the cold grew steadily stronger; the more they proceeded, the more difficult it became.

Some two hours away from Kouga, it took them eighteen hours to return. All day and night, they struggled with the ice to open up a pathway. When they finally arrived back at the hut, more dead than alive, they collapsed onto the floor to sleep.

The Swamp froze over completely. Communications ceased. The canoes couldn't circulate; and neither men nor food supplies reached them anymore. Far from the friendly southern shore and huts, those guarding Kouga found themselves cut off.

With food diminishing and running short, they were forced to make smaller portions and measure every mouthful. Hunger set in.

And since they couldn't transport wood to warm themselves, they had to cut grass and reeds to burn. The smoke choked them, yet when they opened the oil-cloth door for it to escape, the hut froze again.

The strenuous life of the Swamp became agony.

No one complained, though, or sought to leave. The commander's endurance gave heart to the men, who suffered without speaking.

"Thank God that Captain Agras is gone!" Captain Teligadis would exclaim from time to time. "He'd have died if he remained here . . ."

Apostolis had brought news from Toumba that Agras was recovering ever so slowly and had to be restrained from leaving for Kouga. Distressed at not being back in the fighting, he needed to be watched in order not to set off.

Soon after Apostolis' departure, when the lake was a sheet of ice, sentries on the lookout toward the Bulgarian section reported that the enemy was expanding further in their direction.

The next day Captain Nikiphoros put on his long boots that came up over his knees and started out with five select youths, including Captain Pandelis, to see for himself. All were armed with a rifle, pistol, and cartridges.

The commander left instructions for the men remaining at Kouga to inform the neighboring Greek huts to fire all at once if gunshots erupted. That way they'd confuse the enemy.

The ice was thin as the six rebels departed at midday. At times it gave way under their weight, so that they sank down into the water—which often rose as high as their waist.

They'd climb onto some plants then, shake themselves, and raise their feet to empty the water from their boots. Dry reeds were everywhere; and frozen, they crackled when they broke.

The men advanced slowly—over ice, inside the water, and through vegetation—pausing at intervals to strain their ears and scrutinize in every direction. If all appeared clear, they pressed on again.

* * * *

As it began to grow dark, Nikiphoros got a look at the new, half-constructed hut from inside the reeds now sparse from the cold—close enough to see and hear the workers out on the deck.

Signaling to his men to halt and approach with care, he drew ahead in the water a few meters and lay flat on some broad-leafed plants. Captain Pandelis followed and did the same, as did the other men.

Everyone lined up side by side, silent and motionless. The slightest sound would betray them.

And once more Nikiphoros got up and they all crept forward, one after the other, until they arrived almost to the hut.

Raising his hand, the commander gave the sign.

Suddenly a volley burst forth, a second one, and a third—succeeded by shrieks, moans, and cries for help from the Bulgarians.

Heavy gunfire started up from the nearby Greek huts. Inside the tumult, Nikiphoros and his five men emptied ten rounds each at the half-finished hut, firing from close range.

The daring assault brought such turmoil to the enemy that they failed to hunt down the exposed men who were on foot.

While the Bulgarians gathered up their wounded and dead, the six Greeks managed to make their way back to Kouga—intact, but ready to drop from fatigue and the cold.

The next day they awoke to rain.

"At least the ice will melt!" Captain Pandelis exclaimed with relief. "Now we'll be able to travel by boat again! See what the water and plants did to me yesterday!"

The most orderly of the company, he resented the damage his clean but worn outfit had suffered the night before.

"There, there!" Mihalis sympathized. And he called out:

"Heat the iron so Pandelis' jacket and breeches can be ironed!"

All the men laughed—foremost among them Captain Pandelis, who ran his hand over the wrinkles to smooth them out.

"Don't tease Pandelis!" the commander said good-naturedly. "Would that you all were as neat as he is. We'd go to death like Leonidas' Spartans did—clean and spruced up like bridegrooms."

Looking up toward the black clouds descending in cascades, he remarked: "Who knows if, with this weather, our neighbors will attack us tomorrow . . ."

However frightened by yesterday's sudden assault, the Bulgarians didn't stir.

* * * *

For three days and nights it rained. The ice melted. It dawned sunny and bright the fourth day—a delight! The fresh lake sparkled, with diamonds mounted on every branch, shrub, and reed.

Boats were now arriving with food supplies and ammunition, and delivering information back and forth as well. Agras was better. Full of enthusiasm, he'd written to Nikiphoros:

"Brother Yianni,

I've received your wonderful letter! A little more patience and effort, and we'll drive our friends out. Your action was brilliant. The results will be decisive. When you're able, come to Toumba; we'll be awaiting you.

Reinforcements are due today. Thus you can replace those who need it most. Let the others remain, either at the hut or outposts.   Yours, Agras"

In the meantime, Apostolis had journeyed to the coast to meet and guide the reinforcements the Center sent them.

"Good news!" Nikiphoros announced, with an encouraging glance at the men around him. "Some of us have need of rest."

Many were tired, and others had a fever. Still, who would admit it as long as Nikiphoros put up such resistance himself? They all threw back their shoulders and protested that no one would go. No one would leave their commander.

But with the ice melted, the situation at Kouga grew worse instead of improving. Water descended in torrents from the mountains, raising the level of the lake and flooding the huts.

Kouga—old, poorly-constructed, and heavy—rested on the lake's shallow bottom; it didn't rise with the water and float. On the contrary, it became more inundated all the time. From the new warehouse to the south, canoes constantly transported reeds, wood, and empty cases, which were piled onto the floor to elevate it. Inside the hut, there was no room to stand upright. Moreover the door had been reduced to a hole.

The water rose higher and higher . . .

Everyone had taken off his boots, as they no longer served for protection. Bare to above the knees, they all moved about in the icy water hunched over, sat down on a case for a while, and then got up again to circulate in order not to freeze.

It was impossible to lie down or sleep.

The men spent two days and nights inside the rising water. Life grew unbearable. Pain tortured them in all their joints.

An exhausted Nikiphoros sat with water up to his waist, leaning against the wall of the hut, pretending to sleep. The others tried to imitate him. But just as sleep overcame them, the cold woke them up. Their teeth chattered and their bodies grew numb. Hands, feet, waist and back all ached, stiffening and losing their flexibility.

Occasionally Bulgarian bullets whistled in their ears. However no one responded, not wanting to provoke an attack that would be catastrophic at that point. Fortification of the hut now remained slight . . .

The following day Nikiphoros chose about a dozen of those who were sick and worn-out, and whether they wished it or not, had them go to the Lower Huts. At the same time, he notified Agras to have reinforcements ready at the first call.

He'd been left with only twenty-one men and a few villagers to protect the huts and resist a possible Bulgarian attack.

That night Nikiphoros didn't sleep.

On his feet, uneasy and feverish, he made plans for a battle. Sentries were stationed towards the Bulgarian huts, while a steady stream of canoes brought earth for the embankment and a supply of cartridges for the fighters.

"Sit down, Commander," Captain Pandelis said, setting up a case for him. "You won't last if you continue this way. What's more, your feet are swollen."

Worried, the commander replied:

"I can't sleep or relax. I have a foreboding they'll strike us."

The sentries reappeared, uneasy themselves. There was an unusual amount of activity at the Bulgarian huts, they reported, with canoes coming and going.

"Something's up, Commander."

"In such cold?" one of the lads asked.

"Since they're more experienced than we are, they've constructed their huts better. They're not suffering this way," Captain Teligadis stated. "They may attack us."

"I'm certain they will. We don't have a moment to lose," Captain Nikiphoros declared. "I feel it in my bones."

And separating six out of the twenty-one men, he provided them with two boats and ordered the first to hide in the reeds to the right of the hut, the other to the left. Only when he gave the signal—if the Bulgarians approached and Kougas was in danger—only then were they to shoot.

* * * *

It was seven in the morning. Day had dawned. From the direction of the Bulgarians, movement was perceptible . . . gliding and the dipping of oars. Firing, the sentries withdrew towards Kouga.

At that moment, volleys fell upon them from different points. Bullets hissed and splashed in the water around the hut.

But Nikiphoros was prepared. He made a sign that no one was to fire. And fortified behind their embankment, the men waited, well-disciplined.

The gunshots heated up. Bullets burst upon the deck and the hut. An evzone who started to crawl back to take something from the hut, dropped dead.

Nikiphoros gave a command for just a few rifles to answer, so that the Bulgarians would be misled into thinking Kouga didn't have strength.

Joyful and triumphant, Bulgarian voices cried out:

"Get them! Get them all! There aren't many!"

The boats would have been numerous and close. Although invisible themselves, the enemy could see the hut. Because bullets were falling onto the deck; they were pounding the earth barrier.

"Fire away!" the commander ordered all at once.

Pandemonium burst forth.

The whole lake reverberated! . . . Kouga was enflamed from one end to the other. Rifles spewed out fire and iron—but blindly, into the reeds from where the enemy bullets were coming. On their stomachs behind the low earth embankment, the rebels fired away.

Nevertheless the Bulgarians continued to gain ground. With every sacrifice, they were determined to capture this bastion of Greek resistance, which had become such a thorn to them. Sometimes one of their canoes tried to venture out from inside the sparse reeds, but such an outburst of shots greeted it that it was forced to retreat.

* * * *

Time passed. Nikiphoros knew that it would be a while before help could reach them, as fast as the men from the Lower Huts hastened there. They had to endure until then.

The left side of Kouga, full of thick vegetation, bothered him. From the shallow water, the Bulgarians could approach on foot to throw grenades. And that would be disastrous.

He gave the signal for the canoe on the left to fire.

But exposed and suffering as the men were in the two hidden boats, they'd pulled back.

"So! We'll manage . . . Courage—hold firm!" . . . the commander shouted.

However from the smoke of the old Gras rifles with their black gunpowder, he couldn't see anything now.

"Captain Pandelis, take the left side yourself with Evangelos, in case they attack us from there! And the rest of you, cease firing!" he called out.

It was as though he'd said: "Commit suicide!" to the two youths, such a hail of bullets was descending everywhere! . . . But neither of them hesitated. Getting up from the embankment, they took over the left side—all the while shooting at the Bulgarian canoes.

Before an opening in the earthwork defense, Nikiphoros made out the enemy boats appearing and disappearing inside the reeds, growing closer all the time and tightening the siege.

Two villagers, panic-stricken, ran into the hut and stuffed their heads into bundles of Swamp grass, thinking they'd escape that way.

Nikiphoros saw them. Feeling the nervousness of his men—who'd been lying motionless behind their low barrier for so long, firing from inside water—he was fearful that the villagers' panic would spread to them. Suddenly he was struck with an inspiration.

"Captain Zeza's song, all together!" he commanded. "Let them hear who we are!"

And in unison, like a single person they began to sing the song that was on the lips of all the mountain rebels. Electrified, they rose bravely to their knees with new courage and determination, took aim, and fired.

One youth who was wounded, ignored it and went on singing. Another who fell, said to his companions:

"Fire, take back my blood!"

Like a cheerful echo, a distant battery sounded.

"Courage! Courage lads!" the commander shouted, intoxicated with joy. "Help is coming to us! Take aim and fire away!"

All of Kouga spit forth fire, iron, and death.

The men readied hand grenades; and the Cretans took out their knives, willing in their enthusiasm even to jump into the water at the first order.

But abruptly the enemy bullets started to thin out, and the angry voices subsided. Oars dipped hurriedly into the water. The gunshots were steadily decreasing.

"They're leaving! They're leaving! . . . Aim and fire! We've won!" Nikiphoros yelled, beside himself.

At the same time a triumphant victory-cry rang out, close now behind Kouga.

"H-u-r-r-a-h! B-r-a-v-o! . . . Hold on, comrades, we're here! . . ."

Opposite them the shooting had completely stopped. Not a word was heard. Only the crushed reeds and the hasty flapping of oars in the water testified to the Bulgarians' rapid flight.

16.

New Arrivals

A quarter of an hour later help arrived—a whole series of canoes with men chosen by Agras, accompanied this time by Captain Kalas. Congratulations, handshakes, embraces, laughter, emotion—those who'd come didn't know how to express their elation to the dead-tired defenders of Kouga for their heroic victory.

Old Pascal had guided them, rejoicing even more, perhaps, than the Greeks at the Bulgarian defeat.

"The ones who need it can get some relief at the Lower Huts now," Captain Kalas proposed. "We'll be sufficient to hold Kouga! . . ."

As if anyone would part from their commander! Victory had fanaticized them. It seemed to have refreshed them from their lack of sleep, the water, and the cold. Not even the frightened villagers wanted to leave.

Seated around a fire late that afternoon [with the hut cleared of water and dry reeds spread over the floor] the fighters stretched out their aching limbs before the flames. Each was describing his impressions of the battle to the others, when all of a sudden sentries signaled the approach of a friendly boat.

Rubbing his stiff back, Captain Nikiphoros went out onto the deck with Captain Kalas to receive the visitors.

Three men sat inside a large, wide canoe. Clean and freshly-shaven, they presented a vivid contrast to the rebels at the hut—whose life was no longer civilized. Standing in the back, an oarsman was propelling the boat forward.

It was Apostolis.

The canoe came up alongside the deck, and the guide leaped up onto it.

"Slowly, Mr. Mitsos," he cautioned the taller young man with the straight bearing, who rose abruptly. "These flat-bottomed boats tip over easily. You have to get accustomed to them . . ."

The youth was spirited and handsome in his brand-new rebel uniform with its leather belt and shiny, criss-crossed cartridge pouches.

He too leaped onto the deck, followed by a white-haired man with deep-set black eyes and stooped shoulders. A boy fifteen or sixteen years old, also dressed as a rebel, came last. In his arms he carried a little white dog that had black spots on its head and face.

Apostolis introduced them:

"Mitsos and Pericles Vasiotakis, and Vasilis Andreadis. They were insistent on coming to fight with you, Commander," he said to Captain Nikiphoros. "I received a command from the Master to go and meet them, and guide them here to Kouga. They're Greeks from Egypt."

Surprised, Nikiphoros looked at the three new arrivals, each so different. Mechanically, he stroked the head of the dog, still in Pericles' arms.

"Dogs are useless and dangerous in the Swamp," he commented. "Their barking can betray us . . ."

"Don't be uneasy about that, Commander," the boy responded. "Mangas has been trained not to bark. I brought him with Captain Agras' permission, once he'd assured himself that the dog could be a help rather than a hindrance."

"You saw Captain Agras?" Nikiphoros asked the tall youth Mitsos, who stood beside him. "How is he? . . ."

"He had a fever . . . I'd say he needs to get away from the lake," Mitsos answered. "You speak, Vasilis. What was it the doctor told you?"

Everyone turned toward the white-haired man who'd remained a little over to the side.

His hair was white and his melancholy eyes were deep-set under thick black eyebrows and a lined forehead. However, his body was lean and firm.

He spoke in a matter-of-fact manner:

"A doctor from Thessalonika examined Agras and told him he should leave the Swamp. He wanted him to give up the rebel life for a while and return to Greece. Otherwise he said he couldn't hope to regain his health."

"Did Agras decide to go?" Nikiphoros inquired.

"He laughed when he heard it. After the doctor repeated it to him, he replied: 'Don't waste your words. My fate is bound up with the Swamp. When we drive the Bulgarians out, perhaps I'll go myself. Meanwhile, I'll stay here.'"

"Has his fever gone, at least?"

"No! Before we set off, it caught hold of him again. His temperature was over a hundred!"

"He appeared exhausted," Mitsos added. "Doctor Antonakis advised him to leave, but Agras wouldn't hear of it."

"Doctor Antonakis!" Captain Kalas exclaimed with a smile. "Then you've met him? He's an important part of the Struggle, but he's no longer posing as a doctor. Did he inform you of how he gets rid of dogs in the villages?" he asked with a nod towards the one in Pericles' arms.

"No," Pericles answered. "He didn't mention it. Why?"

"He has a way of driving them out," Captain Kalas declared. And he related it to them:

"When a Greek force has to pass near a village with a Turkish army, he goes ahead a day or so, as if to visit someone sick. Then he lets out a screech so high and shrill that every last dog takes off. Nor do they return for a couple of days, so that there's no need to fear their barking. You see them running like mad with their hair standing on end. The villagers learned about it and begged him to stop. Antonakis the doctor has provided all kinds of service to the resistance."

Captain Nikiphoros stepped inside the hut with the three new arrivals.

"We'll get you a cup of coffee," he said.

But Mitsos immediately put things in their place.

"We didn't come as guests, Captain Nikiphoros. We're here to enlist in your force and fight with you."

Christos the Cretan stared disdainfully at Mitsos' new uniform and shiny leather belt and cartridge pouches.

"Ask him if he's ever been tested in battle," he whispered to Captain Pandelis, who was admiring the uniform and its accessories with something like jealousy in his eyes.

Mitsos heard it, although it had been said in a low voice—and he smiled.

"No, I've not yet been tested in battle," he replied, "since there wasn't one during the time I grew up. I was in the army for two years, though, and I come from a military family. My father was wounded in '97, while my cousin's great-grandfather—and he nodded toward Pericles—fought in the Greek Revolution.[36] As native Cretans, we're trained with a rifle."

Ashamed that his words had been overheard, Christos started to move away. Yet he didn't stop casting glances at Mitsos' new uniform. Perceiving it, Mitsos felt the need to explain:

"I'm not to blame if my uniform's brand-new! It's just come from the tailor's. But I hope it gets stained from gunpowder soon like that of my friend Vasilis," he added, slapping the white-haired man fondly on the shoulder. "He fought with Captain Zezas—he was beside him until the end!"

The men's attention shifted from Mitsos' uniform, to Vasilis.

"Really?"

"You knew him?"

"You fought with him?"

"We just sang his song in battle . . ." Captain Nikiphoros began.

But a shout from outside interrupted him.

"Commander! They're asking for you!" Mihalis called.

Nikiphoros stood up and went out onto the deck. In a few minutes he returned, frowning and troubled.

"Who will accompany me on a patrol?" he asked.

All the men flew up.

"I will, Commander!"

"I!"

"I!"

"I!"

Forgetting their pain and fatigue, everyone wanted to go.

"I'll take just a couple with me," Nikiphoros said. "Both Apostol Petkoff and Hadji-Traios had a part in the battle today— two chieftains that won't be put down easily! We may have a surprise attack in the night . . ."

"How did you find out?" Kalas inquired.

"Manolis and his companion came and told me. And for Manolis to report it, you can be sure he knows. Besides, he's here from the western shore of the lake, near Zervohori."

Kalas stood up. "I'd like to see him, myself," he said.

"They've left," Nikiphoros answered. "They were in a hurry and didn't even get out of their canoe."

"Where were they going?"

"To the Lower Huts. They have some work there, it seems."

"Was it the Manolis who killed Stavrakis?" Captain Kalas wanted to know.

"Yes," Nikiphoros replied.

"And the other?"

"I don't know him. He's tall, dark . . ."

"Aha . . . The Bulgarians will have a time of it," Kalas responded.

"You know his companion?" Nikiphoros asked.

"They appeared together to see me. His companion's the one who strangled a comitadje leader at Zervohori. He's equal to Manolis in both strength and bravery!"

"Manolis is determined—and clever and shrewd as well!" Nikiphoros added. "When he puts his mind to something, he always succeeds. But his companion seems to be still more daring. He's incredibly strong! A superman!"

And changing the subject:

"Come with me, Vangelis," he ordered the giant Macedonian. "You're a master oarsman. And you, Christos," he said, choosing the Cretan from all those pressing to follow him. "I can't take any others. We must proceed quickly and quietly."

The men had all crowded onto the deck to view the commander's departure. Hardships and cold had taken their toll on them during the last few days. Still, this didn't stop anyone from readying more boats, supplying them with arms, and climbing inside, up to three in each. At the first sound of gunfire, they'd be prepared to race to assist their leader.

The sun was just disappearing behind the mountains when the commander's canoe set off.

* * * *

Wild-ducks and water-hens were returning to roost in the Swamp. Along with martens, water-snakes, the rustling of wind and snapping of reeds in the cold—even snow falling from branches and splashing onto the water—they formed a concert of loud and soft sounds that covered up the gliding of the canoe. In the stern, Vangelis rowed silently, leaning slightly forward and then back again. Christos knelt in the middle of the boat, with the stock of his rifle resting on his shoulder and his finger on the trigger, set to fire.

Seated in front in the prow, Nikiphoros guided them by means of gestures, his revolver in his hand.

Not one of them spoke, or hardly breathed. Complete silence.

They arrived down under the enemy's central hut without the sentry noticing them.

No activity could be detected inside the hut—only a droning voice saying something in Bulgarian, and another answering wearily.

Turning his head, Nikiphoros mutely questioned Vangelis, who replied with a motion of his hand: "Nothing."

Calm and gloom in the hut.

At another indication from the commander, the Macedonian changed the movement of his oar. Instead of drawing ahead, he backtracked the boat in the narrow path, and they withdrew and slipped away.

Once out of the danger zone, Nikiphoros asked for an account of what the Bulgarians had said.

"They're disheartened," Vangelis stated. "It seems they suffered a tremendous blow. They're on guard in case we attack them. But not a word about an assault. They've been crushed."

The men were waiting in canoes and on the deck of the hut to greet their leader when he appeared. All were happy and relieved to see him.

That night, lying on dry reeds, old and new fighters slept side by side.

* * * *

As was his custom, Captain Nikiphoros got up early in the morning to see if all was in order, with the guards in their places. With astonishment he caught sight of Pericles in a small canoe, oar in hand. Standing before him, Apostolis was instructing him how to use it. With his ears raised, the dog was seated in the prow watching—following Pericles' every movement, lifting up and lowering his nose in sequence. Upon seeing the commander, the two boys sprang to attention.

"What are you doing here at such an hour? Why aren't you sleeping?" Captain Nikiphoros questioned them.

"Apostolis is teaching me how to handle the oar, Commander," Pericles replied with the respect of an old military man toward his superior.

"So early?"

"We've returned, Commander," Apostolis answered with pride. "We went up to the Bulgarian huts."

Captain Nikiphoros grew serious.

"This I forbid!" he exclaimed. "Without a command, no one has the right to go off from here."

And observing the boys shrink back, he added:

" . . . You could suffer some misfortune."

Pericles replied again respectfully:

"That's what we came for, Commander—my cousin, Vasilis, and I—to undergo hardships."

Nikiphoros was touched by his words.

"I don't doubt it," he answered. "However, one person is in charge at Kouga. As brave as my men are, they're obliged to submit to my orders and follow them! Apostolis, you should know the procedures here. It was up to you to advise Pericles, who's new!"

"Apostolis isn't to blame, Commander," Pericles said, still at attention. "I led him astray. From close up, I wanted to see the huts you surveyed yesterday . . ."

"All right! I won't scold you the first time!" the commander responded. "Were you at least armed?"

The two boys took out their weapons to show him. Apostolis' revolver was old. Captain Agras had given it to him. Pericles though, had a striking Braouning.

"Do you know how to use this?" Nikiphoros inquired after he'd examined it. "Yes? Where did you learn? . . ."

"In Crete," Pericles replied, "from my grandfather—actually my great-grandfather who brought me up. He gave it to me and taught me to use it. I'm experienced in target-practice!"

Thoughtfully Nikiphoros stroked his short beard.

"It was foolish to take the dog with you," he remarked.

"On the contrary, Commander," Pericles answered, "he's been trained to inform me when we approach someone. That way, we were able to avoid all the Bulgarian sentries."

"How does he inform you?"

"If it's a friend, he wags his tail and strains his nose forward. If it's an enemy he also strains his nose forward, but he uncovers his teeth with a fury. However he doesn't bark."

"How is he able to distinguish an enemy from a friend?" Nikiphoros inquired.

Pericles took the dog in his arms. "He comes from a good breed—the fox terrier," he replied; "and he learns whatever I want to teach him. By the way I alert him, he understands if there's danger. And then there's his sense of smell. The dog picks up the scent of strangers. This dog, especially, has a strong instinct to distinguish a friend from an enemy."

"You've spent a lot of time on him?" Nikiphoros asked with interest.

"Yes. I love Mangas. He's my best friend. When I'm with him, I don't fear anything or anyone. We went down under the central hut of the Bulgarians with Apostolis and avoided all the guards."

"What did you see there?' the commander wanted to know.

"Apostolis overheard conversation."

"What did they say, Apostolis?"

"There were a few men in the hut, but we didn't get a look at them," Apostolis replied. "They must have been wounded, although they were working inside. Those severely wounded had been transferred to Zervohori. The ones remaining were complaining about their leaders."

"Did they name them?"

"I heard the name of Hadji-Traios. The other they spoke of only as 'chief.'"

"Why were they complaining?"

"Because so many men had been killed. They thought they'd find a small force here, and your resistence shattered them. They've suffered heavy losses!"

The Bulgarians had in fact suffered substantial losses. They weren't about to undertake an assault now. Clashes were occurring regularly, almost every day, for Captain Nikiphoros wouldn't let them catch their breath. Wherever they ventured, they stumbled upon Greek patrols that attacked them. And intimidated as they were, they didn't resist but fled inside their dark, twisting pathways.

However, neither did the Greeks make assaults anymore. The courageous failure of Agras had taught them that without machine guns, they couldn't capture fortified huts. And they had no machine-guns.

* * * *

A command arrived from the Center, which had received reports from Agras and Nikiphoros. The action of the Greek forces was to be divided. Captain Nikiphoros would take charge of the western lake—of Kouga, the Lower Huts, and Toumba; while from a base at Tsekri, Captain Kalas would assume command of the eastern lake and the defense of those villages under attack from the comitadjes.

This order displeased Captain Kalas. Kouga's fame had spread over the whole western region of the lake. Whoever remained there to defend the hut, acquired glory and became the essential leader of the lake forces. Kalas had been sent to the Swamp as General Commander. How was he now to accept a secondary position? Seeing him so down, Nikiphoros generously suggested that they switch districts. If the Center approved, he'd return to Tsekri; and Kalas could stay at Toumba as commander of the western division.

The Center accepted it. And after leaving a deputy-commander with sufficient strength at Kouga, Kalas departed for Toumba with his force. Nikiphoros left also to go back to Tsekri with his men and the new arrivals from Egypt.

On the way they stopped at Toumba in order to bid farewell to Agras, who had received word from the Center to go to Naousa and undertake the administration there.

They discovered the once perpetually cheerful Agras, sad and glum. Fever had consumed him. Weak and pale, with dull, sunken eyes, he stared at the still fresh volunteers from Egypt and the thin but fit fighters from Kouga.

Affected by the sight of him, Captain Telegadis kissed his hand without a word. A knot had gathered in his throat and he couldn't speak. Agras smiled at him, then said sadly to Nikiphoros:

"I'm useless now, Yianni!"

"Why useless?" his friend protested. "Do you think the administration of Naousa is insignificent? First of all, the force there remains without a commander since Captain Panayiotis left. Besides, all Hellenism from Vodena and below will rely on you. All the comitadjes come from there to flood the Swamp. When you're in charge, you'll prevent it!"

"Yes, but the resistance and the action are at the Swamp. As proof, all those from the outside enter here," Agras responded— and he looked over at the two cousins and Vasilis.

With his heavy step and stooped shoulders, Vasilis approached him:

"Commander," he said, "I'd like to ask you as a favor to take me along with you."

"To Naousa? Just what will you do there?"

"I'm from those parts. I have some old accounts to settle," Vasilis replied.

"We're with you, Pericles and I! . . ." Mitsos interjected.

A motion from Vasilis stopped him.

"No, Mr. Mitsos," he declared. "For the work I have to attend to, it's better we're not together. I'm going to Naousa to find a certain Pazarenze . . ."

"Pazarenze? They killed him a few days ago!" Agras exclaimed.

"They killed him? Who?" Vasilis asked.

His face had hardened.

"An unknown avenger of yours, it seems. He went with his friend—the now renowned Captain Manolis—and strangled him."

"Manolis! He took my prey!" Vasilis grew agitated, breathing heavily and clenching his fists and teeth.

Then swallowing his anger, he continued:

"Pazarenze isn't the only one. I have other reckonings."

Slowly and deliberately, rotating his glance back and forth from the captains to the men, he said:

"There's a Botsos . . ."

"Botsos?" Apostolis burst out. "Is he short, dark, fierce? . . ."

"Yes! Do you know him?"

"He's at Bozets. He's committed no end of crimes," Apostolis replied.

"At Bozets? East of the Swamp?" Vasilis responded.

And addressing Mitsos:

"You see, Mr. Mitsos, it's good you're here with Captain Nikiphoros to keep track of the eastern section while I'm searching in the west."

He was gritting his teeth.

Mitsos gave him a couple of reassuring slaps on the shoulder.

"Don't worry, Vasilis—whatever you wish. Go with Captain Agras! And after you've succeeded with your plan, when you've found who it is you're seeking, come safely back to us at Tsekri."

17.

Agras

FIRST NIKIPHOROS HAD STARTED OUT with his force for the eastern hut of Tsekri; and in the afternoon Agras left for Naousa with Captain Teligadis and those faithful evzones that remained with him— not much more than a handful in all. Apostolis the guide and the white-haired Vasilis accompanied them.

They traveled by the secret pathway Captain Panayiotis had opened up in the high reeds, which ended at Yianzista.

Agras went ahead in the first canoe with Mihalis and Apostolis, Captain Teligadis came next with Vasilis and Christos, and the other boats followed with three in the larger one and two in the smaller.

In a low voice, since sounds carried over distances in the water, Agras asked Apostolis:

"Who is he?" motioning with his eyebrows towards Vasilis in the canoe six meters behind.

"I don't know," Apostolis whispered back.

"Why does he address the two Vasiotakis youth—who are younger than he is—as 'Mister,' while both of them simply call him Vasilis?"

"I don't know," Apostolis said again. "I imagine, though, that he's their employee. Because when he refers to Mitsos' father, he says 'the boss.' Here, however, he directs them and they follow his advice."

Pensive, Agras remarked:

"That's natural, since he's a seasoned fighter. But why did the others come? They're not from the military, and one's under age."

Once more, Apostolis didn't know.

And he was bothered that he didn't.

Smart and curious, an experienced observer and scout dedicated to the Struggle, he'd learned to draw conclusions from his observations—conclusions which rarely proved wrong.

He'd gone down to the sea as ordered by the Center and met the three Egyptians, along with some Cretans the Command in Athens had sent. In guiding them to the Swamp, and then to Kouga, he hadn't ceased wondering himself about the relation of the two cousins to the white-haired old warrior. Yet wanting to form his own conclusions without laying himself open to others, he hadn't asked anything.

"But I'll find out, Commander," he declared to Agras in a low voice. "I'll find out and tell you, provided you allow me to stay with you."

"With me?" Agras burst into his former carefree, youthful laughter. "What will I do with a youngster like you?"

Apostolis stroked the pistol he'd stuffed in his belt.

"Try me, Commander," he answered proudly.

With fondness, Agras said to him:

"Well-spoken. I observed you during the attack upon the central Bulgarian hut."

At that, the boy's eyes grew misty. Whatever the commander would order him to do now, he'd give his life for him! . . .

The commander didn't order anything, and thus they reached the Yianzista shore alive and intact. A makeshift landing-cove, it had been dug in a deserted spot, from where the men emerged hidden inside the reeds.

An oarsman tied the canoes to each other and brought them back to the Lower Huts, while Agras dispatched Apostolis to investigate. Knowing the Macedonian dialect and the surroundings as he did, he was to locate a road for the small force to take, without entering the Bulgarian village of Yianzista.

* * * *

It was night when Apostolis returned to the shore of the lake. Agras was feverish again; but ignoring it, he had them depart. According to the regular night marches, they formed a line with the guide in front and the commander directly behind.

The men were thin and tired and had undergone many trials. Weakened by fever, each also bore scars from one or more wounds that had healed. Nevertheless, they'd become used to their demanding life as rebels; and like Apostolis, they stood ready to throw themselves into fire or water for their leader.

At a shallow point, they crossed one of the tributaries flowing into the lake and began their ascent.

However, no longer accustomed to footmarches, they found the road arduous and difficult, with thick weeds, rocks and stones.

As they approached a village, houses could be distinguished in the dark.

"We'll stop here," Agras announced.

"What! Bulgarians are here, Commander!" Apostolis exclaimed. "This is Upper Kopanos!"

"We'll stop here," Agras repeated, "whether they like it or not!"

When they arrived at the first house, they rapped on the door.

A window was lit up, but the light went out at the first rap.

Agras beat on the door again and called out in Greek:

"Whoever you are, open up! We want to enter and rest inside."

From the window, a hoarse Bulgarian voice sounded:

"Set fire to my house and burn it down if you will, but I won't open the door for you!"

"Smash the door in!" Agras ordered.

With two kicks and a couple of blows from their gunstocks, the men broke the door down and burst into the house.

In the lead as always, Agras was heading up the stairs in the dark when two pistol shots rang out next to him. The bullets hissed in his ears.

Footsteps were heard running, a skirmish followed, and curses flew back and forth. Someone struck a match and ignited a lamp.

Two of Agras' men, Vasilis and Mihalis, had seized an old man by the arms and were dragging him up before the commander. Furious, the Bulgarian stared at the Greek leader.

"Did you fire?" Agras questioned him.

"I did," the old man replied in Greek.

"Why?"

"To kill you!" he answered.

"Why did you want to kill me? Have I done anything to you?" Agras asked.

With hatred, the old Bulgarian said:

"Aren't you from the Swamp? Weren't you the one that killed my son?"

"Who was your son?" Agras inquired.

The old man didn't reply. He had his jaws clenched to such an extent that his teeth were near the breaking point.

Agras looked at him; and the childlike kindness that characterized him returned to his gaze.

"Free him!" he commanded.

Mihalis let go. Vasilis, though, became pale under his white hair. His black eyebrows appeared even blacker.

"Commander . . ." he started to say.

Agras cut him off:

"Free him! . . ."

Through his clenched teeth, the old Bulgarian declared:

"Don't think you can sway me! Kill me if you want. But if you let me go, know that I'll try to shoot you again!"

Agras showed no concern.

"We'll see. In the meantime, Vasilis, release him and let him go."

Unwillingly, Vasilis loosened his hands. The Bulgarian fled towards the door and was lost in the dark outside.

Agras observed Vasilis.

"Don't carry on like that," he said to him. "We killed his son. It's to be expected that he hates us. You'd hate him too, if he killed your child."

Vasilis face grew as white as his hair. Yet he kept silent. Well-disciplined, he went out with Captain Teligadis and took up a position at one corner of the house, while Teligadis guarded the other. When an hour later others came to replace them, he reentered the house and lay down at the bottom of the wooden staircase—protecting his weary commander with his own body, even as he slept.

* * * *

In the morning they set off from the village. Not until Naousa where the Greeks had been notified to await them, would they meet up with the Turkish army. As for the Bulgarians along the way, Agras didn't bother about them.

Resuming their ascent, Apostolis proceeded first, with Agras immediately behind. The guide was anxious. While he admired the commander's generous treatment of the enemy, he feared some ambush on the road. The old Bulgarian could easily have set up men at various spots to murder them. From the evening before, he'd had ample time to alert the village. Once they reached Greek Naousa, there'd be no more danger. Meanwhile they continued to meet Bulgarians and pass by Bulgarian villages. And armed woodcutters were appearing on the mountain.

Apostolis' eyes darted in all directions, scrutinizing the rocks, low trees, and thick shrubs, alighting on shadows and ferreting out wild animals. Every noise was suspect, even the wind passing through the branches.

All of a sudden, he threw himself in front of the commander to shield him.

That same second a gunshot erupted, and in a flash, a second one. A bullet pierced Captain Agras' cloak.

The men, seeing the smoke inside the bushes, had rushed forth. Once more they hauled the old man of the previous night up before their commander.

"Why did you shoot, you scoundrel?" Agras reacted angerly.

"To kill you!" the old man answered as before.

"Let's see you kill me!" Agras said mockingly, extending his rifle out to him.

Right away the Bulgarian grabbed it, ready to pull the trigger.

With a back-handed slap, Vasilis sent the rifle flying from his hand; and they dragged the old man aside.

"Bind his hands behind his back and bring him along to Naousa," Agras called out.

And he drew ahead with Apostolis and Teligadis.

They hadn't gone far when another shot shattered the calm of the mountain.

Agras halted, shaken.

"Who fired?" he shouted.

A moment of silence followed. One by one, the evzones came out of the bushes and approached.

"Who fired?" Agras asked again.

No one answered.

Agras turned back and penetrated the thick wooded area from where the gunshot had arisen.

On the ground, the old Bulgarian was lying with a hole in his head. Beside him with bloody hands, Vasilis was tidying him up— crossing the dead man's hands over his chest and closing his eyes.

"Who killed him?" Agras yelled, beside himself.

Vasilis got up.

"I did, Commander," he replied in his steady manner.

"I'd forbidden it! He was to be brought to Naousa," an infuriated Agras exclaimed.

Vasilis spoke without raising his voice:

"You treated him fairly yesterday, Commander. He told us he hated us because you killed his son. You didn't even know who he was, or if you actually did kill his child. What can I say, since he murdered both my mother and wife, and perhaps my child as well?"

"What!" Agras burst out. "You know him?"

"Both him and his son, who I'd sworn to kill. Manolis or his companion robbed me of my revenge."

"This old man? He's the father of Toman Pazarenze?"

"Yes. You gave Toman his life once. And as an answer, he and some others like him took the lives of eight unsuspecting lads at Tekovo."

"You're sure Toman did it?"

"He and his father and his whole family! Don't pity a Bulgarian, Commander. Wherever you find one, crush him like a snake!"

Vasilis spoke slowly, but the unrestrainable hate that overcame him made his voice tremble—and his lips and large hands as well.

"Listen, Vasilis," Agras said, trying to calm him. "You're in such a condition that you may not be judging correctly. How did you find out who killed the lads at Tekovo?"

"He told me, himself."

"Who? This old man?"

"Yes! And do you want to hear how heartless he was, Commander? With my rifle aimed at him, I asked: 'Did you destroy Asprohori, you criminal?' Do you suppose he put up a defense? He replied: 'Yes, I destroyed it. I stabbed your wife to death, too. And Toman killed your mother!' I restrained myself and asked again: 'What did you do to my child?' The beast began to laugh and said: 'Your child? The Greeks drowned him in the Aliakmon River along with the Bulgarians they captured!' Then I fired. Do as you please to me, Commander. I shot him."

The men had all gathered around to listen to the commander's exchange with Vasilis—aroused and incensed.

All at once Apostolis sprang up among them.

"They drowned him?" he cried, very agitated. "No, they didn't! Your child wasn't on the boat at the Aliakmon River with the Bulgarians that drowned! He escaped—to the monastery. I know where he is. His name is Takis, isn't it?"

Vasilis' whole body was shaking.

"No, his name isn't Takis. What does a name mean, though? They could have changed it. We called him Theodore since he was born on the feastday of St. Theodore. But how do you know this?" he inquired abruptly. "How is it that you know my lost child?"

Excited, Apostolis related as much as he'd seen and heard from Miss Aspasia, the teacher at Koulakia.

"And someone else is searching for him," he added, "someone disguised as a priest, with a false black beard. However, he was in a hurry and didn't have time to speak with the boy. He said he'd return . . ."

"How old is the child?" Vasilis inquired.

"I'm supposed to know? . . . Seven, eight . . . Maybe more, maybe less . . . I didn't ask."

Very pale, Vasilis rubbed his forehead as though dazed.

"Forgive me, Commander," he murmured softly. "The news was so sudden . . . I'd given up all hope of finding him . . . I came back to Macedonia seeking revenge."

Compassionately, Agras patted him on the shoulder.

"Sometimes we're sent unexpected blessings," he said kindly. "Let's be on our way now to Naousa. You can easily go back to Koulakia from there."

18.

Captain Akritas

"Do you know these parts well, Apostolis?"

"These here, not so well. That is, I'm familiar with the footpaths and shortcuts, but I don't know the people."

"The paths and hideouts, the caves and secret roads, I know myself. It's the people I'm asking about."

"Who is it you're seeking, Mister Vasilis?"

"It's better to ask 'which ones?' Because a good many had a hand in destroying my village. And I've sworn to take care of them all—as I did old Pazarenze."

"Give me a name . . ."

"Have you heard of Sloupias?"

"No."

"Zlatan?"

"No, not him either."

"Botsos?"

"Is he short and dark? He's at Bozets."

"Yes, you told me. However, there are still others. Kronos? A Tané? Pio?"

"Angel?"

"Yes."

"He's the uncle of my apprentice."

Vasilis' eyes flashed.

"You work with Bulgarians?"

"We're so intermixed . . . You know it better than I do, Mister Vasilis. Even though my apprentice is Bulgarian-speaking, he's our own—and he's just a child! Besides, wasn't Captain Kottas

Bulgarian-speaking? And Gonos? Do there exist more genuine Greek patriots than they are? What does it mean if my apprentice is Pio's nephew? His mother might have been Greek. He hates the Bulgarians, and he's learned to speak Greek. I've sent him to stay with Miss Electra, the teacher at Zorba. His name is Jovan. We'll make it Yianni."

"Really?" Vasilis replied, his mind elsewhere.

"Don't count such a youngster out," Apostolis said, bothered by his elder's indifference. "This Bulgarian-speaking tot went and unearthed Apostol Petkoff at Zervohori when they thought he was at Ramel. And all by himself with a canoe, he discovered Captain Agras at the Lower Huts."

"Would he be able to find Zlatan from the village of Golesiani, if we set him to it?" Vasilis asked, attentive to this last piece of information.

"Who is Zlatan?"

Vasilis' eyebrows shot together, the sign of an impending storm. But he didn't answer.

The two resumed their way in silence.

Where it was they were traveling, Apostolis wasn't sure. Supposedly they were headed for the Swamp. Yet the road they were following among tall bushes and over the slopes of hills, at times led them unexpectedly to Bulgarian cottages and at other times buried them in thick brush full of thorns and brambles. Then again it brought them to a village square, where under the pretext of buying something or asking a question, Vasilis quizzed the villagers. He was as fluent in the Slavic-Macedonian dialect as a native.

Apostolis still hadn't "sized up" Vasilis well, as he put it. Taciturn and unsociable, always ready for difficult tasks but not for conversation or holding forth, Vasilis remained closed to him.

They'd only spent a few days together, though.

* * * *

When Agras had reached Naousa, the Greek community headed by its doctor welcomed him with enthusiasm. It was then that

Apostolis realized the fame the commander's name had acquired, spreading fear among the Bulgarians and inspiring Greeks wherever he passed. He'd become the legendary hero of the Swamp.

Although sick, thin, and ravaged by the fever that had ruined his health, Agras immediately got to work at Naousa. He organized a recruitment of youths, armed them, and provided military instruction. Within a couple of days, he'd galvanized the whole region.

Always prepared to execute a command, Vasilis had roamed the countryside and furnished the commander with whatever information he'd sought; and he'd transported weapons and cartridges for him. But Apostolis perceived with his natural shrewdness that the older warrior was preoccupied. With his lost child, he wondered?

One day Apostolis said to him:

"I should leave. The commander hasn't given me any work here. Perhaps they need me at the lower Swamp."

"Wait," Vasilis had replied. "We'll travel to Koulakia together."

After the first week ended and things settled down more or less, Vasilis requested the commander's permission to go down to Koulakia with Apostolis. He wanted to see the child called Takis, who'd escaped drowning at the Aliakmon River and was now living with the teacher Miss Aspasia.

Agras granted permission, and Vasilis set off with Apostolis.

But they didn't go straight to Yianzista, in order to pass by the Swamp to Kryfi and from there to Koulakia. Instead they took a route so strange that Apostolis was completely baffled.

In broad daylight they proceeded northeast from Naousa, then east, due south, and west again—passing by huts and sheepfolds and back onto the mountain, sometimes at heights where the forest was dense and green. And everywhere Vasilis made inquiries. He was constantly asking questions.

The day before, an armed rebel had stopped them, bursting forth from an area thick with brush. In Greek, Vasilis said to him:

"I surrender. Take me to Captain Akritas."

It jolted Apostolis, for he knew that Captain Akritas had left Macedonia. After two years of daring activity as leader of a force at Naousa, he'd returned to Greece. The Turks were on his trail, and his lingering in the mountain area would have endangered the whole Struggle.

Without protest or hesitation, the man led Vasilis and Apostolis to a rebel hideout.

Vasilis didn't speak or give a name; he simply made a secret sign. One of the rebels, a large, dark-skinned, bearded man, stood up at once and approached him. With obvious agitation, he looked him in the eyes, suspicious and uncertain.

"Yes!" Vasilis exclaimed.

The other let out a strangled cry and threw his arms around him. For a moment they remained speechless, overcome.

Then the rebel, said:

"Your white hair . . ."

Again Vasilis exclaimed:

"Yes!"

The two of them withdrew and conversed together privately for some time.

Apostolis was left with the rebels, who offered him stale bread and cheese. Next they questioned him: From where had he come? Where was he going? And who was the white-haired man? Trained not to reveal what he knew, Apostolis replied disjointedly: He didn't know him ...Not even his name ... No, they'd met on the road.

But like Vasilis he too was preoccupied now. His mind was on Captain Akritas, who'd suddenly reappeared on the mountain— with a small band, true, yet a well-armed one. Apostolis kept looking in his direction.

He saw Vasilis take a wallet from his friend's hand, remove something from inside, stare at it for a long while, and afterwards turn it over . . . Could it be a map? . . . Then he gave it back to Captain Akritas, who wrote something on it—what Vasilis told him.

Where could he have seen him before? He didn't know Captain Akritas, but he'd heard enough about him. Growing up

around the Swamp, he'd followed the illustrious captain's action—
at Mt. Vermio with the heroic Garefis, at Naousa, and elsewhere.
Where hadn't Captain Akritas operated! However Apostolis had
never chanced to meet up with him.

This one, he'd seen somewhere. But where? His black, fiery
eyes, his large, strong hands, his tall, straight bearing and powerful body, all muscle and nerves, lean and firm . . . And that over-
riding stride . . . Where had he encountered them before?

He began asking questions in turn:

How long had Captain Akritas been hiding out here? Why
did he leave Mt. Vermio for such a time . . .?

Just as Apostolis had done, the rebels promptly clammed up,
answered in monosyllables, didn't want to speak . . .

The two friends walked up arm-in-arm, like they couldn't
decide to separate. The rebel raised his hand and placed it down
heavily on Vasilis' shoulder.

"Come what may," he declared, "Good luck!"

Apostolis had heard that deep, resonant voice before. Where,
though?

The two friends parted, and Apostolis set off with Vasilis. For
the rest of the day, Vasilis didn't speak to him again except to say:
"We'll sleep here!"—that is, inside the forest when it grew dark—
and "It's time to be off!" upon awakening.

All the next day they walked without exchanging another
word until the sun went down—when abruptly Vasilis wanted to
know if he was familiar with the surroundings.

While it wasn't his own territory, the guide had traveled a
couple of times to Naousa. Moreover once he'd passed through a
place, he could find the most secluded paths again, whether night
or day. Now with night descending, they trudged on.

Vasilis appeared to know the landscape well. They weren't
following a frequented road, or even a footpath. Still, he proceeded
with certainty, seemingly at home.

Leaving the forest behind, he headed left in a northerly direction. In a short time a light glimmered in a wooded spot beyond—
from the slightly-opened upstairs window of a cottage.

Vasilis halted for a moment, hesitating, then said to Apostolis:

"They claim you're smart and trustworthy. What's more, you're light on your feet and have the reputation of being fearless. See that cabin before us? Draw up to it without a sound. The stable is on the lower floor. Without their detecting it, find out how many animals are inside. Return and tell me."

Apostolis couldn't have asked for anything more. Vasilis had scarcely finished speaking and the guide was halfway there—moving swiftly and stealthily.

Vasilis watched his stooped, shadowy figure approach the hut, until he lost sight of him inside the brush.

It wasn't long before the boy sprang up from a nearby bush.

"Three mules and a horse that has traveled some distance," he reported, "and traveled fast."

"How do you know?" Vasilis questioned him.

"It's in a lather and so worn out it can't eat—only drink water."

"How do you know?" Vasilis asked again.

"The stable door doesn't close at the top, for ventilation it seems. I climbed up and entered inside. Two of the mules were rested, but the horse had just arrived. The horseman didn't even have time to remove the saddle-pack. The others would have been waiting for him."

"What others?"

"Those conversing in Bulgarian behind the window."

"Did you hear them?"

"A few words. They were speaking in low voices."

Vasilis patted his head as a way of saying thank-you. And with that, he completely won him over.

"Let's go have a look," Vasilis said in a voice unusually gentle for him.

"Follow in my footsteps," Apostolis replied, "so as not to trample any brush underfoot."

They made their way up to the hut, the guide choosing soft ground to absorb the sound.

A simple villager's cottage, it was constructed of boards and branches, with dry Swamp grass covering the roof—a rustic refuge concealed among the trees.

Beneath the almost closed window, they stopped to listen. But only murmuring could be heard. From time to time they could distinguish a word or two.

Vasilis glued his back to the wall of the cottage and made a sign to Apostolis to step up onto his interlocked hands. The guide did so—and from there up onto his shoulders until his head just reached the narrow opening of the shuttered window.

Fixing his eye upon the open slit, he saw four men seated on stools around a plank table, where a peasant's oil lamp was burning.

Three of them were dressed in the customary village clothes of the region: a wool tunic and jacket, short fur-trimmed cloak, and knee-breeches. Wool gaiters were stuffed inside their pigskin shoes.

All three had beards; they were unkempt villagers.

The fourth, whose back was turned to the window, was better dressed, with blue woolen pants, long black boots, and a red belt. Expensive fur decorated his cloak. As he gestured—speaking to the others as a leader to subordinates—Apostolis observed a gold ring on his third finger.

After holding forth for some time, the man rose and bid the three villagers good-by, one by one. When he faced the light, Apostolis saw that he was shaven.

Hurriedly, the boy knelt back down onto Vasilis' shoulders and slipped to the ground. Seizing his older companion by the hand, he led him into the forest behind the thick shrubs. From there, they were able to observe the scene without being visible themselves.

At the rear of the cottage, outer wooden stairs creaked; and two shadows issued forth from the corner. Opening the stable door, they entered inside. At the same time in front of the building, the shutters on the upper floor window were drawn back, pouring light into the darkness outside. Two armed men leaned out and inspected the illuminated section before the cottage.

Tramping sounded in the stable. One of the men who'd entered rode out slowly astride a mule, enveloped in his cloak. Looking around carefully, he pulled his fur cap further down onto his face, then circled the cottage and departed.

"Apostol Petkoff," Apostolis murmured in Vasilis' ear. But Vasilis covered the boy's mouth with his hand.

The other villager walked out of the stable, locked the door, and climbed up the back stairway, which creaked again under his footsteps. The two armed men withdrew from the window and closed the wooden shutters. And the light went out inside.

Tiptoeing away, Vasilis and Apostolis emerged from the bushes and passed silently down a steep descent leading to another wooded slope.

Vasilis sat down on the ground and signaled Apostolis to do the same.

"Speak now," he said. "Who were the others?"

"I don't know them!"

"They didn't give any names?"

"No!"

"Petkoff? You know him?"

"No! I recognized him by Jovan my apprentice's description of him—a shaven face and a gold ring on his middle finger. Besides, the other three called him 'chief.'"

"Was one of the three a redhead?"

"Yes, with a red beard. I couldn't see his hair because he had a handkerchief tied around his head. But one of his eyes was smaller than the other, as if half-shut."

"That was Zlatan! What were they talking about?"

"It was impossible to understand. They were hunting for someone. They know where he is, although they didn't say. The conversation was ending. Apostol Petkoff said: 'We'll catch him, either dead or alive—however we'll get him. It's better, though, to capture him alive.' He told them he'd take one of the three mules because his horse was half-dead and he had a distance to go."

"So he's the one that came so far at such speed. We don't have a mule or horse to pursue him. But let's go on to the Swamp; they're expecting us."

The two got up and continued their journey.

On the way, Vasilis broke the silence:

"A little beyond that cottage was my house—along with just ten to fifteen others. There's no longer a trace of them. And do you think I'll ever forgive what happened?"

It was said thoughtfully, more with pain than anger. Affected by his words, Apostolis didn't reply.

* * * *

It was two or three in the morning when they arrived at the reeds in the Swamp. Vasilis let out a cry like the cackling of a water-hen. A wolf's howl responded a little to the south. Squatting in the bushes, Vasilis and Apostolis waited, with Vasilis repeating the water-hen's cackle from time to time.

Farther down, the ground had been dug up to form an oblong hollow area, flooded now by the lake's water.

Another, softer wolf's howl sounded close by. Vasilis replied with a subdued cackling; and the prow of a canoe came into view from the reeds and entered the hollowed out space. There was but one oarsman. Without a word Vasilis climbed inside, followed by Apostolis. The canoe backtracked, disappeared in the reeds, then reappeared in a pathway.

A second boat was waiting there with two armed men inside. In the bottom, a third person was lying with his arms bound behind his back and his mouth stuffed with a cloth.

No one uttered a word. Both Vasilis and Apostolis had seen the man tied up in the bottom of the boat, yet neither asked anything. Silently the two canoes proceeded along the dark path.

Apostolis had recognized Captain Panayiotis' secret road, which began near Yianzista and ended up at the Lower Huts.

In fact, it wasn't long before they arrived at Agia Marina. Vasilis and Apostolis got out onto the deck; and for a moment they stopped, expecting the others. But only the one canoe with its oarsman was there. The other boat had stayed inside the reeds, from where the indistinct sound of a struggle was heard, then a chilling gurgling, and afterwards nothing.

Vasilis rubbed his forehead a couple of times with the palm of his hand. A few seconds went by.

Softly he said to Apostolis: "Better to enter the hut."

However Apostolis didn't budge. A disagreeable curiosity held him outside on the deck. Vasilis didn't insist; he appeared to have forgotten him.

In a short while, the second canoe passed slowly out of the reeds and drew up alongside the deck. One of the two armed men climbed out, carrying a large sack over his shoulder.

Apostolis' curious eyes searched for the canoe in the dark. The other armed man remained alone inside with the oarsman. The bound prisoner was missing.

"Who was he?" Vasilis asked the one carrying the large sack over his shoulder.

"Sloupias," a deep voice answered.

Apostolis shuddered. It was Captain Akritas. While he didn't know him—the rebel who'd embraced Vasilis at the mountain refuge—nevertheless that voice was familiar to him.

Rising, it declared:

"I've relieved you of some dirty work!" whereupon the man set the sack down on the floor.

"Sloupias was the least dangerous," Vasilis stated.

"Today he proved the most dangerous," the other informed him. "He'd trailed us and overheard our conversation. Spies . . ." and he slashed the air with a horizontal movement of his hand.

"Wouldn't a single shot have done the job as well with less hassle?" Vasilis inquired.

"Too much of a commotion. At such an hour, we'd stir up both Turks and Bulgarians. The knife's quieter."

Apostolis considered himself to be hardened, well fortified, prepared to see and hear about every atrocity. But the sack in a heap below so turned his stomach that he sat down on the floor in the shadow of the hut to recover.

Nobody paid any attention to him.

Akritas strode over to the edge of the deck, where the canoes were being tied up.

"You'll have to set off again for the shore with him, Manolis," he said to the tall, strong, solidly-built man in the second canoe.

"No, not me," Manolis replied, crossing onto the deck. "I've done my work. Let Mitris go. Besides, there's the battle tomorrow."

"What battle?" Vasilis asked.

"If Captain Kalas finally decides to attack them and capture the new hut they're secretly building to the northwest of Toumba . . ."

"Really? You've joined up with Captain Kalas?"

"No," Manolis replied. "I'm with Captain Gonos at the lake. But given that Gregos and I are here, we'll both fight wherever there's a battle."

"And after that you'll return to Matapas, Gregos?" Vasilis inquired, looking at Captain Akritas.

The hunting dog instinct brought Apostolis to life, conquering his indisposition. Captain Akritas' name was Kostas, and this one was called Gregos. He'd rightly suspected that it couldn't be Captain Akritas!

The resonant voice replied:

"It depends on you and your boss's son."

Apostolis pricked up his ears in the dark.

A little window was now opening up into the mystery of Captain Akritas. He knew Mitsos. And Pericles, too, he wondered?

The Captain turned towards the boat where the oarsman stood waiting for a further command.

"You'll take care of him, Mitris?"

"I'll go. But I won't manage alone."

"Then pass by the Vangeli hut. And since you're going there, inquire about poor Petris."

Together with Manolis, Gregos lifted up the sack and lowered it into the canoe, while Vasilis watched.

"Where did you catch Sloupias?" he asked.

"Inside the reeds, coming to pick you up," Manolis answered. "We'd been after him all day. I'd caught him before in the morning, in a clash on a reconnaissance. Thinking he was wounded, we pulled him from the water. As thanks, he stabbed Petris who was sitting next to him—one of our finer lads—and then jumped inside the reeds. Since it was shallow, he escaped. We discovered him again on shore. Fortunate for us, Gregos was there waiting for you. He spotted and captured him as he was making a break for Yianzista. Had he succeeded, tomorrow the Swamp would have swarmed with comitadjes."

Manolis took out a cigarette and lit it up. By the flame of the match, Apostolis was able to catch sight of a handsome man with soft brown eyes and a kind, sympathetic look.

"Here it's a fight for survival," Manolis went on, "while I have to avenge my Thracian village . . ."

Once more the hunting dog's instinct threw Apostolis into turmoil. So this handsome, good-natured youth was the Manolis who'd killed Stavrakis in the middle of Thessalonnika, at a funeral with hundreds of people! . . .

In the dark Apostolis observed him by the faint light of the stars; and he gathered his impressions.

Thus you can have a gentle, guileless face, soft, appealing eyes, even a pleasing voice—and yet stab someone, cut off heads dispassionately, and bury bodies on some desolate lake shore . . .

He remembered the words Nikiphoros had spoken when he first arrived at the Tsekri hut:

"Captain Zezas didn't kill anyone. Let him be our example . . ."

To which Captain Pandelis had replied: "With his own hand he didn't kill anyone. But have you asked about his men?"

Agras had given Toman Pazarenje his life. However Manolis' companion, this huge Gregos—the false-Akritas—had strangled him. Moreover he'd acted with Manolis' approval and cooperation. Agras had also given old Pazarenze his life and freedom, and Vasilis had shot him. Yet Agras didn't punish him. On the contrary, he'd felt sympathy for Vasilis—who sought revenge for slaughtered women and children . . .

This was the *Struggle*. And so the Struggle for one's country—war and the fight for freedom—covered and excused all?

The three friends entered the hut, closing the oilcloth door after them. They didn't notice Apostolis huddled in the background; and he didn't get up to go inside. Wrapped in his cloak, he lay down upon the reed floor and reflected, trying to make sense of it all . . . until he fell asleep.

A clamor awoke him in the morning. Canoes were assembling around the deck, and men arming themselves for a campaign—filling their cartridge-pouches, polishing their weapons, and lowering ammunition into the boats.

Always ready to lend a hand, Apostolis assisted in the loading. Someone brought him black coffee in an earthen mug, along with bread and cheese.

"Eat," he said. "We're setting off for a battle. You may not have food again for some time. You're to be our guide."

"Who gave the order?"

"Captain Nikos has his own guide," the rebel answered, nodding towards Captain Agras' former officer who was in charge at Agia Marina. "But he," and he gave another nod towards the false-Akritas, "said we should take you."

"Who is he?" Apostolis inquired, feigning ignorance.

"Who knows! They call him Captain Akritas. But the real Akritas is in Greece now; and he's little. This one's a giant."

"You've met the real Captain Akritas?"

"Yes! He took care of arming and readying us when we left from Greece."

"When did you come?"

"Just lately, with the new lads."

He started to leave, but Apostolis stopped him.

"You said that Captain Akritas—that is, the false-Akritas—wants to have me as a guide?"

"Yes! He claims you're familiar with the paths."

"Where did he learn it? How is he acquainted with me?"

"Well, why don't you ask him? How am I to know? I've never seen him before."

Contemplating, Apostolis ate his bread and cheese while cleaning a short-barrelled Mannlicher they'd given him.

He cleaned the rifle and carried bullets and hand-grenades from the deck to the canoes, climbing back and forth between them.

However his gaze followed Gregos.

Although newly-arrived at the hut, he was directing everything; and the men all obeyed him—even Captain Nikos, in command now of Agia Marina's defense.

Apostolis watched him carry the heaviest loads on his back, striding effortlessly from the deck into a canoe—and he marveled that his rapid movement didn't overturn the boat. He observed his dexterity in turning and lighting a cigarette, amazed that his powerful hands didn't crush it to pieces as it disappeared like a crumb in his strong fingers.

Then he lost himself in his thoughts. Where in the devil had he seen that masterful and at the same time subtle touch?

Approaching, Gregos looked him in the eyes and announced: "Get ready, Apostolis—you'll guide us." And again the boy remembered both the voice and the flashing eyes, only now they'd softened into what seemed to be a mocking smile.

Everyone entered the boats; and they set off to the northeast with Captain Akritas in the lead and Apostolis as guide.

Only a few turns had been made inside the zigzag paths, when heavy gunfire broke out in the distance before them.

Gregos rose and strained his ear.

"Kouga?" he asked Apostolis, who was rowing.

"No. They're firing to the east, towards Toumba."

"Faster," Gregos ordered. "However it is, we have to go to their aid."

The shots were deafening. The whole lake vibrated.

Volleys fell one after another, then suddenly decreased and died away as silence spread over the water. The quiet was such that the chirping of a bird building its nest was audible.

"Hurrah! Our men took the hut!" a rebel voice shouted from one of the canoes in the rear.

The oarsmen were making time, ascending the branches of the river and its tributaries towards Kouga, in order to prevent a Bulgarian' withdrawal. All together, the men had begun singing a rousing victory-song. But after the first two lines, a drawn-out cry from inside the vegetation broke their momentum.

"Ba-a-a-ck! . . ."

Oars were lifted out of the water. Each rebel secured his rifle on his shoulder and his finger on the trigger in anticipation of a battle.

A canoe issued from a path, a second one behind it, and a third and fourth. Others followed—a whole series of them.

In the first boat, Captain Kalas was seated with two oarsmen. Raising his hand, he called out:

"Back! Don't anyone go forward."

"Kouga?" Captain Nikos shouted. "What happened at Kouga?"

"No one's attacked Kouga! Kouga's not in danger! Huts aren't taken that way!" Captain Kalas said with a frown.

"You weren't fighting at Kouga?" Manolis inquired. "Where was the firing, then?"

"At the new hut . . . beyond Toumba . . ."

"You captured it?" ten voices burst out together.

"Huts aren't taken that way," Kalas repeated, scowling. "The Bulgarians fortified it before they finished building it. Huts don't come cheaply! Words do!"

"Didn't you have grenades? Or maybe they didn't explode again?" Captain Nikos asked, exasperated.

"We had them. But . . . we were at a distance . . . The grenades failed to reach the hut . . . They fell in the water."

In a low voice, Apostolis scoffed:

"They'd reach it if it were Captain Agras . . ."

Startled, he threw himself back. Captain Akritas' threatening hand was shaking next to his ear.

"You, an infant, dare to have your say about your superior?" the rebel hissed, his eyes blazing.

Dipping his oar into the water, Apostolis acted as if he were guiding the canoe. Just who was this Akritas? . . . An officer, in any case . . .

The deputy-commanders were seeking information and directions.

No, huts weren't captured that way, Captain Kalas said again. They'd lose too many men. Two of his lads had already been wounded. He was taking them back to Toumba. It wasn't a good policy to be on the offensive. Defense only was required. Kouga had been strengthened, and Toumba as well. They would construct still another hut between Kouga and the new Bulgarian one—and they'd ensure communications. To do more was unnecessary and dangerous. They'd suffered great loses and damage, etc., etc. . .

* * * *

The boats traveled slowly to Toumba. In one of the last canoes, two men sat glumly, one with his head bound, the other with his arm hanging limp.

An out-of-spirits Captain Kalas was in the lead canoe, giving instructions to the men of Agia Marina, who mechanically complied.

However, when they arrived at a crossroad of paths, Captain Akritas addressed Kalas for the first time:

"Do you need us, Commander? Could you use support? If there's not going to be fighting, we have other work!"

No, there wasn't going to be fighting, Captain Kalas responded, and he had no need of support. They had sufficient strength at the Toumba huts.

Disorder occurred in the line at that point. A number of boats turned back towards Agia Marina with Captain Nikos, while others took the road to Toumba. In the shallow water, Manolis got out of his canoe. Stepping onto a cluster of plants, he walked up to Gregos.

"Switch places with me," he said. "Vasilis wants you."

And once he was alone with Apostolis, Manolis asked if he knew the way to Tsekri.

"Yes, I know," Apostolis said.

"Start rowing, then. The three of us are headed there."

Apostolis felt somewhat freer with Manolis.

Not worrying much, seeing the second canoe far enough away and noting the oarsman awkwardly striking the bottom of the lake without being able to maneuver the boat, he asked:

"What is the name of your companion, Captain Manolis?"

The other immediately became uncommunicative.

"Captain Akritas," he replied curtly.

"Captain Akritas is in Greece. He armed and sent off the last mission . . ." Apostolis began to protest.

But the other interrupted him.

"They misinformed you," he said sharply. "This is Captain Akritas."

Apostolis didn't answer. However he reasoned that having operated in the Naousa district, Captain Akritas wouldn't be found alone at the Swamp without his force. Silently he dipped the oar in the water and made a few strokes. Yet Manolis' mild expression renewed his courage, along with an appetite for conversation.

"You killed Stavrakis, Captain Manolis?" he inquired.

"Certainly I did!"

"Weren't you afraid?"

"What should I be afraid of?"

"That the police would catch you!"

"So?"

"They'd hang you!"

"So?" Manolis repeated.

Apostolis had seen and heard of many brave acts. But the unassuming, even-tempered indifference of this rebel astonished him. He remained a little dumbfounded.

Calmly Manolis said:

"Stavrakis was a national threat. He had to be eliminated. The cost of doing away with him didn't count."

"And if they killed you there inside the crowd?"

Manolis shrugged his shoulders.

"Let them kill me! What does it matter?" he answered, unperturbed. "The order was to dispose of Stavrakis. Keep your eye on the goal."

He was smoking, relaxed and easy-going, casting smoke up towards the still budding leaves on the new shoots and tips of reeds. Pensive, he was staring straight before him, his brown eyes full of kindness and childlike goodwill.

"Who gave the command?" Apostolis asked.

"That's not your business."

"It is! Because I work for the Master, too."

Manolis focused his gaze on the boy who was rowing.

"Why are you asking, then?" he responded with good-humor. And he added: "We're all struggling for the same end. Each of us doesn't need to know what the other is doing."

True, Apostolis reflected. He knew this rule. All the Struggle's organization depended on it. The left hand wasn't to know what the right hand was about. Yet how curiosity gnawed away at him! . . .

He threw a glance at the two rebels behind them in their canoe, the white-haired Vasilis who'd come to find his lost child, and his companion. The captain had taken his cap off, revealing his broad forehead with his thick brownish-black hair and two deep lines between his well-proportioned eyebrows. Who could he be?

* * * *

When they arrived at Tsekri, they didn't find Nikiphoros. He'd gone with Mitsos to Niki, a sizable new hut built south of Kryfi. It was located almost at the edge of the lake in order to train the youth from the Greek villages and teach them marksmanship.

Although Nikiphoros was missing, they did find a well-dressed girl with a decisive manner and slender white hands. She knew the names of all the men and spoke familiarly to them, like they were related.

It was Miss Electra. Jovan accompanied her; and he went over shyly and took refuge next to Apostolis, slipping his hand inside the older boy's.

However Apostolis was looking at his peer, Pericles. Dressed like the others, he stood out from them; and Apostolis tried to understand why. His outfit now had lost its freshness and showed signs of wear. Certainly his trousers had been ripped above the knee and were sewed together with thick thread. Still, he appeared exemplary—clean, well-groomed, and smart.

Could the way he held his head high be what distinguished him? Apostolis wondered. All the men seemed to consider him a friend. They spoke to him as an equal, as though they'd forgotten the difference in his age—that he was but a teenage boy like Apostolis himself . . .

Just as Vasilis climbed onto the deck, a white dog with black spots on his head flew out of the hut and started to jump up around him, up to his chest. The dog sniffed the other two a couple of times, Captain Akritas and Manolis, and then turned back to Vasilis.

Vasilis picked him up, and the introductions began.

Miss Electra had come from Zorba to see Captain Nikiphoros and ask him to keep Jovan at the hut.

"Why?" Apostolis inquired.

But Miss Electra didn't want to say.

"Because!" she replied, putting an end to further questioning.

The three newly-arrived men stared at the child. What would Nikiphoros do with this tot?

The "tot" didn't dare open his mouth. Bashful, as though to blame for something, he lowered his eyes and tried to become as small and inconspicuous as he could, burrowing inside the folds of Apostolis' cloak. Only when Vasilis spoke did he venture to look up at his white hair in surprise, as if it were the most curious thing at the hut.

Vasilis was looking at Jovan, too.

"Is he your apprentice, the little Bulgarian?" he asked Apostolis.

Jovan heard and grew red. Apostolis observed it and felt sympathy for him.

"Don't call him that . . . Have pity . . ." he said in a low voice. But Vasilis cut him off:

"And you gathered him from the likes of Angel Pio?"

Vasilis' eyes flashed. Turning his back to Apostolis, he walked further down.

Jovan had overheard him. He kept silent, turning away himself by the other side, pretending to watch the canoes going back and forth from the nearby oven.

Nikiphoros had left Manolis the Curlyhead in charge of the hut.

"Listen, Miss Electra," he said to the teacher. "The child can't remain here! We'll be making raids on the villages. And no one knows who will survive! Why don't you send him to Thessalonika, and from there they'll take him to Greece to one of the orphanages or schools they've opened up for the Bulgarian children we dispatch to them from time to time?"

Miss Electra extended her hand and stroked the child's head.

"Because!" she repeated with affection, "I'd like him here close-by."

"The commander must decide, then," the Curlyhead declared. "Do you want to go to Niki to see him? Panos, who's a good oarsman and knows the way, can take you."

"We'll go along too," Captain Akritas said with a gesture that included both Manolis and Vasilis. "He's the one we came to see."

It was settled at once. Leaving Jovan with Apostolis, Miss Electra entered a canoe with Vasilis and Panos. Behind in a smaller boat, Manolis followed with Gregos.

19.

Comitadjes

ABOVE NIKI, A LARGE, SOLIDLY-CONSTRUCTED HUT with a wide, fortified deck, the blue and white Greek flag was waving, unfurling in the cool, late-afternoon breeze.

The youths were at target-practice, firing at a square piece of wood they'd set up at a distance on a patch of waterlilies. Niki-phoros, once more shaven, clean, and well-groomed, was seated cross-legged on the floor, writing. Captain Pandelis and Mitsos, both with rifle in hand, were instructing the recruits how to handle their weapons.

Mitsos' handsome new clothes no longer distinguished him from the other rebels so much. On deck around the clock as he was, often inside the water and at times on long marches over the plain, his outfit had lost the freshness which was the envy of Captain Pandelis. The sun and wind had put color into his face and arms, and the simple, monotonous food at the hut had slimmed him down and made him firm and strong.

Suddenly a cry arose from the reeds:

"Cease firing! A v-i-s-i-t . . ."

Everyone stood with his weapon lowered, delighted and eager. The rare visits to Niki that occured were a welcome change and diversion.

Two canoes drew up. Recognizing Miss Electra, Nikiphoros got up.

"To what do we owe this pleasure?" he inquired, extending his hand to assist her onto the deck.

And immediately he introduced her: "Mitsos Vasiotakis, Miss Electra Drakou, a heroic colleague . . ."

"Not at all heroic," she said, greeting Mitsos.

Vasilis made an affirmative sign; and the three rebels—Vasilis, Akritas, and Manolis—climbed up on deck as the oarsmen tied up the canoes. Gregos couldn't take his eyes off Mitsos. But he didn't address him, or speak at all.

"What help do you seek from us?" Nikiphoros asked Miss Electra.

"You tell me what you can do to help," Miss Electra answered. "The comitadjes are ravaging the countryside and our Greek villages. They've burned down houses, killed the teacher Sophocles, and threaten everyday to do the same to Father Chrysostomos if he doesn't leave Bozets. Yesterday they entered my school—I don't know how—planted a bomb and ignited the fuse.

"As they rushed out, an article of clothing must have fallen and caught fire. Jovan, who's staying with me, smelled the burnt cloth, searched the kitchen, and snuffed out the lit fuse with his foot. What a scare! I don't want him there anymore. Alone I'll be freer, as I can fight better without the worry of the child. He shouldn't suffer."

"He's the nephew of . . ."

". . . of Angel Pio," Miss Electra interjected.

Vasilis was listening. His face twitched.

"And you want to save him?" he responded.

"How is the child to blame if he was born a Bulgarian?" Miss Electra asked, "and if his uncle is a comitadje?"

Vasilis didn't answer. His hands were shaking. Mitsos observed it and turned to the teacher:

"How does Pio's nephew happen to be with you?"

Miss Electra gave an account of his arrival one cold, rainy day at dusk with Captain Agras' message for Nikiphoros.

"Did you make sure it was really the message?" Mitsos inquired.

"Yes, it was," Nikiphoros replied. "And since then, he's done still other work for us . . ."

"You trust an offshoot of Pio?" Vasilis asked, his voice trembling. "He'll deceive you all and betray you."

For a moment, the others stopped short. Decisively, Miss Electra declared:

"No, he won't betray us. He's given evidence at the risk of his life that he's devoted to us."

Manolis spoke up:

"Why don't you believe, Vasilis, that he can become Greek?"

"Because, as the proverb goes: 'The wolf may grow old and white, but underneath he remains the same wolf as before,'" Vasilis replied. "How much more so with his offspring who's been reared in the rot of deception and treachery and hasn't yet suffered himself?"

"You're wrong," Captain Akritas' deep voice sounded, grown suddenly tender. "I observed the little Bulgarian. He appears both troubled and suffering, and sensitive as well. His big black eyes have a disturbing effect. He reminds me of one of my sisters . . ."

"Don't blaspheme!" Vasilis exclaimed angerly.

"It's not blasphemy. He resembles her, whether you like it or not," Gregos answered softly.

"Why don't you accept that he can become ours, Vasilis?" Manolis asked again. "It's occurred with others that are Bulgarian-speaking. Look at Captain Kottas and Captain Gonos! Didn't they join us? A perceptive child could be swayed to attach himself to us. And he could hate them."

"He hates them," Miss Electra assured him.

Vasilis kept quiet. His lips trembled from his passion. Nikiphoros changed the subject.

"Did you inform the police of the attempt to blow up your school?"

"Go to a Turk? Of course not! . . ." Miss Electra replied.

Mitsos, still unaccustomed to the Macedonian scene, looked at her inquiringly.

"If you don't ask for help from the authorities in charge, where will you seek it?" he wanted to know.

Miss Electra smiled, and it enlivened her somewhat austere face.

"From you," she answered. "From Captain Nikiphoros."

Nikiphoros scraped a little dried mud off his boot.

"You do well to rely more on us," he said. "But we must be informed in time."

Miss Electra smiled again.

"That's the reason I came. To tell you to send help right away if you, the Kryfi, Petra, or Apostoles huts hear pistol shots. Seeing that you're nearby, you'll arrive in time. I'll defend myself."

Once more, Mitsos stared at her with uncertainty. How could this girl defend herself? She was perhaps twenty years old. What did she know about war?

Miss Electra asked Nikiphoros:

"What will you do about the child? I'd like him to stay close."

"All right," Nikiphoros agreed. "Something can be arranged. Spring is coming. We'll fix him up somewhere. However why don't you go to Thessalonika, since the comitadjes are after you?"

"Leave my school?"

She said it with an air of such determination that Nikiphoros didn't insist.

"You judge . . ." he responded.

"Yes, I'll judge. And now I judge it necessary to set off in order to arrive back before dark, if possible. Could you let me out at the Petra landing-pier? It's closer to Zorba."

"We'll accompany you to the school," Nikiphoros replied.

Two canoes were readied immediately. Nikiphoros climbed into one, along with an oarsman, and assisted Miss Electra down into it. Mitsos followed in another, with an armed rower. Gregos jumped in beside him.

"You're coming, too, Captain Akritas?" Mitsos inquired to make conversation.

"Yes, Mister Vasiotakis," the rebel leader responded; and his deep voice seemed moved.

Mitsos reacted with surpirse.

"Why do you call me Mister?"

Instead of answering, Gregos asked in turn:

"How did your mother allow you come here with Vasilis? Doesn't she realize that it's a struggle to the death?"

Mitsos smiled.

"She realizes it. But she'd never stop me from a duty."

"And your father considers it your duty to find Vasilis' child?" Again Gregos' voice seemed to reflect emotion.

Mitsos became curious.

"Perhaps you know my father?"

At once the other curbed his tongue.

"Vasilis told me your father was seriously wounded in a battle . . . in '97," he said, feigning indifference.

"Yes, he was wounded. He almost died. But why are you interested, Captain Akritas? Could you have fought in '97, yourself?"

"No!" Gregos replied abruptly.

His behavior aroused Mitsos' curiosity even more.

"What is your relation to Vasilis?" he inquired. "You seem like the best of friends. However he's a Macedonian from the heart of Macedonia, while you're an Athenian, Captain Akritas . . . How did you become so close?"

Gregos shrugged his shoulders.

"We know each other," he said indifferently.

He fell silent, lost in contemplation, which it didn't seem right to Mitsos to interrupt now.

In the meantime at Niki, Vasilis was out on the deck with Manolis, watching the canoes disappear.

"Who does the girl live with?" he asked.

But Manolis didn't know her. It was Captain Pandelis who replied:

"She lives by herself at her school."

"The priest, at least, is nearby?"

"Zorba doesn't have a Greek church. The priest is Bulgarian."

"Does she have someone? Neighbors? Friends?"

"Everyone in the village is her friend," Captain Pandelis responded. "The same holds true in all the surroundings. But God protect her! If the help she sought from us today doesn't get there in time, she'll go the way of Katerina Hadji-georgiou."

"What happened to her?" Vasilis hadn't heard about it.

"She was a teacher; and because a Greek village to the north, inside Bulgaria, had been left to its fate, she opened up a school there. The Bulgarians warned they'd kill her, but she paid no attention and went on with her work. Then late one day the comitadjes encircled her school. For two hours she defended herself, pistol in hand, whereupon the Bulgarians set fire to the school. Suffocating from the smoke, Hadji-georgiou leaped from the window, along with two girls. All met a cruel death.

"First thing the next day, a force of ours retaliated by burning down the two Bulgarian villages where the murderers had taken refuge. You can be sure they took care of the criminals. Yet what did that mean? The brave Hadji-georgiou was gone, as were the others trapped in the school with her."

Manolis clenched his fists. "After all this, Captain Agras can still talk about sparing lives and offering second chances!"

"Captain Nikiphoros, too, wanted to use the gospel and the cross," Pandelis added. "But one or two trips to the outlying villages persuaded him, I think, that the Struggle won't be fought without bloodshed. Every day elders, priests, and teachers, even Turks, come to request our help after new Bulgarian atrocities. . . Let the Center give the sign and all together they'll pay for their crimes. We've had it up to our ears! Moreover we know where they're hiding. Bozets, Kourfalia, and a number of other villages are comitadje dens. Just let us get there . . ."

For a time, the three men were silent.

A tense Vasilis spoke up:

" . . . And the teacher from Zorba is trying to save a Bulgarian child!"

Late at night, they were still seated conversing when the canoes returned with Nikiphoros, Captain Akritas, and Mitsos. They'd accompanied the teacher to her school. All was peaceful in the village—but for how long?

"What I admire," the commander declared, "is the self-possession of this girl. She lives alone, closed up in her school, and acts as though it's nothing. The women of the Struggle are truly remarkable!"

* * * *

Back at Tsekri, sitting on the floor beside Apostolis, Jovan related what he'd seen and heard since the two boys separated. The child was worried. Petroff the coal-dealer had appeared at the school two times at night to secretly urge Miss Electra to leave. He was a member of the committee that was threatening the Greeks—and the Bulgarian priest was, too.

Yet Petroff didn't want anything to happen to Miss Electra, who'd cared for his daughter when she was sick, staying up a whole night to keep watch over her. He wanted the teacher to be aware that she'd suffer if she failed to go.

Laughing, she answered him: "Very well, Petroff!" and ignored his warning. Then yesterday, while removing the stew from the fire, he'd smelled burnt cloth. Under a stool near the window, he'd discovered a black iron ball with a lit fuse and a piece of burnt clothing. He remembered the time Bulgarians from an enemy faction had planted such a ball at Angel Pio's. The comitadje had trampled the fuse to put it out; and he'd beat Jovan for not noticing it and putting it out on his own. The ball, he said, would burn the house to the ground if it exploded.

"Are these balls what they call grenades, Apostolis?"

"More or less," Apostolis replied. "Only the grenades burst when they hit the ground, and they're smaller. Our grenades at the Bulgarian hut didn't go off. For that reason, Captain Agras wasn't able to capture it, in spite of all his daring. But what did you do with the bomb, seeing that you snuffed out the fuse?"

"Miss Electra wanted to bring it here. She said we shouldn't lose it."

They'd hidden it in a basket, covered it with parsley, and carried it with them.

Apostolis had spoken without focusing too much attention upon the child. His mind was on his peer Pericles, who was engaged in showing four or five men how to load their rifles more rapidly.

With good-nature, these veterans of the Struggle said to him:

"We'll make you a deputy commander, Pericles. Only let's see a moustache on you, so that they respect you when you shoot them!"

Pericles was lean and tall for his age, but still without a moustache. Nevertheless, he seemed able to impose his authority upon the war-seasoned rebels.

He'd imposed himself upon Apostolis as well. At first the guide had been struck by his composure, and by his spotless new uniform like Mitsos's. The two cousins had appeared out-of-place, like foreign elements, among the others who were sooty from gunpowder and smoke. That image didn't last long, though, amidst the rigorous life at the lake.

However Pericles remained well-groomed, and he was a crack shot—even surpassing the older, experienced rebels. It was as if he'd spent his life among battles, gunpowder, and bullets. And when he fixed his steady gaze on the men, with his head held high, he impressed them as a born leader. This bothered Apostolis somewhat. Still, at the same time it attracted him. He resolved to get to know him better in order to understand him—this boy who was his same age.

Withdrawing a little from the rest, Pericles had settled himself upon the deck with his dog on his lap, and was gazing thoughtfully at the river flowing before the hut. Apostolis stood up, told Jovan to wait, and approached and sat down beside him.

"Is this your first time here in the Swamp?" he asked casually.

"Yes!" Pericles answered. "Why?"

"How is it that you're so skilled with a rifle? Have you fought before?"

"I've never fought," Pericles replied. "However I was up in the mountains of Crete with rebels who had. And my grandfather who brought me up fought in the Revolution of '21. He raised me with a rifle and pistol, just as he'd been raised when even younger than I am, he went to war."

"Are you acquainted with Captain Akritas?"

"The one who came with Vasilis and left with the lady? No, I'm not. It's the first time I've seen him. Why do you ask?"

"Because . . . Does your cousin know him?"

"I'm not sure. But I don't think so."

"You're from Crete?"

"Yes."

"And your cousin?"

"He is also, but he lives in Alexandria, Egypt now—where I've been staying, too, with his family."

"Why did you come here?"

"We're seeking someone."

"I know—Takis, Vasilis' child. He's at Koulakia. I'll take Vasilis to see him."

"You're sure his child's at Koulakia?"

"I encountered him at the village school. According to the Master's command, I took someone disguised as a priest from Koulakia to Kleidi . . ."

"Matapas?"

"How do you know Matapas?"

"I don't know him, yet I've heard of him. Didn't he pretend to be the abbot of a monastery for four months before he entered the Swamp?"

"Yes! And after that?"

"After that, I don't know. Are you aware of where he is?"

"Yes! I didn't see him, but I know. Do you want to meet him?"

"Do I! When will you go there again?"

"I'm setting off now with Vasilis to find his child."

"I mean to go along!"

"Fine! From there it's easy."

"Where is he?"

"I'll guide you if the commander consents to it," Apostolis said cautiously.

Pericles smiled.

"You do well to be on guard. You don't know me."

A little embarrassed, Apostolis explained:

"No . . . but . . . I've taken an oath. It's the rule for those who've been sworn in not to speak out or ask questions. There are thousands of us. But no one knows about his fellow members who've been initiated. That's how the organization operates. If one of us is caught and questioned, even if he'd like to, he's not able to answer. With secret signs we understand if the person we're talking to has been sworn in. You haven't, nor has your cousin. Vasilis has."

"How do you know?"

"Vasilis responds to secret signs. You and your cousin don't."

Pericles paused to reflect. Then he inquired:

"Is there anyone here to swear me in?"

"I don't know. None of us do—that is, of us 'soldiers.' Perhaps the commander knows."

For some time Pericles contemplated.

"Would it be right for you to tell me who initiated you?"

"No! We give an oath not to reveal it."

Again, the boys remained silent.

Then Pericles said:

"I left my uncle's house without his permission. He's kind and he forgave me. His mother assured me of it. She left with us and is in Thessalonika now. The Macedonian Struggle drew me here; however I never imagined it would be so exciting!"

"You see? And you still haven't fought in a battle! If you'd been up close to Zervohori when Agras attacked the hut! . . ."

A deep growl from Mangas on Pericles' lap, interrupted him.

Pericles bent down over his dog.

"What is it, Mangas?" he asked, stroking the dog's head. With his ears pricked up, the dog went on growling softly but angerly, wrinkling his nose and uncovering his teeth.

Pericles raised Mangas' head and looked him in the eyes:

"Bad?" he asked.

The dog's growling grew more intense.

"Softly, Mangas," Pericles said. "We'll find him . . ."

The dog wagged his tail, got up poised to spring forward, and continued growling, only lower.

"Stop, Mangas," Pericles ordered.

The dog stopped. But all at once he uncovered his teeth further and shook all over, swaying on his back legs, prepared to dart away.

"Why is he acting that way?" Apostolis inquired.

"He smells an enemy," Pericles answered, staring at a canoe which appeared from a Swamp path.

Apostolis turned and observed the canoe.

"It's our lads with a Turk," he said.

Captain Manolis the Curlyhead, in charge of the hut during the commander's and Pandelis' absence, had also noticed it. Rising, he waved. However as the boat pulled up, Mangas became nearly uncontrollable.

The Curlyhead looked around, saw him, and chuckled.

"Aren't you ashamed, Mangas?" he exclaimed.

Pericles was holding the dog by his collar, trying to quiet him.

"It's the first time you've seen Ali, eh?" the Curlyhead responded with a smile. Leaning over, he petted the dog. "But he's good, good . . ." he continued reassuringly. "He's with us . . ."

The Turk had climbed up onto the deck and greeted the men in a friendly manner. Nevertheless Mangas went on softly growling and trembling.

"Is he always this way with strangers?" Apostolis asked.

Pericles shook his head "no."

"Like the Cretan that he is, then, it seems he hates Turks . . ." Apostolis commented in a low voice.

"No, he's not Cretan. He's an English breed," Pericles replied. "Besides, he doesn't especially hate Turks. Yesterday another Turk arrived and he received him well enough. A dog's instinct doesn't deceive him."

Apostolis laughed.

"Miss Electra says I have a hunting dog's instinct," he said. "This time I agree with Mangas. I don't like this Turk."

One of the men who was nearby overheard his last words.

"You're mistaken," he told him softly. "First, he's not a Turk—he's Albanian. Second, he's in the commander's service. On many occasions he's brought us important news and information . . ."

The Curlyhead said to Ali:

"The commander's not here, but you can inform me."

"Better, you tell me where the captain is," Ali insisted.

"I don't know. For him to be late, he's about some work. Say what you've got to say to me."

"What will you give me if I tell you where Chief Apostol's hiding out?" the Albanian asked.

"Go to the devil!" the Curlyhead responded. "You're paid two liras a month to report these things to us, and you want even more?"

"I won't speak, then!"

"As you please!" Captain Manolis answered with a shrug of his shoulders. "But at the end of the month, don't come to take your liras because the commander won't give them to you!"

Mangas let out another angry growl. Ali glanced at him, unconcerned, then said to the Curlyhead:

"Tell your boss that Petkoff was in Ramel yesterday—a piece of information for you."

"Do you know anything else?' the Curlyhead questioned him.

"If it were the captain, I'd say more," the Albanian replied in jest.

"All right. Sit down and we'll have a cup of coffee—while you tell it to me," the Curlyhead said, easy-going now.

Mangas was so agitated that Pericles stood up.

"Let's go and row," he said to Apostolis. "Bring Jovan along."

When they returned, the Albanian had departed. Pericles inquired and learned that Ali worked for Captain Nikiphoros, providing him regularly with news of the Bulgarians' movements and serving as a link between Nikiphoros and the Turkish beys of the region. For the beys often sought support from the Greek forces against the Bulgarian bands; and in exchange, they sent food, tobacco, and above all ammunition.

Ali had brought still other news this time. Two known comitadjes in two different villages in the western area of the lake had been found killed in the same way, each with a knife driven into his heart. A third had disappeared. The Turks were all upset. Such murders had occurred in the northern villages, but the murderer had left no sign to enable the Turks to discover him. The Bulgarians, for their part, were terror-striken, saying that the Eviscerator had passed through their villages.

Ali had affected reluctance to say all this; however, the Curlyhead coaxed him and gave him a gift of food for speaking.

"Naturally, we hear what we want to learn," Captain Manolis remarked, "without our telling either this Albanian or the Turk yesterday more than we're willing to reveal. You saw that we didn't disclose where the commander was."

"Then Mangas and I were deceived?" Apostolis asked Pericles later.

Pericles, though, only shook his head and didn't reply.

The two boys became bound more closely that evening than all the other days they'd been together. It was a chilly night at the end of February, and they'd wrapped themselves in their cloaks and reclined outside on the deck with Jovan, conversing until it was late. Apostolis related his life story to Pericles—one of perpetual activity as a child with no home, working from a young age to earn his bread. Pericles in turn introduced him to the history of the '21 Revolution. Jovan, too, listened insatiably; and when they dropped off to sleep that night, their heads were full of new knowledge and yearnings.

Suddenly, towards two in the morning a series of pistol shots, one after the other, awakened the hut. After falling silent for a spell, they started up again, and then volleys split the air.

"Those are Gras rifles . . ." the Curlyhead stated. "They're at a distance, towards Petra, perhaps Kryfi . . . Maybe Niki . . ."

Apostolis licked his finger and held it up to determine the direction of the wind.

"It's blowing from the southeast. The firing is coming from the shore."

"Nasos!" the Curlyhead shouted. "Take a canoe with . . . with . . . Who is the most skilled oarsman?"

"I am!" Apostolis cried. "And I know the paths. I'll go!"

"So will I!" Pericles said.

The volleys had stopped, yet the pistol shots, along with on and off rifle fire, continued.

"Go down to Niki, then, and find out what's happening," the Curlyhead ordered. "In the meantime, I'll go out on land with ten men. Wherever the battle is, we'll find the scoundrels!"

Armed, the two boys were already in the canoe, moving off, when Mangas leaped in next to them.

At the edge of the deck, with his hands clasped together, Jovan watched them in agony. But Apostolis had forgotten him. He'd grabbed the oar and, together with Nasos, was rowing with all his strength, steering the boat towards a deep fork in the Loudias River.

The gunshots kept up, at times intense, then again sporadic. They didn't end, though. No one in the canoe spoke. With anguish they were listening to the firing, trying to imagine what was taking place.

All at once the Gras shooting ceased, and silence spread over the lake.

Time passed. And once more, repeated pistol fire as if calling for help.

But from where?

Resolutely they rowed on, striking the bottom of the lake where the water was shallow.

Steady firing . . . Then bright light burst out on shore. Nasos crossed himself.

"Fire! . . ." he murmured.

Gunshots, one after another again . . . followed by constant volleys . . .

"Gras . . . and now Mauser rifles," Pericles said. "Two opposing forces are battling on shore."

"Well, let's go," Apostolis shouted.

"The command was for Niki," Nasos replied. "Yet can you get there for sure, when they're fighting so close?"

In his anxiety, Pericles stood up.

"Take it upon yourself, Nasos!" he exclaimed. "Let's go to the battle! Look how Mangas is leading us on!"

The dog, with his hair raised and his nose strained forward, broke into strangled cries. His eyes were fixed on the fire to the left. He too was in distress. Nasos made his decision.

"We'll go!" he declared, "whatever happens . . ."

He turned the boat to the left in the direction of the shore, now illuminated by the fire. The gunshots continued, grew faint, and died out . . . Pericles consulted his watch. The firing had lasted for two hours.

With an onrush they approached the shore, passing among the reeds that Pericles opened up with his hands from the prow. Casting the dugout on the ground, the three set out to orient themselves. But Mangas sped away, running along the shore and barking to call them. They rushed after him up to a landing-cove, where many canoes were gathered.

An oarsman was guarding them. Upon seeing the three rebels, he pointed to the fire.

"It's over," he said. "They're coming back."

"Who?" all three asked simultaneously.

"Captain Nikiphoros. He went to Zorba."

Pericles bent down to the dog.

"The commander, Mangas! The commander! Hurry! Find him!"

Like an arrow Mangas took off towards the fire, with the two boys and Nasos behind him. They'd almost reached the village when a shadow rose up before them. A rifle flashed.

"Halt!" the guard shouted. And he added in Greek: "No one's to pass."

"Let us by, Andreas. I'm Apostolis the guide, and these two are Captain Nikiphoros' men," Apostolis answered. "We're here to help."

"Look, they're already returning!" Andreas said. "Their work is finished."

In fact, a couple of men were nearly there, with a band of armed rebels appearing after them.

"What did you do, Commander?" Nasos inquired.

In the lead, Nikiphoros had a worried look.

"We beat them," he said. "They're gone; they've scattered. But the teacher . . ."

He raised his hand in a sorrowful gesture.

"Did they kill her?" Apostolis cried out.

"We put out the fire at the school. The barn is still burning," Nikiphoros replied. "However we didn't find her, either dead or alive."

"The school burned down?" Apostolis responded, more and more disturbed.

"A part of it, not the whole school," Mitsos answered, drawing near. "The villagers assisted us. They extinguished the fire, while Captain Akritas hunted for the comitadjes. But the teacher was nowhere to be found."

"Miss Electra isn't dumb," Apostolis said, aroused. "For her to surrender—she'd never do it. Let's go back! We'll find her."

"Forward, Mangas," Pericles ordered. "Be about your work!"

They raced back to the school with Captain Nikiphoros, Mitsos, and all the force. Apostolis was in the lead.

The wall enclosure of the school still held firm, although the outer door had been smashed with axes and fallen inside. A classroom window had its shutters broken and burnt; and the school door stood wide-open.

The villagers had dispersed. To one side, much of the barn was in ashes.

"Do you know where her clothes are, Apostolis?" Pericles asked.

"Yes," Apostolis replied.

He went straight into Miss Electra's bedroom. Destruction and havoc. The mattress was burnt, the chairs half-burnt, the cabinet battered in, and the clothes strewn around. Pericles took an article of clothing, rolled it up, and gave it to Mangas to smell.

"Search, Mangas," he said. "Search!"

Half-crying, anxious, nervous, Mangas jumped into the cabinet and out again. Sniffing the floor, he darted into the next room, up onto the ledge of the now open window, back down, and on into the kitchen.

Nikiphoros followed with some of the men.

"I knew it! I knew it!" Apostolis shouted, unable to control himself from his excitement.

And turning to Captain Nikiphoros:

"Commander," he begged. "Send your men away. Have them go outside, and you come with Mitsos."

Captain Nikiphoros, the two boys, Mitsos, and Captain Pandelis entered the kitchen and closed the door.

"Search!" Pericles exclaimed again and again, inciting the dog.

Mangas, though, no longer had need of incitement. He dashed right to the fireplace. Half-barking, half-crying, he scratched at the floor.

"I knew it, I knew it!" Apostolis repeated in a strangled voice. "Mister Mitsos, Pericles, help!"

On his knees, he shoved away a sack of sand that had fallen and spilled. With his hands, he brushed the sand aside and uncovered an iron ring. Mangas couldn't be quieted now. He burst back and forth—barking, crying, biting at the iron.

"Quickly," Apostolis said, taking hold of the ring.

With Nikiphoros' aid, he raised a trap-door and uncovered a black hole.

"Miss Electra!" Apostolis called in agony.

But no one answered.

"Is there a candle?" Captain Nikiphoros inquired.

Apostolis had sprung onto a stool and seized a little oil lamp still standing up on the shelf. Nikiphoros struck a match and lit it.

"Hold it, Pericles," he said. "And you, Apostolis, since you're shorter I'll lower you."

Nikiphoros lay down on the floor, while Apostolis hung from his hands and descended into the black hole. Pericles lit the way from above.

"She's here," Apostolis' strangled voice sounded. "I can't manage alone, though. Wait and I'll put up the ladder."

Indeed, he lifted a ladder up from inside and leaned it against the edge of the trap-door. Mitsos didn't wait for it. Suspending himself by his hands, he leaped below. Captain Nikiphoros, slower in his movements, climbed down the ladder; while from above Pericles cast light on them.

For a moment nothing was heard. Then the voice of Nikiphoros exclaimed:

"She's alive! But we must remove her from here."

A few minutes elapsed. Slowly, with difficulty, Captain Nikiphoros made his way up the ladder carrying a body over his shoulder. Mitsos supported it from behind.

Captain Pandelis helped the commander bring her out through the trap-door, and Mitsos and Apostolis both climbed up. All together they lay her down.

Miss Electra was dressed as a man. Her jacket was blood-stained on the shoulder, and her black braid soaked with blood.

"We need to take her outside to get some air," Captain Nikiphoros said. "First of all, we must revive her. After that, we'll see."

"And the hiding-place has to be closed up, Commander," Apostolis declared, never losing sight of his work. "It's the best hideout in the village. They mustn't discover it!"

When the trap-door was back in place, Apostolis hunted for a piece of wood on the floor. Finding it, he covered the ring and poured and spread sand from above.

As soon as the night air entering freely from the window reached her, Miss Electra recovered. Opening her eyes, she saw her friends hovering over her uneasily; and startled, she sat up.

Sharp pain in her shoulder reminded her of what had happened.

"How did you find me there?" she asked, glancing over at the hiding-place.

*Slowly . . . Nikiphoros made his way up the ladder carrying
a body over his shoulder.*

"We'll talk about it later," Nikiphoros replied. "However your wounds need to be tended to."

"Not here! We'll get embroiled with the Turks! Let's be off! Let's go!" Miss Electra cried. "They'll overtake you."

"How can you walk in the condition you're in?" Mitsos asked.

Miss Electra laughed.

"Do you take me for the kind of a woman who becomes frightened by a little blood?"

She made an effort to rise, had some difficulty in getting up, then grit her teeth and succeeded.

"Let's be off!" she repeated. "Immediately!"

She was so determined that the men didn't argue.

Leaning on Nikiphoros' arm, Miss Electra passed into the courtyard where the rebels were waiting.

"Tie your rifles together. Make a stretcher to carry the lady . . ." Nikiphoros began.

"For shame, Commander," the teacher interrupted him. "I'll walk. Only hurry."

They all went out into the road. Miss Electra threw a final glance back.

"My poor school!" she murmured.

She was the first to proceed. But they'd only taken a few steps when other rebels rushed up to them.

"Quickly! Quickly! The Turks are coming!"

"From where?" Captain Nikiphoros asked.

"From Plati and Koutalar. Villagers have come out to calm them down. They'll tell them the Bulgarians burned the school and then left, so that there's no need for the army to advance. Perhaps they'll delay them a little, but they won't stop them. Make haste! We have to be off!"

A deep voice could be singled out from the others, asserting itself:

"We'll manage, provided we move fast."

"Captain Akritas! Vasilis! You've arrived in the nick of time," Nikiphoros exclaimed. "Captain Akritas, you're the strongest. You carry the young lady."

Miss Electra tried to protest. Without more ado, Gregos lifted her in his arms like a child; and together they all fled toward the Swamp. The countryside was bare, without a tree. At times shrubs relieved the stark plain. A couple of men hid behind them to guard their withdrawal, then pulled back to other shrubs—a process that was continued until they reached the edge of the lake.

It was daybreak.

Gregos all but flew into a canoe with his load. The others packed in, abandoning Nasos' dugout tied further down shore. They headed for Niki, Captain Nikiphoros' large, well-built new hut that was concealed among thick beds of reeds.

As soon as they got there, Miss Electra fainted again, leaving the men at a loss. No woman was nearby. And they were primarily fighters; they didn't know how to care for her.

"Will you let me take charge of her?" Pericles asked. "In the mountains of Crete, far away from any hospital, my grandfather taught me how to bandage wounds."

"If you can help her, do so," Nikiphoros said, used to waging war but not to treating injuries.

After a pause, he added:

"Only be careful not to hurt the poor girl . . ."

Gregos carried the teacher inside the hut.

"Ask for bandages and an antiseptic," Pericles whispered to Apostolis. "And then return to assist me."

With a penknife, he cut Miss Electra's jacket at the shoulder, exposing a small hole where the blood had dried.

"The bullet is inside," he informed Apostolis—who was helping him with his skillful, yet gentle hands. "But the head? What can we do with so much hair?"

"Wait," Apostolis responded. "We'll remove all the hairpins and find the wound . . ."

"There's no need," Pericles interrupted. "See! It's not a head wound. A bullet took away the upper part of her ear."

"So much blood?" Apostolis wondered.

"Don't you know? The ear puts out a lot of blood. She'll remain a little scarred, but the scar will be her glory."

Miss Electra recovered consciousness before Pericles finished the bandaging. Seeing the two boys, she became alarmed.

"What are you doing to me!" she cried, trying to cover her bare shoulder.

And complaining, almost in tears, she added:

"Why do you let them undress me, Apostolis?"

Apostolis stroked her hands.

"Don't carry on that way, Miss Electra," he pleaded. "We had to wash your wound, and Pericles is experienced."

Fully recovered now, Miss Electra made light of her initial fear.

"Thank you very much, boys. However, such a fuss for a simple scratch wasn't necessary."

"It's not a simple scratch, Miss Electra. You have a bullet inside your shoulder that a doctor must remove," Pericles stated. "Do you want the commander to come inside? You should depart as quickly as possible."

"It would be preferable for all of us to go outside," Miss Electra answered. "It's a beautiful day."

With her shoulder bandaged and her arm hanging limp, she got up herself and cheerfully stepped out on deck. Worried, the men were conferring together in low voices. When they saw her, they were shaken.

"We were considering how to transport you, and here you're walking!" Nikiphoros exclaimed.

Miss Electra sat down on an empty, overturned case that Mitsos provided.

"What are you plotting without consulting me?" she asked.

"We're plotting to take you to Thessalonika today, at once," Nikiphoros replied.

"Does it matter if it's tomorrow?" the teacher inquired, half-laughing, half-serious. "I have a slight headache . . ."

Nikiphoros turned to Apostolis.

"The hair . . ." he said.

But the teacher broke in, feeling the thick braid that crowned her forehead:

"I know; it's still bloody . . . and damp. Yet I don't want to loosen my hair. It's a nuisance, and I'm not able to wash it here . . ."

"But neither can you remain without a bandage," Mitsos said.

Miss Electra smiled at Pericles.

"My doctor tended to me," she replied, placing her hand on a gauze attached to her ear with sticking plaster. "It's not my head that was hit. A scratch on the ear caused such confusion and blood."

"But how were you wounded?" Nikiphoros asked. "And how is it that they didn't find you?"

Miss Electra slowly moved her limp arm. Refllecting, she said:

"There are some good men among them. One is the Bulgarian coal-dealer Petroff. I'd gone to bed, when I heard beating at the window. It took me back since I'd locked the outer door of the courtyard. Where could they have entered? Getting up, I called out to see who it was. It was Petroff. He'd climbed up the wall—a man no longer young—to warn me that comitadjes were on their way to kill me. He brought the men's clothes I'm wearing, so that I could escape with him. I put the clothes on, but couldn't bring myself to leave. I figured that if you came in time, I'd save my school.

"Just as I heard them in the road, I let off a succession of pistol shots, as we'd agreed. They responded with a volley of rifle fire—to scare me, I guess, because they were outside and couldn't see in. I didn't answer. Then they broke down the outer door and surrounded the school. With the butts of their rifles, they tried to smash in the inner door. Dressed as I was in men's clothing, I went over to a window and fired into the crowd. One fell. The others drew back. They'd found a man where they didn't expect any and took fright.

"Still, how much can one pistol do? Once more, they approached the school. I fired from all the windows, one after another, like there were many men inside. Were they fooled in the beginning? I don't know. They came closer, but didn't enter—shooting off volley after volley. At one window, a bullet hit me in the shoulder—the left one, fortunately, so I could continue to resist. But they brought axes and started chopping at the shutters. I fired and struck where I could. When someone fell, the others retreated for a little.

"However they returned. The barn had been set in flames; and realizing they would come in and catch me, I ran to the kitchen. A bullet pierced my ear and I grew dizzy—although I succeeded in opening the trap-door and climbing down. But I could hear the gunfire, their voices and their racing around. I'd been able to remove the ladder; and from below I made out your volleys. When you arrived, I tried to put the ladder back in place to climb up, then became dizzy again and fell. After that, I don't remember."

The men listened, fascinated. Apostolis was following the narration with all his senses, eagerly awaiting the words from her lips.

"How many did you kill, Miss Electra?" he asked, holding his breath.

Softly she said:

"No one, I hope. It's horrible to shoot to kill. A battle is dreadful. Yet I had to give you time to arrive."

The men were stirred. There was silence. But Mitsos broke it:

"One thing I don't understand. Before he found the ring for the trap-door, Apostolis removed some sand that had poured onto the floor. Who poured it?"

Smiling, the teacher cast a glance at Apostolis.

"Ah, this is our pride!" she said. "Apostolis and I practiced and practiced to learn how to do it. Upon entering the hiding-place, we had to cover it up. Otherwise it would be to no avail. Therefore we placed a sack of sand at the edge of the hole, tilted slightly towards the part with the ring. In closing the door, we tugged at the sack so that the sand would fall slowly and spread. Another time we'd had no trouble. However today I was dazed and pulled hurriedly at the sack. Some sand spilled into the hiding-place, and I was uneasy the ring might not be covered up. When I heard them running back and forth in the kitchen, smashing furniture and plates, I broke into a cold sweat. Imagine my relief when I heard your firing."

"Then you knew that help had arrived?" Nikiphoros asked. "We didn't find you, though. We were leaving, thinking they'd killed or captured you. If this child hadn't appeared," he added, indicating Apostolis, "we wouldn't have discovered you."

"You're still new at this war, Commander," Gregos declared in his deep voice. "Now that you're going out into the villages, keep in mind that there's not one without its hiding-places. When you fail to find the beast you're after, seek his cave. If you don't find it, set fire to the house and he'll be trapped like a mouse in his hole. That's how one of the worse criminals terrorizing the Greek villages ended up, along with his force. The Bulgarians know these tactics well; they're aware that hideouts exist everywhere. Why do you think they burned Miss Electra's school?"

"Frightful," Mitsos murmured.

Nikiphoros raised his head.

"Yes, frightful. I'm still not used to these mutual slaughters . . ."

Enunciating his words, Vasilis spoke up:

"If they'd killed your mother, wife, and child, you'd understand, Commander . . . and you'd grow used to it."

No one uttered a word. Then, in order to divert the men's thoughts, Nikiphoros said:

"Our first job now is to see how to take Miss Electra to Thessalonika. Apostolis, since you brought Captain Agras, what is the easiest way?"

Without hesitating, Apostolis replied:

"By canoe to Kryfi, and from there we'll descend the Loudias River to Plati. After that, by train to Thessalonika. This evening we'll be there."

"Is the station at Plati near the river?" Nikiphoros inquired.

"No," Apostolis answered, a little disconcerted. "We'll have to walk."

Gregos cut him off with a motion of his hand.

"It doesn't matter. The girl won't walk," he said with his deep, warm voice. "Don't worry, Commander. In any case, Vasilis and I want to get going today—Vasilis for Koulakia and I for the retreat . . . You know."

Troubled, Nikiphoros said:

"It's not right for them to catch sight of you at Plati, Captain Akritas."

"Don't worry," Gregos replied. "With Turkish clothes, Vasilis will pass. Once it turns dark, I will, too. Eh, Vasilis? It won't be the first or last time for us. Only we need Apostolis as a guide."

"Who will accompany her to Thessalonika?" Captain Niki-phoros asked.

"I will, of course!" Apostolis said. "I have a written pass from Halil-bey to come and go freely to Thessalonika."

"Where will you be afterwards?" Vasilis inquired. "You'll take me to Koulakia this time?"

"Certainly! We'll set a day for you to hide at Plati. I'll tell you where."

Once more Gregos raised his hand.

"We'll discuss it on the road," he said.

* * * *

In the afternoon they started off. Pericles wanted to go along.

"Didn't we come to find your child?" he asked Vasilis.

"Yes, Mister Pericles . . . But things at the Swamp aren't as simple as in Alexandria. Many men can't move around together. You and Mister Mitsos wait for me here, providing the commander gives his permission. And I'll meet up with you again when I return—if we find the child . . ."

"Aren't you hopeful, Vasilis?" Miss Electra asked sympathetically.

But Vasilis didn't answer.

20.

Takis

THE DOCTOR'S HOUSE IN THESSALONIKA was the center, the *nest* of the Struggle. A friend of the beys and generally of the Turks, the doctor was trusted and consulted whenever they became ill. And every time a Greek found himself in difficulty, the doctor intervened on his behalf, often rescuing him.

"That one? But I know him; he's a friend! . . ." he would exclaim.

He saved many rebels from frightful Turkish dungeons and other ordeals with the authorities, and from harassment by the European Powers who sent agents and police to Macedonia under the pretext of putting Turkey's internal affairs in order. Each Power sought to benefit itself at the expense of the Christian minorities subject to the corrupt Turkish yoke, especially the Greeks.

Upon arriving in Thessalonika with Apostolis, Miss Electra went directly to the doctor's house, where she received care, hospitality, sympathy, and companionship—as well as support and encouragement.

"You mustn't leave," the doctor told her. "We removed the bullet from your shoulder, and we'll rebuild your school. The General Consul will find the money, since the building didn't burn down completely and only needs repairs. Rest in bed, get well, and don't worry about anything else . . ."

Relieved when he heard it, Apostolis left her with the doctor's kind wife and returned to Plati. Coming out of the station, he set off for the bridge, expecting to meet his companion. However Turkish soldiers were on guard at that hour, and no rebels appeared.

Apostolis kept his wits about him. With his hands in his pockets, he crossed the bridge along with villagers and soldiers, and resumed his way—seemingly nonchalant. Suddenly a running child stumbled against him, fell down at his feet, and threw him to the ground, too. Before Apostolis could succeed in getting up again, the child stuffed something into his pocket, leaped to his feet, and was off again running towards the bridge.

Apostolis was familiar with these maneuvers. Unruffled by the incident, he headed towards a deserted spot and searched in his pocket. He discovered a piece of paper with "Kara-Azmak— riverbank" written on it in pencil.

It had rained the evening before, so that the marshy plain was muddier and stickier than usual. Traipsing through the mud, Apostolis followed the edge of the riverbank and drew to the south in desolate country. He'd walked for about half an hour when, by a bush with thorns, a man stood up. It was Vasilis. Apostolis looked all around—no one else.

"Captain Akritas? . . ." he asked.

"He has other work," Vasilis answered. "Let's go to Koulakia to ease our conscience."

"Don't you believe Takis is your lost child?" Apostolis inquired.

"That the Bulgarians saved a Greek child?" Vasilis responded, shaking his head.

"They didn't save him," Apostolis replied. "Our captains— Bouas, Akritas, and Garefis—caught some Bulgarian bear-trainers, who were then put on a boat that sank at Kokova. And it happened that Takis wasn't on the boat at the time the Bulgarians drowned. One of Captain Akritas' lads happened to go to the monastery nearby, and he took the child with him. Thus Takis escaped. Seeing that he's such a friend, didn't Captain Akritas tell you about it?" Apostolis added with a touch of irony, stressing Captain Akritas' name.

But Vasilis ignored the question.

"How did he come to be at Koulakia?" he asked.

"He was at Koulakia because the Bulgarians burned Nisi, where the mother of Miss Aspasia, the teacher at Koulakia, was living; and she happened to have the child with her. All the inhabitants of Nisi migrated to Koulakia."

"That's a lot of things that *happened*," Vasilis declared with disbelief. "Did the child ever speak to you about me? About his house? About his mother?"

"No," Apostolis confessed. "That *didn't happen*! I'd seen Takis on a couple of occasions at Miss Aspasia's school, without paying attention to him. When I learned his history, that he wasn't related to her but had been taken in from kindness, I didn't have time to question him. I had work to do and left right away."

"With the fake-priest you accompanied to Kaliani?"

Apostolis gave a start.

"How did you know I took him to Kaliani?" he inquired.

Vasilis stopped short. However he remained composed.

"Didn't you tell me?"

"I? Certainly not! I never talk about the work they give me."

"I imagined it, then," Vasilis said.

Apostolis made no reply. His restless mind began to ponder.

Seemingly indifferent, Vasilis pursued the conversation:

"Where did you bring the fake-priest, since it wasn't Kaliani?"

"I didn't say it wasn't Kaliani. I wondered how you guessed it! . . ."

"You would have taken him somewhere with a church. Perhaps that's why I hit upon Kaliani . . ." And he went on, unconcerned: "How far is it from here to Koulakia?"

"We'll get there quickly," Apostolis replied. "But the Axios River has overflown; we'll have to make a detour."

* * * *

They continued their journey in silence. As usual, there wasn't much talk with Vasilis. He trudged through the mud without a word. After a hasty snack of bread and cheese, they pressed on—often into water that flooded their path. Late in the evening, they reached Koulakia.

Apostolis led Vasilis straight to Miss Aspasia's house.

A light was burning at a window. Apostolis threw a stone against the closed shutter and called out:

"Open up, Miss Aspasia."

The window opened and a woman's form came into view, lit up from inside.

"Who is it?" she asked.

"It's Apostolis the guide, Miss Aspasia!"

"At such an hour! Wait, I'll come down! . . ."

She closed the window again; and in a short time the door unlocked and Miss Aspasia arrived, holding up an oil lamp. Observing a man in the dark, she hesitated, uncertain.

"You're not alone?" she murmured.

"Don't be afraid. Let us in, Miss Aspasia," Apostolis replied. "We're seeking a lost child . . ."

"Ah! You're with Father Gregory?" she interrupted, smiling.

An abrupt movement from Vasilis cut her off. She stopped, paralyzed, lamp in hand.

Apostolis was startled as well. A memory flashed into his mind. Miss Aspasia had heard almost the same words before from the so-called priest: "I'm seeking the lost child of a friend!" They were said in the same deep voice that had declared: "Come what may, good luck!" to Vasilis at the hide-out in the mountain. And with the same warm tone that had assured them: "The girl won't walk, don't worry, Commander!" at the Niki hut.

Shaken, Apostolis asked:

"Is Gregory the name of the priest I accompanied the last time I was here? The priest who was also looking for a child . . .? Was he called Gregory?"

Miss Aspasia froze. She'd raised her lamp and was staring at Vasilis, who stared back at her in silence.

"Do you think I can remember all the priests that travel by here?" she countered, groping for words. "Rather, you tell me what you're about and who the man with you is."

Meanwhile she'd brought them into the kitchen. Without waiting for an answer, she remarked:

"You'll be hungry. What can I offer you?"

"We don't want anything, thank you," Vasilis replied. "Apostolis says you have an orphan at your house. Can you give me details about him?"

Apostolis had seated himself at the table, his elbows on the wood plank and his chin in his hands. He didn't seem to be listening. His mind was busy searching and probing . . . The fake-priest was called Gregory, the false Akritas, Gregos . . .

"You're referring to Takis?" Miss Aspasia responded. "He's been with me for two and a half years now. However there are many things I don't know about him. Nor does he remember much himself. He knows that the Bulgarians took him, but where he was before, I haven't been able to learn."

"Could I see him?" Vasilis inquired.

"Now? He's sleeping in the loft. He was exhausted and went to bed early. Won't you stay here to sleep, and see him tomorrow?"

"What do you think, Apostolis?" Vasilis asked sharply. "Aren't you listening to Miss Aspasia?"

Hearing his name, Apostolis was caught unawares.

"No! I was thinking about something else. What did you say Miss Aspasia?"

"That you should sleep here. I don't have a mattress to give you, but at least you'll be protected if it rains."

"We're used to sleeping on the ground," Vasilis answered. "We'll stay. Thank you."

He spoke wearily, as though he was tired and it didn't much interest him if he did or didn't see the orphan who might be his child.

Miss Aspasia, too, seemed in a hurry to be off. Leaving the lamp with them, she went out the door and back up to her room.

Putting out the light, Vasilis lay down on the floor and didn't speak again.

* * * *

Apostolis' thoughts returned to his last visit to Miss Aspasia's school. He sought to tie together countless small observations that had no continuity, but that bothered him. Until sleep overcame him . . .

When he woke in the morning, he found the door open. Stepping out into the courtyard, he saw Vasilis. Washed and tidy with his clothes dusted off, he was sitting on the ledge of a well, contemplating. Hurriedly Apostolis also washed up, with water from the well.

"Did you see anyone, Mister Vasilis?" he inquired.

"No," Vasilis replied.

Removing bread and goat's cheese from his sack, he gave it to the boy.

"It's still early," he said. "I'll wait for him here."

Once more, he fell into his accustomed silence.

After a while footsteps sounded, descending the stairs. Miss Aspasia's head appeared at the door. Viewing her two visitors, she turned back and called:

"Takis, come quickly!"

Apostolis noticed the color drain from Vasilis' face and his hands begin to tremble.

Miss Aspasia entered, holding Takis by the hand. Approaching, she bid her two guests "good-morning."

However without answering, Vasilis raised the child's face and looked into his eyes.

"No," he said. "His eyes are green. My child's were black, like his mother's."

Without another word or even thanking Miss Aspasia, who seemed stunned, he went out onto the road and left.

Dumbfounded by Vasilis' behavior, Apostolis tried to justify him.

"He's a very unfortunate man, Miss Aspasia. Don't be upset with him."

"I'm not upset with him," Miss Aspasia responded. "Only I'm sorry he didn't find his child, and Takis his father."

She smiled with tears in her eyes, and added:

"What a wonderful end to a novel it would have been."

And stroking Takis' head, she murmured:

"My poor orphan!"

All at once Takis threw his arms around her waist and burst out crying.

"I was afraid! . . . Ah, how I was afraid you would give me to that fierce man with the black eyebrows! . . ." he said between sobs. "And I don't want, I don't want to leave you, Miss Aspasia! . . ."

* * * *

Shaken to the core, Apostolis departed.

Look! he reflected. You can do bad, attempting to do good! How hard Takis cried! And how much affection Miss Aspasia showed him, in tears herself! . . . Imagine if he'd really been Vasilis' child! His little heart would have broken had they taken him away! . . .

At his regular pace, his hands in his pockets, Apostolis set off to find Vasilis. He made a round of the village, entered two coffee-houses, and lingered in the square—but to no avail. Vasilis was nowhere to be seen. He'd vanished. What could he do now to find him? Where could he look? Returning to Miss Aspasia's, he encountered only the old lady cooking. He tried the school, he asked Miss Aspasia, he hung around until midday. However Vasilis didn't show up.

On foot, then, he set off for Thesssalonika, directly to the doctor's to consult with Miss Electra. But she wasn't there. She'd gone to visit an elderly lady, Mrs. Vasiotakis—"grandmother" to the Vasiotakis household—who'd rented a home next door.

He discovered Miss Electra alone.

"What should I do?" he asked her, after explaining the situation.

Miss Electra was always a haven for him. Thinking it over, she replied:

"Let's ask Mrs. Vasiotakis. She knows Vasilis well, since he was the gardener at Mitsos' house. She'll advise us."

Together they walked into a little salon, where a white-haired lady with a gracious smile was seated. Miss Electra introduced Apostolis to her, and gave an account of the difficulty he was in. Upon hearing the entire story, Mrs. Vasiotakis inquired about a few more particulars, then shook her head slowly and said:

"As I know Vasilis, he's suffered a great disappointment. Yet he won't want to show it and he won't return to Miss Aspasia's. Don't lose your time seeking him."

She asked for news of Mitsos and Pericles—how they were and whether they'd adjustied to the work and hard life at the lake. And she wanted to learn where Apostolis would go . . . and what he'd do . . . If he didn't have a place to stay, he was to understand that there would always be a bed and food for him at her house, whenever he passed by Thessalonika . . .

Mrs. Vasiotakis was elderly but not old; moreover she was very sharp. With curiosity as well as sympathy, Apostolis observed her smile that had remained so youthful; and he recalled Pericles' words: "She's a Cretan; she has a great spirit . . ."

"Consider your mission finished," Miss Electra said to Apostolis, once they were alone again. "Go to the Consulate and see if they have other work for you . . ."

But Apostolis had something weighing on him, which he wanted to tell her.

"Miss Electra, perhaps you know who Captain Akritas is—the commander who came and saved you with Captain Nikiphoros?"

Miss Electra didn't know.

"Why do you ask?" she responded.

"Because I have reason to believe that Captain Akritas isn't Captain Akritas, but someone else hiding under his name."

"It's possible," Miss Electra said, deliberating. "Still, don't forget that since you took an oath, you're bound not to speak about your work or inquire into what they don't want to tell you."

Not to inquire—all right. But not to ponder the matter? . . . As he strode towards the Consulate with his hands in his pockets as always, Apostolis couldn't stop thinking and reflecting about it. He recalled and again heard the fake-priest's deep voice uttering almost the same words he'd said himself in seeking Vasilis' lost child . . .

* * * *

At the Consulate he requested Mr. Zoés. Ali welcomed him.

"Why haven't you come in such a long time?" he asked. "Tell me, how is the rebel in Turkish clothes?"

Apostolis replied in disjointed sentences; and Ali brought him to Mr. Zoés's office and announced him. The official was alone.

"Apostolis the guide?" he inquired. "Do you bring news from Kleidi?"

"No," Apostolis answered. "I'm here from the Swamp to ask for work."

He described the comitadje attack at Zorba to him as well as the fire.

"We're aware of it," Mr. Zoés replied. "And we know that the comitadjes escaped. Only two were killed by the courageous teacher. Apostol Petkoff and Botsos got away."

"Petkoff was there again?"

"That's what we learned," Mr. Zoés stated. "He doesn't seem to stay two days in the same place But listen. Can you set off immediately and go find Captain Nikiphoros?"

"Immediately! . . ."

"You'll deliver a letter to him. Where will you hide it?"

"In the sole of my shoe, if you like," Apostolis said. "Is there a need, though? I speak Turkish and Bulgarian, and I'm a carpenter. I pass where I want. For the Turkish patrol, I have a travel permit from Halil-bey."

"My advice is, it's best to conceal it in your shoe. Wait until I finish the letter, and then leave at once."

While Mr. Zoés wrote, Apostolis waited. But he was itching to talk.

"Captain Akritas was also in Captain Nikiphoros' force," he informed him.

"I know," Mr. Zoés replied, without pausing in his writing.

"They don't call him Kostas, just Gregos," Apostolis commented.

Mr. Zoés turned. He stopped short for a moment, then burst out laughing.

"So?" he said.

"He's big and powerful," Apostolis continued. He'd taken the plunge and couldn't stop. "Captain Akritas is small, and he's in Greece."

Mr. Zoés folded the letter and placed it in a long, narrow envelope.

"You're a careful observer, I see; and you perceive even more. They're useful qualities for the work you're about. However first of all, you have to know when to keep quiet."

"I'm only saying it here, for information," Apostolis responded.

"Well, I'm only saying it to you, for explanation. In the mountains and countryside, we still have need of a Captain Akritas. Do you understand?"

Seriously, Apostolis replied:

"I understand."

And he added:

"But now I know that last December I guided this Captain Akritas from Koulakia to Kaliani, at your command."

"All right," Mr. Zoés said, good-heartedly. "It's enough that you know it, yourself."

Apostolis was proud and in good spirits as he left the Consulate, heading for the Swamp at dusk inside the mud. He'd solved half the puzzle. It remained to discover who Gregos was, and why he concealed his identity so insistently.

Deep into the night he arrived at the fisherman's cabin situated at the point where the small tributary joined the Loudias River. The fisherman welcomed him and put out a mattress for the exhausted boy to sleep. Early in the morning Apostolis set off again—for Plati and on to the Swamp. He arrived without incident that evening in the dark. Canoes were coming and going, transporting earth to strengthen the embankment at Niki. Climbing into one of them, he started up a conversation.

Captain Nikiphoros was no longer at Niki, they told him; he'd returned to Tsekri. Thus Apostolis left the men with their canoes full of earth, and made his way alone in a small dugout directly to Tsekri. However he was very tired, the night was dark, and he had no other oarsman with him. Tying his canoe up at Petra, where there was a guard, he went to sleep there.

In the morning, he started off and was almost to Tsekri when gunfire erupted from the water's edge, jarring him. Carrying no other weapon than his pistol from Captain Agras, without a moment's hesitation he drew for the shore.

Two canoes appeared, returning rapidly from the land. Upright in one, a rebel was aiming inside the reeds and firing.

In another small canoe, Pericles sat with Nasos as oarsman and Mangas in the prow, his hair set on end and his teeth exposed, growling incessantly. Other boats followed behind, with Captain Nikiphoros in one of them.

All were hastening toward Tsekri, but by sideroads—firing at intervals before changing direction. Apostolis trailed them until they reached the hut. When they were all there safely, Nikiphoros called over Pericles and Nasos who were standing awkwardly off to the side. Patting the dog that was lying on the deck near him, he said:

"Explain to me how you suddenly came to be at the landing-cove with Mangas."

Pericles spoke up. "Please, Commander, I alone am responsible. I disobeyed your command that we all stay here and led Nasos astray by assuring him your life was in danger."

"It was in danger! How did you know?"

"The men you sent to investigate the signal—a pistol shot from land—reported back that Ali the Albanian wanted you to come to shore. Isn't that right?"

"Yes. What about it?"

"It hadn't occured that way before . . ."

"No! Generally Ali comes here to the hut."

"Didn't you suspect anything?"

"I did. However it seemed cowardly not to go."

"Mangas, though, was wary. One by one he sniffed the three men who'd gone to see about the signal; and he grew furious. It appears they'd taken hold of Ali's hand and he'd given them tobacco. Mangas flew into a rage trying to take the tobacco away.

"Knowing my dog, I became suspicious. And I remembered what you said, Apostolis—that you have a hunting dog's instinct and that you didn't trust Ali. You'd departed, Commander, and we had no time to lose. I hustled Nasos into a canoe, Mangas leaped in, and we took off. The day before we'd been reprimanded for drawing towards Zorba instead of going to Niki as instructed— but we were forgiven because Miss Electra was found.

"I felt that today you'd punish us. Yet what did it matter? We had to save you. The two of us rowed like crazy to get there in time, as Mangas' behavior frightened us. He'd rushed to the edge of the prow, ready to jump in the water, growling and showing his teeth. I had to threaten him to prevent him from howling. Before we could get out—while you were speaking unawares in the secluded spot Ali had lured you to—Mangas sprang onto shore. With his usual light-crying that warns of danger, he sped in the direction of the Turkish soldiers' trap, then back again to summon me.

"Suddenly we saw the Turkish soldiers creeping up to cut off your retreat. Your men had also observed them, and they called out to you. It was a real feat how you all managed to get into the canoes and plunge them back into the water! . . ."

"That traitor Ali!" one of the men who'd followed Captain Nikiphoros murmured. "I wonder if any bullet of ours hit him?"

"It's sufficient that we deceived the Turks with our firing, zigzagging as we did; and that their bullets missed their mark," Nikiphoros replied. And seeing Nasos huddled over to the side, he laughed and said: "I certainly should punish the two of you, both you and Pericles, for disobeying me. You deserve it! But then it's the second time your disobedience has ended up well! . . . Before, it was the teacher at Zorba—today, me. Still, you mustn't repeat these initiatives without serious cause. Because a military force can't survive without discipline. Instead of scolding you as I should, let me clasp your hands. Ali betrayed us, and the dog was onto it. I wouldn't have escaped if the Turks had succeeded in blocking my retreat from their trap!"

The two guilty ones glowed with pride.

"Give us a chore for punishment, Commander," Nasos said. "That way we'll have our conscience easy . . ."

"Very well," the commander replied. "Go help Elias the Baker take out the bread. It's just coming from the oven!"

* * * *

Touched, Nikiphoros watched them; and when they'd gone off, he got up himself to begin his work. But Apostolis stopped him.

"From the Center, Commander," he said, handing him a letter.

"You've been to Thessalonika?" Nikiphoros asked.

"Yes."

"Who gave you the letter?"

"Mr. Zoés."

Nikiphoros opened it, sat down again on the deck, and read it attentively.

"Did he entrust you with any other order?" he questioned Apostolis.

"No, Commander."

Nikiphoros was worried.

"I sent the little boy—your apprentice, is he?—to Miss Euthalia, the teacher at Bozets. What bad luck that the worst comitadjes are gathered right there!"

"And Apostol Petkoff as well, it appears," Apostolis said.

"Both he and all his gang—with that criminal Delithanas who's terrorized all the region as their host!"

* * * *

Troubled, Nikiphoros called Captain Pandelis; and the two of them entered the hut, where they conferred for some time. When they emerged again, Pandelis summoned two of their brave youth and spoke with them privately. Right away the two set off in a canoe with an oarsman, headed for the Tsekri landing-cove—all three, heavily armed.

Apostolis looked for Mitsos, but discovered only Pericles reading a letter from home.

"Has Vasilis come by here?" he inquired.

Pericles was taken by surprise.

"Did he find his child?" he responded.

Apostolis gave him an account of Vasilis' meeting with the orphan and his reaction upon seeing that the child had green eyes.

"What a disappointment! . . ." Pericles exclaimed. "And you have no idea where he could be—or if he had something in mind, leaving that way?"

However Apostolis didn't know.

21.

Bozets

THAT AFTERNOON NIKIPHOROS DIDN'T FIND A MOMENT'S PEACE. Turkish beys, Greek villagers, elders and priests arrived to see him. The beys sought protection for their estates and villages from plundering Bulgarian bands; the villagers wanted their differences with neighbors and kin settled; and elders and priests came to denounce the murders and disappearances occurring in the countryside.

Tsekri had become the headquarters of the entire region.

The villagers also kept the commander informed of Bulgarian activities—as did the Greek rebels, and Turks who were paid for information. Youth from Greek-speaking and Greek-sympathizing villages volunteered for training and service in reinforcement units, while Greek priests and teachers approached Nikiphoros secretly for guidance and counsel on how to save the exposed villagers from the comitadjes' killings and arson.

The captain's force now numbered seventy-five, not counting the village youth being trained in arms. He continually traveled back and forth from Tsekri to Niki to see Captain Pandelis, who was instructing the recruits; and to Kryfi, Petra and the other huts—seven sizeable centers scattered in the upper lake inside the tall reeds. Then at night he set forth with small units on land tours of the villages. Alerted in advance, the villagers awaited him at the teacher's, priest's, or a notable's house, where he conversed with them, encouraged and directed them, and aroused their enthusiasm. Always by dawn, he was back at the Swamp.

It was difficult, rigorous work. Moreover Captain Nikiphoros no longer possessed his earlier endurance. He'd paid a price for his stay at Kouga in the ice and water. Like Agras he suffered from fever; and his rheumatism bothered him so much that he was often compelled to ride horseback on his rounds from village to village.

With the end of winter, the insects began to flutter about and multiply ominously, especially the mosquitoes. To drink water, the men had to filter it through the porous leaves of a native shrub to keep tiny leeches out. A blood-letting resource for the merchants, the leeches created constant danger for the Greek rebels.

In addition to all the natural perils, at times the men had to cope with the Bulgarians disposing of a corpse in the lake. Nikiphoros had given an order for the huts to boil their drinking water. However when the rebels left Tsekri, they didn't always carry it out.

That day was a lively one at Tsekri. And in the evening Mitsos arrived from Niki with news that the villagers hadn't been appearing for training. The Turks had grown suspicious and were on the lookout for them.

"Exactly when I needed you. It's the moment for action!" Nikiphoros confided to him. "I have a major operation in mind."

The same evening, the two armed youths sent out by Captain Pandelis returned with a stranger. Known as Uncle Tasos, he was short, stout, and darkened by the sun—a Bulgarian unable to speak a word of Greek. The best guide in the northeastern part of the lake, he'd once worked with Apostol Petkoff. But for a minor offence, the fierce chief had beaten him until his back was bloody and he fainted. From then on, like Pascal, Tasos had sworn undying hatred for the comitadjes. Fond of Captain Nikiphoros, whenever the commander summoned him, he abandoned everything to serve him.

Tasos had a big flaw, though. He drank! And like a sponge! For Captain Nikiphoros to make use of him, his most faithful men had to keep watch so that the guide wouldn't find wine or spirits. Because he became blind-drunk, which rendered him worthless, or even a risk. While he didn't know Greek, he did speak Turkish along with Bulgarian. His communication with Nikiphoros took place through an interpreter.

* * * *

Without telling anyone his destination, Captain Nikiphoros prepared for an expedition. Only to Captain Pandelis and especially to Mitsos did he reveal his plan to go to Bozets. Orders from the Center were to clear the territory from the scourge of comitadjes, who every so often carried out a new crime—killing villagers in their fields, attacking young girls at school, or tormenting women who refused to inform on their husbands. Or else they slaughtered flocks of sheep and burned down sheepfolds. Above all, they persecuted the priests and teachers who strove to preserve Greek morale in the villages.

Only heroic Petrovo, with Father Manolis as its leader, had never succumbed to the Bulgarian propaganda or consented to renounce the Greek Patriarch. Those defiant Petrovo inhabitants who persisted in asserting their Greekness suffered as in no other place. The rest of the lake's northern villages, or nearly all, had become Bulgarian, some from persuasion but most of them from fear.

Bozets and Kourfalia, in particular, were dens of comitadjes.

Bozets was difficult to attack, situated as it was far from the lake. The Greek force had to cross a bare plain and pass by scattered Bulgarian sheepfolds, Turkish pastures, and the Turkish army patroling the villages from Giannitsa. And while the Turkish army never managed to prevent a crime, it could destroy the Greek force by cutting off its withdrawal as it returned to the lake.

The undertaking was as risky as it was bold. Without delay, Captain Nikiphoros made up his mind; and with his usual speed and courage, he put the plan into operation. Brave, dedicated Father Chrysostomos served as his agent in Bozets, where he lived pistol in hand night and day, alone like a pariah. Only three villagers and the teacher Miss Evthalia went defiantly to see and consult with him. Intimidated, the other Greeks feared to approach him openly.

Nikiphoros notified these three villagers along with Father Chrysostomos that he would come out the next evening, and to be ready to meet and assist the force.

All the preparations were conducted in secret.

But the young rebels, as if aware of the commander's plan, began to arrive one by one from the other huts: Cretans wearing silver chains around their necks, well-groomed Captain Pandelis, Evangelos with his long curly hair, and Nikolas from Chalkidiki,[37] among them All were completely dedicated to their leader. In fact, between the last two, a rivalry had sprung up to determine which could be of most service to him; and Nikiphoros took care not to show any partiality that could cause jealousy.

They'd all assembled at Tsekri in hopes of accompanying him. In vain, he explained that it was also brave and useful to remain behind to guard the huts and landing-coves. Everyone wanted to leave and fight. Finally Nikiphoros chose twenty-five men and ordered the others to abide by his decision.

The sun set. Those chosen entered into twelve canoes; and Nikiphoros was ready to descend into one of them when the baker Elias appeared, begging to be taken along.

"But it's far! And you're no longer young!" Nikiphoros protested.

Elias went on pleading and entreating him.

"I left all my children to come and fight with you, and you won't take me? After all I've endured from the Bulgarians, I can't go with you to have my revenge and share in the danger?"

Yielding to his plea, the commander included him.

Apostolis hadn't spoken. Observing the others' insistance upon going, he realized that he had no hope, himself. In the end, he slipped unseen into a canoe beside Captain Manolis the Curlyhead.

"What do you, an infant, want with us?" the rebel asked.

"Sh-h-h! Don't give me away!" Apostolis implored. "I can see at night. Tasos may be a good guide, but the other two aren't worth anything. They're from the lake villages; and it's possible they'll betray us."

"Do you know the way?"

"No, but I tell you I can see in the dark, and I'll follow Tasos."

"All right," the Curlyhead said. "However you're responsible if you suffer anything."

"Of course!" Apostolis replied.

Upon reaching the landing-cove, he remained lying down in the bottom of the boat so the commander wouldn't notice him. Captain Nikiphoros gathered his men together and spoke to them.

"We'll go to Bozets," he announced, disclosing his plan for the first time. "Still, Bozets is far and we must get there and return before dawn. I know that each of you will do his duty. That's not enough, though! We must also be victorious in order to raise the spirits of our comrades. We'll struggle, but we have to succeed. Is everyone willing?"

"All of us, commander!" the men exclaimed with one voice.

"Forward, then, with God's help."

"Show us the road, Tasos," the interpreter said, overjoyed as if going on a pleasure trip. "Forward! Lead us on!"

But with a yearning look, the guide stared at another rebel, his glance fixed longingly on his sack.

The commander saw it and understood.

"Give him a small glass, but only one and no more."

Dutifully, the man removed a bottle from his sack and treated the guide to a little cognac.

* * * *

It began to grow dark. Tasos proceeded first, followed by Captain Nikiphoros, Evangelos, Nikolas, and the others one after another in a long, human chain. In the middle Captain Pandelis headed the second section, and below the Curlyhead led the third, just as the commander had divided them. Apostolis brought up the rear—watching, searching, and attentive to every direction Tasos gave. The Bulgarian was truly a fine guide, which Apostolis could appreciate better than anyone else. He never exposed them, but selected a path through ravines and low areas, preferably behind hills. Thus the folds of the landscape concealed them.

All at once, a little before they crossed the Giannitsa-Thessa-lonika highway, the tramping of horses sounded. The guide gave a signal, and they all fell to the ground. The news traveled quickly down the line.

"Turks!"

"The army!"

"Betrayal!"

No one stirred, though. Flat on the ground, the men took aim and waited for the order to fire. A little to the side to avoid the commander's gaze, Apostolis crouched on his knees, trying to see.

"It's not an enemy," a voice near him whispered.

Apostolis stopped short. He'd recognized Pericles.

"How did you get here?" he whispered back.

"I hid . . . like you did. And I came . . . It's not an enemy. Look at Mangas!"

Half-concealed in Pericles' cloak, the dog had his nose sticking out; and with one paw stretched onto his master's arm and his ears pricked up, he sniffed curiously in the direction of the tramping. However he showed no anger or uneasiness. At a distance before them, the commander had risen to his knees and was examining the countryside with his binoculars. Beside him, Tasos was trying to pierce the darkness with his trained eyes.

The deputy-commanders, along with Elias the baker, had drawn up close to Captain Nikiphoros.

"An army?" they inquired.

"Betrayal?"

Yet no one appeared. The shadow of a galloping horse went by, but without a rider, then another, and then many all together, their hindquarters bare. As if frightened, they ran helter-skelter over the plain.

The guide chuckled and threw up his arm.

"Albanian pastures," he said. "Their horses were grazing and we scared them!"

After the translator explained, the captains let out a sigh of relief. Once more the news was transmitted back down the line. And cheerful and carefree again, each one resumed his position and the march continued.

Bozets was a considerable distance away. Out-of-condition for foot-marches, the weary men of the Swamp advanced slowly, halting every hour for five or six minutes before setting off again. Tasos kept pressing them to hurry.

"It's a long journey. We must be back before the sun rises! . . ."

Ignoring fatigue and pain, the men would start walking again, careful to always head against the wind when passing sheepfolds and villages. Leaving behind hills and ravines, shrubs and bare plain, at last they approached Bozets. All at once, with a motion of his hand, Tasos stopped the entire force.

"Men up ahead . . ." he murmured.

Immediately the chain of rebels dropped to the ground.

It could only be Turks, or a Bulgarian band. Robbers and brigands didn't venture out at that hour, nor did innocent folk. So fearful were the natives of the irregular forces that no one risked appearing. It would be the comitadjes—or the army.

Again the rebels awaited the commander's order, with their finger on the trigger. Quietly Nikiphoros instructed a couple of men to proceed ahead and investigate—when suddenly a shadow arose and ran up to two other half-hidden shadows that were larger. And quickly the three—silent, happy, and smiling—drew up to the commander.

"It's Father Chrysostomos and Dionysios," Apostolis said, daring to reveal himself for the first time.

Nikiphoros was so delighted that he failed to rebuke Apostolis, or think to ask him how he got there. Dionysios was one of the three courageous villagers of Bozets who didn't fear to show themselves as "Grecomans," as the Bulgarians referred to Slavic-speaking Greeks. He visited Father Chrysostomos freely and every so often journeyed up to Tsekri.

Recognizing him with the priest, Nikiphoros greeted the two men with emotion. For they hadn't hesitated to leave their village to meet the force, regardless of the danger of being seen and betrayed. And taking them aside, he conferred with them.

Chrysostomos advised that they burn the village except for the Greek houses, as the Bulgarians in Bozets were fanatical. Nikiphoros didn't want to.

"Not needless bloodshed and destruction," he said. "We'll punish only the criminals! . . ." It was his will that prevailed.

With his force divided into three, he sent a division with Captain Pandelis and a second one with the Curlyhead to occupy two points in the village, in order to put down resistance. Then he had Father Chrysostomos and Dionysios go back.

"Make haste!" he told them, "in case anyone spots you with us and you pay for it tomorrow!"

Allowing them time to withdraw, Nikiphoros and the third division made their way to Delithanas' house—which Dionysios had pointed out—and circled it.

One of the rebels, flat against the wall to escape any bullets fired from the windows, beat upon the door with the butt of his rifle.

"Open up!" he shouted in Bulgarian. "Surrender!"

But nothing was heard from inside the house. Nikiphoros waited. Absolute silence . . .

"Call for them to put the women and children out," the commander ordered.

Once more the rebel shouted to them in Bulgarian. As an answer, firing burst forth from all the windows and bullets whizzed by. At the same time, from the house opposite and others in the neighborhood, more shots erupted. The Greeks' situation—unprotected as it was on the road—became critical.

"The kerosene! Set a fire!" Nikiphoros commanded.

A cart laden with straw was standing in the road, as if ordered.

"Quickly! We don't have time to lose!" Nikiphoros' voice sounded amidst the tumult.

A Cretan brought over a can of kerosene, which the rebels carried with them on such raids. Pericles, appearing unexpectedly, helped form bundles of straw to dip in the oil and stuff in any cracks or gaps discernable in the windows or shutters. The men competed with each other to show who was bolder. One, defying the bullets falling all around, sprang onto the low, slanted roof and threw a grenade inside the chimney.

But again it didn't explode . . .

"Bring straw, sponges, and kerosene!" he yelled to his companions.

More agile than those who were older, Pericles leaped onto the roof himself, laden with sponges and straw doused with kerosene to throw into the holes opened up. Within a few minutes the roof was engulfed in flames with the house burning from three sides.

The battle had now extended to the roads. Armed, the villagers had rushed out. However, finding themselves before Pandelis and the Curlyhead and their men, they retreated towards the village center.

With his noisy old Gras that kicked furiously, Apostolis was firing at the house opposite when all at once someone tugged at his clothes. Startled, by the light of the fire he saw Jovan shouting to him:

"The other house! The other house!"

"Get away, hide!" Apostolis ordered him in a loud voice.

But the child didn't let go of his clothing.

"Botsos, the fierce, dark Bulgarian who came to Zorba—he's there inside! . . ." he cried through the thunder of the rifles, gesturing towards the burning house.

At the same time, the door opened. Women and children with reddened eyes and terrified faces black from smoke, emerged onto the road. The rebels grabbed hold of the women and stopped them. Imperatively Nikiphoros' voice ascended above the din of the battle:

"Let them leave!"

The rebels obeyed. Yet at that moment two or three men dashed outside of the burning house, following the women closely.

Thick gunfire greeted them. Two fell. A third rushed into the road, pursued by the rebels, and was able to escape by a sideroad. However he ran headlong into Captain Pandelis' force. Riddled with bullets, he collapsed in a heap. It was the fearsome Delithanas.

The firing was widespread, making it difficult to hear commands. At Apostolis' side, a screaming Jovan stamped his feet, beside himself.

"Botsos! . . .Botsos! There he is! And behind him Angel Pio . . .!"

Two men appeared inside the flames. One was short, dark, and scorched from the fire. He burst forth and fired, trying to open up a path.

"Botsos! Botsos!" Tasos who was next to Nikiphoros yelled. "It's Botsos!"

A battery was heard, a woman's shriek responded, and Botsos stumbled, staggered, and dropped to the ground.

The house seemed to groan and tremble inside the flames. Its roof had caved in.

A woman all soot and blood fled outside, and after taking a few steps, fell beside Apostolis. Apostolis saw Jovan falter, say something in a strangled voice—of which he distinguished only the word "mother"—and crumple at his feet.

The whole scene lasted but a few seconds, unobserved. In the fury of the battle, the men chasing the comitadjes who were fleeing the flames, hadn't noticed anything. Apostolis bent over Jovan to determine if a bullet had struck him. Alongside him, he suddenly saw a young, delicately-built woman lift the child into her arms. Sagging under the weight, she sought to leave.

"Help me!" she said to Apostolis. "The school is nearby. He got away . . . Let's return there! . . ."

Apostolis caught hold of Jovan's dangling legs; and together with bullets whistling all around them, they carried the unconscious boy to a house a little beyond. The door had remained open, and inside an oil lamp was glowing.

When they'd put Jovan down, the woman unbuttoned his shirt. Apostolis stared at her.

"Are you Miss Evthalia?" he asked.

The young woman was taken by surprise.

"How do you know me?" she inquired.

"I don't know you. I know your name, though, and that Jovan stays with you . . ."

The teacher had opened up the child's clothing. No wound was visible.

"He became frightened," Apostolis said. "He's often afraid . . ."

The teacher had risen to her knees. With her two hands, she pushed her hair back from her forehead.

"This one?" she said. "He doesn't fear anything. Father Chrysostomos uses him as his right hand, as small as he is. It was he who discovered that Botsos had assembled all the men of his family here, in order to burn Petrovo and get rid of Father Manolis. That child afraid? Bah! He experienced something else."

Jovan was recovering. Opening his eyes, he recognized Apostolis and stretched out his hand to catch hold of his.

"Don't leave! . . ." he said to him. "They're killing women! . . ."

The firing had subsided in those parts. Farther on, the other two divisions were still fighting, but even there the shooting had let up. Miss Evthalia wiped Jovan's perspiring forehead.

"Are you better?" she asked.

The child stood up. His legs shook a little, although he dismissed it.

"Let's go, Apostolis, to the battle."

"By no means will you go back," Miss Evthalia scolded him, more out of affection than in anger. "And you're a naughty child for disobeying me and slipping away. Hadn't I told you to be off to bed?"

"Well, you'd gone out . . ." Jovan began sheepishly.

The teacher interrupted him:

"What I do is another thing."

And, worried, she asked Apostolis:

"You're Apostolis the guide?"

"Yes!"

"You see I know you, too, from what this one told me. Listen! They sent the child here, but tomorrow Father Chrysostomos and I—and perhaps poor Dionysios and his two cousins as well—we'll all be in jail . . ."

"Why?" Apostolis exclaimed.

"Because we're Grecomans. It's clear as daylight to the Turks that we guided and assisted the rebels in wiping out the Bulgarian strength at Bozets. Take Jovan then, as quickly as possible, and return him to Zorba."

"Miss Electra isn't there. She was wounded and is in Thessalonika under doctor's care."

Miss Evthalia grew still more upset.

"What will become of this child? I don't have anyone to send him to, and it's not wise for him to remain here alone."

Troubled, she inquired:

"Don't you know anywhere else to bring him?"

"To the Swamp. It's better there again . . ."

"Take him. If you set off immediately, you'll arrive before dawn . . ."

The two boys went out together. Delithanas' house, in ruins, was still burning in places. It cast light on some corpses that had fallen in the road. Jovan leaned over and showed one to Apostolis.

"Botsos," he said. "The comitadje who came to Zorba. But Angel Pio must have escaped. He's not here."

"The others farther down could have killed him. But I wonder if they got Apostol Petkoff?" Apostolis asked.

"Petkoff? Chief Apostol? He wasn't here at all. I didn't see him."

Counting the corpses, Jovan saw the dead woman again. Gasping, he covered his eyes. Trembling he passed by her.

"Won't you tell me?" Apostolis asked with compassion. "Is she your mother?"

"No," Jovan murmured.

"Why did you call her 'mother?'"

Jovan didn't reply right away. All at once he broke out crying uncontrollably.

"Don't ask me! Don't talk to me!" he said between sobs.

Apostolis didn't insist. Besides, another worry occupied him—how to find Captain Nikiphoros.

Once he'd taken a path, Apostolis never forgot it. Departing from the now quiet Bozets, he headed with Jovan for the ravines and hills where the force had passed with Tasos as guide. But as fast as they went, they didn't catch up with the rebels or observe a trace of them.

When the boys reached the Swamp, it was still dark. They'd walked rapidly, almost running. The canoes, drawn up on the ground, were all waiting with oarsmen.

"Where is the Commander?" the men asked anxiously. "And the others?"

Yet Apostolis was even more anxious. They'd destroyed the village and wiped out the criminals. But he hadn't met up with Captain Nikiphoros' force on the trip back. What could have happened?

Along with the men, the boys sat and waited beside the canoes, becoming more and more uneasy. Returning, they'd passed by Albanian pastures, villages with a Turkish army, and Romanians on foot—customary betrayers of the Greek forces, united with the Bulgarians in seeking to crush them.

"Could they have been ambushed?" Nasos, who'd remained behind with the boats, murmured.

Each one offered his view.

It started to grow light. Suddenly a dog jumped up on Apostolis, joyfully wagging its tail.

"Mangas!" the guide exclaimed.

Everyone leaped up. A shadow could be detected in the plain, and behind it a second, a third, and another and another—a complete line, a human chain approaching . . . It was Captain Nikiphoros' whole force, with Tasos in the lead. The stocky little guide was stretching his short legs to their utmost.

The men rushed up to welcome them with nervous laughter.

"You're late!"

"We were worried!"

"What happened to you . . ."

"Quickly! To the boats and off to the hut! Day has broken!" Tasos replied.

"Why are you late, Commander?" Nasos asked, pushing his canoe into the water. "Apostolis is here, and he didn't see you coming back."

"Tasos brought us another way for greater safety—in case anyone saw us going to Bozets and informed on us," Nikiphoros answered. "Besides, Apostolis is faster . . . Any villager could travel back and forth in less time than we did. We're no longer in shape for marches . . . What a return journey it was! Our legs have given out . . ."

In a long series all the canoes drew towards Tsekri, with the paths in daylight now. To both sides of them, the still budding leaves of the reeds were just turning green.

22.

MATAPAS

WHILE THE SUCCESS AT BOZETS SHOOK THE TURKS and the representatives of the European Powers, it terrified the Bulgarians and Romanians. And the Greek population received such a boost that whole villages dared acknowledge their return to Hellenism. Renouncing the Exarch, they declared themselves patriarchal.

In all the Greek huts at the Swamp, and above all at Tsekri, the days following the bold undertaking turned into a general celebration. Those who'd gone to Bozets never ceased giving an account of it; those who'd been wounded became heroes. Mitsos, his outfit stained with blood, was now Captain Mitsos to his companions. A little embarrassed about the praise he heard all around him, he tried to hide his arm—which was in a sling—under his cloak. Yet he didn't wash the blood that decorated his sleeve like a medal. His uniform, now sooty from gunpowder, had lost its former luster that Captain Pandelis so envied.

* * * *

Apostolis slept the entire day after the Bozets' operation. When he awoke, it was evening. He started to turn over again, when he perceived Pericles seated next to him, staring out at the water of the lake.

"You're not sleeping?" Apostolis asked him.

"Did you see Angel Pio's body anywhere?" Pericles replied in return.

Apostolis sat up.

"No," he answered. "He was with Botsos. But we didn't discover him among the dead in front of Delithanas' house. He must have been killed, though . . . Why?"

"He wasn't killed," Pericles said. "In the confusion of the battle, he escaped. Captain Manolis got a glimpse of him leaving the village and fired at him. But Pio disappeared in the dark. We didn't find him anywhere. Nor would I have given another thought to him, if little Jovan hadn't awakened me, crying in his sleep. When I shook him to wake him, he cried out: 'Angel Pio, don't hit her anymore!' Who do you suppose he was pleading for? I woke him up; and seeing me, he began to cry all the harder. How does he know Pio?"

Apostolis glanced around for Jovan. Guessing his thought, Pericles responded:

"He's not listening. He went to the oven with Christos. But how does he know Pio?"

In a low voice, Apostolis answered:

"Pio is his uncle. Don't say anything, though. It hurts him that he has such an uncle, and he hates him. I took him myself from Pio's sheepfold. His uncle is a comitadje and a beast."

"The poor child . . ." Pericles murmured.

The two remained silent. Pensive, Pericles wound and unwound a bandage on his left hand, which had a burn on the palm.

"No one saw Apostol Petkoff either. Once more he got away," Pericles said.

"He wasn't there," Apostolis replied. "Jovan knows him, and he informed me that Apostol didn't come to Bozets. He never exposes himself. He only goes to the slaughters where there's no danger."

That night the two boys slept side by side. In the morning at daybreak, upon opening his eyes first, Apostolis saw Jovan sleeping huddled up beside him, as if for protection.

Apostolis had dreamt in his sleep; and once awake he began to daydream. He felt refreshed. Not used to a settled existence, he was ready to embark on new adventures.

But the commander had forbidden all activity. The evening before, a message had come to him that the Turkish army was on the move, searching for the Greek band that burned down Delithanas' house with Botsos hiding inside. All the male relatives of the comitadjes at Bozets had lost their lives. No one was to leave the Swamp. Until the storm passed and it quieted down, they had to lay low.

While the rebels couldn't go out, frightened villagers were secretly arriving with news. Their disaster had overwhelmed the Bulgarians, who hadn't forseen such a daring operation. They'd been preparing to burn the Greek village of Petrovo themselves—when suddenly a thunderbolt struck them from the distant Swamp!

The Turks had arrested Father Chrysostomos and Miss Evthalia, as well as the villager Dionysios, although nothing developed from the interrogation. Meanwhile the beys, experiencing relief after the murder of the Delithanas and Botsos clans, notified Nikiphoros to be patient. It wouldn't be long before the teacher, the priest, and Dionysios would be out of jail.

* * * *

With the messengers, a thin, pale man seemingly exhausted from hardships and hunger appeared, wanting to enter into Captain Nikiphoros' force. His name was Andonis and he was from Volos. A volunteer from another rebel band in Macedonia, he'd fallen into the Turks' hands and rotted in Turkish prisons for a whole year. Finally he'd succeeded in breaking away; and from the General Consulate where he fled, they'd sent him to the lake.

"Let me join with you and you won't be sorry, Commander," he said to Nikiphoros. "I'm set on getting even for all I've been through!"

Nikiphoros accepted him and enlisted him in his force.

The next day, vague rumors reached Tsekri. A couple of comitadjes had been found dead around Verria, each with a knife driven into his heart. Other news mixed with it seemed overblown and confusing. Captain Matapas reportedly had rid the area of eleven Bulgarian criminals posing as coal-dealers. The Turks were hunting him down to wipe him out, along with his band.

Apostolis was galvanized into action. Pericles' words had aroused suspicion in him. Was Pio alive? If so, he knew Matapas and without doubt he'd inform on him. Botsos and Delithanas had been killed. But Pio?

He went to Nikiphoros.

"Permit me to leave the lake, Commander," he said to him. "I'll scout around and bring you information about Captain Matapas, or else guide him here if I find him."

However the commander put forth objections.

"There's no safety in the countryside now," he declared. "Moreover the Turks won't show any mercy."

"I have Halil-bey's pass to present to the Turks," Apostolis replied "What's more, with the Bulgarians I get by wherever I want as one of them. Allow me to go on shore and learn about Captain Matapas."

"And the child? What am I to do with him?"

"I'll bring him with me. It's safer with two of us, especially since he's small . . ."

Alarmed about Matapas, Nikiphoros consented to let him leave.

* * * *

Early in the morning Apostolis set off in a canoe with Jovan, who couldn't contain himself from his pride and delight. For the first time he'd be alone with Apostolis again; he'd be "working" with him. They headed for Kryfi, and from there got off at the landing cove and drew inland. Up to Plati they took the usual road, passing by the carriage bridge. From Plati, though, they left the road and made their way over the plain, avoiding pastures and the occasional cottages along their path. Seeing the Roumlouki plain again where he'd been so isolated and lonely, Jovan recalled his life with Angel Pio; and he shuddered. Hesitantly, he asked Apostolis:

"Where are we going, Apostolis?"

It was the first time the child had questioned the older boy. Obedient and trusting, he'd been following after him through the deserted, dismal countryside with its sparse shrubs and solitary trees. Devoid of leaves, their thorny branches resembled skeletons with their arms raised high.

"We're on our way to Kleidi," Apostolis answered. "From there, we'll see."

Uncertain, fearful, the child inquired:

"Did you learn if they killed Angel Pio?"

"No, they didn't kill him," Apostolis responded. "He seems to have escaped."

Jovan was quiet. Apostolis saw the color drain from his face.

"That's why I came," the guide confessed, "to see if he's at his sheepfold."

Jovan put his hand on the bigger boy's arm.

"I'll come too," he said.

Apostolis looked at him and observed his pale lips.

"And if he recognizes you?" he asked.

Jovan cast a glance at Apostolis' belt.

"You'll give me your pistol . . ." he murmured.

The older boy laughed.

"What next! Now you, a tot, know about pistols!"

Jovan didn't reply. However he caught hold of his older friend's hand as they continued walking.

* * * *

The two of them were tired. The sun had set and night was rapidly descending. Sitting down, they ate the cold meat and bread they'd been given at Niki. Jovan fell asleep during the meal, and Apostolis spread his cloak out on the ground and carefully lifted the child onto it. Reclining next to him, he formed a pillow with his two arms.

But he wasn't sleepy. As he stared at the domed sky above him, his mind was active. He'd take Jovan to Mister Thanasis and leave him there; it would be more sensible to travel to Pio's alone tomorrow. Perhaps there'd be news about Matapas. And Mister

Thanasis might know . . . Or would it be better to go to Koulakia? Or to a patriarchal shepherd?"

A slight noise behind them startled him. He sat up to investigate at the same moment that a white dog jumped up on his chest.

"Mangas!" he cried out.

In the starlight, he could distinguish a Turk still some distance away, approaching on the run. It was Pericles in Turkish clothes.

With Apostolis' cry and the dog's jumping, Jovan woke up.

Amazed, he saw a very tired Pericles sink to the ground next to them.

"How I raced here!" he said, panting. "From the Kryfi landing cove, I've been running to catch up with you! . . ."

"Why didn't you come with us, since you wanted to?" Apostolis asked.

"Because the commander didn't give me permission. Bad news had to arrive after you'd gone, for him to let me leave!"

"Bad news?"

"Yes! That the Turks captured Matapas! It was then that he allowed a couple of the natives to set off to learn what had happened. Since I know Turkish, he let me go, too! . . ."

"How did they capture Matapas?"

"The information isn't clear . . ." Pericles said. "That's why Nikiphoros permitted us to leave—to find out. It's rumored that they caught him in Thessalonika . . . in Verria . . . in the mountains. No one's sure . . ."

"Matapas isn't the kind of a man to be caught in Thessalonika," Apostolis interrupted, "or in Verria, or on the mountain. He'd fight and die rather than surrender."

"The commander said the same thing. However it was reported that they'd discovered him hidden at Kleidi. I thought you would come by this way, so I landed at Kryfi."

"How did you find me in the open plain?"

Pericles stroked his dog's head.

"It wasn't hard," he said. "I had Mangas. And I let him smell this . . ." He held out a handkerchief to Apostolis with a red A embroidered in one corner. "You forgot it in your haste to be off. Mangas led me this far at full speed."

"How did you pass over the bridge? Didn't they stop you?"

"I'm fluent in Turkish. My clothes deceived them. No one even asked who I was. With a 'Good-day' in Turkish, I passed with no trouble."

"Where did you get your clothes?"

"At Kryfi. Villagers and messengers were coming and going. A Turk there supplied them. But where are you headed?" Pericles inquired.

"To Kleidi, in order to deliver this child—and from there, I have some other work ..."

"No, Apostolis!" Jovan cut in with unusual boldness. "Don't leave me at Kleidi! Take me to Angel Pio's . . ."

His voice quivered and there were tears in his eyes.

Two pistol shots, one after the other, split the silence of the countryside. The boys flew to their feet. Pericles just managed to grab Mangas in his arms. The dog's ears were straight up and he was ready to dash forward. In the distance to the right, a light glowed dimly in the dark.

"A fire! . . ." Pericles murmured, "with thick smoke. Did the shots come from there, I wonder?"

"No! They were closer," Apostolis answered.

"The shots came from Angel Pio's sheepfold . . ." Jovan said, pointing with a trembling hand.

"Then where is the fire?" Pericles asked.

"At some other farm," Apostolis replied. "There's no village in that direction."

"Let's go see!" Pericles said decisively.

The two boys made their way toward the fire with Jovan. As they drew near, they could see the flames and smoke better, issuing from a two-story house. Around it, haylofts and sheepfolds were also burning, hurling flames, smoke and sparks into the wind. Except for the rasping of the fire, the plain was silent.

All at once, like a spring uncoiled, Mangas leaped from Pericles' arms and set off. Pericles started to run after him; however Apostolis shoved him forcefully onto the ground.

"Gunbarrel in front of us! Don't move! . . ." he whispered.

Jovan had dropped to the ground too, and waited, his eyes scrutinizing the horizon.

Three men rose from behind a bush and proceeded towards them. Mangas was circling them, jumping up and down happily. Pericles stood up immediately.

"Friends!" he said. "Let's go and meet them."

It was Vasilis with Captain Akritas and a priest, all of them armed.

"How is it that you're here at such an hour, Mister Pericles, dressed up as a Turk?" Vasilis asked. "It was lucky Captain Matapas didn't shoot at you."

"Captain Matapas! . . ."

From his emotion, Pericles' voice broke. But it was dark and he couldn't see him. Without stopping to think, he struck a match, casting light on Captain Akritas and the priest.

This was Matapas? The famous, the legendary Captain Matapas?

Short, dark, and ugly, with eyes reddened and inflamed from the conjuntivitis he'd caught at the Swamp, the priest stared at the boys. A smile softened his harsh face with its unkempt rebel beard.

The match went out and fell to the ground.

"We're here from the Swamp because of you," Pericles said to him, very moved. "They told us you'd been captured."

Captain Matapas laughed:

"They'll never catch me alive, don't worry!" he replied. "But do you have weapons?"

Pericles took out his Brauning, and Apostolis his old pistol. Matapas treated the pistol with disdain.

"Fit to be fired at Easter with the firecrackers—nothing more!" he said, giving him his own revolver. "I have a rifle. Do you know how to get us to the Swamp? You're a guide, I hear."

"Yes! I know the way. However we can't go by Kryfi tonight. The Turks are on guard at the bridges."

"The Hell with the bridges! We'll go to Terkovista! By way of the doctor's property . . ."

"Are you joking, Commander? Or could it be you're not aware that the Turks have seized it?" the guide responded.

"We'll talk later, Captain Matapas," Captain Akritas said somewhat impatiently. "The house burned. There might be some injured persons inside . . ."

"What time is it, I wonder?" Matapas inquired.

To check his watch, Pericles lit a match again. That same instant a shot sounded—and a second one. Bullets whistled through the air, putting a hole through Captain Matapas' headdress.

All together, they raced in the direction of the firing. The dog ran first, with Pericles right after him, revolver in hand. The others followed, straight towards the fire—Jovan hanging onto Apostolis' belt. Then abruptly Mangas turned and darted into some brambles next to Apostolis.

A blaze, the blast of a gun—and a bullet whizzed close to Apostolis' ear. Simultaneously Jovan let out a choked cry. Grabbing Apostolis' old pistol from his belt, with his two hands he raised it, fired into the brambles, and fainted!

But Vasilis had rushed there and caught hold of the neck of a man who was trying to remove his hand from Mangas' teeth. Dodging a second shot, he hit him between the eyes with his fist.

The struggle was fierce. Vasilis squeezed the neck of his adversary as he was attempting to take out a knife. Seizing it, Vasilis dragged the man from the brambles, threw him down, and knelt on his chest. With clenched teeth, he hissed:

"Angel Pio, do you hear me? I'm Vasilis Andreadis from Asprohori. Are you listening? Your turn has come to pay! . . ."

And drawing out his revolver, he shot him!

The entire scene was over in seconds. Apostolis had followed it with the unconscious Jovan at his feet. Captain Matapas, Captain Akritas, and Pericles were off pursuing another Bulgarian who'd leapt up from the bush.

"Alive! Capture him alive!" Matapas called out.

Picking up the unconscious child, Vasilis hastened after his companions with Apostolis. He reached them just as they'd caught the other Bulgarian and were tying his hands behind his back. Young, seventeen or eighteen years old, he was shaking throughout.

"Mercy! Spare me, Father! I'm not to blame!" he cried to Matapas in Bulgarian.

Pistol in hand, the captain replied in the smattering of Bulgarian he knew:

"We'll show mercy if you speak the truth! Who burned down the farm?"

"Zlatan! Angel Pio led him to it! Gionis was patriarchal. Angel Pio said the Eviscerator and Captain Matapas were hiding there. They'd come down from Mt. Olympus and killed Bulgarian comitadjes.[38] But they didn't find him. And they put so many to death unjustly!"

"How many? Tell us what you did or I'll fire!" Matapas shouted.

"By God, I didn't lift a hand. I didn't strike anyone! I didn't kill!" the Bulgarian cried out, falling to his knees. "They put us on guard, my brother and me. My brother didn't want to, and Pio slashed him with a knife! I was scared. I stood where they told me. And I saw . . I saw . . . ."

His nerves had broken. He began to cry like a child.

"What did you see? Tell us and you won't suffer anything," Vasilis said in a milder tone, speaking Bulgarian like a native.

"I saw old Gionis. He opened the door. He was hospitable to them. His two married daughters were with him. They said Captain Matapas hadn't come, nor anyone else. Then the comitadjes killed and beheaded them. When the house started to burn and some children ran outside, they threw them back. A woman jumped out of a window and they killed her, too. Go see if you don't believe me!"

"Zlatan, where is he?" Matapas asked, gritting his teeth.

"He had a horse. He left for Zervohori."

"How do you know?"

"I watched him go . . . The signal sounded from Angel Pio's property—two shots, one after another. Didn't you hear them?"

Matapas stole a glance at his companions.

"And you wanted me to take pity!" he muttered to Gregos. "You wouldn't let me tie up the two females at that murderer Pio's! As if women don't inform! As if there's nothing to fear from them! You saved their leader—and might have buried us all for good," he added angrily, his always painful, reddened eyes flashing.

Vasilis continued the interrogation.

"What did the two pistol shots mean?" he asked.

"That there was danger, that the Grecomans had arrived—and that they should disperse. The others scattered and Zlatan fled. But Angel Pio said his wife was alone with her best friend[39] at the farm, and that he had to get to her and bring them to Zervohori. I tried to break away. He seized me by the back of the neck and forced me to follow him. Making our way hunched over, we noticed a faint light in the plain. Did one of you light up a cigarette?"

"Go on!" Matapas ordered without answering.

"Angel Pio was on the lookout. After you lit a second match, he fired two shots. You'd cut off our road. He wanted to frighten you, but you came after us. Pio held me by the neck so I wouldn't flee. You started to pass us; however just as he thought he'd escaped, the dog found him and one of you threw him down and finished him off. Then I made a break—and you caught me. Mercy! Forgive me! I'm not to blame! . . ."

"Did anyone escape from Gionis' farm?" Vasilis asked.

The Bulgarian shook his head "no."

"They wiped them out before burning it," he said with a shudder.

"Let's go and see!" Apostolis exclaimed.

"We'll go together," Vasilis replied. "Guide us!" he ordered the Bulgarian.

In the meantime Pericles was trying to revive Jovan by sprinkling water onto his face. Captain Akritas had also bent over him and was rubbing his feet. Pericles marveled at how gentle Gregos's powerful hands could be, hands that seemed made only for the use of lethal weapons. When Jovan opened his eyes, the captain inquired kindly:

"Are you better?"

Vasilis didn't delay in returning with Apostolis, dragging the tied Bulgarian along with him. As much as the youth had told them proved to be correct. They found his brother fatally slashed with a knife; and they discovered the body of the woman who'd jumped from the window. Nothing remained of Gionis' farm. Humans and animals had been reduced to ashes inside the flames. The dying fire still shed a dull glow in the plain.

Matapas took out his watch.

"How long is it from here to the Swamp?" he asked.

"Have Apostolis tell us," Vasilis answered.

"Four hours to Kryfi. But we can't get through."

"I'm asking about Toumba at Terkovista!" Matapas said sharply. "And naturally we'll avoid the villages!"

"Eight to ten hours, if we hurry!" Apostolis replied.

"It's two now. We'll be out in the country when day breaks . . ." Matapas said, scowling.

Captain Akritas cut him short:

"Isn't there a monastery or chapel in the surroundings? Do you know, Apostolis?" he inquired, supposedly indifferent.

Apostolis' heart leaped to his throat.

"Yes, I do," he replied in a strangled voice.

"Where?" Captain Matapas asked.

"At Kaliani," he answered, trying to seem indifferent himself, his eyes fixed on Gregos. "It happened that I guided someone disguised as a priest there. He left his beard and robe inside the church. However, I don't have the key . . ."

"Good!" Captain Matapas interrupted him. "Get us there and we'll see about keys!"

Gregos hadn't lowered his eyes. With an ironic smile that revealed his white teeth inside his rebel beard, he met the boy's gaze.

"There's the child, though . . . He won't be able to walk far," Pericles said. "And then the prisoner . . ."

Embarrassed, Jovan sprang to his feet.

But before he could speak, with one hand Gregos grabbed hold of him by the belt and seated him upon his shoulder.

"I'll tend to the child," he said cheerfully. "You take charge of the prisoner, Vasilis. Who's leading us?"

"I am," Apostolis responded. "But there are Albanian pastures along the way. Don't anyone light a cigarette . . ."

"We know, youngster!" Matapas broke in. "It's your companion dressed up as a Turk that doesn't. He's the one who lit a match in the plain! You go first and I'll follow—with the others each three feet apart. Step lively! And not a word!"

* * * *

It was still dark when they arrived outside Kaliani. A strong north wind was blowing. Apostolis passed south of the village with his companions so the dogs wouldn't detect any scent or sound. Making a loop, he brought them to the white chapel. They'd covered the eyes of the Bulgarian to prevent him from seeing where they were going.

23.

The Chapel At Kaliani

IT WAS ALREADY ROSY-HUED IN THE EAST . . .

Without trying to conceal it, Gregos took a key out of his pocket and opened the door.

"Everyone remove his shoes," he ordered, "so that we don't leave mud on the clean pavingstones."

Indeed, the church was spotless, as though the Christians of the village didn't set foot inside.

Carrying their shoes, they all entered the deserted chapel, with Mangas in Pericles' arms. Gregos closed the door quietly and locked it. He'd assumed command.

"Someone has to stand guard at each window," he declared. "I wouldn't put it past the Turks to seek us even here. They'll find a problem between the burnt farm of the patriarchal Gionis and the dead Bulgarians; and they won't know who killed who."

Half-serious, half-mocking, he called to Apostolis:

"Come help me hide the beard and robe of the fake-priest in a better place. We don't want them to give us away."

Apostolis wasn't expecting so provocative an admission. He hesitated, a little bewildered.

"Under the corner pew," Gregos directed him. "Hurry up!" And he winked!

Apostolis gathered up the bundle from where he'd left it three months earlier and handed it to Gregos to dispose of.

"Pay attention to this, too!" Gregos continued.

And moving the altar with its altar cloth to the side, he exposed the pavingstones beneath it. One of them had its corner

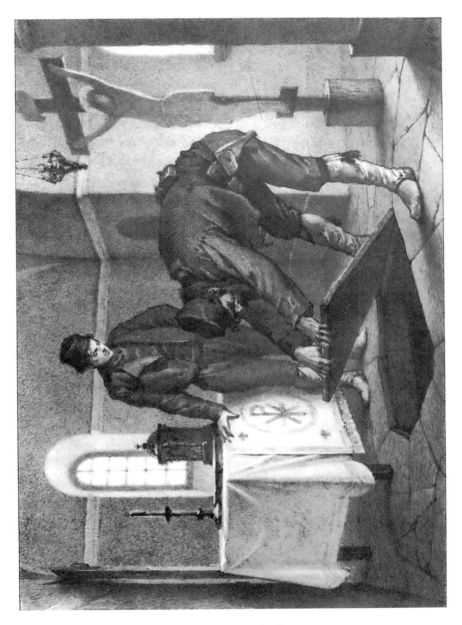

. . . like a feather, he raised the heavy stone . . .

broken off. He thrust his finger into the hollow, and like a feather, raised the heavy stone that rested on secret hinges, uncovering a stone stairway. Then he got up, shook the dust off his hands, and said with a smile:

"There are hiding places even you don't know about, Apostolis. However you're smart and observant, since you recognized me . . . It's good for you to be aware of this corner."

Agitated, Apostolis asked:

"But who are you? Because I know Captain Akritas is in . . ."

Abruptly Gregos put his hand over the boy's mouth.

"Shh! What does it matter to you who I am? Believe, or pretend to believe, that I'm Captain Akritas. Who I am is of no interest to anyone."

He went on giving orders: "Bring the child below to sleep—and the Bulgarian as well. We'll keep watch up here in case the Turks appear."

Captain Matapas climbed down into the hide-out with Jovan and the bound Bulgarian. Vasilis remained in the church with Captain Akritas and the two boys. Half of them would get some sleep, while the others stood guard at the windows.

"How do you happen to be with Captain Matapas, Vasilis?" Pericles inquired. "Apostolis lost track of you at Koulakia."

"I had nothing more to do there, once I assured myself the orphan they showed me wasn't my child," Vasilis replied. "Nor do I hold any hope of ever finding him. I headed for Mt. Olympus, following secret signs that Gregos left, and located him with Captain Matapas. Since then I've been with them."

"How is it that you're back here?"

"Crimes had been committed. Matapas came down from the mountain and discovered a nest of comitadjes at Vougadia and the Petra Monastery nearby . . . Acting as coal-dealers, they'd murdered patriarchal Greeks, one after another . . ."

"Mister Vasilis," Apostolis broke in. "Did you realize Pio was in the vicinity?"

"No! I thought he was at Bozets. When we learned that Captain Nikiphoros had burned Bozets, we felt he'd eliminated him. I lamented it, as I wanted to be the one to do away with him . . ."

With a secret gesture, Gregos interrupted Vasilis and resumed the account himself.

"A crime had occurred which opened our eyes. They put a husband and wife to death near Kleidi, and left their bodies in a frightful condition—with their limbs all twisted up! When we heard about it, we knew immediately that Angel Pio had contrived it, as he'd done the same before. Captain Matapas flew into a rage; and leaving his force in the hands of his deputy-commander, he came down from Olympus with Vasilis and me. The two of us had some old business to settle with Pio as well. At his farm, there were only two women . . ."

"Besides the dogs? . . . There are two ferocious dogs! . . ." Apostolis exclaimed.

"Ferocious and as strong as lions," Gregos said. "We took care of them."

"But not easily," Vasilis added. "No shots could be fired that might betray us. However Captain Akritas is a master with a knife."

With admiration, Apostolis stared at Gregos' large, powerful hands. Noticing it, the Captain laughed.

"After you've been pitted against lions and panthers, of what consequence are dogs?"

"You've really killed lions and panthers, Captain Akritas?" Pericles couldn't help asking.

"And elephants, yes; and worse—cannibals!"

"You've lived in Polynesia, then?"

"It's of no concern where or how I lived—although I'm well-traveled. But we're not speaking of me now."

"We're talking about Pio, though," Pericles said. "How did you find him, Vasilis?"

"Since he wasn't at the farm, he had to be somewhere in the area, Mister Pericles."

"How did you discover that he wasn't at the farm?"

"Captain Matapas knows both the comitadjes and their tricks," Vasilis replied.

And speaking slowly—as deliberate with his words as he was with his movements—he gave them details:

"There was an open window all lit up. 'A trap, a signal!' Captain Matapas warned. At the first barking of the dogs, the light at the window went out. At such times, speed and decisiveness are crucial. We didn't know what we'd find inside. But we climbed in by the window, with Captain Matapas in the lead. Near the fireplace, he discovered two women huddled up. They didn't have time to put out the fire, which was burning and throwing off light. Seeing a priest, they fell at his feet, seeking help.

"Both Captain Akritas and I had come in; and knowing Bulgarian better, I asked who they were waiting for. Crossing themselves, they swore that Angel Pio wasn't at home. The younger one, Pazarenze's widow—you've encountered her, Apostolis—had more courage. She said she wanted to be hospitable, taking us for fools! . . . We inquired where Pio was. 'In Yianzista, where he sells his cheeses,' they answered. And the window—why was it open and lit up? . . .

"The old woman, Pio's wife, got confused and started to cry. The other one declared that the child hadn't returned, that they were expecting him. 'What child?' I demanded. They stopped short. 'My nephew,' the old lady replied—as if we didn't know about her nephew, the little Bulgarian! That is to say, Captain Akritas had been informed of how Pazarenze's wife received some of the child's clothes back and thought Captain Agras killed him. Right, Apostolis?"

"Yes, I heard her mourning him at Zervohori."

"Captain Akritas told me," Vasilis went on. "I inquired if perhaps they'd set up the light for Angel Pio's dead nephew . . . At that point, they lost their heads and swore at our feet that they were alone and didn't know Angel Pio's whereabouts. Captain Matapas had grown angry and wanted to tie them up. But Captain Akritas pitied them.

"From the window we saw a fire, and rushed outside. Just as we left, the women fired two pistol shots. Like our prisoner said, it was the signal for the men to flee. Then we met up with you. If Mangas hadn't burst upon me, we might have shot you, we were so certain it was Pio."

"He was out there!" Pericles remarked. "Only not with us."

Thoughtfully, Vasilis said:

"The little Bulgarian saw him first and fired at him! He did so in a fury!"

"Jovan hates him," Apostolis explained. "He fears and hates him."

"Why?" Pericles asked.

"His uncle mistreated him."

"He beat him?"

"One time I saw him whip him with a strap. I saved him with some lies. Since then, the child has followed me faithfully. Yet he never speaks about his uncle. Who knows why the comitadje took him into his house! . . . Perhaps to graze his sheep . . . The child was always hungry . . ."

Vasilis cut him off. Tired and dispirited, he lay down to sleep on the flagstones, as did Pericles—while Apostolis and Captain Akritas stood watch at the windows.

The day passed without any trouble. Every two hours, they changed guard. The sun was about to set, when at one of the windows Pericles silently gave the signal.

Danger! . . .

At once, they all rushed over to the hiding-place. Gregos, the last one, returned the altar to its place and descended a few steps below. Keeping the stone slab ajar with his back, he listened.

The church door opened. Footsteps and Turkish conversation filled the room.

"No," a man's voice maintained in Turkish. "I haven't conducted a service for two Sundays because I was sick. However I carry the key with me. No one enters inside."

The footsteps drew near. Searching and more questions followed. And again the priest spoke, complaining:

"You've dirtied the flagstones with your muddy shoes!"

"True! There was no need for us to lose so much time on these stones that no one's walked on," another voice responded with a laugh. "If the infidels had hidden here, they would have left tracks . . ."

Yet the voices grew closer.

"Sometimes they don't leave tracks," the other Turk replied. "Search! Search everywhere!"

Quietly Gregos lowered his shoulders, and without a sound the slab adjusted into place under the altar.

There was more shuffling back and forth. After that, it became calm and the church door closed heavily.

* * * *

Gregos didn't stir. For an hour he remained motionless, straining his ear. A soft growling sounded behind him, which was stifled immediately. Someone started to come up in back of him. It was Apostolis. Like a hook, Gregos' iron-like hand restrained him. Another hour went by.

There was a noise—that of the church door opening again and closing.

Gregos bent over to Apostolis' ear. The boy was standing right behind him, pinned there by his powerful hand.

"Don't budge! Don't anyone say a word! The dog musn't growl . . ." he whispered to him.

Slowly, without any creaking or sound at all, he raised the stone slab and stood there immobile on the stairway. Then in the dusk that faintly lit up the church, Apostolis watched Gregos' huge body undulate out of the trap-door like a snake, and lie down under the altar cloth. For such a strong man, his agility and control were astonishing. . . Suddenly Gregos sprang up and charged out from under the altar! . . . A battle could be heard, silent and harrowing. And afterwards calm again . . . Apostolis drew himself out of the hole, raised the altar cloth, and saw Gregos kneeling on a man's chest, tying him up like a sausage.

Seizing his old pistol, Apostolis ran to help.

"Don't fire, for God's sake! No noise! . . ." Gregos said.

On the ground, tied-up and incapable of moving, his mouth stopped up and his eyes closed, a Turk appeared dead.

"Did you kill him?" Apostolis asked.

"Not yet," Gregos replied. "If there's any resistance, though, I'll settle with him!"

And he ordered:

"Go over to the window . . . See if you notice a shadow . . . If need be, we'll cut down this Turk, along with the Bulgarian, and make an assault . . ."

Apostolis went over to the window. He didn't see anything. He passed to the opposite window. Once more, nothing.

"If I open the door a little, will you go and scout around?" Gregos asked.

"I'll go."

"Wait until it's dark . . ."

Before long Apostolis slipped through the door, crawled outside, and disappeared in the night.

When he returned shortly, Gregos half-opened the door again, and the guide crept back into the church.

"They've gone to the village to the coffee-house," he told Gregos. "But they'll be back. They left their sacks close by. Cigarette butts are on the ground. There don't seem to be many men—a patrol."

"Fetch the others. Let's be off! Can we reach Toumba before daybreak?"

"Impossible!"

"Where should we go?"

"To Kapsohora. I know of some reliable lodging there."

"We're off, then, for Kapsohora!"

Yet it wasn't so simple. The rebels emerged from their refuge—with Matapas leading the blindfolded Bulgarian, and Vasilis and Gregos carrying the tied and gagged Turk. Outside, they headed west in the plain.

Far from any habitation they uncovered the Bulgarian's eyes, then untied the Turk's feet and removed the cloth from his mouth. But when they ordered him to walk, he refused.

"Tie him to a tree and leave him," Vasilis told Gregos.

"And when they find him?" Gregos asked. "It's not to our advantage to lose the hiding-place at Kaliani."

"Walk with us," Pericles said in Turkish. "We won't harm you. However we can't leave you."

As an answer, the Turk let out a cry:

"Infidels! Help! . . ."

He didn't succeed in saying more. Gregos' large hand fell hard upon his mouth, and he raised his revolver.

"Walk or I'll fire!"

The Turk sat down.

"I won't go," he replied in a choked voice. "Fire if you dare!"

Gregos hesitated. A gunshot would wake the whole countryside.

Matapas approached him.

"We have no time for discussion," he said, "nor the resources to lose Kaliani. Do what has to be done! . . . Forward!" he commanded the others.

They proceeded in silence, leaving Gregos behind with the Turk. Jovan tottered and fell down. Vasilis picked him up with a certain affection and saw that he was crying. He spoke gently to him:

"You raised a pistol against your uncle. You were so brave. And now you're crying?"

The child didn't answer. He went on crying softly, his face buried in his arm. They traveled at a rapid pace, without speaking. With great strides, Gregos caught up to them—alone. No one asked him what had become of the Turk. It was almost at a run that they continued.

The night was advanced, two or three in the morning, when they reached a house on the outskirts of Kapsohora—trudging through muddy swamp-land in a roundabout way.

In the lead, Apostolis gave a soft cry that resembled the muffled wail of a jackal.

A window opened part way.

"Who is it?" a man asked in a low voice.

"Apostolis the guide!"

"Alone?"

"No!"

"Bring them!"

Turning to his companions, Apostolis led them to the door of the house. It opened silently, and they all entered into a dark room.

"How many are there?" the same masculine voice inquired.

"Seven—including a child," Matapas answered. "What's more, we're hungry and dead-tired!"

"I can't light a lamp here," the man said. "Come downstairs. I'll get you some food and water."

"Be careful!" Apostolis said, guiding them. "We'll descend by a rope-ladder."

One by one, they climbed down into a room with a dirt floor. They were so weary that they stretched right out on the ground.

In a little while, the master of the house brought bread, cheese, yogurt and water—and a small lantern as well, which he lit. An old man with white hair, he was short and hunched over, but his blue eyes radiated goodness and he had a smile on his lips.

"I don't have other food in the house," he said, as if to excuse himself for the simple but ample meal. "At least no one will search for you here. Eat and sleep in peace. I'll be on guard."

He stopped for a moment before Gregos, like he wanted to say something to him. However he didn't speak. He only looked him in the eyes, and then went back upstairs and closed the door behind him.

The rebels were in a dirt cellar below ground, with a wood ceiling and no window. No one inquired about the old man. Untying the Bulgarian's hands, they gave him his share and retied his hands. Everyone lay down to sleep.

Apostolis was next to Pericles.

"The 1821 revolution," he whispered, "where your grand-father lost his arm—was it as fierce as this Struggle?"

Pericles reflected:

"It was fierce, too." he replied. "Yet I think this Struggle is worse."

"Why?"

"There it was a war. Here it's murders."

Gregos, who had an ear out for the boys' conversation, sat up and put his arms around his knees, which he'd drawn up against his chest.

"What do you youngsters know about atrocities?" he asked them, without any irony or edge to his voice. "Have you ever seen hungry men eat a living person? Have you seen them smear honey over someone and throw him, alive, into an ants' nest? What do you know about savagery?"

The boys kept quiet. A serious Gregos continued:

"Every struggle is fierce! . . . Without exception! Take the Greek Revolution. We don't know all about 1821, because those who saw it and those who wrote about it omitted many ugly deeds from their accounts, or they played down the atrocities. That way, the Revolution became a legend, which isn't always dependable. The same thing will happen when they write about this Struggle. The Bulgarians will say we're beasts—and we'll claim to be angels. However all of us—do you hear!—as many as have joined the Struggle, we've been compelled to spill blood, some of it justly, some unjustly. All struggles are fierce. Either you kill or they'll kill you. What's more, the means the enemy uses, willingly or not, you'll use yourself if you don't want to be destroyed."

Once more, the boys kept silent. And Captain Matapas, guessing that the fate of the Turk was on their minds, spoke up:

"Here we're fighting Bulgarians and Romanians on the terri-tory of a third enemy, the Turk, who seeks to divide us in order to better assert his own control. Wherever he can he'll wipe us out—separately, and together."

A thoughtful silence followed. Again Matapas broke it:

"How did you realize that poor Turk hadn't left the church with the others?" he asked Gregos.

"I had my suspicions. Besides, the church door reclosed as if they hadn't all gone out together the first time. And I heard the dog growl. In the silence of the church, something indefinable told me it wasn't empty. In Uganda, you learn to perceive secret movements, even smell them when you don't hear them . . ."

In a low voice, Apostolis asked Pericles:

"What does Uganda mean? Do you know?"

"It's a place in the center of Africa with many wild animals, and wild tribes in some parts."

"And Captain Akritas went there?"

"It appears so. Ask him tomorrow."

But the next day Apostolis didn't ask him. All their minds were preoccupied. In the morning, the old man ran and shut the trap-door. Silent and motionless, the rebels heard conversation and a commotion above them that lasted throughout the day. It was a Turkish patrol. Soldiers had come; and they stayed to eat, drink, and sleep at the old man's house. They had no idea seven persons were hiding under their feet. No sound or movement could be discerned.

To be on the safe side, they'd tied the Bulgarian prisoner's hands and feet and gagged him. Towards evening, though, with no air in their hole in the ground, it became stifling to such a degree that Vasilis took the gag off so the Bulgarian wouldn't suffocate. He sat beside him, himself, with his knife ready should he start to speak or stir.

Everyone waited. The air became increasingly unbearable. They were all lying down, without water or air. How long could they endure it?

In the early evening, a clamor sounded above their heads. The soldiers were collecting their weapons and equipment to depart.

The house emptied out. Moments passed, and the trap-door opened. Fresh air poured into the hideout, reinvigorating them. Quietly the old man descended the rope-ladder with more food and water.

"They're going to Gida," he said, "but in a couple of hours, others will be here. I informed them that I'd seen you yesterday heading for Nikhori. They'll search for you there. However others are on their way from Kaliani. You must leave at once."

Captain Matapas wanted to give the old man money, but he was obstinate in refusing it.

"My child is in the Greek Army. I won't be paid for rendering such aid."

"What is your name, so at least we know who we're indebted to?" Matapas asked.

"What does my name matter to you?" the old man replied.

Turning his guileless blue eyes towards Gregos, he added:

"Only know that I'm not the offspring of a Turk! . . ."

Gregos grew pale. But he inquired calmly:

"Could your son be called Yiangos?"

The old man smiled.

"He might be called Yiangos," he replied. "Perhaps you know him?"

"I know a Yiangos who has blue eyes like yours," Gregos said, assuming a look of indifference.

The old man spoke up again, addressing Captain Matapas:

"The men here think I'm one of them—an Albanian, a Turk! Let me do what I can for our Struggle in secret."

Matapas squeezed his hand.

"Greek patriotism raises its head at such times," he declared. "And we have still another favor to ask of you. Hold this one! He's a burden to us in our hasty flight,"—and he indicated the Bulgarian prisoner.

But upon hearing that they intended to leave him behind, the Bulgarian fell at Matapas' feet. Crying, he hugged the captain's knees.

"Don't leave me! Take me with you! I'll give my life for you!" he begged. "I don't want to return to the Bulgarians! Look at what they do to us to force us to fight with them!"

Opening his shirt, he displayed three or four half-healed knife wounds.

"That's what they did to my brother! And to me!" he said. "No matter how we feel about it, we have to follow them. Take me with you! I don't want to fall into their hands again!"

Matapas fretted and fumed. He was impatient and hesitant.

"Take him with you, Commander," Gregos intervened. "He might be telling the truth. I'll vouch for him. And if he goes astray . . ."

With the palm of his hand, he slapped the revolver that was stuffed into his belt.

Matapas relented:

"What is your name?" he asked.

"Christof Bozan!"

"Come along then, Christof Bozan," he said to the prisoner in his broken Bulgarian. "However if you make a move to betray us . . ."

The Bulgarian knelt and kissed the captain's knees.

"Do with me as you will!" he exclaimed. "I'll be devoted to you!"

Hurriedly Apostolis led them over the most deserted parts of the plain. He made detours and chose ravines and irregular terrain—passing through gorges, even into the water when there was a risk that someone would see or hear them.

It was still night—day hadn't yet broken—when they reached the landing cove at Terkovista.

Two successive pistol shots brought a few canoes to the shore. Quickly the exhausted group entered the dugouts. And before dawn they were stretched out, free and secure, on the deck of the large Toumba hut, beyond the Bulgarians' revenge and the Turkish authorities' pursuit.

24.

Kourfalia

ON A MARCH MORNING, THE LARGE TOUMBA HUT was in a state of agitation. For days Captain Akritas had been ready to depart, exasperated that Apostolis wasn't back from Olympus where he'd guided Captain Matapas. He threatened to go off "to his work" without any guide, along with Vasilis who'd remained with him.

The work of Captain Akritas, a commander still without a rebel force, proved a mystery to everyone. Yet who would have the nerve to ask for an explanation from the powerful rebel with the flashing eyes, if he didn't choose to give it himself? He declared that he was fed up waiting, that he'd be on his way—and he got ready and ordered a canoe to let him out at the landing-cove.

Meanwhile, in the southern plain the Turks had been thrown into turmoil by the discovery of Angel Pio's corpse, as well as that of a Turkish soldier with a knife plunged into his heart. Confused, they didn't understand the sequence of who killed who, since that same night the patriarchal farm of Gionis had been burned down and all those inside slaughtered. As always the Turks searched, arrested innocent people, and failed to find anything out.

"It doesn't matter to me!" Gregos told Captain Kalas, who characteristically advised caution and delay. "I'll leave without a guide, whatever happens!"

That morning Apostolis finally arrived. And now Captain Akritas no longer wanted to set off.

For Apostolis had brought unexpected news.

Everyone—men and captains alike—realized that the Macedonian Struggle was at a critical point. The brilliant commanders,

338

seasoned by the hardships and dangers of the war, had reached their limits. Sick and exhausted, they were requesting replacements—replacements which hadn't come.

All the rebels were aware that the security force dispatched by the governments of the European Powers, allegedly to instill order into Turkey's internal affairs, supported the Bulgarians when it served their interests—or the Romanians or Serbs. But they never favored the Greeks, who as a more progressive element thwarted their propaganda . . .

The men knew that the Turks, pressured by the foreign powers, were abandoning their half-hearted policies and hunting down the Greek forces with a vengeance. Posted at the borders, they followed and obstructed their movements and supplies, protesting and complaining to the Greek government that the rebel chiefs were army officers.

Thus the authorities in Greece were forced to recall many of the commanders, above all those well-known to the Turks.

Apostolis had stopped at various villages to ply his trade as a carpenter. He needed to earn some money to buy new shoes . . .

"Why didn't you ask me to give it to you, instead of making me waste so much time?" Gregos said with a frown.

"Ask for a handout?" Apostolis responded indignantly.

"You wouldn't be asking for a handout, since you'd be working for me," Gregos answered.

Apostolis recalled the two gold liras the fake-priest had put in the fisherman's hand when they'd crossed the Loudias River. However to be paid himself? For a service to the Struggle? To stoop to that? . . .

Without replying, he resumed his account.

He'd undertaken repairs in the villages he passed through, but also gathered information and listened to the villagers' views and complaints. And he'd visited Zorba and seen Miss Electra. With her school still in ruins, she couldn't return to it. The Master had promised to rebuild it for her; yet how would he manage to do so?

Faced with all these difficulties, the General Consul had decided to alter his strategy, although he remained resolute in not giving ground. Since the officers and men arriving from Greece were limited now, he'd recruit villagers trained with a rifle and appoint local deputy-commanders—ones who'd fought with the great captains and knew rebel warfare first hand. But they needed money . . . which they didn't have . . .

Apostolis waited until Captain Kalas had gone, then spoke in a low voice to Vasilis and Gregos, busy loading their equipment, ready to set off.

"I saw Pericles at Niki. He told me to inform you that Captain Nikiphoros sent secretly for guides from all the surrounding Greek villages, and that without letting the men in on it he's planning a new raid. Pericles didn't know where, though. The commander wants all the fighters to meet at Tsekri."

As soon as he learned it, Gregos changed his mind about departing. He wouldn't go either to Olympus or anywhere else— but to Tsekri.

"Here at the lake, the Struggle has declined," he said to Apostolis. "There's no longer any action!" In his anger he put aside the difference in the boy's age and suddenly spoke to him as an equal.

"The Bulgarians found it tough-going with Kouga forti-fied and new Greek huts sprouting up in all the corridor this far. They've abandoned their hut nearby and confined themselves to their complex at Zervohori. Moreover with Agras gone, Kalas has adopted a purely defensive role from his base at the two Toumbas. He's taking it easy until he gets the permission he sought to return to Greece."

"Captain Agras has also asked for a replacement . . ." Apostolis interjected sadly. "And Captain Nikiphoros."

"Who informed you?" Vasilis questioned him.

"Miss Electra. Captain Agras is worn out from his constant fever, and Captain Nikiphoros requested to be sent to Naousa in his place. He wants to leave the Swamp. He's suffering from rheu-matism, and from fever and a cough—what's more, he has trouble walking. His replacement has arrived."

"Then he's through? We'll go to Tsekri for the new commander?" Gregos was becoming more and more dispirited.

Softly, Apostolis replied:

"Pericles said it will be a bold undertaking. Mitsos is in on it; however he didn't reveal the location, even to his cousin. Pericles has guessed it, though."

"What did he guess?"

"That it's Kourfalia!"

"I'll be damned!" Gregos responded in his deep voice, recovering his spirits all at once. "Do you know what an expedition to Kourfalia means?"

"It's a nest of comitadjes, isn't it?" Vasilis spoke up.

"Yes! It's their strongest village, with a Turkish army stationed there. All the villagers—and there are many of them!—are armed. At night sentries keep watch so that no one approaches. Matapas wanted to descend from Olympus and strike them. But he doesn't have enough men."

"Pericles says that Captain Nikiphoros has seventy-five regulars now, plus many locals instructed in firearms!" Apostolis reported. "And one day the commander told Mitsos he couldn't accept leaving Kourfalia, the most difficult and dangerous operation, to his successor. For this reason, Pericles suspects he's preparing to go there."

"What is his successor like?" Vasilis inquired.

Apostolis didn't know. He hadn't seen him."

Gregos got up.

"What does it matter?" he asked, shaking his hands that were numb from lack of activity and stamping his feet on the floor. "We'll follow Captain Nikiphoros wherever he leads us. Go get a canoe, Apostolis, and guide us to Tsekri!"

In the meantime, a dugout had drawn up alongside the deck. From Tsekri, it brought news for Captain Kalas. After hearing it in private, Kalas reappeared and summoned his men.

"Captain Nikiphoros is seeking volunteers at Tsekri," he announced. "Who would like to join him?"

Most of them did, including the Bulgarian prisoner Christof Bozan. But they brushed him aside. Captain Kalas selected those who weren't indispensable to the safety of Toumba; and with joyful voices, the men got ready to leave. At last they would be on the move again! The whole deck was exhilarated.

* * * *

A series of canoes, one behind the other, headed along the lake paths. However when they reached the deeper water of the Loudias River, they encountered a complete fleet of other canoes on their way to Nikhori. Captain Nikiphoros was with them.

In order to mislead the Turks, and at the same time celebrate the planned operation on its eve, he was taking his men down to the most heavily Greek populated village. Its inhabitants were awaiting him with lamb on a spit and lute music.

"Whoever wants to come with us, follow along," Nikiphoros said to Kalas's men.

Only one canoe failed to join the fleet. Instead, it continued north. It was Gregos' and Vasilis' boat, with Apostolis as guide. The boy refused to leave them.

"Better for them not to see us," Gregos had commented, making a sign to Vasilis.

Vasilis agreed.

* * * *

Few men had remained at Tsekri, only as many as were needed to guard the hut. Yet no one knew the destination of the campaign.

"Where is the little Bulgarian, your apprentice?" Gregos asked Apostolis all of a sudden. "Pericles got him from Toumba to bring him here. Where did he put him that I don't see him?"

He'd stretched out on deck and was sunning himself lazily.

"Miss Electra has him again," the guide answered. "She says that she wants to take him to Thessalonika to Pericles' grandmother, Mrs. Vasiotakis, to make him a Greek."

"Has he gone?" Vasilis inquired.

Apostolis didn't know. He'd left him at Zorba with Miss Electra, at the home of her pupil Evangelia.

* * * *

Lying on his back with his hands under his head, Gregos murmured a name over and over . . .

"George Vasiotakis . . . George Vasiotakis . . ."

It sent a shiver through Apostolis, who'd never seen Gregos like that. His reflective, almost sorrowful air disturbed the boy.

"Not George—Pericles!" Apostolis said. "And his cousin Mitsos!"

Gregos didn't answer.

"You don't know," Vasilis said. "George is the name of Mitsos' father. I was the gardener at his house in Alexandria."

"Is Alexandria in Uganda?" Apostolis asked. He never forgot a word once he'd heard it, but he didn't know much geography.

Gregos sat up.

"How do you know Uganda?" he asked in return.

"You said one day . . . when you caught the Turk in the church at Kaliani, that in Uganda you learn to both hear and smell sounds."

Gregos looked at him half-mockingly, his hands clasped around his knees.

"A hell of a memory!" he responded. And he added: "Do you like to travel? Would you like to go to Uganda?"

Apostolis' eyes shone. But he restrained himself.

"Now I have work here," he answered. "I can't leave."

"I also have work here . . . as does Vasilis . . . and all of us . . ." Gregos said, becoming preoccupied again.

He fell silent, gazing out at the water and the green bed of reeds beyond.

Curiosity was eating away at Apostolis. He wanted to ask Gregos a thousand things, yet he didn't dare. Freer with the mild-mannered Vasilis, he inquired again in a low voice:

"Is Alexandria in Uganda?"

344 Secrets of the Swamp

"No. It's in Egypt," Vasilis replied. "Uganda is a long way off."

"How does Captain Akritas know your boss?" Apostolis whispered even lower, a little frightened by his boldness.

But Gregos heard him. Truly, as he'd said, he smelled as well as heard sounds. Unperturbed, he answered:

"I knew him in '97. He'd come as a volunteer to fight."

Apostolis' breath was taken away.

"Here? In Macedonia?"

"No, in Greece. We all fought then. But we were defeated."

He seemed angry when he said it. Silence followed.

Then Apostolis spoke up—deciding to risk a beating in order to learn:

"Captain Akritas, Pericles related many things to me about the war of '97, where his uncle was wounded. However I never understood, nor did he, why the Turks won. In the 1821 Revolution, a few Greeks defeated many Turks. Here, when a Greek force fights a Bulgarian one, the Bulgarians get the worst of it. Why in '97 were the Greeks defeated? What made the difference?"

"The difference between now and '97 is that here the Master is in charge, while in '97! . . . In '97, the officers called all of us from Turkish-occupied territory 'Turkish offspring' . . . Our leaders then were elite boors in polished boots who abandoned Larissa and fled as though making off with stolen chickens . . ."

Gregos stopped and bit his lips that trembled.

"You were there!" Apostolis exclaimed, ignoring Gregos' blazing eyes in his longing to hear more.

Vasilis made a sign with his hand.

"Let it be," he said softly to Gregos. "Why repeat it?"

"It doesn't bother me to talk about it today," Gregos replied, regaining his composure. "At Kourfalia, if we go, many of us won't return. Besides, I saw the sorcerer in my sleep yesterday."

"What sorcerer?" Apostolis asked eagerly.

Gregos began a narrative:

"Uganda is a strange place in Africa with different black tribes. Among them are Christians, and cannibals who hide inside the thick forests and kill strangers with poisonous arrows or lances. There are sorcerers, too, that perform magic to bring rain or cast curses and fearful punishments upon their enemies. I once saved a sorcerer from some cannibals who were preparing to tear him apart . . ."

"How did you save him?" Apostolis inquired breathlessly.

"It wasn't hard. I had a revolver and they were short, so-high people! With a back-handed blow, I threw down three, and with a gunshot I dispersed the others."

"And the sorcerer?"

"The sorcerer fell at my feet and asked what I wanted as a gift. 'Tell me when I'll die,' I said. 'When I come and visit you in your sleep, get ready!' he answered. 'In three days, you'll die!' Last night as I slept, he came. But I still have a debt to pay off . . ."

Vasilis interrupted him.

"A shame, I took you for smart," he said. "And you believe such tales, spun by old women . . ."

Gregos laughed, unconcerned.

"Whether I believe them or not doesn't alter fate," he stated.

"What does that mean?" Apostolis asked.

"As we would say, what's written. And it's written for me that I won't return to Greece."

"Why? Why?" Apostolis cried out.

"Because that's the way it is," Gregos declared in a manner that cut off further conversation.

Enclosed once more in his accustomed secrecy, he lay back down and shut his eyes.

* * * *

All that day, again and again Apostolis thought about Gregos' words. Concerning Uganda, he'd ask Miss Electra. She knew it all—even about the wild tribes. But the sorcerer's prophesy shook him to his depths. For Gregos to die! . . . Such a big, powerful, invincible man! Who would dare attack him? A bullet? With his hand, he'd scoop them up like roasted chick peas . . .

At night when the men returned singing and laughing from the festivity at Nikhori, their pleasure seemed jarring to him.

There was a lot of laughter. At Nikhori, the villagers had roasted lamb and treated the rebels to wine and ouzo. They'd even called over some Turks passing by with two policemen and entertained them!

Captain Nikiphoros had had his lads guard the Turks all evening—while the villagers were to prevent their leaving Nikhori the next day or the following night. That way, they couldn't reveal the force's movements and create suspicion with the authorities. Afterwards they'd be free to go.

Together with Nikiphoros and his men, an elderly Greek in rebel's clothes with a heavily lined face ascended to the Tsekri hut. It was Captain Nikiphoros' newly-arrived successor, with the military name "Nikiphoros the Second."[40] The Bulgarians weren't to learn that the commander had been transferred to Naousa, and take courage that the man who'd instilled so much fear in them would be gone.

But the rebels hadn't yet developed affection for the new leader, Pericles informed Apostolis when he inquired. "He's a little abrupt—he comes on at us too strong. Besides, everyone is inconsolable that the commander is departing. Let's hope Captain Akritas, at any rate, remains with us . . ."

Embarassed, humbled by his ignorance, Apostolis asked:

"Do you know, Pericles, if the sorcerers of Uganda are wise?"

"The sorcerers of Uganda? I know nothing about Uganda and its sorcerers. Where did you hear about them?"

Apostolis related what Captain Akritas had said that day about the prophesy of the sorcerer of Uganda, the '97 war, and the insult "a boor with polished boots" had given him. He added that it was "written" for the captain not to return to Greece again.

Pericles raised his eyebrows doubtfully.

"Why won't he return to Greece? Who will stop him? Didn't you ask why it was 'written' for him not to return?"

"I asked him. And he replied: 'Because that's the way it is.'"

The two boys contemplated the matter. Still, Apostolis didn't tell him: "He's not Captain Akritas; he's called Gregos." Nor did Pericles confide to Apostolis that for some time he'd suspected that the powerful giant who turned up here and there according to the needs of the Struggle—always alone, a leader without a following, a captain without men—wasn't the real Captain Akritas but someone hiding behind his name. Each of them kept his reflections and suspicions to himself.

* * * *

The next day in the morning, initiated youths from the surrounding villages began arriving, along with a number of men from the hut at Boura. Where they would go, they didn't know. Captain Nikiphoros had summoned them; and willing to meet their death, they rushed where they were ordered—some to the Apostoles hut, others to Tsekri.

After consulting with his second-in-command, his captains, and his guides, the commander set the departure time for the undertaking at five in the afternoon, then started off for the Apostoles hut with his force.

Fortunately many villagers had responded to his call. Nikiphoros separated sixty to guard the various huts and the Tsekri and Apostoles landing-coves, where boats would await the rebels' return. Both coves had to be free and protected when they got back to the lake from their dangerous expedition.

At five, Nikiphoros and his men descended at the Apostoles landing. There were sixty-eight in all—all of them dedicated to their commander. Andonis from Volos was among them. Upon hearing he was to be left behind, he'd put up such an outcry to be allowed to avenge all he'd suffered in Macedonia, that Captain Nikiphoros relented and took him along.

"Who of us will consent to stay behind!" Mitsos whispered to Vasilis.

Under his breath, Pericles murmured:

"Who will consent to it?"

Because once they'd reached land, Captain Nikiphoros had taken Pericles and Apostolis aside. It would be a difficult and risky operation, he said, and he refused to bring two such young boys with him. For the first time he disclosed to the men that their destination was Kourfalia. He'd found out that the Turkish army had left there and was hopeful new soldiers wouldn't have time to replace them. The moment was ripe to strike the village.

In the dark, in the silence of the deserted shore, the commander spoke to his youth, urging them to keep calm, be brave, and stick close to their captains.

"The great danger of night operations," he told them, "is the splitting up of the force and misunderstandings that result from it."

Emotion swept over him, it being the first time he'd led so many men on such a hard campaign. The knowledge that his own lack of care or thought could cause them to be lost, troubled him. Nevertheless, he assumed responsibility without hesitation or fear; and he felt pride and pleasure that he'd be their leader.

"A Greek force hasn't dared attack this nest of comitadjes," he went on. "But seeing that we're determined to defend our comrades at Kourfalia, we must enter the village and hold the Bulgarians accountable for their crimes. Remember, retaliate only against those with murder on their hands, and those who support them. I entrust our success to your bravery and patriotism!"

His emotion had been transmitted to his men. He crossed himself, and they did the same. No one uttered a word. All, though, resolved to fall rather than shame their commander.

"Let's go now," Nikiphoros declared. "Forward! . . . at a brisk pace!"

Apostolis was visibly moved by the commander's words.

In a hushed voice he asked Pericles, who'd been listening beside him:

"He didn't give you any job? . . ."

"No. None . . ."

"You brought Mangas?"

"Yes. He's in the canoe."

"Get him and let's go on our own. It's dark. They won't notice us. Mangas can follow their trail," Apostolis said.

* * * *

The human chain had left, with Tasos as guide. Captain Niki-phoros was second in line, and after him all the others from the commander's division. Silently, the remaining sections followed with their guides and captains. Vasilis and Gregos, who hadn't been included, were concealed among them.

"But who of us will consent to stay behind?" Vasilis repeated, next to Mitsos.

Gregos didn't speak. Impassive, he proceeded with his eyes fixed on Captain Nikiphoros' first division.

The moon came into view, requiring more caution on their part. For they'd pass the Apostoles village with its Turkish army, as well as other villages and farms and two Albanian pastures where they could be betrayed. Once alerted, the Turks would cut off their retreat to the lake when they returned. Again Tasos showed his capability, selecting the secret recesses of the landscape and guiding the long, human band through shielded areas behind hills or inside ravines. At a woody section in ancient Pella, the men sat down to rest, hidden inside the trees.

Bypassing the Apostoles village, they experienced no incident. Then shifting course, they continued their march all the way to the foot of a hill about fifteen minutes from Kourfalia, having traveled some three and a half hours. Behind them, stooped over at times and then upright—or crawling or even face down on the ground so as not to be discovered—the two boys trailed them. Next to Pericles, as if he perceived the need to hide, Mangas ran lightly and quietly.

Concealed by some low shrubs, Pericles observed the now motionless group of rebels. In the moonlight it couldn't be distinguished from the nearby hill.

"What are they doing?" he asked Apostolis, who was at his side. "Can you see?"

"They're not doing anything. They're having a break. That curved tree on the hill is the commander surveying below with his binoculars."

Pericles grew nostalgic at the sight of Nikiphoros.

"He reminds me of my grandfather. That's the way I remember him during an uprising in Crete when I was small. We'd taken to the mountains and he was watching the Turks from a hill, before firing broke out from the Greek side. It was '97, the year of the shameful Larissa flight . . ."

The curved tree on the hill shrank and disappeared.

"The commander's lying down. He's resting . . ." Apostolis said. "When he starts up again, we'll do so, too."

His penetrating eyes remained fixed upon the human band that slowly unfolded, separated, and proceeded almost imperceptibly towards Kourfalia. Rising, the two boys approached the hill and crawled up on it.

"The commander has stationed sentries," Apostolis murmured. "They'll see us if we stand up . . ."

"Wait for the shooting to begin," Pericles replied.

Catching hold of Mangas, he stuffed him under his arm, covering him with his cloak.

Activity could be detected in the village.

"The Bulgarians have sentries, too . . . They're withdrawing . . . However, they don't seem frightened . . . They'll have seen our men and mistaken them for the Turkish army," Apostolis explained, following every movement in the village roads below.

* * * *

Suddenly a division of rebels poured into a main street. A cry sounded, a signal! Armed villagers flew from their houses and sprang out of the sideroads. The firing lit up.

At the same time other rebels arrived on the run, leaping over barriers and ditches.

"The commander! The commander! The tall one there ahead . . . Come, Pericles! . . ." Apostolis said, all choked up.

The two boys rushed down the hill, gave the secret sign, and passed by the guards without anyone stopping them.

* * * *

Terrified, the Bulgarians had retreated and scattered. The boldness of the raid had dazed them. They needed time to recover, to assemble their forces and reorganize. In the meantime the rebels were burning designated comitadje houses. Evacuating the women and children, they grabbed hold of the armed youth and tied up those who wouldn't submit. The ones that attacked them, they shot. At a house in flames, where despairing women were trying to save some of their belongings, a few rebels lent a hand.

Meanwhile the Bulgarians had regrouped. Armed to the teeth, they counter-attacked the Greeks from various points. The battle raged—with lightning-like flashes erupting from the windows and direct clashes breaking out in the roads. The din was fearful. Gunshots burst forth like thunder, while shouts, commands, and moans filled the air.

* * * *

The two boys had hidden among the rebels and were fighting, themselves. Pericles had his rifle, but Apostolis was trying to manage with the pistol Agras had given him.

Carried away by the battle, Pericles cried out to him:

"Enter a house, take a rifle, and come back."

Apostolis climbed through a low window of the first house he encountered. Before him, he saw an elderly villager watching the battle from the far end of the room. The old man seemed to be following the shooting in the road more from curiosity than from fear, with a revolver in his hand.

Like a wild animal, Apostolis rushed at him, hung onto his arm, and grabbed his weapon.

"I won't hurt you," he said in Bulgarian, "but let me have your gun."

The man answered him in Greek:

"You fool! Do you think you'd succeed in taking it away from me, if I didn't see you were a Greek? Leave me my weapon; it won't be of use to you as it doesn't shoot far. Open the case over there and remove the Gras rifle from inside. There are cartridges as well."

Taken back, Apostolis stared at him.

"You're Greek?"

"Yes, there are a fair number of us here. Yet why do we talk! We've been waiting for you so long! Finally you came!"

Looking out at the road, he went on:

"If you win tonight, the village will become patriarchal again. If you're defeated, though . . ."

And turning to Apostolis:

"Who is your commander?" he inquired. "Tell him to capture Mitris Tané and burn his house down. But before he burns it, he should find Zlatan's letters."

"Which house is his?" Apostolis asked quickly, all his hunting dog's instinct aroused and ready.

"In the third road to the left, the fourth house with the tiles. There, take the Gras," he added.

Opening the case, he gave him the rifle and cartridges.

"Hurry," he said, "and get hold of the letters. Zlatan's preparing some outrage."

Apostolis had already jumped out the window. However, when he reached the road the old man had told him about, he saw that Mitris Tané's house was on fire. A fierce battle was underway, with shooting back and forth between those at the windows and the rebels outside. Captain Nikiphoros had raced up; and a couple of others were throwing hand grenades at the entrance and windows. The door opened and some women dashed outside, followed by two men. The Greeks caught hold of the women, then shot the men before they could flee.

Apostolis attempted to enter the house through a burnt window. Yet at that moment, the roof collapsed with a loud crash, hurling flames and sparks high up into the sky. It was too late. The whole house had become a sea of flames.

* * * *

The fighting persisted amidst great danger. A Turkish army was stationed an hour and a half away—which could appear at any time to block the Greeks' withdrawal. The deputy-commander guarding outside the village sent three men to inform Captain Nikiphoros that Bulgarians were shooting somewhere nearby, and to advise him to leave in case the Turks arrived. But the Captain had become intoxicated from the battle and the unexpected success of the operation.

Bulgarians were fleeing from all sides, or surrendering. The commander had captured hostages and interrogated them. He'd punished, burnt down, and devastated the comitadje nest. Defeated and disheartened, the villagers had given up. Nikiphoros remained another half hour to finish his work and ensure victory. Finally, drawing some youth and children with him as hostages, he departed from the village.

But a couple of old men followed him. Wailing, they pleaded: "The children! The children!" over and over again.

In response, Captain Nikiphoros ordered the children to be left behind. He took only five youth with him as hostages, in order to prevent reprisals against the Greek inhabitants of Kourfalia.

* * * *

The force returned rapidly with Tasos in the lead. Stretching his short, stout legs as fast as they'd go, he made a number of turns—keeping at a distance from the Apostoles village with its fifty or so Turks and an officer.

They went straight to the Apostoles landing, which had men on guard and canoes waiting for them. Day was just dawning. With its stagnant water, thick spring growth, water-lilies and old, rotted plants, the Swamp emitted fumes and a stench of decay and mould that caught in their throats. It was more noticeable now, after their foray into the clear, country air.

"We've lived for seven months in this hell! . . ." Captain Pandelis exclaimed, viewing the myriad of winged insects that, not yet grown bold, shot up and darted back down again, fluttering and whirling about the water-lilies and lake water.

Captain Nikiphoros hastened them on.

"Everyone into the canoes!" he ordered. "Count up. How many are we?"

There were sixty-eight of them, the number that had set off.

With astonishment, Captain Nikiphoros saw Vasilis.

"How did you get here?" he asked.

And he commanded: "Count up again. Another man has been added. We're more now."

The men recounted. Once again there were sixty-eight. From those that had started out, one person was missing.

Mitsos Vasiotakis was no longer with them.

25.

Gregos

FROM MITRIS TANÉ'S HOUSE, which had been destroyed by fire, Apostolis returned to the old villager's without achieving anything. He found him as he'd left him, staring out into the road with the revolver in his hand.

"The house burned down. It was too late," he said, panting from his run back. "I didn't get the letters."

"Did they kill Mitris Tané?" the old man inquired.

"I don't know him. However, they killed two men who came out of his door."

"Wait for me here. I'll go and make sure. Just don't let them see us together. It's possible he has a letter on him. I'll search," the old man said.

And he went outside.

In the road, they were still fighting. Apostolis watched the battle without being visible himself. Suddenly a dog bounded inside and sprang up on him with happy cries. At the same time, Pericles, too, entered the room through the window.

"What are you doing here?" he asked. "I had a terrible time finding you! Without Mangas I'd still be looking. The commander almost caught sight of me . . ."

Apostolis told him as much as he knew and explained that he was waiting for the old man.

A container of water stood on a shelf. Pericles grabbed it and gulped it down.

"We left without a water-bottle," he said, "like inexperienced schoolchildren. This water stinks! Poof! But listen! Mitsos saw me and scolded me . . ."

"Will he give us away?" Apostolis asked anxiously.

"No! He told me where we can find him outside the village in order to return together. The commander was right. The danger lies in the force splintering and in misunderstandings. Our own sentry didn't distinguish who Mitsos was as he jumped over a ditch with Tasos and two others; and he shot at him."

"Did he hit him?" Apostolis cried.

"No! Fortunately it was cloudy. In his haste, the sentry didn't aim well. The bullet missed its mark. Now Mitsos' division is fighting nearby. I made off so as not to be seen and recognized . . ."

The old man was coming back. He'd viewed both corpses, neither of which was Tané. They were his two followers. Tané had either perished in the fire, or escaped. But the rebels had won, and they'd burned down five or six houses. The worst comitadjes had fallen. The others had taken flight, were in hiding, or surrendered.

By then the battle had died down. The firing was steadily decreasing. From time to time, a couple of gunshots rang out in the distance, and then stopped abruptly. The boys walked out into the road and found it deserted. Everywhere fear and silence reigned. All the windows and doors were closed. Occasionally a woman's wail could be heard behind wooden shutters, before silence returned.

The old man had followed them.

"Where are you headed?" he inquired.

"For the hill."

"Don't go that way. There's a row of Bulgarian houses; and they'll be watching in back of the shutters. Take the upper way, make a loop, and you'll come to a ravine that puts you out at the hill. Farewell, lads!"

The boys did as the old man instructed. Yet they'd lost time. When they reached the hill, they discovered Mitsos alone. The entire force had left. However faithful to his word, Mitsos had stayed behind to wait for his cousin and Apostolis.

"In the dark, we won't find them again," he said, worried.

"I'll locate the road," Apostolis answered. "When I've traveled a path, I never forget it . . ."

"Besides, we have the dog," a deep voice near them said.

"You again, Captain Akritas!" Mitsos exclaimed. "Why are you always close by tonight? And how is it that you remained behind?"

"Didn't you stay back to accompany these two foolish boys?" Gregos responded calmly.

Moved, Mitsos said:

"Captain Akritas, you saved my life once when you knocked the rifle out of a Bulgarian's hand. Then you saved me again . . ."

"Wouldn't you do the same?" Gregos countered. "Let's not waste time. We have a long journey to the Swamp."

"Why are you still here?" Mitsos asked.

"The commander isn't aware that I set off with him, so he's not looking for me. Better two men than one, I figured. Moreover, it's not certain we'll find the road clear . . . and the children don't count."

The children counted to themselves; and they were offended by Gregos' words. Apostolis meant to show his usefulness. Taking charge, he hurried down the hill and caught up with the road they'd arrived on. Mangas ran beside him, sniffing and smelling the ground. No one spoke. Gregos came second, Pericles next, and Mitsos last. They went by an Albanian pasture unobserved, and kept on traveling until they approached the Apostoles village.

Following Tasos' example, the guide descended into a ravine to provide cover. Then Mangas started to show signs of agitation, running up and down while sniffing the ground. He darted up to Pericles, cried out softly to him, and continued running up and down without distancing himself.

"Danger . . ." Pericles murmured.

Gregos passed the word to Apostolis, and they all lay flat on the ground. Nothing could be heard—only Mangas' low growling.

The clouds had glided by, revealing the implacable light of the moon.

"We don't have time. Whatever happens, we must be off," Gregos whispered.

Without a sound, they resumed their way inside the ravine, with Gregos bringing up the rear.

All at once, Mangas burst into a bush. That same second, there was a flash and the hiss of a bullet. Gregos leaped past Mitsos who was in front of him, shielding him with his body—just as a second flash and a second shot erupted.

"Don't fire!" Gregos ordered those with him.

And hopping with one foot and dragging the other, he plunged with all his weight inside the bush.

The two boys and Mitsos also rushed there. But the struggle was over. Down under Gregos' large hands that were squeezing his neck, a man appeared in his death throes.

"Stay back! . . ." Gregos said with clenched teeth.

A couple more spasms shook the other man's body; and he became still. Yet Gregos didn't let go. Like hooks, his hands gripped him by the neck.

Then abruptly he released him, rolled over onto his side, and fell backwards with his arms outstretched.

"Now be off," he said to Mitsos who was leaning over him. "You still have time."

Horrified, Mitsos saw in the moonlight that he was covered with blood. With trembling hands, he drew a knife out of Gregos' chest.

"Be off," Gregos repeated. "Tell Vasilis that Mitris Tané paid for the blood he shed."

"Tané?" Apostolis cried out. "This is Tané?"

Gregos tried to lift his head.

"Perhaps you know him, youngster?" he said mockingly.

Apostolis had already unbuttoned the Bulgarian's jacket and was emptying his pockets and rummaging around his belt.

Brushing aside Mitsos' hands that were trying to stop the blood welling up from his chest, Gregos raised himself on his elbow.

"Aren't you ashamed?" he said to Apostolis. "You're robbing a dead man?"

"His papers, yes! He had dealings with Zlatan!"

Gregos smiled.

"Damn kid . . ." he murmured. "You'll become a great captain if you survive."

He collapsed onto his back again and impatiently pushed Mitsos away as he sought to apply a make-shift bandage.

"Don't lose time," he said. "I'm finished. The bullet broke my leg. I can't walk. Get going . . ."

"We won't leave you, Captain Akritas," Pericles said in a strangled voice.

Speaking low, Mitsos ordered:

"With the three rifles and our belts . . . a stretcher . . ."

Infuriated, Gregos sat up.

"Be off!" he said, gritting his teeth, "or I'll fire!"

He grabbed his revolver from his belt.

"Fire at us, if you want," Mitsos answered, "but we won't abandon you to the Turks."

In a milder tone, Gregos replied:

"You won't leave me to the Turks . . . The third day that the sorcerer said has dawned. Mitsos, tell your father I repaid my debt today."

"What debt?"

"Just tell him that. Vasilis knows. And inform Vasilis that Zlatan is still living, that it's up to him to kill him . . . Now be off. Goodbye!"

Mitsos had put the three rifles down on the ground and was preparing to untie his belt . . . With his sound foot, Gregos kicked it.

"Will you get going?" he growled, enraged.

"We won't abandon you alive," Mitsos replied.

"Ah, that's it?" Gregos scoffed.

And raising his revolver, he placed it against his temple before anyone could stop him.

The discharge was muted. Gregos fell back dead, his skull in fragments . . .

* * * *

This violent act was over in minutes.

No one spoke. Quietly Mitsos knelt, took the revolver from the dead man's hand, picked up his rifle from the ground, and turned to leave. Without a word, as if in shock, the two boys followed him.

Silence spread over the countryside . . .

Time passed . . . The cold, indifferent moon at times was concealed by fleeting clouds, and then again it lit up the fatal ravine with the two enemies fallen almost side by side, reconciled in their final sleep. In the deep quiet of the night, there was a slight crackling in the bushes—a crackling that ceased and then started up again. A low shadow that seemed to be crawling, emerged from the bushes and stealthily approached the dead men.

All of a sudden, a stone flew out from another bush and struck the shadow on the side. The wild animal sped away fearfully and disappeared. A child slipped out of the bushes, glanced up and down the ravine, and tip-toed up to the dead men. He eyed the Bulgarian for only a second, before kneeling down beside the Greek rebel. With a trembling hand he touched his bloody chest and face, then sprang back, frightened. Once more he bent over the dead man and whispered:

"Captain Akritas! . . . Captain Akritas . . ."

Nothing was heard. The dead don't answer.

Again the child extended his hand to the dead man's chest, where it met something hard. He searched and discovered a watch, along with a worn leather wallet. Shaking, the child opened it—a simple wallet with two pockets, one empty, the other with just a photograph inside. In the pale moonlight he made out a young girl wearing the headdress of the Gida village, smiling with her hand on her hip and her head slanted back a little.

The child's hands shook more and more. Turning the picture over to the other side, he saw a fine line, and below it words in a heavier writing, one under the other. He didn't know how to read well. And there was no light, for clouds had covered the moon again. Removing a match from his pocket, he ignited a dry stick and took another look. Dizziness overcame him. He attempted to kiss the photograph but didn't succeed in doing so. The flame went out; and falling forward, he fainted . . .

* * * *

It was daybreak when Apostolis reached the Apostoles landing-cove with Mitsos and Pericles. Captain Nikiphoros had been by with his force and gone on to the hut. Only Vasilis with an oarsman and two canoes awaited the latecomers.

Vasilis sighed when a white dog jumped up on him and he recognized Mangas. Stepping out from the reeds, he saw three very tired rebels advancing.

"Mister Mitsos! And you, boys! Thank God!" he exclaimed with relief. His gaze searched the plain beyond with its reeds and bushes. "There's still someone missing," he added.

Suddenly he saw blood on Mitsos' clothes and hands.

"Were you wounded?" he asked uneasily.

Mitsos made a vague sign with his hand. Hoarsely he said:

"It's not me. But the one who's missing won't return."

Vasilis grew pale. He struggled to speak, yet his throat had tightened so that no words would come out. Silently they entered the first canoe and drew for the Apostoles hut. Behind them, the other boat followed with its oarsman. Upon arriving, they climbed out onto the deck in silence. Captain Nikiphoros had already set off with his force for Tsekri.

Quietly Vasilis headed straight for the flagpole where the flag had been raised, and lowered it to half-mast. Without speaking to the rebels, who'd come out to welcome them and stood there as though frozen, he went inside the hut with Mitsos and Pericles and closed the oilcloth door.

One of the men, the oarsman Nasos, stopped Apostolis as he was getting ready to go after them.

"What's the matter?" he asked. "Who are we mourning?"

"Captain Akritas," Apostolis replied; and with the backside of his hand, he wiped away a tear.

That day the Tsekri hut celebrated a great, unhoped-for victory—the destruction of the comitadjes at Kourfalia. Greetings poured in . . . presents, congratulations, even compliments and expressions of thanks from beys and other Turks. Captain Nikiphoros had delivered the region from terrorism.

At the Apostoles hut, in contrast, silence reigned. Vasilis had lowered the flag, and everyone knew his love for his dead friend. The rebels didn't dare raise their voices, but withdrew to the side to learn from Apostolis how the legendary commander met his death.

"Captain Akritas is dead! Captain Akritas is gone! . . ." they whispered.

"The brave rebel! . . . What bad luck! . . ."

"Our invincible giant. It shouldn't have happened."

Gregos had commanded respect from them all with his fearlessness and strength, with his forceful air that marked him as a leader, his decisiveness and his flashing eyes. Those who hadn't seen him in battle or on a bold operation, but had heard of the feats that made his name renowned in Macedonia, lived with the hope of knowing him and perhaps fighting with him.

But now Captain Akritas was dead. He'd killed himself because a bullet had broken his leg, and he didn't want the others to be caught by the Turks . . . those Turks hunting down the Greeks that burned and cleansed Kourfalia . . .

Meanwhile, enclosed inside the hut, Vasilis listened to the two cousins' account of what had taken place without opening his mouth or articulating a word. When Mitsos repeated Captain Akritas' last message for him—that Zlatan was still alive and that it would be his job to kill him—again Vasilis didn't speak. And when Mitsos asked:

"Did Captain Akritas know my father? How was Captain Akritas indebted to my father?" Vasilis made no reply.

With his eyes fixed on Gregos' revolver and rifle that Mitsos had given him, he seemed to neither see nor hear what was going on around him.

The two cousins fell silent and lay down to sleep, while seated on the floor with his arms around his knees, Vasilis continued to stare out into space, lost in his gloomy reflections.

But the cousins didn't find any sleep either. Their nerves were overstrained. Mitsos turned Captain Akritas' words over and over in his mind. And he recalled how many times the captain had saved his life. At Kourfalia he'd rescued him twice, once by sending a Bulgarian's rifle flying from his hands, the other time by dragging him away from a flaming roof that was collapsing.

He remembered that night at Zorba, too—how the captain had left to chase the Bulgarians and asked Captain Nikiphoros to give Mitsos another task. The work had seemed humiliating to him, like a guarantee for the safety of his life.

Beside him, a sleepless Pericles was also lost in his reflections, his eyes fastened on the conical roof above his head. From the night's tragedy, Pericles had grown more mature, become still more of a man. He'd deeply felt the grandeur of Captain Akritas' sacrifice. For if he hadn't blown his brains out, he might have been saved from the knife wound in his chest and the bullet in his leg—he had such a strong constitution! But the delay of their return would have endangered the others. With stoic disdain for his life, the captain had released them from taking care of him.

Reclining on the reed floor of the hut, Pericles felt the same disdain of life, the same indifference toward death that so easily seized hold of brave men like Captain Akritas.

His regard for the dead rebel was so high that he made him his idol. The knife Mitsos pulled from his chest, Pericles had gathered up, bloody as it was, folded it in his handkerchief, and concealed it at his own chest. Mitsos had presented the dead man's revolver and rifle to Vasilis. But Pericles hadn't mentioned the Bulgarian's knife—he didn't want to surrender this priceless treasure which reminded him of the hero. As Zezas was the example and ideal of Captain Nikiphoros, in the same way this stoic rebel would be an inspiration for him. Pericles hadn't shed a tear when they'd left the dead captain on the ground beside the Bulgarian he'd strangled. Now, though, just thinking about him brought tears to his eyes.

He recalled Captain Akritas' past words, along with those Apostolis had related to him. The sorcerer of Uganda had prophesized his death. It was "written," the captain said, that he wouldn't return to Greece. He'd fought in '97, and some boor with polished boots had called him "an offspring of a Turk." An atmosphere of mystery enveloped his former life and activities. Who was he? Who was hiding under Captain Akritas' name? Because for some time Pericles had wondered about the fearless fighter's identity . . .

A guard's shout disturbed the silence of the hut.

"A v-i-s-i-t! . . "

Vasilis didn't stir. Mitsos, who'd raised himself, dropped back down next to Pericles. Let the men outside who were fresh take care of the visitor. After a sleepless night, the three of them weren't in any condition to see him. It was rest they needed.

But when the oilcloth door was pulled aside and a woman appeared in the opening, they all scrambled to their feet.

It was Miss Electra with Apostolis, holding Jovan by the hand. Not greeting anyone, she entered and closed the opening to the door. Serious and somber, pale as if from lack of sleep, she sat down on a case they used for a stool.

"I buried him," she said sadly to Vasilis.

Mechanically Vasilis asked:

"Who?"

Without knowing anything, he'd guessed what had happened.

"Gregos. He couldn't stay that way; the wolves would have eaten him . . ." Miss Electra replied.

For a second no one spoke—as if a solemn secret had suddenly been revealed—as if they were all at a funeral.

Then a grim Vasilis asked:

"How did you know he was called Gregos?"

"Jovan told me."

"How did you know, Jovan?"

Jovan didn't answer. He was trembling all over. As always when he didn't want to speak, he shrugged his shoulder.

Miss Electra emptied her pocket.

"I was at the Apostoles village," she said. "The Center transferred me to Bozets until Miss Evthalia gets out of jail and my
school is rebuilt. I'd stopped at the Apostoles village to see about
leaving this child with Father Mihalis, the village priest. At night
at my host's I couldn't sleep, as the priest had informed me that
a rebel force passed by and that the Turks were aware of it. However no one knew if it was Greek or Bulgarian. Earlier I'd learned
that Captain Nikiphoros had summoned our lads from Koulakia,
Nikhori, and our other villages, so I was alarmed that the Turkish
army might come out and cut off their retreat.

"After putting Jovan to bed, I went over to Father Mihalis', a
little outside the village. We remained up all night on the lookout,
the old priest and I. Very late—two or three in the morning—gunshots sounded. Stealing away in the direction of the shots, we came
to a ravine. Fortunately I had a flashlight, because it had clouded
over and we couldn't make out where we were going. We proceeded haphazardly. All at once I saw this child before me, calling
me! . . ." And she nodded towards Jovan who stood with his head
down. "He'd arrived before me and discovered two dead men, a
Bulgarian and Gregos. The child was very upset. He found these
and gave them to me. They belong to you, Vasilis."

She held out a silver watch with two intertwined letters—G
and T—inscribed on it, a leather pouch with gold coins, and a key
to an outer door.

"I opened the purse," Miss Electra added, "and saw the money
just as it is, the key which the child claims is to some church, and a
paper that says they're all for you . . . Take them, Vasilis."

With his hands shaking, Vasilis unfolded and read the paper
written in Gregos' large, characteristic handwriting: "I leave my
possessions to Vasilis Andreadis, all of them." It was signed G. T.
Nothing else.

Apostolis leaned over to look at the writing. He recognized
the easy-to-read, distinctive handwriting of the fake-priest he'd
guided to the Kaliani Church—which he'd seen again in Thanasis'
hands at Kleidi.

"Where did you discover these, Jovan?" Vasilis asked, enunciating his words clearly.

The child, however, raised his shoulder again without answering.

"In the pocket of the dead man's jacket," Miss Electra replied for him.

"There was nothing else?" Vasilis asked again, his eyes upon the paper. "A notebook? A wallet?"

"No, I dug into his pockets, myself."

Slowly, haltingly, Vasilis asked once more:

"How did you know . . . Jovan . . . that Captain Akritas was called Gregos?"

"I knew it, too!" Apostolis exclaimed. "I was aware he wasn't Captain Akritas!"

"You knew both this and many other things," Vasilis said. "You realized that you'd guided him disguised as a priest one night to Kaliani, crossing over the Loudias River. But how did Jovan know his name? Did you tell him?"

Under Vasilis' suspicious gaze, Jovan appeared ready to cry. Apostolis felt for him.

"No, I didn't tell him," he answered, "because we're forbidden to repeat what we know. But the same way I learned it, he must have learned it, too. In speaking among yourselves, you never called him Captain Akritas or Kostas—but always Gregos. The night you killed Angel Pio, you would have addressed him by his name. Eh, Jovan?"

But again, the child didn't answer. He only raised his black eyes to Apostolis, with tears of gratitude.

Affected by the scene, Mitsos turned to Miss Electra.

"Who buried him?" he inquired, cutting off Vasilis' questioning.

"We—Father Mihalis and I. It was slow work, since we didn't have any tool. With thick branches and our hands, we opened up the hole. And this one helped," she said, placing her hand on Jovan's head. "He carried stones. The hole was long and shallow, as Gregos was a giant. In order to prevent wild animals from discovering him, we covered him with all the stones we could find.

"The priest gave a blessing, and we left in daylight—he for the village in an indirect way so as not to meet up with the Turkish army, and I for Tsekri. They informed me there that you hadn't gone, Vasilis—that you'd be at the hut here. So I came."

"And the Bulgarian? What became of him?" Pericles inquired.

Miss Electra raised her eyebrows with a pained expression. However Apostolis sprang up in the middle and took some papers out of his shirt pocket.

"It doesn't matter if they didn't bury him and the wolves got him! He was a criminal!" he declared from the black and white perspective of his youth. "He was Mitris Tané! Moreover I found these on him, Vasilis. He had dealings with Zlatan. Before I bring them to the commander, do you want to see them?"

They were insignificant papers—bills for small purchases and notes without any meaning. Only one held Vasilis' attention, which he translated into Greek as he read it aloud. It was poorly written, from an uneducated man.

> "Dear Comrade," it said in Bulgarian, "Greetings. Know that it's not to our interests to attack the commander of the Greeks directly, because we won't succeed. But there are other ways, and the chief has begun the work. The Greek has the weakness of his countrymen in that he doesn't want, he says, to spill more blood. You bear up at Kourfalia and we'll do the same at Zervohori, provided that he doesn't descend upon us. If the Turks don't foil our plans and drive us out of the Swamp, we'll catch the scoundrel alive. You watch your man in order to prevent a repeat of what happened at Bozets, and don't worry about ours . . ."

There were some further greetings to this person and that, and it concluded: "Your brother," followed by a seal with two bones crossed. No signature or date.

Thoughtfully, Vasilis studied the seal.

"Is it Zlatan's?" Mitsos inquired.

"I don't recognize it," Vasilis replied. "But Captain Niki-phoros captured some hostages. Perhaps they'll know."

"The 'your man' is obviously Nikiphoros," Mitsos stated. "Yet who is the 'commander of the Greeks'? Could he mean the Master who directs everything?"

"No," Apostolis said decisively. "It's not the Master."

Taken by surprise, Mitsos asked: "Do you know?"

"I don't know anything," Apostolis replied, his sharp eyes lit up. "From the letter, though, it seems that it's someone on the western side of the Swamp, since they're guarding Zervohori. It's necessary to learn where Zlatan is, what relations he has, and what schemes 'Chief' Apostol has begun. He's the invisible source in back of all that happens. Besides, they know as we do that no operation occurs without a command from the Master. He'd never say that the Master has the weakness of the Greeks not to spill blood. Someone else is meant. And to find him, we must first of all find Zlatan . . ."

With curiosity, Vasilis stared at the boy and listened to his reasoning.

"You'll die very young or you'll become a great captain," he declared.

Embarrassed, Apostolis moved away and stepped outside. Jovan followed him faithfully.

"Gregos said the same thing," Mitsos added. "However Apostolis reasoned correctly."

"Only he shouldn't speak that way before the little Bulgarian," Vasilis said. Deep wrinkles lined his forehead.

Miss Electra, who had leaned back wearily against the wall, shot up.

"Don't suspect him anymore, Vasilis!" she protested. "He hates the Bulgarians!"

"He hated Angel Pio, certainly, and wanted to kill him even though he's his uncle," Vasilis agreed. "Still, can he hate his country?"

"He can! This child hides some mystery," Miss Electra replied. "I don't know why he hates his fellow countrymen so much; he keeps it to himself. Yet he hates them with a passion—believe it, Vasilis! I'd entrust my biggest secret to him . . . But where did Apostolis take him? . . . Jovan! . . ." she called.

Shyly the child appeared at the door.

"Come and sleep, Jovan!" the teacher said gently.

Mitsos spread a cover on the floor.

"You're also very tired, Miss Electra, and Jovan seems exhausted. Sleep here, both of you. We'll go outside."

"You must be tired, yourselves," Miss Electra responded.

Mitsos blushed.

"You've put us to shame. We three men abandoned him for the wolves, as you said. While you, a woman, went and buried him . . ."

He left the hut with Pericles and Vasilis and closed the oilcloth door. Lying on the deck to sleep, each one in his corner, they kept their melancholy thoughts to themselves.

Apostolis had settled down near the door, without being able to sleep. Endless reflections rushed through his restless mind. Stretched out on the reeds, he tried to piece together Vasilis' life, which he didn't know well, with Gregos's, which he didn't know at all. Gregos was without doubt a close friend of Vasilis'. When Gregos saw him at the mountain retreat, though, he hadn't recognized him and needed secret signs to understand . . .

A stifled sob inside the hut shook him. He raised a corner of the oilcloth and peered inside. Miss Electra was sleeping with one arm under her head. Seated cross-legged beside her, Jovan was staring at a paper in the palms of his hands, crying softly. His little face was so sad, he was so immersed in his sorrow, so distant and withdrawn, that Apostolis was ashamed he'd seen him—that he'd pried uninvited into the child's hidden grief. Quietly he lowered the raised corner of the oilcloth and shut his eyes to go to sleep.

Late in the afternoon, when Miss Electra appeared with Jovan and turned him over to Apostolis to get something to eat, the older

boy treated his small companion with unaccustomed affection. Yet
he didn't ask him why he was crying earlier.

They'd seated themselves off to the side, and Jovan had
stuffed his hand inside Apostolis'. Whispering, the child described
the tragic events of the past night. Miss Electra had tucked him in
bed, but he'd suspected something after overhearing a few words
from her host, the president of the community. And he'd watched
her leave. In the dark, he put on his clothes and climbed out the
window.

"Weren't you afraid, alone in the night?" Apostolis asked,
throwing his arm protectively around the child.

Jovan gave him a questioning look.

"Didn't I sneak out alone from Angel Pio's farm to meet you?
Besides, Angel Pio was living then. Now that he's dead, what do I
have to be afraid of?"

"You're right. Well, continue. Where did you go once you'd
climbed out the window?"

"To the priest's, as I knew Miss Electra would be there. However Turkish police were guarding in the road. So I circled around
them, and that was when I heard gunshots. The firing came from
the ravine. I headed there, only I hid so they wouldn't see me.
Because I didn't know who was doing the shooting. No one was
there, though—just a wolf prowling. I followed it and saw the
animal licking something like it was hungry." Shivering, the child
stopped. Apostolis squeezed him closer.

"And then?" he inquired.

"Then I threw a stone at it. The wolf got scared; and when
it ran off, I went over to see. There was a moon and I made out a
Bulgarian and a rebel. Both of them had been killed. I recognized
Captain Akritas and called out to him. But he was dead . . ."

"Afterwards?"

"I don't know after that."

"How is it that you don't know? You found his watch and the
liras!"

"Yes," Jovan said hesitantly. "But . . . but . . ." He stopped for
a moment and burst out crying.

With compassion Apostolis asked:

"Where did you find Miss Electra?"

Jovan choked back his sobs and resumed his account, chopping up his sentences:

"She came . . . I think I grew dizzy—I don't know . . . It was dark, but I noticed a little light darting here and there . . . It fell on Miss Electra's dress—and then I knew her and called to her . . . She came with the priest . . . and they buried Gregos . . ."

"Jovan, how did you know that Gregos was his name?" Apostolis interrupted.

Jovan cast a frightened look at Apostolis without answering.

"Perhaps you heard Vasilis? Or his friend Manolis?" Apostolis questioned him again.

Once more Jovan didn't reply. All at once, burying his face in his hands, he broke out crying again.

Curious, Apostolis watched him sobbing, his shoulders heaving up and down.

"Why won't you tell me?" he inquired, a little hurt.

Amidst his sobs, Jovan murmured:

"Don't ask me! . . . Please don't ask me! . . ."

Apostolis remembered a similar scene at Bozets when he wanted to know if the dead Bulgarian was his mother.

Suddenly Jovan threw his arms around Apostolis' neck.

"Apostolis!" he exclaimed in anguish. "Let's go together to find this comitadje they call Zlatan."

Apostolis was startled.

"How do you know Zlatan?" he inquired.

"I don't know him. But I didn't know Apostol Petkoff either, and I discovered him. If you want, I'll find Zlatan!"

"I know him," Apostolis said. "He has red hair and his one eye is smaller than the other."

The child marveled, wide-eyed.

"You've discovered where he is?"

"No. However if you like, we'll go track him down. Maybe Vasilis would like to come, too."

He repeated Gregos' words before he shot himself:

"'Tell Vasilis that Zlatan is still living and that it's his job to kill him!"

"He shot himself?" the child murmured, shuddering.

"Yes, so that we'd escape. He feared the Turks would capture us."

And he related Gregos' heroic end to Jovan.

The child listened in silence, with horror expressed on his face. His one hand tremblingly searched for something at his chest. When Apostolis had finished his story, Jovan didn't speak. Staring out at the lake, he became absorbed in his thoughts.

And when Apostolis asked him: "What are you thinking?" Jovan replied in a low voice:

"I'm thinking that I'd like to be big and strong like Gregos in order to kill Zlatan, myself!"

"Why do you want to kill Zlatan, since you don't even know him?" Apostolis inquired.

The child didn't answer.

26.

Meeting At Kouga

"WHERE IS IT THAT YOU'RE GUIDING ME?"

"To the Kouga hut."

The Bulgarian drew back his foot from the prow of the canoe, which was halfway out on shore.

"That is, into the wolf's den?" he responded.

The oarsman laughed. He stood upright in the stern with the oar dipped part way in the water.

"You wouldn't know the wolf," he said.

"Don't forget what he and his blood-brother from Tsekri are capable of," the other reminded him.

"Well, he's not the same man," the oarsman declared. "Speak up, Kasapje!"

"He's right, Zlatan! . . ." Kasapje replied.

"Still, he's far from harmless!" Zlatan persisted. "What about the fires he set at Zervohori, or the battle at the Central Hut, which he would have captured if his grenades hadn't been defective? . . . As if Agras has turned into a little girl!"

The men who were gathered around their leader, chuckled.

"No one said he's a little girl," Kasapje said seriously. "Only he believes you if you talk nicely to him, and he's changed his view about the Struggle in Macedonia—as you know. Unfortunately, he now has evidence he can succeed. Didn't a few of our villages recently become patriarchal again with his message of reconciliation? And aren't some of our men who shifted to his politics seeking an understanding with him? Haven't they become enthusiastic and now work together with the captain? Why do you think

Apostol Petkoff is uneasy? For what reason has the Committee decided to send you to talk to him? Agras is aware you can't be conquered. His greatest ambition is to bring you over to his side and persuade you to cooperate with him."

Pensive, Zlatan stroked his reddish-blond beard.

"All right," he agreed, giving way. "However if he's out to set a trap for me precisely because he knows I won't yield?"

Once more the oarsman laughed.

"The wolf's no longer on the prowl!" he assured him with a guffaw. "And he's a most unsuspecting man. That fool Christof Bozan told me so—the one Captain Matapas took as a prisoner. Since he'd been spared his life, Bozan nearly went over to the Greeks, himself. We've put him as a spy close to Agras."

"Besides, you won't be alone, Zlatan," Kasapje added. "You'll go, but we'll follow you. We'll be near if he turns nasty."

Zlatan's cunning eyes rested on his men for a moment.

"Two in the canoe with me, the other two in the second boat!" he instructed them.

And climbing into the dugout in front of him, he sat down in the middle.

"First to our hut at Koraka," he ordered. "We'll inform them to be prepared to come if they hear firing."

* * * *

It was a sunny morning in May. The green Swamp hummed with life—with birds, insects, and wild animals. Water-lilies competed with broad, leafy plants and stalks of slender reeds as to which would grow thicker and spread their juice-swollen shoots further. And the water teemed with water-snakes, fish, eels, frogs, and leeches; while butterflies flitted to and fro.

Everywhere a swarm of mosquitos buzzed about—in the branches, on the surface of the water, in the reeds, the brambles, and the Swamp grass. Fierce and aggressive, they carried fever and death with their slight prick.

Inside the two canoes, the men made their way cautiously, scrutinizing the reeds so as not to fall into an ambush. Yet nothing disturbing appeared. They entered the snakelike Grounandero and from there into the tributary leading to Kouga, without incident.

They hadn't gone far, however, when sentries stopped them.

"Halt! Stay where you are. The commander will come here in order to speak to you."

A glance persuaded Zlatan that the "commander" was well protected. Guards were visible all around inside the green foliage. The tributaries and paths to Kouga also had a sentry posted at every turn, with a rifle in his hand, pistols in his belt, and a knife handy.

From a pathway, a canoe issued forth with two villagers at the oars. A third man, seated down in the middle, was staring calmly before him. Bareheaded, he had thick brown hair that curled in a disorderly fashion on his forehead, according to how the wind blew it. He had no rifle or any other weapon, and he seemed in good spirits.

In a low voice, Zlatan asked:

"Is that Agras?"

"That's him," the oarsman responded, "the one sitting in the middle without a cap."

Agras saw the two Bulgarian dugouts and got up.

"Good-day, Chief Zlatan!" he greeted him in a lively manner, his boyish, openhearted smile lighting up his face. "You came armed, I see! For a battle or a peaceful conversation did you prepare yourself?"

Zlatan stood up also, careful not to overturn the dugout. He replied in Greek, pronouncing his consonants with a thick accent:

"I came for an agreement, Captain Agras. But we fighters have our rifle as a companion! . . ."

Agras made a sign to his oarsmen. Immediately they pulled up alongside Zlatan's canoe.

"Enter inside, Chief," he said to the Bulgarian. "And let my lads climb in your canoe with your boys. What I have to tell you is only for the two of us."

And observing Zlatan hesitate:

"Bring your rifle since you can't be separated from it," he declared cheerfully. "Don't be afraid. I haven't even a pistol with me."

Fully armed, Zlatan entered Agras' boat and the two oarsmen switched into his. Agras took an oar and pushed the canoe further out in the water. Below, the men eyed each other suspiciously. Few words were exchanged; there was no sympathy between them. Mistrustful, one kept watch on the other. Both stole glances at their leaders—following their movements, ready to kill each other at the first indication of a clash between the captains.

Their minds were so focused on the canoe alone in the middle of the tributary that no one noticed two black, almond-shaped eyes in a pale childish face behind the green reeds. They too secretly watched the two leaders who were off by themselves, and then shifted back to the oarsmen in the two boats—attentive to words, movements, even glances.

When the commanders' private conversation ended, Agras took up the oar again and signalled for the oarsmen to approach. After each leader was back with his own men, the sentries came out of their hiding-places to accompany the Bulgarians up to Grounandero, while Agras drew for Kouga. With the light rustling of the wind among the grass and shrubs, again no one observed a little dugout that silently slipped through the green vegetation like a lizard.

From a distance, the small, narrow dugout trailed the two Bulgarian canoes without being seen, as far as the final twisting of the waterway towards Zervohori. Once the child guiding it had assured himself that the Bulgarians were disembarking and heading for the village, he turned and took the tributaries that descended to the south. Entering Captain Panayiotis' path, he emerged at the secret landing-cove next to Yianzista. Jumping from the canoe, he wailed softly like a jackal and waited, concealed among the reeds at the edge of the lake. From time to time he let out another soft wail and then paused to listen. Finally, tip-toeing sounded, the reeds parted, and an older boy stepped out and sat down beside the child.

"You're late," he said. "Did you at least find him?"

"I found him," the child answered, "but he wasn't at Zervohori, Apostolis. That's why I'm late. I searched for him there, as you told me. However, I discovered him at Plasna and followed him secretly almost to Kouga."

Stunned, Apostolis whispered:

"To Kouga? What work did Zlatan have at Kouga?"

"Captain Agras was there . . . It seems they had an understanding . . . Captain Agras came and they met on a pathway. He took Zlatan into his boat, where they spoke together. They'd sent the oarsmen away and talked by themselves."

Apostolis grasped the child's arm in alarm.

"Jovan!" he said in a strangled voice. "We must stop him!"

"How?" the child asked sadly. "Who will listen to us?"

For a short while Apostolis considered it.

"Everything's going wrong! . . ." he muttered. "Pericles' illness! . . . Did he have to drink that filthy water at Kourfalia and come down with typhus? . . . Captain Nikiphoros' departure . . . Mitsos' quarrel with Nikiphoros the Second . . . You'd say the force fell apart once our commander, Captain Nikiphoros, left!"

"What could Captain Nikiphoros do, Apostolis, if he'd stayed at Tsekri?" Jovan asked despondently.

"I don't know. Yet we'd have someone to see in order to report what's happening. Now we don't—we're not even aware where Vasilis is . . . whether he's still in Thessalonika . . ."

"And my uncle died . . ." Jovan murmured absent-mindedly.

"Your uncle? What does your uncle have to do with it?" Apostolis responded, flaring up. "Do you think we'd go to Angel Pio for advice?"

Apprehensive, Jovan murmured:

"No, certainly not to Angel Pio . . . I didn't mean to say . . . Don't be angry, Apostolis . . ."

But Apostolis was too preoccupied to follow the child's train of thought.

"Listen, Jovan," he said, worried. "There's one person who could give us good counsel—Captain Matapas! He's far away, though. Mr. Zoés could as well, but he's also far away. Since we don't have time to travel either to Olympus or Thessalonika, we'll have to manage by ourselves. Were you able to make out what the two captains said in the canoe?"

"No. They were speaking secretly. I only heard Captain Agras ask Zlatan if he came for a battle or a talk, since he was carrying a rifle. Captain Agras wasn't armed; he didn't even have a pistol on him . . ."

"Always the same!" Apostolis said, stirred by that piece of information. "His bravery borders on madness! ...The other Bulgarians—those who accompanied him. Did they say anything?"

"No. They were watching the rebels and didn't speak. Our own men were on guard and kept quiet, too."

"And when the commanders parted?"

"Captain Agras headed for Kouga, and Zlatan for Zervohori. I came here."

"Then Captain Agras will pass by this way on his return to Naousa . . ." Apostolis figured. "There's no other way that's safe. We'll wait for him here. Look, I brought you a bite to eat. Wherever he goes, we'll trail him."

But the whole day went by without anyone showing up. Hidden in the reeds, the two boys waited. Sometimes Apostolis stayed awake on the lookout, while Jovan slept on the ground; at other times Jovan kept watch, and Apostolis caught some sleep. It was dark at night with Jovan on guard, when the light scraping of a canoe inside the reeds sounded. The child woke Apostolis; and huddled side by side, the two boys saw the tip of the canoe rise onto the landing. Three men jumped out.

One of them, small and quick on his feet, returned to the canoe and bent over towards the reeds where the boys were concealed.

"Someone's here!" he whispered. "A visitor's anticipated us! A dugout! . . ."

Apostolis sprang from his hiding-place, holding Jovan by the hand.

"It's us, Commander! Apostolis the guide and Jovan, my apprentice," he said, breathless from his excitement.

"The two children! What are you doing out here at such an hour?" Agras inquired.

"We were waiting for you, Commander, to guide you where you want to go!" Apostolis answered decisively.

"You knew that I'd come by here?" Agras asked.

"It's our job to learn when the captains have need of us," Apostolis replied.

Such strong feelings gripped him that his voice cracked.

Captain Agras put his hand on the boy's shoulder.

"If that's your job, you know and execute it well," he said. "I thought I entered the Swamp unknown to all, and two children discovered me! . . ."

In the dark, Apostolis secretly pinched Jovan's ear—it was his thank you.

"My faithful Toni Mingas is with me. However, you say that you can see in the dark," Captain Agras went on. "Could you manage to guide us to the mountain—and get us to Naousa before dawn?"

"I can."

"Don't lead us by a round-about way, though. I'm no longer in a condition to endure it . . . These fevers . . ."

"I'll take you by shortcuts, don't worry, Commander!" Apostolis said with a lump in his throat. "We'll be able to rest up on the road! . . . and still arrive before daybreak!"

Two other canoes had arrived with five rebels—who along with the guide Mingas accompanied him. Bidding the oarsmen good-by, they lined up—Apostolis first, then Mingas, Jovan, Captain Agras, and one-by-one his five evzones. Taking their customary precautions for night marches, they headed towards Vermio.

During all the journey, Apostolis perceived that Agras wasn't the commander of old. He walked erect as always, brave and indomitable; yet he was often compelled to stop because he was out of breath. Observing his fatigue, every so often his companions pretended to have difficulty themselves—one that he'd struck his foot, another that he was tired, a third that he wanted to prepare a coffee. Thus they halted among some bushes and sat down for a few minutes to allow the weary captain to recover from the climb.

But Agras wasn't deceived. They'd reached the woods outside Naousa and seated themselves under the green foliage for the last time to rest, when the commander said to Teligadis:

"Fortunately a new captain[40] will be here soon to lead you in the future! I've lost my powers!"

A clamor arose. Distressed, the men protested and assured him—swore to him—that they'd never feel for anyone else the way they did for him. It was Captain Teligadis, who never left him, that summed it up:

"You urged us on with your great spirit! We'd go through fire for you, Commander."

Touched by his words, Agras slapped him on the shoulder.

"I'm aware that you're all devoted to me," he said. "You must be the same to your new commander."

He got up and took his rifle.

"It's enough that I leave the region in peace for him . . . as I want it! . . ." he added.

"Forward, lads!"

At the end of their journey, though, they weren't so guarded with their words. Whispers and murmuring flew back and forth among the rebels:

"We mustn't leave him!"

"He shouldn't believe them!"

"They're treacherous!"

"They're liars and traitors! . . ."

Fragments of what they said reached the ears of Captain Agras, next in line after the guide now. He smiled his innocent, boyish smile, but didn't speak.

Only when they see for themselves will they be persuaded . . . he contemplated, continuing along his way.

Before dawn, as Apostolis had promised, they arrived in Naousa at the house where Agras was to be a guest. The exhausted commander went straight to bed, trembling from fever in the heat of May.

* * * *

The following morning Captain Agras had a meeting with the notables of Naousa—Doctor Perdikaris who was president and soul of the town's Greek community, and two or three priests and teachers from the district.

In the next room, Apostolis sat gluing two detached bars onto the host's wooden bookcase. All of the discussion was audible to him, although the door had been closed.

Each person was given a turn to speak about what had occurred during the last few days—in the community, the school, and the parish. The new position of Captain Agras had attracted and appealed to many people. The farming population, above all, was fed up with the Greek-Bulgarian fighting, the Romanian betrayals, Serb propaganda, and Turkish pressure. Unable to stand it any longer, many had declared themselves gypsies, not wanting to be known either as Greek or Bulgarian. They didn't even send their children to school, so as not to be catagorized and fall victim to the opposing side's revenge.

In the towns, the ethnic animosity continued to hold firm, pitting Bulgarians and Greeks against each other like wolves. But in the country, the hatred wasn't so intense. A number of Bulgarian-speaking and oriented villages had moved towards Agras' peaceful politics and were calling for reconciliation, cooperation, and united action against the Turks, the common enemy and tyrant. Fanatical comitadjes had been forced to flee to the mountains, while others who were more moderate sought an understanding with Agras. They too wanted to live in peace—to graze their sheep and cultivate their fields without fearing every night that their enemy would burn their house and crops and kill their sheep . . . or worse, their women and children!

Now and then an objection was raised.

Were those sincere who declared reconciliation?

Wouldn't they all rise up again in unison if Apostol Petkoff or another Bulgarian chief descended? . . . Moreover, wouldn't the revenge be worse then?

Agras' answer had been calm and soft-spoken: No . . . fierce revenge wouldn't establish a foothold if the tortured, tyrannized Macedonians once tasted peace and good-will. The unfortunate villagers in the countryside had shed their blood and suffered much pain, exposed as they were to the Bulgarian violence and the Greek retaliation. And without fail, their mutual enemy the Turk punished them at will . . . pressured, taxed, imprisoned and hung them . . . with the intent of dividing and conquering through terror! . . .

The elders accepted what Agras said, but . . .

"No, there's no 'but'! Leave the 'buts'!" Agras' voice rose. "Spread the gospel—and everyone will be persuaded that only with reconciliation and cooperation of all the Christian populations will Macedonia be free one day! . . ."

Seated beside Apostolis, watching him make repairs, Jovan extended his hand and placed it on the bigger boy's arm.

"Really, Apostolis?" he asked in a low voice, bending over to look his companion in the eyes. "Really, will we become friends with the Bulgarians? . . ."

Apostolis was frowning and he looked mad. Nevertheless he was moved.

"For the commander to say it, that's the way it will be . . ." he said with clenched teeth.

"Even with Zlatan?"

"Zlatan too! . . ."

"No, Apostolis!" Jovan exclaimed.

His voice, his hands, his lips all trembled. He was shaking throughout from emotion.

"What's the matter, Jovan? . . . What's come over you?" Apostolis responded.

"But . . . but Gregos wanted us to kill him!" Jovan burst out; and he broke down crying.

Curious, Apostolis stared at the child.

"Why are you so worked up about Zlatan?" he questioned him. "Moreover tell me, how did you learn that Captain Akritas was called Gregos? Who told you?"

Suddenly Jovan stuffed his hand into his shirt; however he changed his mind. Leaning his head down upon his knees that were doubled up against him, he started to sob.

"Jovan . . . Something's wrong! . . ." Apostolis said sympathetically. "Something you're concealing . . . Why don't you want to tell me?"

"I can't! . . . Oh, I can't! . . ." the child replied amidst his sobbing. "It was so horrible! I can't speak about it! . . . Oh, I can't, Apostolis! . . ."

The voices in the next room were approaching. Someone turned the knob at the door.

Like a frightened animal, Jovan sprang up and ran outside to hide. Apostolis didn't come across him again all day.

He had work of his own to do, for the commander sent him on errands and used him as a messenger. Only in the evening when it was time to sleep did he find himself with the child once more. But Jovan was so pale and crushed that Apostolis pitied him and didn't reopen their morning's conversation.

Besides, he was deeply troubled and undecided himself. Two conflicting forces were struggling within him. He'd listened to Agras' program; and the kindness, the compassion, the generosity and tolerance of his words had rocked him. They'd shaken him throughout. On the other hand, the memory of Miss Electra exerted a profound influence upon him, also. What would Miss Electra say? She certainly wouldn't want reconciliation and cooperation with the Bulgarians, Romanians, and Serbs—she who hated the first two as much as the Turks! Moreover, what Miss Electra said weighed as heavily for him as Captain Agras' message. It was his gospel. Two contrary gospels stood in opposition, rejecting each other's every word! . . .

. . . Yet hadn't he witnessed Agras in battle? Didn't he know how fearless he was? Wounded and bloody, the captain had fought the Bulgarians obstinately and with great courage. For him to alter his position . . .

Restless, Apostolis tossed and turned on his straw mat on the floor, beside the sleeping Jovan. All at once he felt a tremendous longing for Miss Electra—to see and speak with her, to have her put some order into his confused thoughts that were all at odds.

But how could he go to see Miss Electra now? Everything at the Swamp had been transformed. Captain Nikiphoros, so ill he couldn't stand on his feet any longer, had left on horseback for Koulakia with a few of his men. After saying goodby to them, he'd traveled to Thessalonika dressed in fisherman's clothes, along with two Koulakia fishermen. There he'd conferred with the General Consul before making his way down the coast to meet a ship that took him secretly to Greece. Captain Nikiphoros the Second alone remained at the Swamp, together with his deputy officers. Even Captain Kalas had departed.

Pericles, sick with typhus, had been brought to Thessalonika by Vasilis, Mitsos, and Miss Electra—to Mrs. Vasiotakis' house for "grandmother" to care for him. Miss Electra had been in charge of him at Tsekri those first days, as she'd been without work since Miss Evthalia was released from jail. But where would Apostolis find her now to ask her counsel?

The Turks were threatening to drive all the forces, Greek and Bulgarian, from the Swamp. Until now they'd confined themselves to heavy firing from around the shore, like they wanted to clear out sparrows with gunpowder. In their own western corner, the Bulgarians had grown quiet, neither moving about nor bothering the Greek huts—which had adopted a solely defensive position, themselves. The Struggle seemed to have waned.

The tranquil lake water exuded mould, decay, and fever. No longer troubled by the fighting, it was full of waterbirds, water-snakes, leeches, mosquitos . . . and sickness.

The following evening Apostolis experienced new contradictions and turmoil. Once more he was in the adjoining room with Jovan, when Hadji-demoulas, an engineer from Naousa, entered inside. A highly esteemed man, wise and sensible, he'd been requested by Captain Agras to come and speak with him. But where was the commander?

From the next room, Agras had heard the visitor arrive and walked in to get him, leaving the door open behind them. Briefly, patiently, in plain language, he explained to him the reasons he'd changed his view; and set forth the new course for the Greek leaders to pursue in Macedonia. It wasn't to their interests, he maintained, for Greeks and Bulgarians to be at each others' throats. Only the Turks benefited—encouraging the Christian enmity in order to strengthen their own position. The Greek action had to be broader and more penetrating.

"All of us in the Balkans must become reconciled," Captain Agras declared; "and first of all, we Greeks with our distinguished history must set an example. When we Christians are in agreement, we can attack the Turk together and free Macedonia!"

Hadj-demoulas was caught unawares: "Just how will you give them advice? In order to come to terms with the wolf, he has to want it himself."

"He'll want it!" Agras replied. "The more I see of him, the more I dislike this mutual slaughter of Greeks and Bulgarians! We both weaken ourselves, while the Turk alone enjoys it. That way, none of us will see freedom. To achieve the results I want, I've come to an understanding with the Bulgarians to cease this wrangling . . ."

"You've come to an understanding with the Bulgarians, Captain Agras! . . ." Hadji-demoulas exclaimed, shocked.

"Certainly! And I've persuaded some of them. Moreover, tomorrow I'll go myself to meet one of their most important chiefs . . ."

Hadji-demoulas interrupted him:

"Have you lost your mind, Captain Agras? . . ." he cried out, aroused now. "Do you still have your reason? How do you imagine there can ever be an understanding with them? . . . And you say you'll go to meet them? . . . Don't you realize how faithless the Bulgarians are?"

"I know them and I've fought them," Captain Agras answered with his open-hearted smile. "But I'll go! And I'll go alone, without my force! What will they do to me? Whether they like it or not, they'll hear me out!"

"They'll hear you out, you say? You're not in your right mind!" Hadji-demoulas shouted in a fury. "Let me tell you what they'll do to you! They'll deceive you. They'll lure you to their den, capture you, tie you up and lead you around from village to village, from house to house! What's more, they won't say that they deceived you! Instead they'll claim they conquered you in battle—you, Captain Agras, the General Commander of the Greeks, as the Bulgarians refer to you! Thus you'll destroy the Struggle! Throughout Macedonia it will be known that the General Commander of the Greeks was defeated. The comitadjes will become famous as brave fighters and our own people will be afraid. The Bulgarians will rise up again. And you'll be the reason that the Struggle is lost. So much labor, so much blood in vain! . . ."

Hadji-demoulas was trembling and shouting. Tears of anger and exasperation filled his eyes. Opposite him, self-possessed, twisting a cigarette, serious and unshakable, Agras listened to him.

"Don't speak to me like that, I beg you, Hadji-demoulas!" he responded in his good-natured way. "I've made my decision and I don't want to change it! So don't tell me the opposite, and don't get angry . . . I've informed them. I'll go without fail!"

"Don't go! We'll prevent you! You don't have the right! . . ."

"I'll go and you won't prevent me," Agras replied calmly but firmly. "And I won't destroy the Struggle. Nor can the Bulgarians say that they captured the General Commander of the Greeks, or any 'commander.' Because everyone knows that my replacement, who's my superior, will be here in two days and that I'm a simple civilian now."

"Don't do it, Captain Agras! . . . You'll be responsible for all our bad fortune!" Hadji-demoulas cried out.

Agras smiled.

"You natives with all your hatred don't see the larger picture . . ." he said, speaking in an increasingly amiable manner. "I think I see more clearly. And finally, if I fail, what does it matter? . . . At the most, one man will be lost. However if I succeed, the benefit is so great you can't envision it."

"It's a waste of life! You'll lose your head! They'll slaughter you! . . ."

Agras shrugged his shoulders.

"What is one man with such an end in view?" he said tranquilly.

In the adjoining room, Apostolis had followed all the discussion. His heart was pounding, up to his temples. He grew dizzy . . . Grabbing Jovan's hand, he exclaimed:

"Stay here! Keep your eyes and ears open! Don't leave him! . . . I'll go to Thessalonika! . . . I must see Miss Electra."

"To Thessalonika? . . . How will you get there? . . ." a surprised Jovan murmured.

"I'll run to the station . . . down in the plain! . . . The Turks are transporting an army. There's an evening train! . . . I'll catch it and head for Thessalonika! . . . Mr. Hadji-demoulas is right . . . Ah, Gregos is gone! . . . Let's not lose this one, too! . . ."

Choked up, he went outside, descended to the carriage road, and then raced to the Naousa station, five or six kilometers away. There at the crossing, he'd hail the train in the direction of Verria-Thessalonika.

27.

Fears

Mrs. Vasiotakis' parlor in the house she'd rented next door to her friend the doctor, was very peaceful and simple. It had a few pieces of her landlord's old furniture, enlivened by flowers and photographs of her family in Alexandria. She'd left them to be near Mitsos and Pericles when they entered the Swamp with Vasilis and became a part of the Macedonian Struggle.

For weeks now she'd taken care of Pericles, from the day they'd carried him unconscious to her from the Swamp. She only consented to relinquish her place by his bedside to Miss Electra—who, rested and cheerful, provided "grandmother" with time to sleep. Between them, the two women had kept night vigils over Pericles during his grave illness. And yesterday they'd finally allowed him to be up and about—to go to the parlor, spread out on the sofa, and converse freely . . .

The doctor had declared Pericles on the road to recovery and said it would be a matter of days until he gained the strength needed to resume his regular life. Not, however, to return to the Swamp. This the doctor ruled out. At the first opportunity, in five or six days to allow him to grow stronger, they'd send him to Athens, and from there to Alexandria where his uncle, Mitsos' father, awaited him . . . Pericles listened but didn't speak. He never remembered being so nostalgic for his grandfather. Never before had his grandfather's memory disturbed him so deeply.

To leave the Struggle now! . . . To go back to Alexandria to his uncle's well-kept, well-furnished home—to his aunt's motherly care and all his cousins' attentions. But what about Eva, the older of his cousins who longed for brave deeds? She'd written him that she approved and applauded his secret flight to enter the Struggle himself . . . What would Eva say if she saw him come back empty-handed without Vasilis' child they'd all set off to find, and without liberating even a corner of Macedonia? . . .

And Vasilis, what would he do? . . .

From the day Gregos was killed, Vasilis had aged ten years. He didn't open his mouth or speak to anyone. Withdrawn and silent, he applied himself to the work the commander assigned him, and then in the evening fell asleep like a log.

Once Nikiphoros had departed and Pericles' sickness was revealed, Vasilis had taken charge of him, together with Miss Electra. They'd brought him to the train station at Plati in Turkish clothes—and from there to Thessalonika with Halil-bey's help.

After that, Pericles scarcely remembered what had happened. He'd often asked for Vasilis, yet most of the time the rebel was missing. He'd gone off, they told him, to make the rounds of towns and villages—wherever they informed him there was an orphan. Frequently he was away for weeks on end, before appearing once again empty handed, his shoulders a little more stooped and his forehead more deeply lined.

He'd just turned up from such a tour; but Pericles had received only a "good morning" from him. It was grandmother who said that Vasilis hadn't found the child—that he'd returned again without success. Now Pericles was waiting for him to come upstairs in the parlor, where he'd called him while the others were having dinner in the dining-room.

Vasilis arrived with his stooped shoulders, his white hair, and his deep-set, sad eyes that seemed darker still under his thick black eyebrows. The oil lamp had been lit, and he sat down beside Pericles without saying a word. Pericles extended his thin hand and placed it on the rebel's large, weathered one.

"Nothing? . . ." he asked softly.

Vasilis gave a negative sign "no." And the two of them remained silent for some time.

"Vasilis . . ." Pericles began, "What will you do now? . . . What will Mitsos do? . . . Where is the Struggle headed?"

Articulating his words, Vasilis answered:

"Mr. Mitsos returned. The others intervened . . . Captain Nikiphoros the Second repented for his abrupt behavior and asked Mr. Mitsos to come back . . . And the Center advised him to go."

"He's gone?"

"Yes. What's more, I'll leave myself in order to be close to him. I owe it to his father, my boss."

In a low voice, Pericles inquired:

"What about me, Vasilis?"

Vasilis didn't reply.

"I won't go back to Alexandria, Vasilis. I won't accept it . . ." Pericles said, still lower. "I'm well now. Let's go together to the Swamp."

Again Vasilis didn't answer. The two of them were quiet— until once more Pericles broke the silence:

"In a few days I'll be strong again. Don't leave, Vasilis. Wait for me. We'll travel to the Swamp together."

Vasilis nodded.

However he didn't have time to answer and say how and what he'd decided. Grandmother was returning with Miss Electra, and the conversation became general. Both Pericles and Vasilis avoided mentioning the Swamp in front of them.

Despite the women's efforts, though, the atmosphere grew heavy. No one was in good spirits; and they separated early to their respective rooms. In a short while, one by one the lights went off and the house sank into darkness. A single window, in grandmother's room, remained lit up. She was still reading when a ring at the outer door, and a second and a third, set the house in turmoil.

Grandmother appeared at the head of the stairs, ready to descend. Seeing a light advancing to the entrance before the door, she inquired:

"Who is it?"

"It's me, Vasilis," the rebel replied from the lower floor. "Don't be uneasy; I'll open up."

Cautiously Vasilis opened the outer door, but he stepped aside immediately.

"Apostolis!" he exclaimed. "How is it that you're here?"

Apostolis shoved the outer door closed.

"You, Vasilis!" he responded with relief. "I was seeking someone else. I've come from Naousa. Captain Agras . . ."

Observing a woman's shadow, he suddenly cut off his sentence. Upon recognizing her, his words tumbled out:

"I was looking for you, Miss Electra! I'm here for advice! . . ."

"Stop! Stop so I can come down!" Pericles called from above.

He climbed down as quickly as he could. Behind him more slowly, grandmother followed, still dressed in day clothes. The most composed of all, she took the candle out of Vasilis' hand and sent the prematurely-wakened houseservant back to bed. Then she had the others enter the parlor to hear Apostolis.

With the doors closed, Apostolis nervously gave them an account. He'd caught the evening military train for Thessalonika and hastened directly to Mrs. Vasiotakis' to see if Miss Electra was there, in order to receive her counsel.

Agras now wanted to leave the Swamp, he informed them, and meet with the Bulgarians to reach an agreement. There were prominent villagers who favored it. Others like Mr. Hadji-demoulas considered it madness and the destruction of the Struggle. Apostolis described what he'd heard—Hadji-demoulas' anger, along with the reluctance of some of the others including Doctor Perdikaris, soul of the Greek community in Naousa. The boy's voice trembled as he presented Captain Agras' arguments. The commander had spoken like an apostle, ready to sacrifice his life for the success of his great plan for peace in Macedonia.

Apostolis had rushed to find Miss Electra and get her view, since she knew the Bulgarians . . .

"With which Bulgarians did he come to an understanding? . . . Do you know?" Vasilis interrupted.

"With a Romanian called Vasiliou and someone by the name of Kasapje," Apostolis replied. "And at Kouga, he'd met with Zlatan, who he'll see again . . ."

Vasilis jumped to his feet.

"We must prevent him!" he shouted. "By every means! Not with Zlatan!"

Alarmed, Apostolis asked:

"How can we stop him?"

Beside himself, Vasilis repeated:

"Not with Zlatan! Zlatan will betray him!"

"How do we stop him?" Apostolis asked again.

"I'll prevent him, myself! . . ."

Vasilis started to go to the door, shaking all over from his passion.

Miss Electra burst in front of him and caught the door handle.

"Vasilis!" she said in her steady yet imposing way. "You don't have the authority to make a decision. You're a soldier. You should report to the Center!"

Vasilis came to a standstill. Slowly he passed his hand over his forehead a couple of times. All at once he raised his head.

"Where does Mr. Zoés live? Do you know?" he questioned Apostolis.

"Yes, I know."

"Take me there. Miss Electra is right. But tomorrow will be too late. Let's be off immediately!"

* * * *

Mr. Zoés was sleeping. However when he heard what Apostolis had to say to him, he dressed quickly and told Vasilis and Apostolis to accompany him to the General Consulate.

"You must set off right away with Apostolis and stop Agras," he said to Vasilis. "But until the train departs tomorrow . . . Moreover it's dangerous, in case they suspect you and put you down at a station. They're transporting an army now; they're suspicious . . ."

"Furnish us horses, Mr. Zoés—and don't worry!" Vasilis replied.

"Horses? . . . But will they take you as far as Naousa? . . . Especially if you race them?"

"We'll change them at Kavasila . . . I guarantee it!" Apostolis exclaimed. "And we'll ask Halil-bey for a travel permit for Vasilis. He'll give us one."

Mr. Zoés thought it over. Perhaps it would be safer . . .

"Where will they get the horses to you?" he responded. "It won't do for them to be heard on the cobblestones at such an hour . . ."

"We'll come to get them wherever you order, Mr. Zoés. Both of us speak Turkish," Vasilis answered, "and we're up to their tricks. We pass where we want to pass. Just give us horses!"

"Return to Mrs. Vasiotakis' house and prepare to leave," Mr. Zoés said decisively. "I'll arrange it with the General Consul and inform you through Ali where to find the horses."

Vasilis bid him goodby and went outside. But he turned back again.

"Do you have . . . Do you have any hope of our saving him?" he asked hoarsely.

Mr. Zoés threw up his hands. His forehead, too, was lined, and he had a worried look.

"If we catch him in time . . . I'm afraid . . ." he replied. And he added: "I'll go now to see Mr. Andoniou. We'll telegraph to Vodena to the bishop, so he can take measures . . ."

* * * *

At grandmother's house, the lights were still on in the parlor. The two women and Pericles had stayed up.

"We're leaving at once!" Vasilis told them.

Pericles sprang to his feet.

"I'll accompany you!" he exclaimed.

Gently, Vasilis pushed him back onto the sofa where grandmother had settled him.

"You'll be a hindrance, as weak as you are. Gain strength first."

"Will you keep us informed?" Miss Electra asked anxiously.

"By means of the Consulate, yes!" Vasilis answered.

Seated at Pericles' side, grandmother petted his little dog that had curled up beside him. Listening to Vasilis' narration and Apostolis' comments, she'd become troubled and anxious herself . . . So even Mr. Zoés was fearful? . . .

The doorbell rang and Vasilis ran to open the door.

It was Ali with Mr. Zoés's latest instructions.

When Vasilis returned, he said to Apostolis:

"The horses are waiting. Let's be on our way! It's a matter of life and death."

Pericles heard him. He had a crushed look from agony and despair, aware that he couldn't be of use to them in such a tragic hour. Overcome with anger and shame, he suddenly grabbed his dog, curled up next to him on the sofa, and threw him into Vasilis' arms.

"Take Mangas with you!" he said in an agitated voice. "You might not find Captain Agras and need to search for him. Mangas knows you. He'll be useful and can help track him down! . . ."

"You couldn't offer me a better helper! I'll take him along," Vasilis replied. "If only we save Agras!"

* * * *

Yes! Let's save him! Let's save Agras! Apostolis said over and over in his mind as he rode out of Thessalonika on horseback with Vasilis. If only the foreboding, the ugly foreboding of Mr. Zoés' doesn't prove true . . .

Let Agras be saved! Let him be saved! Miss Electra repeated to herself the next day as she hurried to the General Consulate for news.

Let them save Agras! If only they save him . . . Pericles thought again and again, no longer able to remain either lying down or seated, his eyes constantly on the mantle clock. He grew increasingly tense as time passed and Miss Electra was late in returning, as dusk descended and no news reached him.

When she entered inside and he saw her strained, anguished expression, he froze.

"Did they kill him?" he asked in a husky voice.

"It's not clear. He left Naousa at daybreak! After sending his men away, he started off with a few guides. But he's gone! His men returned. However he didn't come back . . ."

"Did they kill him?" Pericles asked again, beside himself. "Tell me! Did they find his body?"

"No. They don't know anything at the Consulate. They received a cryptic telegram signed by Hadji-demoulas and Dr. Perdikaris that says he departed. That's all. But the hope of saving him is slim . . ."

"Miss, Electra . . . Let's go! You and I! . . . We'll rouse the Greeks in the villages and get him back! We can catch the first train . . . And from Naousa we'll find a guide."

"Grandmother won't permit it . . ." Miss Electra responded.

"I'll leave her a note . . . I'll write her to forgive me. She'll understand. I stole away before . . . We'll go secretly . . ." Pericles said softly. "Whatever sacrifice! But let's save him! . . ."

"Yes—Agras must be saved! . . . Let's save him . . ." the teacher murmured, won over despite herself.

It was daybreak and still dark when two shadows crept out of grandmother's house, dressed in villagers' clothes. They proceeded in the direction of the station and boarded the first morning train, which set off whistling and chugging, hurling forth coils of black smoke.

28.

Betrayal

IT WAS STILL SATURDAY NIGHT, before daybreak on Sunday, when Agras started for the forest with a few guides.

Sad and full of bad presentiments, Captain Teligadis had watched him get ready. He'd accompanied him from Kouga with the hope of stopping him. But he'd ceased trying. Agras had declared that his decision was made. And Teligadis knew his commander, that once he'd decided something, no one could change him. As a last entreaty, he said only:

"Take me with you, Commander—and Mihalis, Vangelis, and Christos—for more safety."

However Agras would have none of it. Never one to suspect evil in others, he replied with his engaging, youthful smile:

"One of our agreements is for the two of us to come without our lads. Why offend him by showing distrust?"

"At least carry your weapon, Commander!"

"That I'll do. Both my revolver and my rifle. It's good to have them handy."

And he left instructions for Teligadis:

"Guard the surrounding villages well in case they commit some foul play while I'm away! They're Bulgarians."

"You'll go alone, knowing their faithlessness?" the captain responded, shaken.

Agras shrugged his shoulders.

"I'm just one person . . . It's worth the risk of my life to succeed in such a sacred cause. But the villagers shouldn't suffer! Keep your wits about you!"

396

He set off with his guides, right behind his loyal Toni Mingas who knew Mt.Vermio and its woods like his own home. On all Agras' trips, from the time the commander had left the Swamp and assumed responsibility for Naousa and its region, he'd served as his main guide.

* * * *

The meeting place was inside the forest, west of Naousa at Gavran-Kamini. It was early morning on a cool June day. The woods were very green, the ground covered with flowers, and the trees thick with foliage. The shrubs and ferns had a delicate, spring hue.

A serious Agras proceeded amidst his guides, reflecting on his meeting with the Bulgarian chief, preparing what he'd say to convey his faith and enthusiasm. Agras was neither stupid nor credulous. He was fully aware of the venture he'd embarked upon and the dangers he ran. Moreover he'd weighed all the pros and cons. Certainly he could fail, but it was also possible to bring the others over to his side. If the Bulgarian Zlatan and the Romanian Vasiliu—the two leaders he'd dealt with—were sincere, his plan would prove beneficial. If they weren't, though? . . .

If they weren't, he knew what awaited him. Still, he'd made his decision. His death would be full of torment. But he accepted it. He was operating with an idea, a great and worthy idea—to persuade the Bulgarians to stop the mutual slaughter and bring peace to the countryside in order to save the tortured population. If his plan succeeded, the day after tomorrow he'd hand over a peaceful district to his replacement. The Naousa region would be calm.

And as a result, other Greek captains and Bulgarian and Romanian chiefs would resolve to become friends and work together to liberate bloodsoaked, oppressed Macedonia.

If he failed? . . . What is one man before such a dream? he said to himself.

His heart overflowing with faith and the will to conquer, he drew on with his head high and his eyes heavy with contemplation and hope. Fearless, he was determined either to conquer or fall in the attempt.

A person dies just once. Christ was martyred for a belief . . .

In the lead, Toni Mingas came to a halt, listened, and then turned anxiously.

"Well, why did you stop?" Agras inquired in a lively manner. "Have we arrived?"

"No. But I heard something inside the branches behind us. Perhaps you detected it, too?" he asked the other guides.

"Something's moving," one of them replied. "It could be a wild animal . . ."

"Following us . . . A wild animal following men?" Toni responded.

Agras laughed.

"We're heading for the Bulgarians in front of us," he said, "and you're bothered about what's behind us?"

"If we're being trailed?"

"So? The enemy's before us! Go on, Toni! Don't be faint-hearted. Besides, I can't hear anything. Forward! . . ."

They resumed their way.

Reaching the spot for the meeting, instead of Zlatan they found two armed Bulgarian comitadjes seated on the ground waiting for them. When the guards saw Agras and his guides, they got up and approached them.

"Where are your men, Captain Agras?" they asked, staring with disbelief in the direction from which Agras and his guides had come.

"I didn't bring my men with me," Agras answered disdainfully. "My agreement with Chief Zlatan was for the two of us to meet alone. But where is Zlatan? Why isn't he here?"

The two comitadjes exchanged glances. And with flattering and agreeable words, they invited him to sit down and rest.

"I don't need rest," Agras replied. "I came to see Zlatan and he's not here. Why? What is he waiting for?"

Thrown off balance, disconcerted, one of the Bulgarians began an explanation. However, the second one interrupted him.

"Why should the chief appear alone and unarmed, when Greek rebels are so close?" he asked.

"Greek rebels? I'm by myself with my guides," Agras stated.

"And your force? Isn't one part at Naousa and another on guard towards Paliohori? Aren't other rebels scattered here and there around us? Fire one shot and they'll all rush up to take the chief prisoner! . . ."

Enraged, Agras broke in:

"You're dishonest and deceitful yourselves and you judge your enemy to be the same! I'm a man of my word, and I gave my word to Zlatan that I'd come alone to reach an agreement with him. Why isn't he here? Where is he?"

"He came," the comitadje replied. "But they informed us that Greek bands are keeping watch in the forest. He's farther on, expecting you."

"Farther on, eh? . . . In a safe place? . . ." Agras scoffed. "Take me to where he's hiding. I don't fear him. I'm a Greek Macedonian who's not afraid to walk through our mountains and woods to come to an understanding with another Macedonian, even if he's an enemy! You guide us. We'll be right behind!"

They started off again towards the northern depths of the forest.

While walking, Agras inquired:

"Who are you?"

One was Bulgarian. He only asked for peace and quiet, to work his field and put his rifle aside—to give it away even and not see it anymore!

The other, a Romanian, yearned for his pasture, his sheep, and his children. Ah, if only the fighting would quiet down!

Yes, if it would quiet down . . . Agras contemplated. If Zlatan and the others sincerely wanted it! . . . What a blessing it would be for the countryside!

There was a crackling sound behind him, and a stone rolled down into a ravine. Preoccupied, Agras turned his head. Meeting Toni's uneasy glance, he smiled at him and made a sign: Don't worry!

But the Romanian had heard it, too. Frightened, he turned, himself.

"You fear the foxes, do you?" Agras said, pointing to a bushy, red tail crossing the ferns and hurriedly disappearing behind some shrubs.

With a laugh, they all continued their journey.

* * * *

After they'd proceeded for some time, they arrived at an open space. One of the men whistled a signal; and from inside the trees a couple of others with weapons emerged. Behind them, hesitating, a man with reddish-blond hair and one eye smaller than the other appeared, holding a rifle and armed to the teeth.

Agras called to him:

"Chief Zlatan, why have you set up so many difficulties? I told you I'd be alone. What do you fear?"

The Bulgarian's eyes searched around and in back of the clearing. Slowly he approached and took Agras' outstretched hand.

"I don't suspect you," he answered. "I know you want us to work together in good fellowship and live in peace. Your men, though . . . Where did you leave them?"

"Didn't I tell you I'd come alone? I've kept my word. Why do you need so many armed men surrounding you?"

Zlatan made light of it.

"They're of no consequence, just sentries for form's sake. I've been waiting for you—with Kasapje, Vasiliu, and some other of the chiefs—to come and break bread with us and forget the past."

"Where are the other chiefs?" Agras inquired, glancing around.

"Where the footpath winds behind the hill. We've set a table on the grass. But leave your rifle here and I'll leave mine. We'll go as brothers who've had enough of hostility . . ."

"Let's go," Agras said cheerfully, leaning his rifle on a tree beside Zlatan's pistols and rifle.

With his hands, he brushed his thick brown hair from his forehead and began following Zlatan to where the path wound around.

From a rock close-by on the slope of a ravine, a childish voice split the air:

"Don't go, Mister Commander! Don't go! . . ."

That same moment, the two armed Bulgarians fell upon Agras' back and seized hold of him.

He shook them off and grabbed his revolver. However, another four men concealed among the trees sprang upon him from behind, twisted his arms, and the revolver dropped to the ground.

"Mr. Commander! . . ."

Agras turned and saw Jovan's small, child's body rise up from inside the thick ferns and try to run to the fallen revolver. But a Bulgarian threw him down, and with a kick sent him tumbling head over heels into the ravine below.

Agras had managed to make eye contact with the child. His brown-eyed glance crossed with Jovan's in a *farewell* full of sorrow and concern. And he viewed the little form somersault down onto the stones.

"Pigs!" he said to the Bulgarians gripping him. "What did the child do to you?"

All around him, there was merrymaking .

With shouts of joy, Bulgarians and Romanians sprouted up everywhere. Grabbing hold of the guides, they screamed and jeered:

"The beast is captured!"

"We've caught the Commander of the Greeks!"

"Death to our mortal enemy!"

"Kill him!"

"Impale him!"

"Disembowel him!"

Zlatan stopped the ready knives.

"To the villages!" he called out. "First let them see him in the villages!"

"Yes! To the villages! Let's make a round of the villages!"

A large, coarse man with a sallow, boorish face that seemed bloated, came up and shoved his finger in Agras' chin.

"Do you remember me, you Greek scoundrel!" he asked.

And he spit right in his face.

Agras threw back his head, escaping the spit.

"I remember you, you cheating Vasiliu! I remember you, you Romanian fraud!" he said scornfully. "I know your pasty face that reeks of lies and treachery! . . . and your mouth that never uttered a true word!"

Blows from rifle-butts rained in on him. Vasiliu started to beat him. Constrained as Agras was, he kicked him in the groin and knocked him down.

"Loathsome Romanian! Coward! Acting like a friend, pretending you were a go-between who would bring Kasapje to me! . . ." the rebel prisoner snapped at him.

"Remove his shoes!" someone shouted.

"Yes! Let him dance like a bear!" another said.

With a jerk, Agras freed his arm and brought the backside of his hand down onto a Bulgarian's mouth.

"Tie him up!" Zlatan commanded.

They bound his hands behind his back.

"Why are you doing this to him?" one of the guides asked fearfully.

Zlatan walked over to him.

"Be off!" he said. "We don't wish you harm!"

As he was reluctant, Zlatan added:

"Nor do we wish your leader harm! He's wild and needs coaxing. But you be off. Inform the rebels that tomorrow I'll bring your leader back, myself. Get going!"

They freed them all. One by one they left.

Only Mingas stayed.

"You go as well!" Zlatan said to him.

However, Toni Mingas shook his head stubbornly.

"I won't leave the commander," he declared.

"Tie him up too, then!" Zlatan ordered.

Secretly he instructed one of his men:

"Go stir up the Turks! Tell them Greek rebel bands are pressuring the villages around the forest. Have the Turks disperse them, so they don't get wind of us and attack! . . . "

The clamor and hooting around Agras was intensifying.

"Make him dance like a bear!" the Bulgarian who'd been struck yelled, wiping the blood that was dripping from his mouth.

Agras' hands were tied. With kicks he kept them at bay, cursing them constantly.

"Liars! Cheats! . . . Murderers! Betrayers! . . . Untie my hands and take me on, if you dare!"

"Remove his shoes!" Vasiliu commanded.

It wasn't easy. They had to throw him down, hands bound behind his back, and someone had to sit on his chest while the others took off his shoes.

Then his martyrdom began.

Striking him with their gunstocks and spitting at him, they hustled Agras off to the first village, bound, barefoot, and in tatters.

"Dance like a bear!" they shouted.

As a reply, he cursed them more, and received another hailstorm of blows.

Yet the Greek commander, who was small in stature and weak and thin from his bouts of fever, stood with his head high and a fearless expression on his face.

"Swine! What does it mean to kill one man?" he responded. "Forty will rise up to take back my blood! You'll pay dearly for your treachery! . . ."

Laughter and jeers drowned out his voice. Seizing him, they dragged him to another village, where his degrading torture continued.

Behind, silent and grief-stricken, bound himself and barefoot, Toni Mingas followed, his eyes fixed on his commander. Loyal to the end, he'd made the decision to suffer with him.

29.

JOVAN

IT WAS GETTING DARK WHEN VASILIS ARRIVED at Naousa with Apostolis and the dog. Galloping almost all the way, they'd passed the Axios railroad bridge, cut across the plain, caught narrow footpaths, and reached Kavasila with their horses half-dead. When Halil-bey learned that his friend Captain Agras was in danger, he gave them two fresh horses immediately. At full speed they set off again for Naousa; and by nightfall they were there.

Naousa was in an uproar . . . Captain Agras had left during the night, a little before dawn. With five guides, one of whom was Bulgarian, he'd headed west toward Gavran-Kamini. Three guides had returned, but not the Bulgarian and not Toni Mingas, who'd refused to abandon his commander. All this portended disaster, since they'd seized Captain Agras by force. Zlatan had promised to bring the General Commander of the Greeks back the next day, unharmed. However they'd taken Agras' rifle away, jeered him, and struck him with their gunstocks for cursing them, it was reported.

And now? . . . Where was he?

No one knew. The guides had fled, fearful for their own lives. The Turkish army was on the move, descending to the villages because Bulgarians had complained to the authorities that Greek rebel forces were pressuring them. Not a person dared show himself!

Vasilis ground his teeth together.

"Let's go ourselves, Apostolis! We'll find him, dead or alive."

Together they started out for Gavran-Kamini, with the dog running ahead. Vasilis had no need of a guide. He knew every inch of Mt.Vermio. The two of them had their revolvers concealed, but didn't bring rifles so as not to arouse suspicion if they encountered Turks.

They didn't meet a soul. The forest was deserted at that hour. The stillness of the countryside—along with the perpetual clashes of Greeks and Bulgarians—ensured that no passers-by risked coming out at night. Nor was the Turkish army about to appear in the forest after dark.

With night upon them, Vasilis lit up a little lantern he'd carried. Reaching Gavran-Kamini, they didn't find anyone. Two paths separated there. Which one could Agras have taken?

"Why don't we each follow one?" Vasilis suggested.

A cry from Apostolis interrupted him. He pointed to two branches of low bushy trees that were entangled, one inside the other, at the beginning of the pathway to the north. A little farther on, it was the same thing.

"Captain Agras passed this way! . . ." he said with agitation. "Jovan was with him! . . ."

"How do you know?" Vasilis asked.

"I taught him to leave such signs in the Swamp when he passed over unknown trails. Besides, in setting off, I instructed him not to let the commander out of sight."

And taking Vasilis' lantern, he examined the ground. On the still damp, tree-lined path, he observed many footsteps, as if men had been by.

"Let's head in that direction," Vasilis said, attentive himself to Apostolis' investigation.

When they reached the open space where Agras had gone, they detected signs of a struggle. Sharp, disorderly footprints were dug into the ground at intervals, the grass was all trampled, and branches had been broken. Partly buried in the dirt, a revolver was lying. Apostolis picked it up.

It was the commander's!

Plaintive cries from Mangas arose. Turning, they saw him standing at the edge of a rock, leaning down towards the ravine. Extending first one paw and then the other as if he wanted to descend, he looked over at Vasilis again, and once more let out cries as though summoning him.

Vasilis climbed onto the rock and lowered his lantern towards the ravine. But he didn't see anything. The dog, however, was growing more and more excited, crying and yelping for him to go down.

It was very steep. With the lantern, Vasilis surveyed the ravine.

"He smells something," he said to Apostolis.

"Let's go below," Apostolis answered. "If we wind around, we can make our way down from over there"—and he indicated the woody slope beyond the rock.

Together they took the descent. At times they grasped onto branches of trees to support themselves, at other times they strode over thick ferns, then again they stumbled onto the damp ground . . . And getting up, they resumed their sharp climb below. Vasilis led with the lantern, with Apostolis right behind. They descended to the stream, which was only a trickle that night in June.

Mangas had run on ahead. In the dark they heard him calling them with soft cries.

As he proceeded, Vasilis scrutinized the bushes and ferns. Catching sight of the white fox terrier up ahead, he quickly approached. The lantern lit up a child's little body, collapsed with arms outstretched. The pale face had dry blood on the forehead and one cheek. Otherwise the child appeared to be sleeping.

It was Jovan.

Kneeling, Vasilis pushed him lightly and lifted up his head. But he was unconscious and didn't stir.

Bent over him, Apostolis called out:

"Jovan! . . . It's me, Jovan!"

However Jovan's eyes remained shut.

Lying him down on the ground, Vasilis unbuttoned his jacket and vest, and undid his shirt without discovering a wound.

Tied to a string around his neck, a little white bag was hanging with something soft in it. Vasilis glanced inside. Suddenly his hands began to shake . . . Putting the lantern down, he removed an old, worn wallet from the little bag. He opened it hurriedly, thrust his fingers into a pocket, and took out a faded photograph . . . It showed a young woman smiling, with one hand on her hip, wearing the headdress of the village of Gida . . .

Motionless Vasilis stared at it, as though dumbfounded.

Apostolis was trying to pour a little water from his canteen into Jovan's mouth, but he didn't succeed. Raising his head to seek help, he saw Vasilis squatting there absolutely still, staring at the photograph by the light of the lantern. His paleness frightened the boy.

"Vasilis!" he exclaimed. "Mister Vasilis! What's the matter? . . ."

Like he'd awakened, Vasilis looked up and viewed Apostolis beside him, with the unconscious child lying on the ground. Grabbing the lantern, he placed the photograph next to the child's pale face, throwing strong light on both of them. All at once he lifted Jovan in his arms, pulled his jacket and vest from his shoulders, and drew down his shirt. The lantern lit up the child's back, where between the shoulder blades, a black mole stood out.

Mangas had drawn up and was sniffing in a friendly way, smelling the bare back and clothes.

Gently Vasilis redressed Jovan and said to Apostolis in an altered voice:

"Brandy! . . . There's some in my sack. Open it! . . ."

While he poured a little alcohol between the child's lips, he ordered:

"Wet my handkerchief! . . . Wash his face! And give me vinegar—from inside my sack."

Keeping his eyes fastened on the child's face, with extreme care he rubbed Jovan's legs with vinegar, massaging them with his large hands. Every so often he bent his ear down to listen to the child's heart, then the massaging began again and he gave him a few drops of brandy.

"His head's been struck," Apostolis said, washing the blood off.

"With a bullet?" Vasilis asked, gritting his teeth.

"No, as if from a fall . . . It's cut in two places."

"Clean the wounds with vinegar," Vasilis instructed him.

The vinegar stung. The child issued a sigh and moaned softly. Apostolis leaned over close to him again and called out:

"Jovan! . . . Speak to me, Jovan! . . . It's me, Apostolis! . . ."

The child half opened his eyes. His unsteady gaze fell upon the rebel's face leaning over him, illuminated by the lantern.

"Mister Vasilis . . ." he murmured.

"No! . . . Father . . ." Vasilis answered, enunciating his words.

"What!" Apostolis cried out.

Jovan didn't seem to hear. His eyelids closed again wearily. Vasilis bent closer.

"My Theodore! . . ." he murmured.

His voice trembled, vibrating with emotion.

This word revived the child as neither the rubbing, the alcohol, or the pain had. Opening his eyes again, he fixed them apprehensively on Vasilis.

"My Theodore . . . Don't you recognize me?" Vasilis asked.

The child's glance wandered from Vasilis' eyes and eyebrows to his white hair.

With his two hands, Vasilis propped him up against his knee.

"You knew me with black hair . . . Remember . . ." he said.

Tears flooded the child's large almond-shaped eyes. He attempted to touch the face leaning over him, but his hand fell limp and weak into Vasilis' strong one.

"Yes . . ." he murmured, ". . . Father . . . I remember . . ."

Vasilis lay him down on the ground and stood up. His eyes explored the surroundings, seeking an outlet.

"I wonder where the ravine comes out?" he inquired nervously, with an unusual lack of attention.

The child sighed.

"It goes back . . ."

Vasilis recovered. Recalling, he knelt beside him again.

"Of course it does!" he said. "It leads to Gavran-Kamini, doesn't it? You passed by there?"

"I know! I saw it. It goes where the branches were joined . . ." Apostolis burst out.

Jovan tried to get up. But he couldn't.

"The Commander!" he exclaimed in a strangled voice. "They caught him, Apostolis!"

Vasilis raised him and supported him against his chest.

"Can you speak?" he asked. "Who captured Agras?"

His lips quivering, the child said:

"There were many of them . . . Zlatan . . . They beat him . . . and took him prisoner! . . ."

"Where did they take him?" Vasilis inquired.

The child didn't reply.

"Jovan! Speak! Where did they take him? . . ." Apostolis insisted.

But Jovan had fainted again. Vasilis lifted him in his arms and rose to his feet.

"You hold the lantern and walk ahead," he ordered Apostolis. "We'll head back."

"Where?"

"To a family friend's . . . to the old lady's . . . To Mistress Hadji-sava's."

"Where is it?"

"I know the way. Go forward and light the path."

Apostolis stopped short.

"Captain Agras?" he murmured hestitantly.

"One job at a time! . . ." Vasilis muttered. "First we'll revive the child . . . to learn what he knows . . ."

Mangas rushed ahead, guiding them. Apostolis walked next to Vasilis, throwing light on the uneven ground of the ravine. He was troubled and upset, with countless thoughts struggling inside him. First Jovan, or first Captain Agras? Save the half-dead child, or find the captured Commander? He looked up at Vasilis' gloomy face, with two deep lines between his black eyebrows. Yet despite his worried expression, what love, what affection lit up his brooding, always sad brown eyes!"

"Mr. Vasilis . . . How did you understand that Jovan was your child Theodore?" Apostolis asked, a little uncertainly.

Vasilis didn't reply right away. He was pondering. Afterwards he said decisively:

"Another time. It's a long story . . ."

* * * *

They arrived at a crevice of the hill where, in the winter, mountain water descended into the ravine. Carrying Jovan, Vasilis took a sharp ascent up to the forest. Searching, he discovered a footpath; and in a short while they came upon thick woods. Inside the foliage, a one-story cottage was just becoming visible.

"Here! . . ." he said to Apostolis. "Knock on the door!"

Although it was still dark, it was growing light in the east. Inside the house, everyone was asleep.

"Knock again!" Vasilis ordered impatiently.

A man opened up. Young, he'd been prematurely awakened and seemed somewhat scared by the night visit.

"Tell your grandmother to come!" Vasilis said. "Tell her Andreadis wants her—say it's Vasilis!"

"She's sleeping," the youth stammered.

But the old lady wasn't sleeping. Hearing the knock at the door, she'd wrapped a skirt around her shoulders over her long nightshirt, and made her way out to see who it was.

"Mistress Hadji-sava!" Vasilis said. "Try to recognize me! Try to remember me! . . . Vasilis Andreadis, Haido's husband! And let us come in! . . ."

"Vasilis! You!" the old woman cried out, clasping her hands together.

In her bewilderment she let go of the skirt, which rolled off her shoulders, leaving them bare.

"Vasilis! . . . With white hair! . . . Mother of God! What happened to the child? . . ."

She gave her dazed grandson a shove.

"Run and get your mother. Be quick about it!" she shouted to him. "Tell her to prepare bedding! Can't you see the child is ill? . . . Where did you find the poor thing?"

Gathering her skirt, she wrapped it hastily over her shoulders.

"Enter inside, Vasilis. You too," she said to Apostolis. "Where have you come from? You seem weary . . ."

A middle aged woman dressed in black with a black kerchief on her head had stepped silently into the kitchen, where the old lady led Vasilis and Apostolis, along with the unconscious Jovan and Mangas. Keeping her hands crossed on her apron, she stared at the strangers while waiting for her mother-in-law to speak first. Patient and slow in her movements, she was a silent, living contrast to the quick, lively old lady.

"Mariyé!" the old lady called to her. "Ready what's needed to put the child to bed . . . Hurry! . . . Don't you see he's ill?"

Without a word Mariyé threw a couple of coals on the embers, which reddened in the fireplace. Then she filled an earthen pot with water, placed it on the coals, and went out. Meanwhile Mistress Katerina had bent over Jovan and was questioning Vasilis as he tried to bring him back to consciousness.

"Is it the late Haido's child? How he resembles her! What's the matter with him? . . . Ah, dear Christ! His head's been struck . . . Who hit him?"

Her eye happened to fall on her grandson, standing in the corner watching silently.

"Why are you idle, Thanasis?" she cried out. "Your mother had the good sense to set water on the fire. Run and fetch the basin so we can wash the child! . . . Which one? The one for kneading bread, what do you think!"

While the old lady hurriedly put on her skirt, buttoned up her shirt, and tied a kerchief around her grey hair, Mariyé swiftly and quietly undressed and washed Jovan in the adjoining room with a mother's care and affection. Wrapping him in one of her own clean shirts, she lay him down on the freshly-made bed. Then she poured a little of the brandy Vasilis gave her between his lips, and rubbed him with vinegar. Every so often she dabbed a few drops of the alcohol in his nostrils.

"Why is he this way? Who hit him?" she asked in a low voice, gently raising Jovan's hair from the wounds on his head.

Scowling, dispirited, Vasilis replied:

"I don't know. I found him in the ravine! . . ."

Jovan moaned. Slowly he raised his hand and groped at his chest. But he only felt his skin under the shirt. His face contracted. He opened and closed his eyelids, tried to turn his head, and broke into a wail.

"Where is it? . . . Where? . . ." he complained.

With tears in his eyes, Vasilis leaned over him and put the worn wallet he'd taken from the child's little bag, into his hand.

"Theodore . . ." he murmured caressingly. "My Theodore . . . Do you hear me?"

The child half-turned and his apprehensive gaze halted before the face and white hair bent over him.

"Mister Vasilis . . ." he whispered.

Vasilis got up, disturbed.

"Please leave me alone with the child," he said.

Mariyé went out, followed by Mistress Hadji-sava making her cross and shaking her head. Vasilis placed his hand on the child's forehead.

"Theodore . . . Do you hear me?" he asked again.

"Yes . . ." the child murmured.

"Theodore . . . I'm your father . . . Do you remember me?"

"Yes," Jovan repeated.

"And do you remember your mother?"

Sobs rose in the child's throat. Tears rolled onto his large pillow.

"Ah, I can't . . . I can't forget! . . ." he moaned softly.

"Forget what?"

"Her cries . . . They killed her . . . with grandma . . ."

Vasilis' face was white.

"You saw it?" he asked.

"Yes . . . They killed them . . . in the courtyard . . ."

"Who . . . Who struck them?"

"There were many . . . And Angel Pio took me . . . His knife was dripping with blood! . . ."

He closed his eyes, ready to faint again.

"I'm thirsty . . ." he murmured.

Vasilis stepped out and requested water. He found Mariyé carrying a cup of fresh milk. Entering the room with Vasilis, she poured it spoonful by spoonful between Jovan's lips as he lay there. The nourishment enlivened the child. He tried to get up, but couldn't.

"Don't move!" Vasilis said to him.

He waited for Mariyé, who was discretely withdrawing, to disappear—then took the child's hand that was gripping the wallet.

"Theodore . . . This wallet with the photograph of your mother, where did you find it?" he asked.

Fearful, the child looked at him and didn't speak.

"Tell me . . . Don't be afraid . . . Did you find it in Gregos' pocket?" Vasilis asked.

" . . . I didn't realize he was Uncle Gregos . . . They called him Captain Akritas. But . . ."

"Yes? . . . Go on . . ."

"I loved him . . . He was good to me and hugged me when we were alone."

"Yes . . . He'd noticed that you resembled your mother."

"I didn't know he was Uncle Gregos. Mama always said he was away in a foreign land."

"He was . . . in wild places. It was in order to avenge her murder that he returned . . . You took the wallet from his pocket?"

"I discovered it fallen on the ground . . . all bloody . . ."

Jovan stopped and bit his lips to stifle his tears. The words he uttered apologetically, tumbled out.

"I didn't go to take anything . . . I touched his chest and felt something that was hard . . . Then I drew it out—the little purse with the money . . . Along with it, I found this wallet . . . And I looked inside . . . When I saw mama, I grew dizzy . . . After I came to, Miss Electra arrived . . . I gave her the money . . . But not the photograph . . . I wanted it . . . "

He was unable to go on. Vasilis bent over and planted a kiss on his forehead. Jovan raised his arm and threw it around Vasilis' neck.

"Do you remember? . . ." he murmured. "Do you remember the day you went away for the last time? . . . You kissed me . . . like now . . . Afterwards mama was sad and told me: 'Don't ever forget your father's kiss, because it may be the last one.'"

Vasilis didn't speak. His throat had tightened . . . Jovan tried again to rise, but again he couldn't.

"Mister Vasilis . . ." he began, half-crying, and then corrected himself: "Father . . . Why do I hurt this way?"

"Where do you hurt? On the head?"

"Everywhere . . . On the back . . . And on the head . . ."

"How is it that you were in the ravine?" Vasilis asked. "Who struck you on the head?"

"On the head? . . . No, he didn't hit me on the head. He kicked me."

"Who?"

"I don't know . . ."

All at once, panic filled his eyes.

"Daddy!" he cried. "They caught the commander!"

"How did they catch him? . . . Where were you? Did you see him? . . ."

"Apostolis had told me: 'Don't let him out of your sight.' And I didn't. But Captain Agras left, and I went out with him. He patted me on the head and said: 'Go to sleep; it's still night.' Secretly I followed him . . . On the way, the guides heard me and almost saw me. I hid in the ferns. Two times they heard me . . . Then I went a little farther on . . . When Zlatan spoke to him . . ."

"Where was Zlatan?"

"Inside the trees . . . And do you know? He was one of those who killed mama! . . . It's written on the back of the photograph . . . Did you see? . . ."

"I know . . . I told Gregos. And he wrote down all the names of the murderers."

"You knew them?"

"I learned them . . . all of them . . . The others paid. He . . . he escaped! . . ."

Jovan tried to get up, but only his head moved. He began to cry.

"Let's go to find the commander!" he said to his father.

"Yes, my child. Rest up and we will," Vasilis replied reassuringly. "But tell me what you saw."

"I'd gone ahead of him. And behind the bushes, I crept up to the rock where the path turned. Comitadjes with rifles were inside the trees, a crowd of them . . ."

"Then?"

"Then Zlatan told him they'd set a table for him. The commander had left his rifle and started to walk there. I saw the comitadjes and shouted: 'Don't go!' But they grabbed him from behind and made him drop his revolver. I ran to pick it up to give it to him, when one of them rose up—I hadn't noticed him—and kicked me here, in the stomach . . ."

"After that?" Vasilis asked, clenching his teeth.

"After that . . . I don't remember . . ." Jovan closed his eyes and smiled . . . "After that . . . you said you're my father! . . ."

The child was quiet but the smile quivered on his lips. Holding his hand, Vasilis leaned over him, staring at him, keeping track of his breathing, studying his features. He recalled Gregos' words: "He resembles my sister . . . Whether you like it or not, he resembles her." While he, Vasilis, in his blind hatred called him "the little Bulgarian"—his Theodore! his own child! . . .

"Why did you want to kill Angel Pio since he took you into his house, Theodore?" he inquired.

Jovan opened his eyes.

"He said he was my uncle and that I should tend his sheep. I knew that he wasn't—that I had only one uncle, Uncle Gregos. But he beat me when I said it."

"Did they beat you?" Vasilis asked with a heavy heart.

"Mistress Pio, not so much. Angel Pio, yes, a lot! He said he was feeding me for nothing and that I wasn't worth the bread I ate. They had two dogs as well . . . The dogs were my friends . . ."

Jovan attempted to turn. His face contracted again with sudden pain.

"Daddy," he cried out. "Why don't my legs move?"

Vasilis brushed the blanket aside and uncovered his legs. They were spread out motionless. He started to lift one, but it fell slack on the bed. Raising both of the child's knees, he brought his legs up to his body. Once more they spread out limp on the bed and remained motionless.

Vasilis' color had drained. However he smiled at his child and said in a cheery voice:

"You're tired and in pain because you fell into a ravine. When you've slept, you'll feel better. Can you sleep?"

Obediently Jovan shut his eyes and became very quiet. Vasilis tiptoed out and discovered Apostolis asleep on the floor in the kitchen. The two women were occupied with their household tasks, conversing softly in order not to waken him. At the doorway Thanasis was sawing wood, with Mangas lying next to him.

"Mistress Hadji-sava, do you have a mule?" Vasilis inquired.

"Certainly!" the old lady replied with a nod of her head. "What do you want with it?"

"For him to go—and he gestured towards the sleeping Apostolis—to bring the doctor."

"Why doesn't Thanasis go? This one's dead asleep. He didn't close an eye all night. But he says you didn't either!"

Thanasis had heard his name and entered inside.

"I want Dr. Perdikaris, from Naousa!" Vasilis said, casting a probing glance at Thanasis' decent but almost expressionless face. "Do you know how to find him?"

Without leaving her frying pan or turning, Mariyé replied:

"He knows. Don't regard him as stupid. He's both hard-working and able. He manages what you tell him. Send him, Vasilis."

"Do you know Dr. Perdikaris?" Vasilis asked.

"Aha!" Thanasis responded, nodding affirmatively himself.

Mariyé spoke up again without turning: "Dr. Perdikaris came to our house here when my late husband grew sick and died . . . He's a good, compassionate man. Send Thanasis!"

"Go then, as fast as you can," Vasilis told him. "Inform the doctor that Vasilis Andreadis is seeking him for his injured child. Bring him back . . ."

A cry from the next room cut him off, woke Apostolis, alarmed the two women, and startled Mangas. With his ears pricked up, the dog darted into the room and huddled under Jovan's bed.

Vasilis rushed to his child's pillow.

Jovan was crying. His face was distorted and his eyes wild.

"Apostolis!" he shouted. "Apostolis! . . . Don't let them kill any more women! . . ."

Apostolis had approached on the run.

"No one's killing women, Jovan . . ."

"Yes, they are! They killed her when she came out on the road from Delithanas' house . . ."

"Who?" an upset Vasilis asked Apostolis.

"He's remembering Bozets," Apostolis answered in a low voice, "when Captain Nikiphoros burned it . . . A woman was killed from the shooting. He witnessed it and fainted. Every time he sees blood, he faints . . ."

Jovan continued to cry and call out:

"Don't hit her anymore! Mama! Mama!"

Swiftly, quietly, without any fuss or noise, Mariyé had come in with a bowl of water and vinegar. Wetting a cloth, she stretched it over Jovan's forehead and the top of his head. To Vasilis' unuttered question, she said only:

"He's feverish and delirious . . . It will pass . . ."

Vasilis left the room with Apostolis.

"Take the mule. It's better that you go to Naousa to bring Dr. Perdikaris. You'll be faster than Thanasis," he told him.

But the mule was no longer in the stable. Thanasis had departed.

"I have no need of a mule," Apostolis said. "I'll get to Naousa more quickly on foot. Before it's dark, I'll be back!"

However it grew dark, night descended, and Apostolis didn't return to Mistress Hadji-sava's cottage.

* * * *

The day flowed by, monotonous and melancholy . . . At times Jovan cried out and raved, then again he sank into lethargy. Seated beside his pillow, his father stroked him to quiet him down during his inflamed periods. Once that he'd calmed the child, Vasilis became absorbed in his own reflections—in conflicting and contrary views.

He'd come to save Agras. Not only had he not saved him or found him, but he'd allowed valuable time to elapse without investigating, without devising a plan or even communicating what he'd learned from Jovan to the rebel forces . . . And yet he'd also come to Macedonia to seek his child. Now that he'd discovered him in such a condition, how could he leave him?

In this disheartening mood, Dr. Perdikaris found him when he arrived on horseback with Thanasis astride his mule. He looked the sick child over—raised him up, reversed him, examined him with the stethoscope, moved his limbs back and forth, and inspected his legs, his head, the nape of his neck and his back. He spoke to Jovan and stared at him for a long while, then settled him back on the mattress. And again he looked at him for some time, listening both to his raving and to his lucid words. As he left the room with Vasilis, he was thoughtful and somber.

"The head wounds don't amount to anything," he said. "But his spine is damaged. For that reason, he can't move his legs."

Vasilis was accustomed to pain, to mourning, and to grief. But the doctor's judgement fell upon him like the blow of a club. For a few minutes he seemed dazed. Swallowing a couple of times, he asked:

"Can it be cured?"

He'd posed the question automatically, from a need to hear his own opinion disproved; and he accorded the doctor's answer its proper weight.

"Later . . . with electricity . . . if you take him to Athens . . ."

Vasilis knew that the spine doesn't heal once it's severed. He'd lived long enough in civilized centers to realize what paralysis meant, what it meant to be crippled, immobile, wasted away, perhaps dead . . . With his hands clasped behind him, he stared straight ahead at the tops of the plane trees, golden in the last rays of the sun.

Finally, slowly and grimly he broached his other worry:

"Have you uncovered anything about Captain Agras?"

"We learned . . . The foolish man threw himself into the trap of his own will . . ." the doctor replied sadly. "It's a wild goose chase now . . ."

"Did they kill him?" Vasilis asked.

"God knows."

"Tell me what you've discovered?"

The doctor gave him an account. Villagers had arrived secretly from the Bulgarian villages with reports that they'd taken Agras to Rizovo. They wanted him to dance like a bear, and because he refused and cursed them, they'd beaten him. Barefoot but proud, he'd cursed them all the more, calling them liars, cheats, murderers, and other insults that incensed them. Then they spit at him and ridiculed him, which broke the hearts of our own villagers who saw it. But how could anyone speak up with all of Zlatan's gang surrounding Agras! . . .

From Rizovo they'd dragged him to other villages . . . Vladovo, and who knows where else! . . . Displaying him as some strange beast, they slapped him and mocked him as "The General Commander of the Greeks!"

"But he showed courage! He didn't give up! He kept cursing them," the doctor added. "Don't ask me more . . . I didn't close my eyes all night. Beside myself, I had in mind to sleep in the morning, when all at once the bell rang. Opening up, I beheld two villagers. One was a woman dressed in a man's clothes, the other still a child. They'd come about Agras. The young woman was a teacher from Zorba . . ."

"Miss Electra!"

"Yes. Are you acquainted with her?"

"I know her. Who was accompanying her?"

"A youth, Vasiotakis—who's only a boy . . ."

"Pericles? But he's just out of bed from typhus! He'll have a relapse!"

"He seemed ill, although he assured me—'no'—that he wasn't. I wanted him to stay and rest. As if he'd listen to me! They were off!"

"Off? For where?"

"They didn't really know. To learn where the comitadjes were leading Agras, and then block their road . . ."

"Did they go alone?"

"Yes. They said they'd travel more easily to the villages and escape attention, if there weren't others along. Their idea was to arouse the Greeks in the patriarchal and mixed villages. If they succeed! . . ."

"From Vodena didn't they take measures about Agras?"

"I imagine so. We informed the president of the community and the church authority immediately. But no reply had arrived when I left."

The two men remained silent as night descended.

"I'll go back," the doctor said in a little while. "To get news."

"Will you come again?" a despondent Vasilis asked him.

"I'll come . . . I'll be here tomorrow to see your child."

But the next day he didn't appear.

* * * *

On Wednesday the day broke overcast, depressing and grey.

Apostolis hadn't returned.

Seated beside Jovan, who sometimes burned from fever and raved and at other times looked longingly at his father and murmured affectionate words, a heavy-hearted Vasilis recalled the time he'd wasted next to the "little Bulgarian" without recognizing his child. How much he could have told him! What he would have felt! How much joy he could have put into the life of his orphaned child! How many tears he could have prevented!

"I saw you, Daddy, when you first came to Tsekri," the child had said to him in a lucid moment. "And I loved you right away because you reminded me of my father. But your hair was white, and my own father's hair was black. And when you looked at me, you were always angry and called me the 'little Bulgarian.' I cried. But I was afraid to come near you . . ."

Vasilis reflected . . . Gregos had seen his resemblance to his slain sister, but he hadn't. Blinded by his hate, he'd pushed his child away, failed to recognize him, hurt him and caused him pain . . . He'd give his life now to raise his child up on his feet again. However it might be too late . . .

The hours dragged on, full of heartache, sorrow, and fear.

* * * *

All day Wednesday the child was silent. Lying on his back with his eyes closed, he breathed slowly, brokenly, irregularly. His always thin face had become even more emaciated these four days. Next to his delicate nose, two ashen lines were carved, descending from his waxen nostrils to his pale, half-opened lips, making his bony features still more pronounced.

In the afternoon Dr. Perdikaris came—nervous, worried, and edgy. To the uneasy words of Mariyé, who let him in murmuring that the child seemed worse, he replied:

"The curse of God has fallen upon us! . . . We've lost trace of Agras. We don't know where they've taken him!"

However, once he was settled beside Jovan's bed, the doctor's sense of duty took command. Leaning over the unconscious child, he watched him for some time without speaking. When he raised his eyes and met Vasilis' glance, he answered with only a gesture of his hand.

He's fading away . . .

And at dusk Jovan expired like a little white candle, without a word, without opening his eyes, without pain or agony . . .

"Internal hemorrhage . . ." the doctor whispered to the two women who asked him, not understanding yet crossing themselves silently.

Mariyé washed little Jovan, shrouded him, and lay him back down on the bed. Between his hands that were crossed, she placed a small icon . . .

* * * *

All night long the two women kept a vigil over him, with Vasilis and Perdikaris.

"He's also a victim of our struggle for freedom," the doctor said when he saw him—such a small child, wrapped in his wool cape resembling a rebel's cloak.

They buried him at daybreak. His grave was but a hump on the ground, surrounded by stones. At the head, towards the east, they erected a rough wooden cross that Thanasis had nailed together during the night from two little boards.

Vasilis stood before the grave with his white head bowed and his black eyebrows drawn together. Next to him with his head down, as if he understood the grief and the mourning, Mangas, too, stared at the fresh, rounded earth that covered his friend.

A ray of sun pierced the thick foliage of the trees and fell upon Vasilis' face.

Like he'd awoken from a bad dream, he raised his head and looked at the sky, full of light now; and at the trees, shrubs, and rich vegetation around him . . . Shoving his hair back, he straightened up and levelled his shoulders.

"And now . . . it's ended. We'll go down again . . ." he said with his customary calm.

Vasilis stood before the grave with his white head bowed . . .

30.

Martyrs

"Pericles, you'll suffer a relapse and it will be my fault."

"You're not at fault, Miss Electra. I wanted to come and I did."

"It's been four nights since you've slept! . . . Today's the fifth."

"What are you saying, Miss Electra. Didn't we sleep yesterday?"

"On the ground, out-of-doors . . . Is that the way for someone getting over typhus?"

"It's summer. What do you fear? Besides, forget the typhus! I'm well."

Miss Electra extended her hand and squeezed his.

"You say you're well," she murmured. "If you could see a mirror, you'd be aghast at how your face has wasted away. It's all eyes . . ."

"Even if it's a matter of my dying, I won't stop, Miss Electra," Pericles replied. "Now that we're on his tracks—now that we're aware of the villages he's passed through and have Kasapje's letter that says Zlatan is with him . . . If I were to stop at this stage, Miss Electra, my grandfather would rise up from his grave and curse me as unworthy and cowardly . . . No! You're a woman and you don't hesitate. Apostolis, who's younger than I am, persists. For me to be faint-hearted would be shameful."

They kept their voices low so as not to wake the others— Apostolis who always slept lightly, and the villager who'd guided them to the forest and hidden them. He'd found a vantage point up high to enable them to view the railroad line north of Vladovo, unseen by others.

424

"It's not a question of faint-heartedness," Miss Electra replied, "but of your remaining here until we scout out the surroundings."

Still wearing a man's outfit, that of a villager, she was resting on a layer of moss and leaves on the ground, conversing with Pericles. They'd come into contact with a rebel band encamped on a wooded hill to the north, and had sent their second guide to ask it to descend to their own hiding-place in the woods. Together, they would attack Captain Agras' convoy and free him from the Bulgarians. The guide, however, hadn't returned yet.

"We'll locate Kasapje and Zlatan first. And afterwards you can join in the battle that's sure to break out," Miss Electra added.

Pericles smiled at this simple maneuver of hers.

"You'll tell the rifles: 'Don't fire until Pericles arrives?'"

A rustling sounded among the branches—a running, leaping, and soft, excited cries as Mangas sprang forth from inside the thick foliage. He jumped up on Pericles' chest and with indescribable joy licked his face, his hands, his neck—wherever he could. The dog's elated but muted barking awakened Apostolis.

"Mangas! . . ." he whispered. "So Vasilis is close-by! . . . He'll have met Stavros the guide! . . ."

In fact, human footsteps were approaching. Following the dog's delighted cries, Vasilis drew near and separated the last branches that concealed him.

He was alone.

Miss Electra, Pericles, and Apostolis had all risen to their feet. Further down, the villager hadn't heard anything and was snoring away unawares.

"And Jovan? How is Jovan?" Miss Electra asked.

"Apostolis told us the way you found him. Did you leave him behind?" Pericles inquired.

Vasilis didn't answer right away.

Turning to Apostolis, who uneasy and half-guessing what had happened didn't speak, he said:

"Your apprentice . . . my child . . . he died, Apostolis! . . ."

And he sat down heavily on the ground, removed his cap, and brushed back his hair a couple of times. No one spoke. Vasilis had said it calmly, but in those few words he'd uttered lay the complete collapse of his life. Tears rose to Apostolis' eyes—he who'd witnessed so much tragedy and so many deaths. Quietly he cried.

Vasilis heard him.

"Don't cry . . ." he said. "You loved him . . . And so did Gregos . . . who was his uncle and suspected it . . . Only I failed to understand he was my child . . . 'the little Bulgarian' . . ."

Again, he pushed back his hair several times as if it bothered him. Then, straightening his shoulders, he changed his manner and asked:

"Why are you here? I searched for you at Vodena. But you passed by Vladovo, eh? Mangas picked up your scent and guided me to you. What are you doing up in the forest here?"

Numb, admiring Vasilis' self-control, Pericles asked in return: "Didn't you meet our guide Stavros?"

"No. I've come directly from Vladovo. Where are you headed?"

"Where they've brought Agras . . . Yet we can't accomplish anything alone. We've sent word to Captain Seraphim's rebel force to join us . . ."

"How did you learn where Agras is? . . ." Vasilis interrupted.

"Apostolis managed to find it out yesterday," Miss Electra explained. "He caught up with us on the road—on his way to Naousa from where he'd left you. And he's been our guide."

She handed Vasilis a paper.

"He got hold of this, too. Read it, Vasilis. It's been translated."

Vasilis lit a match and read the Bulgarian letter translated into Greek:

"Dear brothers from our villages,
    I send you the famous Greek—Captain Agras—as a present. I send him to you to avenge Loukas' blood. In this world of ours, as you know, a man lives for such revenge.
        Your brother, George Kasapje"

"This is a death sentence," Vasilis declared. "When was it written?"

"It isn't dated," Pericles replied. "It came into our hands yesterday. But the day before, our villagers saw Agras exhibited and jeered. Like you, we're afraid and in a hurry to reach him."

"We'll start off as soon as Captain Seraphim arrives," Miss Electra inserted; "and of course we'll put up a fight to free him."

Vasilis didn't answer. And seated on the ground, the three of them observed his slumped over shadow by the light of the stars. From time to time, he drew himself up and stiffened his back, then once more his shoulders sagged as if crushed by an invisible weight.

Pericles broke the silence.

"Where did you leave Jovan? When did he die?"

"The day before yesterday, Wednesday . . . His life slipped away . . . The Bulgarians broke his spine."

"Where did you leave him?"

"In the forest. We buried him under an oak tree, and I set off . . ." Without anger, with a certain fatalism, Vasilis added: "There no longer remains anything to hold me in the world. Wife, mother, child, even Gregos—they're all dead. When I kill Zlatan, I'll escape myself."

"Don't talk that way, Vasilis! . . ." Miss Electra entreated.

There was no answer. Night silence fell upon them.

And slowly, softly, Vasilis said in the low-keyed manner natural to him:

"Mister Pericles . . . I leave you with an order. When you return safely to Alexandria, repeat to the boss, your uncle, what I have to tell you . . ."

Pericles interrupted him:

"We'll return together . . . as we departed."

"I don't think so," Vasilis responded. "In the morning we'll meet up with Zlatan. Either I'll take his life or he'll take mine. The two of us won't come out of the encounter alive. Perhaps we'll both remain behind, like Gregos and Mitris Tané—which would be preferable. If Mister Mitsos were here, I'd relate to him what I have to say. But I won't see him now."

Miss Electra started to get up and move away. Vasilis stretched out his arm and held her back.

"Sit down, Miss Electra. And you, Apostolis, don't leave. We're not sure which of us will survive tomorrow. Yet Gregos' message must reach the boss."

Stopping short for a moment, as if to collect his thoughts, he began to speak in a monotone:

" . . . Gregos was rebellious from the time he was small. Unruly and defiant, a rebel in his father's—Father Theodorides'—house, he could never conform to the slavish life under Turkish occupation. Very strong, he had run-ins every day with the Turkish children of the neighborhood, who trembled under his constant blows. Until one day, still a child of seventeen or eighteen, he broke loose and descended to liberated Greece to join the army as a volunteer.

"He, the most undisciplined of natures, chose the most disciplined of careers. And he completed the Non-Commissioned Officers School and came out a second-lieutenant with the highest honors. The Greek Army hadn't seen a more hardworking and dedicated officer, or a more disciplined one. He lived and worked with one ideal—to free Macedonia. The war of '97 erupted; and from a mission to Crete in support of the rebellion there, he returned to Greece and hastened to the Epiros, where he was wounded and almost killed.

"Disciplined, brave, and daring, he was without question. However just let anyone offend his ethnic pride! Bitter and disheartened—in despair over the disaster of '97—he was sent to Pharsala as a messenger by the director of operations in the Epiros. There, some dapper officer happened to catch sight of him, dusty with dried blood still on his tunic, and called him a 'filthy Turkish offspring.' His temper flared up, the old rebel Gregos surfaced, and he slapped the officer. In time of war, such an act could only mean execution.

"The boss was present, wounded and bitter himself from our repeated flights, retreats, and defeats. Sympathizing with Gregos, he helped him flee, as did another young non-commissioned officer, Yiangos, the son of the old man who took care of us at

Kapsohora. Remember, Mister Pericles? While he didn't want to reveal his name, the old man recognized Gregos and told him that he wasn't 'a Turkish offspring' either! Your uncle gave Gregos as much money as he had with him, along with recommendations to acquaintances in Alexandria.

"But the rebellious Gregos didn't want to stay in such civilized parts. His restless nature drew him to adventure, danger, and wild, untrodden places. He departed for the Congo. He went to Cameroon, to Uganda, and elsewhere, living among fierce African tribes, hunting lions and elephants, imposing his will through his strength and skill—always the conqueror, always victorious. We lost track of him inside the wilderness, amid lakes raging with fever and forests infested with vipers and ferocious animals—which brought devastation and death wherever poisoned arrows or spears hadn't already!

"Years went by . . . He'd disappeared. We didn't know if he was living or dead. The Bulgarians killed my father-in-law, disaster struck my house, and in ill health they brought me to Greece. With no money, I remembered the name of George Vasiotakis who'd enabled Gregos to escape. I went into debt, traveled to Alexandria, and presented myself at your house as a gardener, without making my relation to Gregos known."

"Why?" Pericles broke in.

"Because I didn't want your uncle to think that I'd come with my hand outstretched to exploit his good deed to Gregos. After a time I learned from a fellow Macedonian, who'd returned from Uganda, that Gregos was alive and that he'd been living there. I wrote to him that the Bulgarians had killed his father and destroyed my home.

"Abandoning everything, he sold what he had and returned to Macedonia. He saw the Master, entered the Struggle, and wiped out the beasts who'd drenched Macedonia in blood. He quietly cleansed whole areas. The violent life of Uganda had taught him to deal with the enemy swiftly and stealthily, with a stab in the heart."

Apostolis let out a stifled cry.

"He was the one? . . . The unknown avenger! . . . The Eviscerator of Bulgarians . . . always with a stab in the heart? . . ."

"Yes, he was the one!" Vasilis replied. "He never struck the innocent. But he punished the murderers relentlessly."

"How did you know, Vasilis, that Gregos was in Macedonia?" Pericles inquired. "And how did you find him?"

"I didn't know he was here. In seeking Zlatan, one day I learned that Captain Akritas had his hide-out close-by. Realizing that Captain Akritas was in Thessaly at the time, I asked for a description of him and recognized Gregos as the huge, powerful, fearless rebel. We went to his retreat together, Apostolis. Remember?"

"I remember! He had difficulty, though, recognizing you!"

"My hair had turned white. He knew me with black hair. Besides, we were both young when we separated . . . He asked me for the names of the murderers of his sister. I didn't have paper with me. On the back of an old photograph of her that he always carried with him—signed 'to my brother Gregos'—he wrote down the names I told him. He kept the photograph inside a little wallet that . . . my child found on the dead Gregos' body. Therefore he understood who Gregos was . . . I discovered the wallet concealed beneath my injured child's shirt, and I searched him to find a large, dark mole he'd had from birth between his shoulder blades. It was all discovered too late . . ."

Vasilis went on speaking in a droning voice—as if something inside him had died . . .

And returning to his opening words:

"Mister Pericles, I leave you with an order—to tell the boss, your uncle, what Gregos last said. You heard it, and so did Apostolis and Mister Mitsos. Perhaps you didn't understand. The money your uncle gave him, Gregos had sent back from Uganda. Yet he didn't consider his debt repaid. Upon learning that Mister Mitsos was at the Swamp, he sought to follow him as his unknown protector. Thus it was that he followed him to Zorba the evening Miss Electra's school burned down, and hunted the Bulgarians in his place. And thus he saved him two times at Kourfalia—and killed himself to prevent Mitsos and you from staying back and being captured by the Turks. Tell the boss Gregos repaid his debt."

With agitation Pericles listened to him, as he felt at his chest for the knife with Gregos' blood on it. Now he understood his life as well as his death. Gregos was a heroic figure—an example and ideal for every spirited youth—and his own idol.

Footsteps sounded again, approaching cautiously, apprehensively. Mangas flew up, all ears. There was a soft whistle, a signal that awakened the sleeping villager. They'd all caught hold of their revolvers, ready to fire. However the villager whistled softly, too, and came up to the others.

"It's not an enemy," he said. "It's Stavros the guide. He'll be bringing us some news."

And igniting a piece of brushwood, he raised it high in the dark.

The footsteps quickly drew near. Opening a path inside the thick branches, Stavros appeared.

"You're alone? What happened to Captain Seraphim's young men?" Miss Electra asked.

The guide sat down and requested a little water. Apostolis gave him his water bottle. Thirsty, he drank from it as his anxious, frightened eyes rotated from one to the other of them.

"What's the matter? What happened? . . ." Miss Electra inquired once more.

"They killed him! . . ." the guide answered hoarsely.

A shudder passed through them all.

"Who?" Vasilis asked automatically.

"Captain Agras! . . ."

There was no need to say it. They'd all guessed who it was. For five days now, they'd known it would happen; they'd lived in anguish. With this fear they'd sought to find him—to get to him and save him.

"Where did they kill him? . . . How? . . ." Vasilis questioned the guide.

Stavros motioned toward the west.

"They hanged him," he said.

"Where?"

"On the road. On the way from Vladovo, it seems. He was hanged near Tekovo."

"How do you know?" Apostolis asked.

"I saw him!"

Miss Electra sprang to her feet.

"Take us there!" she said.

* * * *

It grew light as they descended to the road and turned right towards Tekovo.

Cool and sunny, it was a beautiful day. A lively Mangas ran beside Pericles who was in the lead with Vasilis. From time to time the dog lingered behind to sniff inside the thick shrubs that bordered the road. Then he raced up to Pericles again.

They'd proceeded for some time, when all of a sudden Mangas let out a mournful wail. Bursting ahead, he took off. Pericles whistled but the dog didn't return. He continued to run and disappeared at the turn of the road. They all rushed after him; and at the bend, they caught sight of him standing with his tail lowered and his neck strained in the direction of the forest. To the side of the road, also looking towards the forest, two Turkish police were seated on the ground, unaffected by what they saw.

* * * *

Pericles ran up first and was the first to view the fearful sight.

From a large branch of a walnut tree, two bodies were hanging, one near the tree trunk, the other a little farther out.

It was Agras and his faithful guide Toni Mingas.

On Agras' chest, a paper was pinned with the classic warning: "Those who resist us, will end up like this," along with two signatures—Kasapje and Zlatan.

Agras' head was leaning back towards the tree trunk, with his hair dishevelled, his eyes open, and his lips parted. His face, deathly white, appeared tranquil.

Mingas' face, on the contrary, seemed leaden—swollen and contracted from agony. His tongue was half out of his mouth, to one side. Both men had their arms tied behind their back; and their bare feet were swollen and bruised from what they'd endured on the road. Their clothes, torn and dirty, hung on them like rags.

* * * *

When Apostolis saw and recognized the commander who'd inspired him with the feeling of Hellenism, with a pride and love of freedom, his heart was shattered. Ignoring the Turkish police, he fell to the ground among the thick ferns and broke down—perhaps for the first time. Pale and silent, Miss Electra knelt at the foot of the tree where the two martyrs were suspended.

The policemen approached and asked Stavros:

"Are these their relatives?"

"No," Stavros replied, intimidated. "But they're Greeks and they feel compassion for their fellow countrymen hanged by the Bulgarians."

One of the police, a noncommissioned officer, shook his head.

"The Bulgarians are a bad lot!" he said with sympathy. "They killed one of my countrymen the other day! . . . Come, take them down since they're yours. We'll go together to Vladovo. The doctor there will examine the bodies."

With the two guides and Pericles' help, Vasilis removed the nooses from their necks and laid them down on the thick grass under the trees.

"Did they torture them?" one guide wondered.

"No," the other replied; "there aren't any knife wounds."

Pericles, white as a sheet, bent over Agras and started to open his shirt. Vasilis pointed to his neck with the skin scraped away by the rope.

"Could it be that they killed him before hanging him?" he asked. "Perhaps he was strangled—who knows? But he died quickly. His face is calm. The other one was hanged. He struggled before he died . . ."

"They hanged them yesterday," Stavros informed them. "On my way to find you last night, I saw them here and fled in fright."

A villager passing by stopped to stare. Others passed and stopped as well. In a short time a crowd had gathered, some curious, some sympathetic, all of them afraid.

"Let's move them to Vladovo," the head policeman said.

They brought mules and the death procession set off . . .

* * * *

In the poor cemetery of Vladovo, they buried the courageous Greek commander. A wooden rail encircled his modest grave. At its head, a wooden cross was placed, inscribed with his war name.

No official followed the last rites. Those brave youths who died in the Struggle fell anonymously. The consuls and clergy who formed the soul of the Struggle were neither to be present at Agras' funeral nor to acknowledge him. They had to mourn the dead rebel—and avenge him—silently without it being revealed. The Organization operated in secret, as did the Struggle.

Quietly and obscurely, then, the villagers of Vladovo lay the national hero to rest . . . the renowned Captain Agras.

His true name, his real identity, had to be concealed.

31.

Doctor Antonakis

THE MURDER OF AGRAS CAUSED PAIN TO ALL GREEKS. His death was a disaster for the Struggle, his loss irreparable. His acclaimed bravery, as well as his military knowledge, daring, guilelessness and boyish charm, had made him a legendary figure. He'd acquired a reputation as being fearless and invincible.

When it was learned that he went to the Bulgarians to reach an agreement with them, only to be deceived, captured, and killed, the initial shock turned to anger, anger to hate, and hate to rage. All of Greek Macedonia rose up as a body to avenge him.

The Center mobilized all the rebel forces and issued a command to wipe out the murderers wherever they were, mercilessly and without exception.

"Zlatan, though, I'll kill myself!" a grim Vasilis said to Pericles, his eyebrows joined in a frown. He enunciated his words as if he were taking an oath to fulfill his life's mission.

From the time they'd discovered the bodies of Agras and his faithful Mingas hanging from the tree, their little group's eagerness to avenge the commander preoccupied them.

Captain Seraphim's rebels were on Kasapje's heels wherever he passed; and from time to time they'd caught a glimpse of him. Afterwards he'd disappeared into unknown hiding-places in Bulgarian villages—before taking to the mountains again for safety in a southerly direction.

However the "bloodhound" Apostolis had investigated and determined that Zlatan had separated from Kasapje. In terror, he'd

435

abandoned Mt. Vermio with its forests that could conceal Greek avengers, and headed east.

"His plan will be to go to Kourfalia and from there to Bulgaria . . ." Miss Electra declared, bent over a map. "He's quaking in his boots! . . ."[41]

At the priest Father Pakomios' house in Stavro, where they'd ended up after days and nights outdoors hunting down the murderers, Miss Electra, Vasilis, and Pericles were waiting for Apostolis to come back. He'd discovered reliable traces of Zlatan, he said, ones that could finally lead to some results.

Yet Apostolis had been away for three days without any more information reaching them.

"If he's not here tomorrow, I won't wait any longer," Vasilis announced.

Vasilis was even more altered than before. For hours on end he'd remain silent and motionless, immersed in his somber reflections, neither seeing nor hearing. At dusk he'd suddenly set off with Mangas, returning at daybreak—worn-out like he'd walked all night. He would fall into a deep sleep then, or else become absorbed in his reflections again with his head down and his black eyebrows set together in a frown.

At Miss Electra's side, Pericles was studying the map, too. The fever had seized hold of him again in this constant pursuit of Zlatan, and he felt his strength ebbing away. Yet he wouldn't confess it for the world. He'd rather collapse than accept that he was incapable of continuing.

* * * *

It was night and Father Pakomios had retired to his little room. Vasilis hadn't gone out that evening; and the three of them were lying on fleece blankets on the floor to sleep, with Mangas curled up next to Pericles. All at once the dog sprang up with stifled cries and ran to the closed door. At the same time, a soft whistle sounded below the window. Miss Electra leaped to her feet.

"Apostolis' whistle!" she whispered. "Don't move! I'll open up for him."

She shook off her shoes and cautiously, so as not to cause the stairs to creak, tip-toed downstairs. Pulling the bolt from the door, she opened it.

The dog had followed her. Two shadows were standing half-hidden in the door's frame. One was Apostolis. Not recognizing the other, Miss Electra was taken back to see Mangas jump up on him happily.

Apostolis entered inside, supporting his companion by the arm, and Miss Electra closed the door. Just as the other man stepped inside, he fell halfway to the ground and leaned against the wall.

"A little water, Miss Electra," Apostolis said in a low voice. "It's Mitsos. Mangas recognized him. He's wounded; we must take him upstairs. I barely managed to get him here . . ."

Miss Electra had bent over Mitsos, trying to see him in the dark.

"Keep holding him!" she exclaimed to Apostolis. "I'll call Vasilis."

However Vasilis had descended with Pericles. Silently, almost carrying Mitsos, the three of them brought him up to their room. Miss Electra lit a lamp and gave the nearly fainted away Mitsos something to drink. Then she boiled strong tea with a dose of brandy for him, and washed his face and head. Beside her, Mangas sat watching his sick master.

Mitsos was very weak with a high fever. Without any discussion he was left to the caring hands of Miss Electra and Pericles, who undressed him and placed him on a mattress that Vasilis took from the sofa in the priest's little drawing room. Mitsos seemed not to comprehend what was happening around him.

"It was hard for him to come this far . . ." Apostolis explained softly. "I thought he'd fall on the road. His will to find you sustained him. But his leg is inflamed from the bullet that's inside."

"How did he get shot?" Vasilis asked. From the moment he'd recognized Mitsos, it was as though he'd emerged from a gloom that had left him numb.

"He was injured in Monday's battle. Haven't you heard about it?"

"What battle?"

They'd huddled around the lamp, a little apart to allow Mitsos to sleep; and they spoke in whispers in order not to disturb him. Next to the mattress, attentive and alert, Mangas kept watch.

"Didn't you learn that Captain Nikiphoros the Second's force was attacked and wiped out by the Turks?" Apostolis asked.

Speechless, the three of them stared at him. Then Miss Electra spoke:

"Could the curse of God be pursuing us? . . . Perhaps we're suffering from pride . . . that we're always the victors? . . ."

Pericles came to life.

"Nikiphoros the First was always victorious! . . . Could Nikiphoros the Second have committed some blunder?"

Apostolis cut in.

"Don't be unjust to him! Nikiphoros the Second died heroically! . . . It was a mistake, yes, for him to venture out such a distance. It didn't give him time to return to the Swamp before daybreak. Besides, the nights are short now and Goumenitsa far away . . ."

"He went as far as Goumenitsa? What madness! . . ." Vasilis murmured.

"Didn't you know that he planned to strike the Bulgarian comitadje Lazo?" Apostolis asked. "The captain realized it was a bold undertaking, but the old man had courage! Mitsos, who didn't think much of him in the past, told me he admired him. Setting off on the raid, he said to them: 'Whoever wants to die, follow me!'

"Ten followed him, one of whom was Mitsos, of course. They went to Petrovo and received an order from the Center to turn back. The commander didn't want to. He was insistent on eliminating Lazo and making his way further north. However he didn't succeed in entering Goumenitsa. Bulgarian villagers had betrayed them, and the army caught up with them. Fighting, they withdrew, but more Turkish forces arrived, along with armed Bulgarian and Turkish villagers.

"The old man had but ten with him, while enemies pressed down on them. The Turks urged them to surrender, but the commander wouldn't hear of it! He fought desperately, for hours on end, and eventually the shooting subsided. But they'd encircled Nikiphoros the Second and his men—who by throwing bombs to scare them off, succeeded in passing the first ravine.

"However the enemy hunted them down and the battle started up again—little more than a handful of rebels against a sizable army plus villagers! It was a massacre. The commander, who'd been gravely wounded, called upon a brave youth to take command, with the order that he gather the men and take flight. . . . Yet he, too, was wounded, as were Mitsos and two more. The rest had been killed. Mitsos tried to approach the others, but bullets kept falling.

"Then, drawing his pistol, Nikiphoros the Second shot himself so as not to be captured alive by the Turks. That moment and what followed were hell, Mitsos said. They threw their last bombs; and while the Turks retreated, the wounded men were able to drag themselves out of the danger zone. Mitsos lost track of them as they headed towards Ramel. Whether they reached it or not, he didn't find out.

"From the haystack where he collapsed, he could view the Swamp in the distance. A kind woman who was reaping, discovered him, hid him, and later her child brought him by mule to the Tsekri landing. I encountered him at the hut as I was leaving, and took him with me."

"What!" Vasilis reacted. "How is it that you were at Tsekri? . . ."

Apostolis looked at him with flashing eyes.

"You've guessed it, Mr. Vasilis. Yes, Zlatan is at the Swamp!"

"Where? . . . Do you know? . . . Speak!"

"They told me he entered secretly from Goloselo, and I set off in search of him. But he'd left and was reported to be hiding at Zervohori. I went to Tsekri to seek help; however Nikiphoros the

Second's devastating battle had occurred, which meant they had no men to give me. I was ready to go Niki when a canoe brought Mitsos, wounded in the thigh and feverish. When he learned you were at Stavro, he didn't want even to get out—his only thought was to find you . . . We departed together for the Vangeli hut, where we were given food and cartridges before being let out on shore opposite Stavro. Don't ask how we got this far. Ten times I felt he'd die in my hands . . ." he added, nodding toward the mattress where Mitsos was lying.

Miss Electra approached and leaned over him.

"Mr. Mitsos . . ." she murmured.

Drowsy, he didn't reply. Miss Electra returned to the others.

"Where shall we take him? How will we care for him?" she wanted to know.

But Apostolis was conversing with Vasilis.

"If you'd like to avenge Captain Agras, we must start off right away!" he said.

"Both Captain Agras and my child . . ." Vasilis replied.

For a moment he pondered, his arms crossed and his eyes fixed on the flame of the oil lamp—before stating decisively:

"We'll go at once! You Apostolis, Mister Pericles, and I! To you, Miss Electra, we entrust Mitsos."

"Where should I bring him?" she inquired, prepared for any action.

"Stay here, I'd say. You'll tend to him better than anyone else, better then the imposter doctor in the village."

"And the priest?"

"He'll help you. He's a good man, dedicated to the Struggle. If you can, arrange for the doctor from Thessalonika to come. You're resourceful, Miss Electra. You don't need counsel. You'll manage, yourself."

Yes, Miss Electra was resourceful, and she lost no time. Upon seeing the three of them off, with the dog in Pericles' arms, she locked the door and headed straight for Father Pakomios' little room.

"At dawn, while I care for the sick rebel," she said to him, "rush to Halil-bey, Father. Tell him that a friend of Captain Agras' is near death. Have him summon the doctor from Thessalonika. He knows him—the one who took Captain Agras into his home and cured him when he left Kouga, wounded. Go Father, and serve our sacred Struggle! . . ."

Immediately the priest set off on foot, without even waiting for dawn; and he reached Kavasila while it was still dark. He started to rap on the door and grew fearful. To wake Halil-bey before morning? The servants wouldn't hear of it—they'd drive him away!

Huddling down behind a hedge, he soon fell asleep.

* * * *

He awoke with a start. It was daylight and hoofbeats sounded . . . Disoriented from his sleep, the priest didn't perceive a horseman draw up and dismount. It was only when the man stood before him, holding his horse by the reins, that he saw him.

"How is it that you're here, Father, at such an hour?" the man inquired in Greek.

All at once Father Pakomios recognized him.

"Doctor Antonakis! You've been sent by God!" he responded, crossing himself three times. "Bless you with many more years. All the saints . . ."

"All right, all right!" Doctor Antonakis broke in cheerfully. "It's my pleasure and my honor if I can do you a favor, Father. Why are you here? Who are you seeking?"

In a few words Father Pakomios gave him an account of the sudden arrival of the wounded fighter at night, and the urgent need to rush to Halil-bey for help.

"What need do we have of Halil-bey?" the doctor exclaimed. "I'm here. What more could you ask for?"

"Miss Electra wants to bring the doctor from Thessalonika . . . a doctor she knows," the priest explained with some hesitation. He didn't wish to offend this imposter doctor's pride by showing distrust. But Antonakis laughed.

"Her acquaintance, her friend—and my friend too! . . ." he said. "I know him. When she was wounded at Zorba, she went to his home. But do we require Halil-bey, I wonder? Can't I get him to Thessalonika if there's a need? Moreover there will be a need. Your house isn't suitable for sick patients. And if the bullet's still in his leg . . ."

"It is," Father Pakomios said. "And it's inflamed! . . ."

Antonakis interrupted him.

"Come! Climb onto the back of my horse, Father!" he said with good humor. "You must be tired, walking so far."

He mounted himself and they drew at a slow pace for Stavro.

* * * *

Doctor Antonakis was short, blond, and cheerful, with handsome features and a shrewd expression. On the road, he conversed with the priest.

"Where did Miss Electra find her wounded rebel?" he asked.

"I don't know. They brought him in the night while I slept. She only told me that I'd serve our sacred Struggle, and I came."

"A minor clash in the Swamp? . . . Or some quarrel?" the doctor asked again.

But the priest didn't know.

"You were fortunate to meet me. Halil-bey wouldn't do anything for you," Antonakis declared.

"Why?"

"Because he's angry—with all the rebels, the priests, the teachers, and the world, since they let the Bulgarians hang Captain Agras."

"He's right," the priest replied sorrowfully. "Yet what could they do? The Center dispatched men and sent commands, money, and promises. But with such—ahem—devils, how can you succeed? They've hunted for the murderers, but it seems they didn't find them."

"They didn't hunt for them properly. I'd have found them!"

"Eh, of course! You know these matters better," the priest said meekly. "Why didn't the Center send you?"

"It was bad luck," Antonakis responded. "Mr. Ionnidis had me go to Roumlouki to make a round of the villages . . . You know . . . weapons and the rest! I was in the midst of a delivery when I learned they hanged him. A great loss, such a figure!"

"Yes, great!" Father Pakomios sighed. "Tell me, though, how is it that I met you outside Halil-bey's house?"

"I was on my way there, like you. They informed me he was furious and creating difficulties for us. I was supposed to calm him down . . ."

Ferocious barking arose. From a sheepfold, two dogs burst forth and rushed at the horse. Frightened, it started to run and stumbled under the double load. The priest, who was frightened himself, lifted up his robe and feet. Antonakis the doctor tried to shoo the dogs away. Not only did he fail to do so, but three more appeared and raised pandemonium.

"Do you want to laugh, Father? . . . Watch! . . ." the doctor said hurriedly.

He let out a long, loud shriek, raising it up to the most piercing, shrillest pitches.

Right away howling broke out. From all around, sheepdogs with their tail between their legs and their head down, sped off and scattered over the countryside.

The priest was dumbfounded. Astonished, he made his cross.

"I'd heard how you drove the dogs away," he said. "But I never imagined anything like this! . . ."

Amused, the doctor replied:

"I wouldn't have done it if my horse hadn't taken fright. I don't do it without good reason, because the dogs flee and leave the sheepfolds and villagers without guards. And that terrifies them! . . . Now for two days not one dog will return."

"A shame," he added, "that we don't have any rebels to bring to the lake today! . . ."

"You have to get our wounded rebel out, though!" the priest exclaimed.

"Good enough. We'll do it quietly. Do you know if he has a permit? Or identification?"

The priest had no idea.

"It makes no difference," the doctor said, tapping his shirt pocket. "Here we have a little of everything, for all occasions. Is he young?"

"Yes."

"Clean shaven?"

"No. He has a beard."

"That won't bother us. We'll shave him. With Doctor Antonakis, all things can be arranged!"

* * * *

Arriving at the village, they dismounted and walked the rest of the way, holding the horse by the reins. The villagers appeared to greet the doctor, but also to complain that their dogs had run off howling.

"Why did you do it, Doctor!" they said over and over. "The village has been left unprotected!"

Seeing that Antonakis had come, however, they tried to bring him home with them—one for a pain in the heart, another for rheumatism, still another for a cough.

But Doctor Antonakis was no longer playing the role of doctor. He was staying in Thessalonika, where he had other work. Yet with a good word here, or on-the-spot advice there, he sent them on their way and entered the priest's house.

They discovered Miss Electra seated beside Mitsos' bed, reading from an old Thessalonika newspaper she'd found in a drawer. Mitsos' fever was almost gone, but his leg wound gave him pain. Pleased to recognize Doctor Antonakis after meeting up with him a couple of times at the Swamp, he shook his hand heartily like they were old friends who shared the same views.

"Now that I've found you, I'll take you to Thessalonika," Doctor Antonakis announced after examining Mitsos' injured leg. "And I'll transport you to the Verria station by ox-cart, so you don't tire yourself out!"

Worried, Mitsos said:

"I can't travel by train. I don't have a passport."

"What do you need with a passport? You have me!" the doctor replied with an air of importance.

He removed a razor from his pocket.

"Give me a little water, Miss Electra," he said, "and some soap. A razor in a priest's house, I certainly don't expect to find. But I carry what's necessary with me. In ten minutes, Mister Mitsos, I'll have turned you into Sotiris Bazoudi, a brown-haired, clean-shaven youth whose identification card is in my pocket . . ."

"Incredible!" Miss Electra cried out. "You're a miracle worker!"

"Naturally! What did you suppose?" Antonakis replied proudly. "Only take off the boy's clothes you're wearing, Miss Electra, and dress like a woman. I think you'll accompany us."

"Of course," the teacher replied matter-of-factly. "Mister Mitsos should have constant care."

Touched, Mitsos extended his hand. Catching hold of hers, he squeezed it.

"You nursed Pericles to health. Now I'm a burden to you . . ."

But Miss Electra interrupted him.

"Let Father Pakomios go and bring us outfits from the villagers," she said to the doctor. "And we'll send for an ox-cart. Can we make the train?"

"We'll be in time!" Antonakis assured her. "Don't trouble yourself. Leave it all to me. When Doctor Antonakis undertakes something, he always succeeds. I've filled Macedonia with rebels, rifles, cartridges, and bombs. Do you think I can't get a wounded man to Thessalonika?"

And he chuckled to himself with satisfaction.

32.

In The Water Of The Swamp

IT WAS WELL INTO THE MIDDLE OF THE NIGHT when Vasilis reached the Vangeli hut with Pericles and Apostolis, having left Mitsos with Miss Electra at Stavro. A pistol shot had brought two canoes to the shore to transport them; and once there, the exhausted men settled down to sleep on the dry Swamp grass the rebels spread out for them.

Waking at daybreak, they consulted with Agras' former assistant Captain Nikos, on guard at the Lower Huts. He didn't know about Zlatan; he hadn't heard anything. But he advised them to go to Kouga—perhaps they'd learn there. Captain Teligadis, in charge of the now-famous hut, would have set his bloodhounds on the Bulgarian's trail . . .

So they departed.

Apostolis was reminded of earlier days when, oar in hand, he'd guided Captain Agras on a search for Kouga. It had been fall then; the reeds were just turning yellow and drying up. Agras with his boyish laugh and sparkling eyes—with a joke here and an encouraging word there—had leaped into the water himself. Awkwardly but eagerly, he'd cut down the half-dried reeds to set an example for the villagers in opening up new paths.

Now it was summer. Juice-filled plants covered the Swamp, swelling up all around. Even from the bottom of the lake, hearty green shoots burst forth, seeking light and warmth at the water's surface.

A melancholy Apostolis rowed swiftly, shortening the distance to Kouga by taking secret paths. Pericles, with Mangas in his arms, was trembling from fever. The dog was on the watch, ready to give the danger signal, while Pericles examined the profusion of vegetation surrounding them. Seated in the prow with his rifle in his hand—its stock on his shoulder and his finger on the trigger—Vasilis scrutinized the reeds and shrubs in case the enemy might be lurking behind all the beauty.

No one spoke. But the whole lake echoed from its distinctive sounds—from warbling and cackling and chirping, and from cries and screeches in the thick undergrowth.

However no man appeared. The canoe reached Kouga before noon, without difficulty or delay.

Plunged in mourning, Captain Teligadis received them. The murder of his commander had crushed him; and he couldn't forgive himself for obeying Agras and allowing him to depart alone.

"If I'd been along, he wouldn't have gone like a lamb that way to the slaughter. I wouldn't have listened to anyone, or let the lads go off or the village leaders abandon him to his fate. There would have been a bloodbath—but they wouldn't have captured the commander and dragged him away barefoot and humiliated him . . . Captain Agras! . . . Captain Agras . . ." he said again and again.

They'd seated themselves on the floor inside the hut: Teligadis, Vasilis, Apostolis and Pericles. Vasilis explained what they were there for—that Apostolis had succeeded in learning Zlatan was at Zervohori, and they felt Teligadis might know where he was hiding . . .

"It's good you came to me," Captain Teligadis declared. "Not only do I know, but I'm preparing revenge!"

Vasilis' eyes shone.

"What are you preparing?" he asked.

"What is it that I'm preparing? . . . Do you think Zlatan's the only cunning one? He'll meet his match!" Teligadis replied.

"No one surpasses him in cunning—or in crimes," Vasilis said. "Don't try to compete there. He'll beat you!"

"Besides, his trickery is contrary to the commander's principles . . . We shouldn't catch him with cunning, but by bravery," Pericles added, rubbing Mangas' ears nervously with his fingers.

Teligadis flared up.

"A one-to-one battle, eh? . . ." he scoffed. "That's what Captain Agras said, too. But such a thing occurs with brave men, not murderers! And Zlatan's a murderer! A fox! . . . bloodthirsty and cowardly! . . . He'd never pit himself against you or me. A stealthy stab in the back—that's his means. We'll only capture him in the same way!"

"It's not fitting . . . The commander wouldn't want it," Pericles spoke up again.

Apostolis didn't open his mouth. His sharp eyes traveled from one to the other as he listened to what each had to say, their conflicting views at loggerheads within him.

"Let's hear your plan, Captain Teligadis," Vasilis said.

Teligadis related it to them:

"Do you remember the Bulgarian Christof Bozan—who Captain Matapas captured one night and spared his life? Afterwards they brought him here from the Terkovista hut. Well, I sent him to Zervohori where Zlatan is—to speak to him and tell him I want to find a solution to our quarrels . . ."

"And he'll believe it?" Vasilis interrupted.

"When the Bulgarian informs him of it?"

"You have faith in the Bulgarian?"

"What are you saying? He owes us his life! . . . Anyone but Matapas and those of you with him, would have killed him!"

"Rightly so! We've nurtured a snake at our bosom!" Vasilis responded. He turned to Apostolis.

"Tell him what you know!"

Apostolis spoke in a broken voice.

"I had a little friend—did you know him, Captain Teligadis?"

"Your apprentice Jovan? Certainly I know him!" Teligadis answered.

"He's dead now . . . They killed him . . ."

"Little Jovan? . . . The poor child!" Teligadis exclaimed.

"I'd sent him to find Zlatan—who came here to speak to the commander," Apostolis continued with agitation . . . "After they separated, Captain Agras returned to Kouga and Zlatan to Zervohori. Jovan followed the Bulgarian, and Christof Bozan was among those accompanying him. He's a spy and a traitor."

Stunned, confused, Teligadis stared at Apostolis.

Vasilis laughed bitterly.

"And you, evzone, want to compete with Zlatan in cunning?" Straightening up, he went on:

"If you want to avenge the commander, join forces with me! I have a personal account to settle with him, as well. He killed my child . . . little Jovan who you knew and we all considered to be Bulgarian . . . Yet that's beside the point . . . although I'll take back his blood. Will you join with me, Teligadis?"

"I will! But what do you have in mind?"

Vasilis looked at Apostolis, then laid out the plan that had been ripening in his mind night and day.[42]

Apostolis would go to Zervohori to where Zlatan was hiding.

"Seeing that you know it, Teligadis, you'll give him directions."

As soon as Apostolis had assured himself that Zlatan was there, he was to race back and Vasilis would set off at once.

"Good . . ." Teligadis reflected. "But you know you won't escape!"

Vasilis shrugged his shoulders.

"So? What do I have to lose! . . . Neither wife, nor child . . . or anything else. When I put him to death, I'll be through!"

And he instructed Apostolis:

"Go right away. When you return, fire two pistol shots in succession should there be a need. We'll start immediately for Zervohori and meet you on the way!"

* * * *

Apostolis departed, and the others sat down to wait. How much time would it take for him to get there? And come back? If he located Zlatan quickly, he'd be back before dark, Captain Teligadis calculated.

Teligadis described the life at the Swamp to them—dull, tedious, and exasperatingly the same from daybreak until sundown. Once Agras and then Nikiphoros left, the Struggle had come to a standstill. Its momentum was gone. Now Nikiphoros had returned to Greece, Agras had been killed, and Nikiphoros the Second's force decimated.

"We hear only the wild animals," Captain Teligadis said. "Even the Bulgarians are quiet."

From time to time he'd go out with a couple of his men and steal up to the nearby enemy huts . . . Only in summer could he do this, with the leaves out . . . Afterwards, for the fun of it, he'd fire a few shots to wake the Swamp up a little—which would be answered half-heartedly by the Bulgarians.

Then he'd return to Kouga, bored and disgusted by the inaction. It was rare that he met up with an enemy canoe or two on his patrols and exchanged a couple of bullets with them.

The Bulgarians had confined themselves to their impregnable complex of fortified huts to the southwest. They, too, refrained from attempting new conquests. It was as though the Swamp had no spirit.

"Those who called Agras the General Commander of the Greeks knew what they were saying . . ." Teligadis commented sorrowfully.

* * * *

Night had fallen. All three went out into the fresh air on deck, each holding a leafy branch to shoo away the mosquitoes.

Pericles had thrown his arm around his dog and was mumbling something.

"What did you say, Mister Pericles?" Vasilis asked.

But Pericles didn't reply. Realizing he was raving and not wanting to betray himself, he closed his eyes and feigned sleep.

"Apostolis is late . . ." Vasilis said.

"He might not have found Zlatan quickly," Teligades responded.

Both of them had lit up cigarettes to keep the mosquitoes away. While waiting, they conversed quietly.

It grew completely dark; the sentries changed and changed again, but Apostolis failed to appear.

After first burning green branches to smoke up the hut and drive out the mosquitoes there, they all went in to get some sleep. In one corner Pericles sank down on the floor, with Mangas anxiously guarding him. Every so often, the dog licked the boy's feverish hands as if he wanted to cool them.

* * * *

Towards morning, while the men and commanders still slept, a dead-tired Apostolis presented himself and asked for a cup of strong coffee.

"I mustn't sleep," he said, "and I'm about to drop!"

"Did you see Zlatan?" Vasilis inquired as he helped him unbutton his vest in order to wash the dust off his face and neck to cool himself.

Apostolis gave a negative sign.

"He'd gone into the Swamp. He's afraid and wants to take off for Bulgaria. But I was hot on his trail; wherever he went I went— under the pretext that Kasapje had sent me to speak with him. In the meantime, I'd learned that Kasapje was killed . . ."

"He was killed? Where?" Teligadis cried out.

"Near Doliani. Captain Seraphim got him."

"Was there a battle?"

"Yes! He was also fleeing—quaking in his boots, as Miss Electra says. Captain Seraphim caught up with him and shot him!"

"So you didn't see Zlatan?" Vasilis said gloomily.

"No. Once he returned to Zervohori, they wouldn't let me enter the hut where he sleeps. He's scared and has guards. However I'll take you there, Mister Vasilis. We must leave at once, though, so he doesn't escape us. His fear that we'll capture him is such that he passes from one place to another! . . . "

Pericles had risen and approached, reeling.

"I'll come with you, Vasilis! . . ." he said.

Vasilis grew alarmed when he looked at him.

"You're sick, Mister Pericles! You must go to the Lower Huts!"

"It's nothing," Pericles replied. "I'll come with you!"

Yet he appeared ashen—his face twitching and his eyes sunken.

"I won't take you!" Vasilis exclaimed. "Stay here and rest. You'd collapse on the way!"

"Give me a coffee, too. I slept badly during the night . . ." Pericles murmured.

Apostolis pulled Vasilis by the sleeve.

"If we're going, we must leave at once! . . ." he whispered. "Or it will be too late. The bird will have flown!"

"Let's be off," Vasilis said. "Captain Teligadis, give me one of your lads . . ."

"I'll go!" Pericles persisted, pursuing him onto the deck.

Vasilis turned, looked at him again, and then said firmly:

"You're a brave patriot, Mister Pericles! Don't hinder us in our work! It will be a toss-up today—one or the other of us will survive. You're sick. We'll be fighting with everything we have! . . ."

Pericles didn't insist any longer. Humbled, in turmoil, and defeated, he watched Vasilis, Apostolis, and the giant Vangelis— nicknamed "the Macedonian" by Agras—climb down into a canoe, proceed to the right, and disappear behind the reeds.

"Two successive pistol shots will be the signal, if help's required," Vasilis told Teligadis as he left.

Pericles sat at the edge of the deck and leaned against the earthen defense. His head hurt, his bones ached, and his legs were trembling . . . Truly he wasn't fit for battle.

"What a shame . . . What a shame! . . ." he murmured. "If my grandfather saw me now! . . ."

Next to Pericles, with his ears raised and his eyes fixed sympathetically upon him, Mangas gazed at his master. As if he wanted to console him, he raised one paw onto the boy's sleeve. Pericles picked him up and buried his face in the dog's fur.

"Mangas! . . . Mangas! . . . How my heart is shattered . . ." he said softly, ready to cry.

All of a sudden, with a leap Mangas slipped away and ran to the other corner of the deck. His fur stood on end and he growled deeply, exposing his teeth—tense, fierce, furious . . .

Pericles sprang to his feet and followed him. Leaning in the direction the dog indicated, he tried to view inside the reeds.

"What is it, Mangas?" he asked in a commanding voice.

The dog turned quickly, glanced at him, and once more faced back towards the reeds. Growling incessantly, he was about to jump into a canoe that was tied to the deckpost.

"An enemy, Mangas? . . . An enemy? . . ." Pericles repeated.

As if the dog understood, he looked around at his master, then leaped into the boat. Without hesitating Pericles crossed over from the deck to the canoe, and untied it. A rebel observed him from the defense above.

"Where are you going?" he inquired.

"My dog appears to be on the scent of something. I'm going to investigate!" Pericles replied.

Dipping his oar into the water, he steered the canoe toward the reeds where Vasilis had disappeared with his companions. In front in the prow, a growling Mangas became fiercer and fiercer. Ready to plunge into the water, he both drew his master on and guided him along.

According to the dog's movements, Pericles navigated the dugout onto a path behind Kouga. Tremendously excited, Mangas was poised to jump into the water again. He let forth an angry bark, with his nose turned towards the wider waterway that cut off the path. Upright, Pericles had grabbed hold of his revolver with one hand while he worked his oar with the other, pushing the dugout towards Grounandero, where it emerged.

A canoe was hurrying away in front of him toward the eastern part of the lake. Two armed men sat inside, the oarsman Christof Bozan and a redhead who was bent over fearfully searching all around . . . Zlatan? . . .

He tottered and sank backwards, overturning the dugout.

With the redhead's rifle aimed at him, Pericles managed to fire off two bullets and see two flashes before him. At the same time he heard a loud, poignant howling.

Mangas is crying . . . he had time to reflect . . . However my grandfather approves of me . . .

He tottered and sank backwards, overturning the dugout.

And the water of the lake flowed over him.

Hesitant, the Bulgarian canoe had stopped. A frightened Christof Bozan now stood in the stern, oar in hand.

"Should I continue or return to the huts?" he asked.

"Continue! We'll have time . . .!"

"Look at the dog, Zlatan!" Bozen interrupted in a low voice. "He dives in over and over again . . . like he wants to save him!"

Another howl from Mangas split the air. Zlatan threw a glance at the dog.

"Better to head back to the huts before they overtake us!" he ordered. "Fast! They'll hear the shots at Kouga . . . and the dog's cries will lead them here . . . They'll close off our road!"

Rapidly the Bulgarian boat turned back—driven away by Mangas' heart-rending wails. The dog came up to the surface to breathe, then dove back into the water.

"You were fortunate to escape again, chief!" Bozan said, thrusting his oar down to the bottom of the lake.

Zlatan was tying his bloody arm with his torn sleeve.

"Fortunate that two bullets hit me? Yet what an eye! If I'd been facing him, he would have gotten me in the heart!"

"That's the reason I said you're lucky. The bullets missed striking any bone and breaking it, since you're moving your arm . . ."

A curse cut off his speech. Startled, he whirled around and confronted another canoe. Coming from the direction of the Bulgarian huts, it appeared in a pathway before them. He seized his rifle, but it was too late. Two shots sounded and Christof Bozan crumpled into a heap. Zlatan started to take up the oar. With a glance, he measured the distance separating him from the other canoe—and understood that he was lost. Giving the dugout a shove, he jumped into the shallow water.

From the other canoe, Vasilis had anticipated him. Jumping into the water himself, up to the waist, he blocked Zlatan's way. The two men engaged in a hand-to-hand battle. Hate multiplied Vasilis' strength as he tightened his grip on his enemy's neck. Zlatan took out his knife and struck. But the pain of his wound from Pericles was disabling him, and the knife went astray and cut the outer skin of Vasilis' shoulder. With all his weight, Vasilis forced him to his knees inside the water, grabbed the knife from his trembling fingers, and caught him by the hair. With a fury, he bent his head back.

"Do you know me, Zlatan, you criminal? Do you recognize me, you butcher? . . ." he hissed.

Zlatan jerked despairingly, trying to free himself from the hands that held him fast. A stroke of the knife hit its mark; and a second one finished him off. He fell inside the water, which grew red . . .

Vangelis and Apostolis had both witnessed the violent scene from their boat, without being able to help. Once they'd moored it near Zlatan's body, Vasilis looked up and saw them. Then he stared down at his bloody hands. Dipping them into the water, he started to say something . . . However his lips were dry and no words came out.

At a distance from them, wailing erupted above the noise of the lake. Vasilis winced.

"It's nothing," Vangelis reassured him. "A dog howling."

"It's Mangas' cry!" Apostolis said, worried. "He's howling desperately."

"He's gotten a whiff of what's happening here," Vangelis speculated.

Another wail was heard, and a third, fainter and more mournful. Vasilis straightened up.

"Where did we leave Mangas?" he inquired.

"At Kouga! . . ." Vangelis replied.

"The cries aren't coming from Kouga! . . . They're coming from Grounandero! . . . " Apostolis said.

Stooping over abruptly, Vasilis lifted up the dead Zlatan and threw him like a sack into the bottom of the Bulgarian canoe with Christof Bozan. Then with brusque movements, he climbed into the other boat beside Vangelis and Apostolis.

"You drag the canoe with the corpses after us," he said to Vangelis. "Apostolis and I will row. We'll go and investigate."

But the howling had ceased.

Apostolis knew all the paths from the time he'd been at Kouga with Agras. Without hesitating or groping, he guided the canoe to Grounandero. As they reached it, they found themselves in the midst of a little fleet of dugouts. To the side in one of them, Captain Teligadis was searching for something down in the water. Vasilis caught sight of him and called out:

"Teligadis! What is it?"

Teligadis rose, troubled and somber.

"An accident," he said glumly.

Standing, Vasilis was the first to view Mangas' white fur on the floor of the other canoe. The dog was lying on his side, his paws stretched out stiffly.

"What did Mangas suffer?" Vasilis asked. "How is it that he's here?"

Teligadis didn't answer. Removing one leg and then the other from the boat, he jumped into the lake. It being summer, the water came up just above his waist. He bent down and brought up a body.

Close behind him, Vasilis and Vangelis helped raise it and place it down in their canoe.

With horror, Apostolis recognized Pericles. His eyes were wide-open, and a little blood still spurted from a wound in his chest.

No one spoke. Rapidly Vasilis unbuttoned Pericles' jacket and vest. Something heavy rolled with a thud onto the keel. None of them observed it. Vasilis opened up the boy's shirt and uncovered the wound. The bullet had found its target; the heart was no longer beating.

The other dugouts with the rebels had drawn near. All were silent, as though in a state of shock. Vasilis dropped down heavily in the prow of his boat.

"Who gave the signal that summoned us?" he inquired.

The men looked at each other. No one answered.

"Who fired two pistol shots, one after the other?" Vasilis inquired again.

"It wasn't you?" Teligadis asked.

"No. We heard them near the Bulgarian hut and raced back."

"None of us fired," Teligadis said. "We were all at Kouga and came after the shots sounded. We discovered only the poor dog, drowned. We'd heard the pistol shots and the howling and hastened here. And one of the lads had seen Pericles leaving with his dog."

"So he fired them himself? Where is his pistol?"

"Something fell before . . ." Vangelis remarked.

Apostolis searched and found the weapon—a triangular knife. On its copper handle a Bulgarian name was engraved: "Mitris Tané." Apostolis remembered it.

"Mitsos took this knife from Captain Akritas' wound—that is, from Gregos' . . . It appears that Pericles kept it," he said, choked up.

Vasilis picked up the knife and examined it. Gregos' blood had almost all disappeared from the blade, washed out in the water. Only in a groove carved into the steel, some dry blood resembling rust remained.

"He wouldn't have made the shots, since he didn't have a pistol," Teligadis stated softly.

"He did! I know! I saw it!" Apostolis exclaimed. "It must have fallen too and stayed at the bottom!"

Hurriedly he entered the water. Next to him, Teligadis searched also. Apostolis soon located the revolver. Teligadis took it, tapped the spring, and opened it.

Two bullets were missing. Without speaking, he showed Vasilis.

"Both of them hit Zlatan. He has two bullets in his arm," Vangelis informed them.

His words roused Vasilis, who was in a trance with his eyes fixed on the two weapons. Raising his head, he stared at the men around him, then said to Teligadis:

"Bring the dog over. Put it down beside Pericles. He loved him. And let's go back to Kouga."

One by one the canoes set off. In front, Vasilis led the way with Apostolis and the dead Pericles. Behind, the death convoy followed, a series of dugouts in the placid water of the Swamp.

They brought the dead youth down to the Lower Huts and took him out on shore, where a priest from a nearby chapel came and chanted the funeral rites.

* * * *

Together with a silent, stooped Vasilis, they buried him, along with his faithful Mangas. Covering the grave with stones, they erected a wooden cross with the boy's name carved on it:

PERICLES VASIOTAKIS

FOR HIS FAITH AND COUNTRY

And the date: *1907*
Nothing else.

* * * *

Afterwards the rebels departed for Kouga. Vasilis left as well, headed for Stavro with Apostolis.

"One of the purest victims of the Struggle . . ." Vasilis said to him—before falling silent once more.

33.

"Again With The Years, With Time"

ON A SUMMER EVENING AT DUSK, a procession was descending towards the coast. Tired, sick, and emaciated, the travelers trudged slowly through the mud, each three meters apart, avoiding the occasional sheepfolds and pastures.

In front a boy was guiding them, while in the rear a lame man limped along, at times leaning on the arm of a white-haired companion who stayed close to him, at other times upon a girl in a skirt and thick, high-buttoned boots. They all made their way in silence, taking care where they stepped; and as it grew darker, their pace toward the coast quickened.

But it was a strenuous, difficult journey. Every so often they were compelled to stop and sit down on their cloaks, which they threw upon the brambles in order not to get them muddy on the wet ground. After exchanging a few words, they resumed their course.

Most of them were leaving the Swamp ravaged by fever. A couple had been wounded as well. They were departing for their native soil, for liberated Greece; yet no one showed any joy.

Once more Apostolis took the lead and Mitsos closed the line at the end, together with Vasilis and Miss Electra. The men had come to the lake fired with enthusiasm. They'd shed their blood, undergone hardship, labored and fought without grumbling or complaining—suffering misfortune, sickness, deprivation and the cold. However things had gone downhill. They were returning home with a certain disillusionment, along with the grievance that the Struggle had reached an impasse. Action at the Swamp had ceased; the heroic pages of battles and victories were over—although their work wasn't finished.

The great captains of the Swamp had fallen or departed. Commands from the Center were now restricted to defense, to maintaining the huts rather than seeking new conquests. For their part, the Bulgarians didn't budge from the western lake where they had their stronghold. Thus life at the Swamp had lost its luster and interest.

"The Struggle died with Agras," Captain Teligadis declared. Despite the August heat, he wore his cloak and was trembling from fever.

One or two of the men protested half-heartedly for the sake of discussion, though no one maintained his opposition. And again they took up their path in the thick mud.

Vasilis had grown still more silent and grim. After burying Pericles, he'd gone straight to Stavro with Apostolis, to Father Pakomios' house. But he'd found the priest alone. His guests had left the day before with Doctor Antonakis, bound for Thessalonika.

Using passports provided by Halil-bey, Vasilis and Apostolis had boarded a train themselves and headed for the city.

* * * *

They went directly to "grandmother's" and discovered it peaceful and cheery, with the wounded Mitsos in bed and Miss Electra and grandmother beside him. The doctor had removed the bullet from his leg and said that, while broken, the leg would mend. That very morning grandmother had exchanged engagement rings between Mitsos, who couldn't imagine life without Miss Electra, and the teacher from Zorba, who'd sent in her resignation to be free to care for the injured rebel of the Swamp.

The news of Pericles' death struck the happy, light-hearted household like a thunderbolt . . .

Mitsos' wound would heal—although he remained lame. This would pass, the doctor assured them, but his life at the Swamp was over. He required calm and needed to return to liberated Greece, or else home to Alexandria. In time his leg would be as before.

Grandmother got ready and embarked from Thessalonika, while the rebels left secretly for Koulakia—and from there for the coast where a ship would take them undercover to Greece. Those who'd entered Turkish territory in secret couldn't get a passport to depart openly in Thessalonika like grandmother.

* * * *

More taciturn than ever, Vasilis proceeded at Mitsos' side; and just as silent, Apostolis led the little group. Grandmother had informed him that she'd take him and put him through school, then send him to the university to pursue studies to enable him to become an important man. Apostolis was happy he'd be educated and have books so he could explain the problems that tormented him—as Pericles had done for him in their long conversations.

Yet his heart ached with the thought that he'd leave so many graves in the oppressed land, especially Pericles' modest one marked by a few stones and a wooden cross, situated on the lake's shore.

The thought of leaving tortured him so, that when he arrived at the sea with his weary companions and they'd found the fishermen—who shook all their hands in good spirits—he couldn't bring himself to exchange lively greetings. Off to the side he watched and listened, without joining in the good-humored conversation or approaching.

One after another the men climbed into the boats, and Miss Electra and the lame, exhausted Mitsos were helped inside. Vasilis was the last to enter. Suddenly Mitsos noticed Apostolis standing alone and solitary on the sand.

"Apostolis," he called to him in a whisper to keep from being heard in the silent plain. "Apostolis, get in; we're departing! . . ."

Slowly Apostolis drew near.

"I won't be coming . . ." he replied. "You go . . . A good voyage to you!"

"You won't be coming? What nonsense! The ship is waiting for us. Enter quickly!"

"I won't be coming," Apostolis repeated. "I'm a Macedonian and Macedonia hasn't been freed. I'm initiated; I took an oath. We vowed to work with all our strength and soul to set Macedonia free. It's not free . . . We've only opened up graves. Besides, another ship is due tonight with new rebels. I'll wait for them here and guide them to the Swamp. I'll stay in the Struggle with them . . ."

"Come inside the boat! We'll talk about it on the way."

"I won't change my mind. You go. I wish you a good voyage and a good return to freedom! I'll remain . . ."

All their words and pressure proved futile. Apostolis had decided. No one could alter his decision.

Wrapping his cloak tighter, Teligadis murmured:

"Agras' spirit hasn't died . . ."

The boatloads of sick fighters started off and moved swiftly away with the sturdy fishermen at the oars. Beneath the tears in her eyes, Miss Electra continued to stare at the unyielding boy, a faint silhouette with his head bowed. The final good-by she threw him encompassed both the faithful guide and the Macedonian land she loved so well.

In ten minutes, they had located the ship, boarded it, and with warm handshakes, parted from the Koulakia fishermen.

* * * *

It was well into the night. Seated in the prow, holding Miss Electra's hand, Mitsos whispered words of affection to her as she cried silently and every so often answered him with a squeeze of his hand. He spoke of his great respect for her tireless and courageous action at her school and at the lake; and of how, seeing her at her work, he'd admired and loved her.

She went on crying silently from emotion and happiness, but at the same time from the sadness of her split with—and good-by to—the intense, vigorous life of the Struggle, and especially of her separation from Apostolis.

"You don't know how fond I was of that child, Mitsos!" she said. "He was so genuine, so sincere . . . An absolute treasure! . . ."

Alone and half-reclining in the stern, Vasilis gazed into the darkness toward the Macedonian soil. Nothing appeared anymore. No light was shining on the deserted plain; and the ship remained dark to prevent any Turkish boat from noticing it and stopping them.

Vasilis recollected the days, weeks and months he'd spent in his oppressed land.

Why had he gone? Just what had he accomplished? . . . He'd found his child and hadn't recognized him. He'd left Macedonia enslaved, as it was when he returned to it. And he'd failed to discover his wife's grave. Thick vegetation covered the place where they'd buried her. Moreover new graves had opened up . . . So many heroes and martyrs, with still others to fall! . . .

Nikiphoros had departed with his health destroyed. Gregos had taken his own life. They'd killed Jovan, his tender little Theodore, who he'd lived beside without realizing it. Agras, the finest hero of the Macedonian Struggle, had been put to death. Of his men, how many had succumbed! . . . So many men, women, and children . . . And they'd shot Pericles! . . . The outcome? . . . Could the meager results he'd left behind him be worth so much blood? . . .

Why was he leaving? . . . Apostolis had stayed. Why didn't he, Vasilis, stay as well to finish up the Struggle? Had he lost his morale? His faith? He'd arrived filled with fire, turmoil, and a will for victory. And now he was departing . . . Why?

Apostolis had remained. But Apostolis was young with all his life in front of him, all his hopes and the faith that he'd liberate Macedonia . . . He himself was defeated . . .

Apostolis had said he was initiated. He—Vasilis—was initiated, too . . . Yet Apostolis had the future before him for action and victory. A child still, he was filled with life and longing. What more did he, Vasilis, have? Neither mother nor wife, nor child nor home. They'd killed his family, burned his village, and worse, taken away his hope! . . .

To stand tall when everything was demolished? . . . To return to his boss without Pericles? To become their gardener again? Did he have it in him anymore? He'd set off from Macedonia once, and now he was leaving it a second time. However then he'd been hopeful that his child was alive. And he'd lived for revenge. Now he'd had his fill of revenge, and he'd buried his child. Where would he find the strength for work? Moreover what work, since his heart remained in his enslaved land? Life had broken him. Life had conquered him . . .

For a long time he stared into the darkness with his hands interlocked, as the sea, agitated by the ship's passing, swished and swirled before him.

My child's grave was a little bulge on the ground, as was Pericles'. A grave like the sea, with the wind whipping the waves into mountains, would suit them better . . . Such a grave would suit him, too. His whole life had been a storm. Let him be buried in one as well . . .

He bent over to look at the turbulent wave raising the ship. From time to time a star appeared reflected in it. Behind him, someone on deck was softly singing a nostalgic song from his village. It was one of the wounded lads on his way back to liberated Greece—a child of poverty returning to hunger and deprivation. Nevertheless he was singing! . . . of freedom and the future! . . . He himself had Gregos' money . . . So much money! Yet what would he do with it now that he'd lost hope? . . .

All that sacrifice and loss of life! He realized that it wasn't in vain—that the blood which had been spilled strengthened the Greek consciousness under Turkish occupation. Captain Agras had once said that the shame of the defeat of '97 created the Macedonian Struggle, and that the Macedonian Struggle would wake up the Greek people!

And who knew? . . . From the depths of the awakened people, someone might rise as a savior to liberate Macedonia and all of occupied Greece—and then unify the freed nation . . . He was aware that the blood shed would produce avengers, others like Agras, ready to suffer death to set their fellow-countrymen free.

. . . Apostolis had stayed. But he himself had departed. Why?

Both Apostolis and the lad behind him singing of his yearning for his village, were young. He would give the wounded lad a little joy! . . .

Mechanically he searched at his chest for Gregos' old wallet and the Bulgarian knife that still bore traces of his blood. Gregos' leather purse was there as well. He took it out, tore a sheet from his notepad, and groping in the dark, wrote down five words:

"Let the lads divide it."

He stuffed the paper into the purse and placed it down on the boards. Gently he stroked the knife at his chest, along with Gregos' old wallet with the faded photograph of Haido smiling down from under the Macedonian headdress. He remembered her eyes—large, black, and almond-shaped like those of his child . . . And he remembered his former life that had been so happy, gone forever . . .

Longingly he bent over the rail again and observed the wake, like a furrow the ship's passage had left behind . . . One decision, one stride across the rail and his trials would be over! . . . Gregos had killed himself. He, also, would put an end . . .

However Gregos had killed himself for a noble purpose— to release his companions and save them, not from weariness or weakness. While if he did it now . . .

"The ship! The ship with the rebels is passing! . . ."

The words were uttered quietly. By the light of the stars, someone had discerned the black, unlit keel and white sails approaching.

"Our fighters! . . . They're on their way to the Struggle! . . ."

Like a war stallion that smells gunpowder and rushes into battle, Vasilis' rebel spirit rose up.

"Captain Tasos!" he shouted, in his excitement forgetting the danger of betraying them should an enemy boat be on guard nearby. "Captain Tasos! Signal him to stop! Lower the rowboat! Pass me to the other ship!"

"You want to go back?" a shaken Mitsos exclaimed, getting up.

"Quickly!" Vasilis urged the skipper. "Don't let him overtake us!"

Two little lights flashed, one after the other. Another two responded from the dark schooner in front of them. Sails were gathered here and there; and the vessels turned, maneuvered, and approached each other.

In the tranquil night, the other skipper's low voice was heard above the frothy wave breaking against the ships.

"Captain Tasos? . . . What's up? . . ."

"Someone wants to go on board! . . ."

Vasilis had drawn near, prepared to leap into the rowboat as it touched the water.

Stirred, Mitsos said to him:

"You want to leave us, then?"

Vasilis stopped short, stirred himself. At his boss' house they cared about him . . . His heart fluttered for a moment, then became incurably heavy again.

"I'm going to find Apostolis . . ." he stated in his slow, deep voice, hardly audible. "My country—Macedonia—is calling me back . . ."

"At our house, you'll find love and rest. And you could return later . . ." Mitsos responded.

Vasilis straightened up.

"You don't know, Mister Mitsos," he said with some reawakening of his old self. "You don't know . . . Because you're young, like the lad who was singing earlier. He too has all his life before him, as you do. . . . I—I'm spent. I've left only graves behind me . . . For a second I contemplated plunging into the waves to sleep—and not wake again . . ."

"Vasilis!"

"Yes! It would be unworthy. One can die, but for something of value, like Gregos did for you to escape. I'll return to the Swamp, or to Mt. Olympus or Vermio, and meet a death worthy of Gregos—one that will help maintain the Greek morale. And 'again with the years, with time,'[43] a leader will appear to liberate us . . ."[44]

Captain Teligades had approached.

". . . again with the years . . . with time," he repeated with emotion. "I'll return myself when I've recovered."

"I'd return with you, Vasilis! But at least rest up . . ." Mitsos began.

Vasilis interrupted him:

"It's not rest that I want now . . ." he said in his calm manner. "I seek danger, work, and struggle. I want my child's grave liberated . . ."

Miss Electra reached out and clasped his hand.

"Let Vasilis go, Mitsos . . ." she said quietly. "He feels the way he should. His place is there, in the Struggle which isn't finished and requires more sacrifice . . . You'd be there today yourself, if you could . . ."

The rowboat was lowered.

"Hurry, Andreadis! . . ." the captain broke in.

Vasilis leaned down quickly and kissed Miss Electra's hand.

"You, a woman, you understand . . ." he murmured.

He embraced Mitsos, turned, and striding over the rail, jumped down into the boat. Setting off, it drew alongside the other ship.

With misty eyes Miss Electra watched him, as hanging by his hands he lifted himself up inside.

The sails opposite them shook lightly a couple of times, unfurled, grew taut, and the wind puffed them out. Then the ship with the rebels started off and left them behind.

It disappeared in the darkness that enveloped the still enslaved land.

THE END

AFTERWORD

In July 1908, the Young Turks Revolution broke out, bringing the Macedonian Struggle to a halt. The uprising of Turkish army officers, begun in Salonika, succeeded in putting an end to the Sultan's autocratic power.

A new constitutional regime promised equal rights for all ethnic groups and a general amnesty—a development greeted with enthusiasm by the Greek forces. Instead, a policy of repressive "Turkification" was adopted.

The guerilla war at Lake Giannitsa had been fought on the Greek side to stop the spread of Bulgarian nationalism in an area historically Greek. Gradually the Greeks succeeded in countering comitadje gains. Bulgaria, for its part, increasingly had to confront enemies on two fronts—Serbs in the north and Greeks in the south—as well as internal dissent.

In 1909, at Goudi outside Athens, Greek military officers staged a *coup* aimed at modernizing their armed forces, corresponding to Bulgaria's and Serbia's strengthening of their national armies. The Cretan leader Eleftherios Venizelos was given authority to enact military and constitutional reforms, and made premier in 1910. A genuine statesman, he became—to Penelope Delta—"the savior to liberate Macedonia and all of occupied Greece," foretold in the final pages of *Secrets of the Swamp*.

In 1912, the First Balkan War erupted when Greece, Bulgaria, and Serbia put aside their differences and formed an alliance to free Macedonia. Nearly all of the Ottoman Empire in Europe, held for almost four centuries, was captured. In the Second Balkan War of 1913, the former allies fought each other over the conquered territory.

Due to Venizelos' astuteness to a large degree, Greece acquired Salonika and the greater portion of Macedonia—51%—in the 1913 Treaty of Bucharest. The northern sections were divided between the other two states without considering the preference of the population: Serbia—39%, and Bulgaria—10%. This disparity contributed to Bulgaria's entering the First and Second World Wars allied with Germany, in hopes of regaining "lost land."

While the Macedonian Struggle (1904-1908) did not have a decisive outcome for either Greeks or Bulgarians, it did set the foundation and create the confidence for Greek success in the Balkan Wars five years later.

NOTES

1. (p.6) *Captain Nikiphoros*—naval sub-lieutenant John Demestikas; *Captain Kalas*—infantry lieutenant Constantine Sarros ; *Captain Zykis*—infantry sergeant major Christos Karapanos.
2. (p.7) *Captain Agras*—infantry lieutenant Telos Agapinos, to whose memory the book was dedicated.
3. (p.13) *Bey*—provincial governor in the Ottoman Empire.
4. (p.14) *Comitadje*—member of an armed Bulgarian guerilla force in the Macedonian Struggle.
5. (p.16) *Fez*—red felt cap, ornamented with a long, black tassel. Headdress of Turks, and of Greeks under occupation.
6. (p.20) *Captain Matapas*—second lieutenant Michael Anagnostakos, at first deputy commander at Lake Giannitsa, then leader of a force at Mt. Olympus.
7. (p.21) *'97*—thirty-day Greek-Turkish war in Thessaly in 1897, where the Greeks suffered defeat.
8. (p.22) *Among the captains*—*Petrilos*, an infantry lieutenant; and *Kapsalis, Kavondoros*, and *Klaras*, infantry second-lieutenants.
9. (p.22) *Captain Zezas*—Greek army officer Pavlos Melas, who volunteered to organize and fight in the Macedonian Struggle in its early stage. His death turned the nation's attention to the guerilla war being fought in the north.
10. (p.27) *Comitadjes' aim*—to make Macedonia Bulgarian, as had been done earlier in East Rumelia.

     (*See also* p.28) *The Greek Synod of 1872*—proclaimed the Bulgarians schismatic who broke away from the Patriarch in Constantinople to follow the Bulgarian Exarch as leader of the Orthodox church.
11. (p.30) *"Water mannas"*—natural pathways formed from smaller branches of the Loudias River running through the

lake. A reference to the miraculous food or "manna" supplied to the Israelites in the Old Testament.

12. (p.31) *Evzones*—members of a select infantry corps in the Greek army, traditionally kilted.

13. (p.37) *Evamgelos Koukoudeos*—rebel youth with dark eyes and long, curly hair, who resembled the Greek revolutionary hero Thanasis Diakos.

14. (p.37) *Captain Rouvas*—2nd lieutenant; and *Captain Vergas*—cavalry lieutenant.

15. (p.37) *Nikolas Zaferiou*—special guard of Captain Nikiphoros, from Chalkidi in Macedonia.

16. (p.60) *Captain Gonos Ziotas*—at first a Macedonian chiefton, then a dedicated, Bulgarian-speaking patriarchal Greek—as was *Captain Kottas* (see p.220).

17. (p.103) *Dr. Antonakis*—"imposter" doctor, dedicated to the Macedonian Struggle, who performed inestimable services for the Center in Thessalonika.

18 (p.107) *Vozelis*—notable at Ramel, killed by the comitadjes along with his family.

19 (p.109) *Germanos Karavangelis*—bishop of Kastoria, devoted to the Macedonian Struggle and integral to it.

20. (p.116) *Captain Paraskevas Zerveas*—artillery sergeant, deputy commander of Captain Kalas.

21. (p.138) *Captain Bouas*—lieutenant Spyromilios, served at the Center in Thessalonika, then as the leader of a rebel force at Vodena. Wounded in the foot in a battle with the Bulgarians, he returned to Greece lame.

22. (p.139) *A brave fighter*—*Admiral Kanaris* at Samos in the navel battle at White Cape during the 1821 Greek Revolution, where one ship pursued a fleeing Turkish fleet.

23. (p.140) *Captain Panayiotis Papatzaneteas*—artillery sergeant, head of the western division at the lake prior to Captain Agras, and then in charge at Naousa.

24. (p.145) *Mani*—mountainous region of Laconia in the Peloponnese.

25. (p.152) *1897 mission commander—Admiral Andoniadis*, killed with all his men.
26. (p.153) *Theodore Askitis*—interpreter at the Greek Consulate in Thessalonika.
27. (p.156) *Lambros Koromilas*—outstanding General Consul in Thessalonika from October 1904 to the start of 1908. He was removed at the Turks' demand.
28. (p.158) *Greek captains—Captain Kavondoros, Captain Petrilos*, and many more.
29. (p.158) *Captain Amvrakiotis*—2nd lieutenant John Avrasoglou, captured at Kilkis.
30. (p.162) *Athanasios Andoniou* and *Alexandros Ioannidis*—officials at the Consulate who administered the western districts. The first—artillery lieutenant Athanasios Exadaktylos; the second—artillery lieutenant Alekos Mazarakis.
31. (p.162) *Mr. Katsanos*—artillery second lieutenant Kyriakos Tavoularis, and *Mr. Zoés*—lieutenant-engineer Demetrios Kakkavos, both employees at the Consulate in Thessalonika.
32. (p.170) *Districts*—of Verria, Naousa, Kozani, etc., down to the Greek border.
33. (p.189) *Greek Revolution*—fought from 1821-1832, after nearly four centuries of Ottoman rule.
    Captains of the Macedonian Strugle—Captain Akritas, artillery lieutenant Kostas Mazarakis, leader of a force at Naousa; *Captain Vardas*, artillery lieutenant G. Tsondas, head of a force at Kastoria; *Captain Makris*, George Dikovimos from Crete; and *Captain Rouvas* (see p.37).
34. (p.191) *Chrysostomos*—also told Miss Electra to forward a cheese to him, should Manolis, who killed the Bulgarian innkeeper Stavrakis, appear. That way, he'd understand that she saw him and sent him to the Kryfi hut to await the priest's instructrions.
35. (p.199) *Manolis from Thrace*—from Stenimachos in Eastern Rumelia, where the Bulgarians persecuted and eventually drove out the Greek population.

36. (p.220) *Pericles' great-grandfather*—fought in western Greece with *Markos Botsaris*, a Revolutionary War hero.
37. (p.300) *Evangelos Koukoudeas* and *Nikolas Zaferiou*—competed in their dedication to Captain Nikiphoros. (See p.37 also.)
38. (p.320) *Comitadjes killed by the captains*—at Vougadia and the Petra monastery.
39. (p.321) *"Koumbara"*—godmother of one's child in a relationship that extends to families of both the godmother and child. (See p.409 also.)
40. (p.380) *Nikiphoros II*—George Papadopoulos, veteran officer of logistics.
41. (p.436) *Quaking in his boots*—fleeing like Cain before the angel's sword.
42. (p.449) *Vasilis's plan*—to kill Zlatan in the house, or hut, where he was hiding. *Captain Garefis* had carried out a similar plan against two Bulgarians—Loukas and Karataso.
43. (p.467) *"Again with the years, with time"*—Reference to the fall of Constantinople to the Turks, which ended the Byzantine Empire in 1453; and to its future resurrection.
44. (p.467) *Reference to Eleftherios Venizelos*—Prime Minister of Greece from 1910-1915, 1917-1920, 1924, and 1928-1932.

Addition: (p. 194) Before Captains Kalas and Nikiphoros arrived as the Swamp, Captain Panayiotis—and later Matapas—had too few men to fight both in the east and the west. No one knew then that the Bulgarians had built huts in the northeast of the lake. But Panayiotis discovered a secret path to a landing-cove where the comitadjes entered and left the Swamp. He'd found bits of bread in the water and traces of canoes among the reeds, which led to an old "floor" and the corpse of a Greek. It was there that Captain Kapsalis had been ambushed—and now with Nikiphoros away at Kouga, the northern villages were again at risk.

About The Author

PENELOPE DELTA is generally regarded as the most widely-read twentieth-century Greek novelist and storywriter for youth.

To the present day, she remains a popular author and an intriguing figure for Greeks of all ages. In the last decades, another volume of her *Memoirs*—published posthumously—and a book of essays on her work from a twenty-first century perspective have appeared, revealing a life deeply involved in the major issues and events of her times.

Delta chose the Byzantine Empire at its height in the "heroic age of Basil II" as a subject for her first two historical novels. Her final and most acclaimed book, *Secrets of the Swamp,* pays tribute to the Greek rebels who fought in the Macedonian Struggle during the declining years of the Ottoman Empire (1904–1908). Both were little-known periods of Greek history she helped open up to generations of young readers.

About The Translator

RUTH BOBICK translated Penelope Delta's novel *In the Heroic Age of Basil II* and has written articles about her life and work. A freelance writer, she is presently preparing an account of the Settlement Movement at Jane Addams' Hull House, focusing on its influence upon social reform in America.